PRIZE STORIES 1974:
*The O. Henry Awards*

# PRIZE STORIES 1974:

## *The O. Henry Awards*

Edited and with an Introduction
by William Abrahams

*1974*

DOUBLEDAY & COMPANY, INC.
GARDEN CITY, NEW YORK

ISBN: 0-385-02993-4
*Library of Congress Catalog Card Number 21–9372*

# CONTENTS

# PUBLISHER'S NOTE

This volume is the fifty-fourth in the O. Henry Memorial Award series.

In 1918, the Society of Arts and Sciences met to vote upon a monument to the master of the short story, O. Henry. They decided that this memorial should be in the form of two prizes for the best short stories published by American authors in American magazines during the year 1919. From this beginning, the memorial developed into an annual anthology of outstanding short stories by American authors published, with the exception of the years 1952 and 1953, by Doubleday & Company, Inc.

Blanche Colton Williams, one of the founders of the awards, was editor from 1919 to 1932; Harry Hansen from 1933 to 1940; Herschel Brickell from 1941 to 1951. The annual collection did not appear in 1952 and 1953, when the continuity of the series was interrupted by the death of Herschel Brickell, who had been the editor for ten years. Paul Engle was editor from 1954 to 1959 with Hanson Martin co-editor in the years 1954 to 1956; Mary Stegner in 1960; Richard Poirier from 1961 to 1966, with assistance from and co-editorship with William Abrahams from 1964 to 1966. William Abrahams became editor of the series in 1967.

Doubleday also publishes *First-Prize Stories from the O. Henry Memorial Awards* in editions which are brought up to date at intervals. In 1970 Doubleday also published under Mr. Abrahams's editorship, *Fifty Years of the American Short Story*, a collection of stories selected from the series.

The stories chosen for this volume were published in the period from the summer of 1972 to the summer of 1973. A list of the magazines consulted appears at the back of the book. The choice of stories and the selection of prize winners are exclusively the responsibility of the editor. Biographical material is based on information provided by the contributors.

# INTRODUCTION

As an unashamed addict of the short story, I find myself increasingly irritated by the exaggerated claim advanced on behalf of the "new journalism" by its most visible practitioners. One can accept from them—as from any group of rising young writers—a fair degree of self-approbation and mutual admiration. One can accept even their high estimate of what they have actually written, for, judged on its own terms—as journalism cool or feverish—much of their work has been remarkable. (Its durability is another question. Journalism by its very nature only rarely outlasts its own day, and it seems unlikely that many of these highly touted productions, however scintillating or newsworthy at their first appearance, will ultimately have a place alongside such classics of the old journalism as *Ten Days that Shook the World* or *Homage to Catalonia*.)

But there is a point at which a line must be drawn, and I think it is at the claim that the outpourings of the new journalism (articles, pieces, profiles on the surface and in depth, non-fiction novels, novels as biographies etc.) have supplanted and surpassed contemporary fiction, making it superfluous, quite as though fiction and non-fiction were interchangeable, impelled by the same motives, and in competition with each other. Only this past year one spokesman for the new journalists explained their achievements and their victory (but in whose eyes but his was there a contest?) in this fashion: that they had rushed in to do the work that the writers of fiction no longer cared to do, and therefore it was they, rather than the fictionists, who recorded the social changes and disturbances of the 1960s at the very moment of their occurrence.

The argument is so simplistic in its premises—the view of fiction as merely another kind of document—and the evidence enlisted to sustain it so flimsy, suggesting only the most casual acquaintance with the serious fiction of the period, that ordinarily it wouldn't need be paid much attention. But the unwary reader, hustled along by the hyperbolic self-confidence of the author's presentation, might well conclude that the decade of the triumphs of the new journalism coincided with a conspicuous decline in the quality of fiction, and that, so far as fiction was concerned, it was a decade barren of achievement.

In fact, limiting myself only to the short story, and confining myself further only to stories chosen for the annual volumes of this series in the past ten years, I can set out an alphabetical sampling of authors that immediately contradicts the notion of an exhausted genre: John Barth, John Batki, Donald Barthelme, Brock Brower, Hortense Calisher, John Cheever, William Eastlake, Jesse Hill Ford, Nancy Hale, Edward Hoagland, James Alan McPherson, Mary McCarthy, Bernard Malamud, Jack Matthews, Leonard Michaels, H. L. Montzoures, Flannery O'Connor, Joyce Carol Oates, Grace Paley, Reynolds Price, Judith Rascoe, Philip Roth, Elizabeth Spencer, Wallace Stegner, Jonathan Strong, Peter Taylor, John Updike, Eudora Welty, and Patricia Zelver. Surely an impressive group, and it might be easily enlarged by a score of other writers—but I have no wish to enter into a name-dropping competition, and the important point, simply, is that the decade has been enriched by a generous production of imaginative short fiction, in which, as the sympathetic reader will discover, the spirit of the age, filtered through the individual sensibility, is a dominant and affecting presence, not as explicit perhaps as a late news bulletin, or on-the-spot reportage, but as something more pervasive, oblique, subtle, truthful, and, in the long view, more memorable.

It is also a fact, as I have had occasion to remark in more than one of these introductions, that throughout the decade there has been a continuing decline of interest in the short story, on the part of magazine editors and readers, and an ever more generous allotment of space and attention to non-fiction: if the two phenomena are related, then in that respect the new journalism has triumphed. But I am not at all persuaded that a certain chill in the air makes for a bad climate in which to do serious writing. As I observed in this space last year, and find the observation as valid now as then, "The cool attitude (when not downright hostile) of editors toward fiction, and the indifference toward it of a good part of the magazine reading audience . . . means that writers are left pretty much to themselves, freed from any preconceptions and expectations but their own as they begin to write." Their stories accordingly give no sense of being "written to order, or to a formula, or with an eye on editorial taboos, restrictions and preferences: each expresses a vision of life and art

that is personal to its author . . . The story in America at the
present time, insofar as one may generalize, thrives in its apparent
neglect, perhaps even because of it."

To venture a further generalization, what is most remarkable about
the contemporary American story is its unselfconscious variety, in
subject matter and technique, as the seventeen stories included here
should make evident. (I accept, as the writers themselves must do,
that this may be displeasing to those readers who are happiest with
preconceived notions—or prejudices rooted in stories read years ago
and not too accurately remembered—of what the story should be: a
tested formula in which approved elements of character, plot, setting, and theme are brought inoffensively and reminiscently into re-
lation.) Offhand it would be difficult to imagine two stories affording
a greater contrast in their methods and intentions than "Brownstone" by Renata Adler and "Lizzie Borden in the P.M." by Robert
Henson. Yet these authors are alike in the integrity with which they
have gone about their tasks, and in their willingness to break free
of the conventional props of storytelling that their subjects might be
thought to have offered them.

Mr. Henson has boldly appropriated material of a sort that the
new journalism has taken for its own: two violent murders, which
actually occurred, a famous trial, Lizzie Borden's, and its aftermath;
and he has shown us what richness and strangeness—art, in a word—
it can be made to yield. The straightforward narrative line, the zip-
zap building of suspense, and all those other *grand-guignol* touches
appropriate to the case are jettisoned. Instead, with a splendid disre-
gard for the lurid particulars of a tale told innumerable times since
the Borden murders (and sung about in street ballads; and danced
about, too, in a famous ballet of Agnes De Mille's) he has created an
intricately crisscrossed exploration of the lives of Lizzie Borden and
her older sister that yet (to my way of thinking) irresistibly leads
one on to a solution of the "mystery." But Mr. Henson's particular
achievement is in creating a story that exists in its own right, within
the margins of the story as he has written it—no matter, really, that
it had its beginnings in the world of fact.

Miss Adler's story, too, relates to a world of fact; or perhaps I
should say a "real" world—it would be difficult (even among the new
journalists) to find a more realistic evocation of the serio-comic tone
and detail of metropolitan life in the 1970s in America. Yet to read it
at this level, for no more than its shrewdly gathered-in particulars, is

to miss the deeper levels that this gifted author's enigmatic art has opened to us, if we wish to see. Miss Adler has been even more ruthless than Mr. Henson in refusing to traffic in the traditional elements of the story as we have become accustomed to them. Narrative hardly exists (there is the faintest thread of "story" carrying us forward through several months in New York); plot there is none. And as for characterization, though a host of characters appear like bright streaks on a gray surface, there is no attempt to give them a dimensionality that would pass muster in a creative writing textbook. As it is, they have no more dimension than shadows (or cartoons), which is what they very likely are. Is that, perhaps, the "point" Miss Adler's narrator is so preoccupied with, and hence the point of the story? "The point changes and goes out. You can not be forever watching for the point, or you lose the simplest thing: being a major character in your own life."

In "Brownstone"—the title itself, suggesting an older world of New York that no longer exists, is but one of a fabric of ironies— there are no major characters. But the effect of the story is strangely moving. One can hardly weep for this cool-voiced narrator, or the lover, faintly visible, with whom she lives now and then. One is not meant to weep for them, or for any of those other lives evoked with so much wit, dispassion, and (yes) sympathy—but the story disturbs us, unsettles us, moves us as it moves (so there is a narrative propulsion after all) to a conclusion of extraordinary power: "When I wonder what it is that we are doing—in this brownstone, on this block, with this paper—the truth is probably that we are fighting for our lives."

Miss Adler's story, at once so unconventional, so bent upon finding its own form and triumphantly succeeding in its search, proves once again that art will discover areas of life that, because they are ours, seem to us wholly devoid of art, are merely those days and nights of quiet desperation that must be gotten through. It is no small pleasure to be reminded once again of how much the story has to offer. Miss Adler and the sixteen other authors in this year's collection have put us in their debt.

—William Abrahams

# BROWNSTONE

## RENATA ADLER

Renata Adler was born in Milan, Italy, and grew up in Danbury, Connecticut. She was graduated from Bryn Mawr College, and received an M.A. from Harvard. Since 1962 she has been a staff writer-reporter for *The New Yorker*. From January 1968 to March 1969 she was film critic of *The New York Times*. She has published two collections of non-fiction pieces, *Toward a Radical Middle* and *A Year in the Dark*.

The camel, I had noticed, was passing, with great difficulty, through the eye of the needle. The Apollo flight, the four-minute mile, Venus in Scorpio, human records on land and at sea—these had been events of enormous importance. But the camel, practicing in near obscurity for almost two thousand years, was passing through. First the velvety nose, then the rest. Not many were aware. But if the lead camel and then perhaps the entire caravan could make it, the thread, the living thread of camels, would exist, could not be lost. No one could lose the thread. The prospects of the rich would be enhanced. "Ortega tells us that the business of philosophy," the professor was telling his class of indifferent freshmen, "is to crack open metaphors which are dead."

"I shouldn't have come," the Englishman said, waving his drink and breathing so heavily at me that I could feel my bangs shift. "I have a terrible cold."

"He would probably have married her," a voice across the room said, "with the exception that he died."

"Well, I am a personality that prefers not to be annoyed."

"We should all prepare ourselves for this eventuality."

A six-year-old was passing the hors d'oeuvres. The baby, not quite
steady on his feet, was hurtling about the room.

"He's following me," the six-year-old said, in despair.

"Then lock yourself in the bathroom, dear," Inez replied.

"He always waits outside the door."

"He loves you, dear."

"Well, I don't like it."

"How I envy you," the minister's wife was saying to a courteous,
bearded boy, "reading 'Magic Mountain' for the first time."

The homosexual across the hall from me always takes Valium and
walks his beagle. I borrow Valium from him from time to time, and
when he takes a holiday the dog is left with me. On our floor of this
brownstone, we are friends. Our landlord, Roger Somerset, was mur-
dered last July. He was a kind and absentminded man, and on the
night when he was stabbed there was a sort of requiem for him in the
heating system. There is a lot of music in this building anyway. The
newlyweds on the third floor play Bartók on their stereo. The couple
on the second floor play clarinet quintets; their kids play rock. The
girl on the fourth floor, who has been pining for two months, plays
Judy Collins' "Maid of Constant Sorrow" all day long. We have a
kind of orchestra in here. The ground floor is a shop. The owner of
the shop speaks of our landlord's murder still. Shaking his head, he
says that he suspects "foul play." We all agree with him. We changed
our locks. But "foul play" seems a weird expression for the case.

It is all weird. I am not always well. One block away (I often think
of this), there was ten months ago an immense crash. Water mains
broke. There were small rivers in the streets. In a great skyscraper
that was being built, something had failed. The newspapers reported
the next day that by some miracle only two people had been "slightly
injured" by ten tons of falling steel. The steel fell from the eighteenth floor. The question that preoccupies me now is how, under the
circumstances, slight injuries could occur. Perhaps the two people
were grazed in passing by. Perhaps some fragments of the sidewalk
ricocheted. I knew a deliverer of flowers who, at Sixty-ninth and Lexington, was hit by a flying suicide. Situations simply do not yield to
the most likely structures of the mind. A "self-addressed envelope,"
if you are inclined to brood, raises deep questions of identity. Such
an envelope, immutably itself, is always precisely where it belongs.

"Self-pity" is just sadness, I think, in the pejorative. But "joking with nurses" fascinates me in the press. Whenever someone has been quite struck down, lost faculties, members of his family, he is said to have "joked with his nurses" quite a lot. What a mine of humor every nurses's life must be.

The St. Bernard at the pound on Ninety-second Street was named Bonnie and would have cost five dollars. The attendant held her tightly on a leash of rope. "Hello, Bonnie," I said. Bonnie growled.
"I wouldn't talk to her if I was you," the attendant said.
I leaned forward to pat her ear. Bonnie snarled. "I wouldn't touch her if I was you," the attendant said. I held out my hand under Bonnie's jowls. She strained against the leash, and choked and coughed. "Now cut that out, Bonnie," the attendant said.
"Could I just take her for a walk around the block," I said, "before I decide?" "Are you out of your mind?" the attendant said. Aldo patted Bonnie, and we left.

I have a job, of course. I have had several jobs. I've had our paper's gossip column since last month. It is egalitarian. I look for people who are quite obscure, and report who is breaking up with whom and where they go and what they wear.
The person who invented this new form for us is on anti-depressants now. He lives in Illinois. He says there are people in southern Illinois who have not yet been covered by the press. I often write about families in Queens. Last week, I went to a dinner party on Park Avenue. After 1 A.M., something called the Alive or Dead Game was being played. Someone would mention an old character from Tammany or Hollywood. "Dead," "Dead," "Dead," everyone would guess. "No, no. Alive. I saw him walking down the street just yesterday," or "Yes. Dead. I read a little obituary Notice about him last year." One of the little truths people can subtly enrage or reassure each other with is who—when you have looked away a month, a year—is still around.

DEAR TENANT:
We have reason to believe that there are impostors posing as Con Ed repairmen and inspectors circulating in this area.
Do not permit any Con Ed man to enter your premises or the building, if possible.

THE PRECINCT

My cousin, who was born on February 29th, became a veterinarian. Some years ago, when he was twenty-eight (seven, by our childhood birthday count), he was drafted, and sent to Malaysia. He spent most of his military service there, assigned to the zoo. He operated on one tiger, which, in the course of abdominal surgery, began to wake up and wag its tail. The anesthetist grabbed the tail, and injected more sodium pentothal. That tiger survived. But two flamingos, sent by the city of Miami to Kuala Lumpur as a token of good will, could not bear the trip or the climate and, in spite of my cousin's efforts, died. There was also a cobra—the largest anyone in Kuala Lumpur could remember having seen. An old man had brought it, in an immense sack, from somewhere in the countryside. The zoo director called my cousin at once, around dinnertime, to say that an unprecedented cobra had arrived. Something quite drastic, however, seemed wrong with its neck. My cousin, whom I have always admired—for his leap-year birthday, for his pilot's license, for his presence of mind—said that he would certainly examine the cobra in the morning but that the best thing for it after its long journey must be a good night's rest. By morning, the cobra was dead.

My cousin is well. The problem is this. Hardly anyone about whom I deeply care at all resembles anyone else I have ever met, or heard of, or read about in the literature. I know an Israeli general who, in 1967, retook the Mitla Pass but who, since his mandatory retirement from military service at fifty-five, has been trying to repopulate the Ark. He asked me, over breakfast at the Drake, whether I knew any owners of oryxes. Most of the vegetarian species he has collected have already multiplied enough, since he has found and cared for them, to be permitted to run wild. The carnivorous animals, though, must still be kept behind barbed wire—to keep them from stalking the rarer vegetarians. I know a group that studies Proust one Sunday afternoon a month, and an analyst, with that Exeter laugh (embittered mooing noises, and mirthless heaving of the shoulder blades), who has the most remarkable terrorist connections in the Middle East.

The New York Chinese cabdriver lingered at every corner and at every traffic light, to read his paper. I wondered what the news was. I looked over his shoulder. The illustrations and the type were clear enough: newspaper print, pornographic fiction. I leaned back in my seat. A taxi-driver who happened to be Oriental with a sadomasochistic cast of mind was not my business. I lit a cigarette, looked at my bracelet. I caught the driver's eyes a moment in the rearview mirror. He picked up his paper. "I don't think you ought to read," I said, "while you are driving." Traffic was slow. I saw his mirrored eyes again. He stopped his reading. When we reached my address, I did not tip him. Racism and prudishness, I thought, and reading over people's shoulders.

But there are moments in this place when everything becomes a show of force. He can read what he likes at home. Tipping is still my option. Another newspaper event, in our brownstone. It was a holiday. The superintendent normally hauls the garbage down and sends the paper up, by dumbwaiter, each morning. On holidays, the garbage stays upstairs, the paper on the sidewalk. At 8 A.M., I went downstairs. A ragged man was lying across the little space that separates the inner door, which locks, from the outer door, which doesn't. I am not a news addict. I could have stepped over the sleeping man, picked up my *Times,* and gone upstairs to read it. Instead, I knocked absurdly from inside the door, and said, "Wake up. You'll have to leave now." He got up, lifted the flattened cardboard he had been sleeping on, and walked away, mumbling and reeking. It would have been kinder, certainly, to let the driver read, the wino sleep. One simply cannot bear down so hard on all these choices.

What is the point. That is what must be borne in mind. Sometimes the point is really who wants what. Sometimes the point is what is right or kind. Sometimes the point is a momentum, a fact, a quality, a voice, an intimation, a thing said or unsaid. Sometimes it's who's at fault, or what will happen if you do not move at once. The point changes and goes out. You cannot be forever watching for the point, or you lose the simplest thing: being a major character in your own life. But if you are, for any length of time, custodian of the point—in art, in court, in politics, in lives, in rooms—it turns out there are rear-guard actions everywhere. Now and then, a small foray is worthwhile. Just so that being constantly, complacently, thoroughly wrong does not become the safest position of them all. The point has never quite been entrusted to me.

The conversation of "The Magic Mountain" and the unrequited love of six-year-olds occurred on Saturday, at brunch. "Bring someone new," Inez had said. "Not queer. Not married, maybe separated. John and I are breaking up." The invitation was not of a kind that I had heard before. Aldo, who lives with me between the times when he prefers to be alone, refused to come. He despises brunch. He detests Inez. I went, instead, with a lawyer who has been a distant, steady friend but who, ten years ago, when we first came to New York, had once put three condoms on the night table beside the phone. We both had strange ideas then about New York. Aldo is a gentle, orderly, soft-spoken man, slow to conclude. I try to be tidy when he is here, but I have often made his cigarettes, and once his manuscript, into the bed. Our paper's publisher is an intellectual from Baltimore. He has read Wittgenstein; he's always making unimpeachable remarks. Our music critic throws a tantrum every day, in print. Our book reviewer is looking for another job. He found that the packages in which all books are mailed could not, simply could not, be opened without doing considerable damage—through staples, tape, wire, fluttering gray stuff, recalcitrance—to the reviewer's hands. He felt it was a symptom of some kind—one of those cases where incompetence at every stage, across the board, acquired a certain independent force. Nothing to do with books, he thought, worked out at all. We also do the news. For horoscopes, there are the ladies' magazines. We just cannot compete.

My late landlord was from Scarsdale. The Maid of Constant Sorrow is from Texas. Aldo is from St. Louis. Inez's versions vary about where she's from. I grew up in a New England mill town, where, in the early thirties, all the insured factories burned down. It has been difficult to get fire insurance in that region ever since. The owner of a hardware store, whose property adjoined an insured factory at the time, lost everything. Afterward, he walked all day along the railroad track, waiting for a train to run him down. Railroad service has never been very good up there. No trains came. His children own the town these days, for what it's worth. The two cobbled streets where black people always lived have been torn up and turned into a public park since a flood that occurred some years ago. Unprecedented rains came. Retailers had to destroy their sodden products, for fear of contamination. And the black section was torn up and seeded over in the town's rezoning project. No one knows where the blacks live now. But there are Negroes in the stores and schools, and on the football team. It is assumed that the park integrated the town. Those black families must be living somewhere. It is a mystery.

The host, for some reason, was taking Instamatic pictures of his guests. It was not clear whether he was doing this in order to be able to show, at some future time, that there had been this gathering in his house. Or whether he thought of pictures in some voodoo sense. Or whether he found it difficult to talk. Or whether he was bored. Two underground celebrities—one of whom had become a sensation by never generating or exhibiting a flicker of interest in anything, the other of whom was known mainly for hanging around the first—were taking pictures, too. I was there with a movie star I've known for years. He had already been received in an enormous embrace by an Eastern European poet, whose hair was cut too short but who was neither as awkwardly spontaneous nor as drunk as he cared to seem. The party was in honor of the poet, who celebrated the occasion by insulting everyone and being fawned upon, by distinguished and undistinguished writers alike. "This group looks as though someone had torn up a few guest lists and floated the pieces on the air," somebody said.

Paul: "Two diamonds."

Inez: "Two hearts."

Mary: "Three clubs."

John: "Four kings."

Inez: "Darling, you know you can't just bid four kings."

John: "I don't see why. I might have been bluffing."

Inez: "No, darling. That's poker. This is bridge. And even in poker you can't just bid four kings."

John: "No. Well, I guess we'd better deal another hand."

The friend of the underground sensation walked up to the actor and me and said hello. Then, in a verbal seizure of some sort, he began muttering obscenities. The actor said a few calming things that didn't work. He finally put his finger on the mutterer's lips. The mutterer bit that finger extremely hard, and walked away. The actor wrapped his finger in a paper napkin, and got himself another drink. We stayed till twelve.

I went to a women's college. We had distinguished faculty in everything, digs at Nuoro and Mycenae. We had a quality of obsession in our studies. For professors who had quarrelled with their wives at breakfast, those years of bright-eyed young women, never getting any older, must have been a trial. The head of the history department once sneezed into his best student's honors thesis. He slammed it shut. It was ultimately published. When I was there, a girl called Cindy Melchior was immensely fat. She wore silk trousers and gilt mules. One day, in the overheated classroom, she laid aside her knitting and lumbered to the window, which she opened. Then she lumbered back. "Do you think," the professor asked, "you are so graceful?" He somehow meant it kindly. Cindy wept. That year, Cindy's brother Melvin phoned me. "I would have called you sooner," he said, "but I had the most terrible eczema." All the service staff on campus in those days were black. Many of them were followers of Father Divine. They took new names in the church. I remember the year when a maid called Serious Heartbreak married a janitor called Universal Dictionary. At a meeting of the faculty last fall, the college president, who is new and male, spoke of raising money. A female professor of Greek was knitting—and working on Linear B, with an abacus before her. In our time, there was a vogue for madrigals. Some of us listened, constantly, to a single record. There was a phrase we could not decipher. A professor of symbolic logic, a French Canadian, had sounds that matched but a meaning that seemed unlikely: Sheep are no angels; come upstairs. A countertenor explained it, after a local concert: She'd for no angel's comfort stay. Not so likely, either.

The Maid of Constant Sorrow said our landlord's murder marked a turning point in her analysis. "I don't feel guilty. I feel hated," she said. It is true, for a time, we all wanted to feel somehow a part—if only because violence offset the boredom of our lives. My grandfather said that some people have such extreme insomnia that they look at their watches every hour after midnight, to see how sorry they ought to be feeling for themselves. Aldo says he does not care what my grandfather said. My grandmother refused to concede that any member of the family died of natural causes. An uncle's cancer in middle age occurred because all the suitcases fell off the luggage rack onto him when he was in his teens, and so forth. Death was an acquired characteristic. My grandmother, too, used to put other people's ailments into the diminutive: strokelets were what her friends had. Aldo said he was bored to tearsies by my grandmother's diminutives.

When I worked, for a time, in the infirmary of a branch of an up-state university, it was becoming more difficult with each passing semester, except in the most severe cases, to determine which students had mental or medical problems. At the clinic, young men with straggly beards and stained bluejeans wept alongside girls in jeans and frayed sweaters—all being fitted with contact lenses, over which they then wore granny glasses. There was no demand for prescription granny glasses at all. For the severely depressed, the paranoids, and the hallucinators, our young psychiatrists prescribed "mood elevators," pills that were neither uppers nor downers but which affected the bloodstream in such a way that within three to five weeks many sad outpatients became very cheerful, and several saints and historical figures became again Midwestern graduate students under tolerable stress. On one, not unusual, morning, the clinic had a call from an instructor in political science. "I am in the dean's office," he said. "My health is quite perfect. They want me to have a checkup."

"Oh?" said the doctor on duty. "Perhaps you could come in on Friday."

"The problem is," the voice on the phone said, "I have always thought myself, and been thought by others, a Negro. Now, through research, I have found that my family on both sides have always been white."

"Oh," the doctor on duty said. "Perhaps you could just take a cab and come over."

Within twenty minutes, the political-science instructor appeared at the clinic. He was black. The doctor said nothing, and began a physical examination. By the time his blood pressure was taken, the patient confided that his white ancestors were, in fact, royal. The mood elevators restored him. He and the doctor became close friends besides. A few months later, the instructor took a job with the government in Washington. Two weeks after that, he was calling the clinic again. "I have found new documentation," he said. "All eight of my great-grandparents were pure-blooded Germans—seven from Prussia, one from Alsace. I thought I should tell you, dear friend." The doctor suggested he come for the weekend. By Sunday afternoon, a higher dose of the pill had had its effect. The problem has not since recurred.

"All babies are natural swimmers," John said, lowering his two-

year-old son gently over the side of the rowboat, and smiling. The
child thrashed and sank. Aldo dived in and grabbed him. The baby
came up coughing, not crying, and looked with pure fear at his
father. John looked with dismay at his son. "He would have come
up in a minute," John said to Aldo, who was dripping and rowing.
"You have to give nature a chance."

"Reservations are still busy. Thank you for your patience," the
voice of the airline kept saying. It was a recording. After it had said
the same thing thirty-two times, I hung up. Scattered through the
two cars of the Brewster-New York train last week were adults with
what seemed to be a clandestine understanding of some sort. They
did not look at each other. They stared out the windows, or read.
"Um," sang a lady at our fourth stop on the way to Grand Central.
She appeared to be reading the paper. She kept singing her "Um,"
as one who is getting the pitch. A young man had already been
whistling "Frère Jacques" for three stops. When the "Um" lady
found her pitch and began to sing the national anthem, he looked at
her with rage. The conductor passed through, punching tickets in
his usual fashion, not in the aisle but directly over people's laps.
Every single passenger was obliged to flick the tiny punched part of
the ticket from his lap onto the floor. Conductors have this process
as their own little show of force. The whistler and the singer were in
a dead heat when we reached the city. The people with the clandestine understanding turned out to be inmates from an upstate
asylum, now on leave with their families, who met them in New
York.

I don't think much of writers in whom nothing is at risk. It is possible, though, to be too literal-minded about this question.
"$3000 for First Person Articles," for example:

> An article for this series must be a true, hitherto unpublished
> narrative of an unusual personal experience. It may be dramatic,
> inspirational, or humorous, but it must have, in the opinion of the
> editors, a quality of narrative and interest comparable to "How I
> Lost My Eye" (June '72) and "Attacked by a Killer Shark" (April
> '72). Contributions must be typewritten, preferably *double-
> spaced* . . .

I particularly like where the stress, the italics, goes.

In Corfu, I once met a polo-playing Argentine Existential psychiatrist who had lived for months in a London commune. He said that on days when the ordinary neurotics in the commune were getting on each other's nerves the few psychopaths and schizophrenics in their midst retired to their rooms and went their version of berserk, alone. On days when the neurotics got along, the psychopaths calmed down, tried to make contact, cooked meals. It was, he said, as though the sun came out for them. I hope that's true. Although altogether too much of life is mood. I receive communications almost every day from an institution called the Center for Short-Lived Phenomena. They have reporting sources all over the world, and an extensive correspondence. Under the title "Type of Event: Biological," I have received postcards about the progress of the Dormouse Invasion of Formentera ("Apart from population density, the dormouse of Formentera had a peak of reproduction in 1970. All females checked were pregnant, and perhaps this fact could have been the source of the idea of an 'invasion'"), and the Northwest Atlantic Puffin Decline. I have followed the Tanzanian Army Worm Outbreak; the San Fernando Earthquake; the Green Pond Fish Kill ("80% of the numbers involved," the Center's postcard reports, "were mummichogs"); the Samar Spontaneous Soil Burn; the Hawaiian Monk Seal Disappearance; and, also, the Naini Tal Sudden Sky Brightening.

Those are accounts of things that do not last long, but if you become famous for a single thing in this country, and just endure, it is certain you will recur enlarged. Of the eighteen men who were indicted for conspiracy to murder Schwerner, Goodman, and Chaney, seven were convicted by a Mississippi jury—a surprising thing. But then a year later, a man was wounded and a woman killed in a shootout while trying to bomb the house of some Mississippi Jews. It turned out that the informer, the man who had helped the bombers, and led the F.B.I. to them, was one of the convicted seven—the one, in fact, who was alleged to have killed two of the three boys who were found in that Mississippi dam. And what's more, and what's more, the convicted conspirator, alleged double killer, was paid thirty-six thousand dollars by the F.B.I. for bringing the bombers in. Yet the wave of anti-Semitic bombings in Mississippi stopped after the shootout. I don't know what it means. I am in this brownstone.

Last year, Aldo moved out and went to Los Angeles on a story. I called him to ask whether I could come. He said, "Are you going to stay this time?" I said I wasn't sure. I flew out quite early in the morning. On the plane, there was the most banal, unendurable pickup, lasting the whole flight. A young man and a young woman—he was Italian, I think; she was German—had just met, and settled on French as their only common language. They asked each other where they were from, and where they were going. They posed each other riddles. He took out a pencil and paper and sketched her portrait. She giggled. He asked her whether she had ever considered a career as a model. She said she had considered it but she feared that all men in the field were after the same thing. He agreed. He began to tell slightly off-color stories. She laughed and reproached him. It was like that. I wondered whether these things were always, to captive eavesdroppers, so dreary.

When I arrived at Aldo's door, he met me with a smile that seemed surprised, a little sheepish. We talked awhile. Sometimes he took, sometimes I held, my suitcase. I tried, I thought, a joke. I asked whether there was already a girl there. He said there was. He met me in an hour at the corner drugstore for a cup of coffee. We talked. We returned to the apartment. We had Scotch. That afternoon, quite late, I flew home. I called him from time to time. He had his telephone removed a few days later. Now, for a while, he's here again. He's doing a political essay. It begins, "Some things cannot be said too often, and some can." That's all he's got so far.

We had people in for drinks one night last week. The cork in the wine bottle broke. Somebody pounded it into the bottle with a chisel and a hammer. We went to a bar. I have never understood the feeling men seem to have for bars they frequent. A fine musician who was with us played Mozart, Chopin, and Beethoven on the piano. It seemed a great, impromptu occasion. Then he said, we thought, "I am now going to play some Yatz." From what he played, it turned out he meant jazz. He played it badly.

We had driven in from another weekend in the country while it was still daylight. Lots of cars had their headlights on. We weren't sure whether it was for or against peace, or just for highway safety. Milly, a secretary in a brokerage office, was married in our ground-floor shop that evening. She cried hysterically. Her mother and several people from her home town and John, whose girl she had been before he married Inez, thought it was from sentiment or shyness, or some conventional reason. Milly explained it to Aldo later. She and her husband had really married two years before—the week they met, in fact—in a chapel in Las Vegas. They hadn't wanted to tell their parents, or anybody, until he finished law school. They had torn up their Las Vegas license. She had been crying out of some legal fear of being married twice, it turned out. Their best man, a Puerto Rican doctor, said his aunt had been mugged in a cemetery in San Juan by a man on horseback. She thought it was her husband, returned from the dead. She had required sedation. We laughed. My friend across the hall, who owns the beagle, looked very sad all evening. He said, abruptly, that he was cracking up, and no one would believe him. There were sirens in the street. Inez said she knew exactly what he meant: she was cracking up also. Her escort, an Italian jeweller, said, "I too. I too have it. The most terrible anguishes, anguishes all in the night."

Inez said she knew the most wonderful man for the problem. "He may strike you at first as a phony," she said, "but then, when you're with him, you find yourself naturally screaming. It's such a relief. And he teaches you how you can practice at home." Milly said she was not much of a screamer—had never, in fact, screamed in her life. "High time you did, then," Inez said. Our sportswriter said he had recently met a girl whose problem was stealing all the suède garments of house guests, and another, in her thirties, who cried all the time because she had not been accepted at Smith. We heard many more sirens in the streets. We all went home.

At 4 A.M., the phone rang about fifty times. I did not answer it. Aldo suggested that we remove it. I took three Valium. The whole night was sirens, then silence. The phone rang again. It is still ringing. The paper goes to press tomorrow. It is possible that I know who killed our landlord. So many things point in one direction. But too strong a case, I find, is often lost. It incurs doubts, suspicions. Perhaps I do not know. Perhaps it doesn't matter. I think it does, though. When I wonder what it is that we are doing—in this brownstone, on this block, with this paper—the truth is probably that we are fighting for our lives.

# LIZZIE BORDEN IN THE P.M.

## ROBERT HENSON

Robert Henson is a native Oklahoman but is now on the
faculty of Upsala College in New Jersey. He's had stories
in numerous literary quarterlies, one of which was included
in *Best Little Magazine Fiction: 1970.*

I read about her death in the local papers—it was news even here—
"Lizzie Borden Again" for the last time, so to speak.

She entered the hospital under an assumed name. They knew who
she was, of course, and she knew they knew. Pure Lizzie, the whole
thing!

No other details—only a rehash of the murders and trial. I read
just far enough to see if the dress was mentioned.

I wrote to Miss Jubb to say I'd heard. On the way home from the
postoffice I fell and broke my hip. That same night, in the hospital,
I dreamed Lizzie pushed me. I was lying on the sidewalk. "*Why,*
Lizzie?"

She said what she had said thirty years before in Fall River jail:
"You've given me away, Emma." Then she turned her face away, as
she had done then, and said again: "Remember, Emma, I will never
give in one inch—never!"

"Well, Lizzie, you never did," I thought, waking. "But neither did
I, though for twelve years you kept after me."

I finally left her—moved clear away—first to Providence, then here.
Miss Jubb sometimes smuggled in a bit of news—"After all, she is
your sister!"—but I never saw her again.

I heard from her once, indirectly, when she threatened legal action
to keep me from selling my share in the Borden Building. I knew
she could have no sound business reasons, with mills closing and

property values going down in Fall River. I sent word through my lawyer that I intended to proceed.

But then newspapers got wind of the suit. I made myself un-available—Lizzie talked: Father had wanted the building to perpetu-ate his name—she could not conceive why I wanted to endanger family ownership—selling would be disloyal to his memory, etc.

I knew that holding onto a poor investment would be even more disloyal to Andrew J. Borden. However, I offered to sell my share to no one but her. I was even prepared to take a loss.

She refused: the building must be ours, not hers.

Ah Lizzie, I thought, will you never give up?

Reporters became more numerous—the past began to exercise its fascination—I capitulated. I did not have her toleration for pub-licity. I knew how she would interpret my retreat, but I had never been able to prevent her misconstructions—I did not hope to now.

She dropped the suit but not all the reporters went away. A young man from the Providence *Journal* persisted. I could not evade him—my address had become too well-known. Yet he was very courteous. He surprised me by asking through the screen door if the *Journal's* coverage of the trial was my reason for refusing to talk to him: "I've been reading our back files—I understand how you may feel. . . ."

"No, that was before your time—I do not blame you."

"The *Journal*, I believe, was your father's favorite paper."

"Yes. Not that that helped when the time came."

"In one thing our coverage was like everyone else's—there was nothing but respect for you. Affection might be a better word," he said.

"I was not the consideration. Most papers—yours excepted—were also well-disposed toward my sister."

"There was perhaps more admiration than affection for Miss Liz-zie," he said, begging me not to be offended.

"Admiration for my sister is surely not something that could give offense," I said, "except perhaps to the *Journal*."

"My erring employer!" he smiled.

I unlatched the screen. "Well, I will speak with you briefly if it will help you."

"At the time of her acquittal," he said, "it was predicted that the verdict wouldn't be acceptable to everyone—hasn't that proved true?"—"Yes, only too true"—"In all these years no one else has ever been arrested or accused or even suspected"—"Well, that is strange, but I do not blame Lizzie for that"—"It played no part in your decision to leave her?"—"I remained with her for twelve years!"—"You never had any reason yourself to find the verdict unacceptable?"—"My lips must remained sealed as to my precise reason for leaving—I remained with her," I heard myself saying, "until conditions became unbearable."

"Unbearable?"

"And now I deserve to be left in peace."

I paid for my indiscretion. Reporters again descended. For a second time I had to call upon Miss Jubb—"It will not die!" I said. She hurried over from Fall River and helped spirit me away. She is the only person who knows my present whereabouts.

She apologized for not coming in person to tell me about Lizzie's funeral. Poor soul! she's old as I am. But I understand what she meant: if she could just *tell* me she could make it seem less—Lizzie. As if I expected anything else!

She wrote that Lizzie had an operation about a year ago from which she never really recovered—in fact, she felt so strongly that she was going to die that she made plans for her own funeral and left them in a sealed envelope with Helen Leighton.

Miss Leighton was her latest close friend—a young woman—from Boston, not Fall River. According to Miss Jubb, people liked her but made fun of her a little after she took up with Lizzie. She became obsessed with the idea that Fall River had mistreated Lizzie, but would maintain in the same breath that Lizzie said and did nothing to influence her.

She faithfully carried out Lizzie's last wishes: the funeral to be held at home—someone to sing "My Ain Countree"—a select list of people to be invited. Miss Jubb was one.

When the mourners arrived there was no Lizzie—only Miss Leighton pale as death. She had just learned that Lizzie had been buried the night before. Lizzie had left the undertaker instructions too—and paid him well to keep them secret. She had not mentioned a funeral service to him. On the contrary she specified that after the laying-out the coffin was to be closed, draped in black and taken by night—it must be the *same* night—to Oak Grove cemetery. There it was to be lowered into the grave by Negroes—dressed in black. She specifically forbade any other attendants.

He had carried out her instructions to the letter, including the malicious timing.

Poor Miss Leighton! Most of the people on that select list came out of mere curiosity. She must have realized too late that Lizzie only wanted to spite them—and she would have to partly admit that they deserved it. I picture her standing in the parlor—she cannot quite condone Lizzie's action—cannot quite condemn it. People file past her in the awkward silence. She is just beginning to understand what was required of a friend to Lizzie Borden.

Lizzie did not exchange class rings with a friend when she graduated from high school. She gave hers to Father. We had just got home from the exercises. "I want you to wear it always."

Father was not sentimental but he was always solicitous of Lizzie's feelings. Perhaps he felt that she had been more disturbed by Mother's death than I was, though she was only two at the time, while I was twelve. And she was only four when he remarried—she found it natural to call Abby "Mother." I did not, and received permission to use her first name. A few years before the murders we both changed to "Mrs. Borden."

Lizzie soon found that attempts to treat her as a mother only embarrassed and alarmed her. From the beginning she could scarcely be prevailed upon to go out of the house or do anything in it except eat. She took to staying upstairs as much as possible—she would come down only for meals or between-meals foraging. Her weight, before many years passed, made even these descents laborious.

Lizzie turned back to me—she came to dislike Mrs. Borden intensely. I did not. I just could never grow fond of her—of her sloth, her physical grossness. I compared her to Mother and found her wanting. I did not, however, think of her as coming between Father and me. The older Lizzie grew the more she behaved as if every token of affection for Mrs. Borden were stolen from her. She fought back.

Father said he would attach the ring to his watch chain—"No, you must wear it on your finger!"—he said it was too small—"Then wear it on your small finger!"—he started to put it on his right hand —"Not that hand, Father!" I remember how he hesitated—the least thing was liable to send her off into one of her peculiar spells—then, silently, he worked the ring onto the small finger of his left hand. It clashed unavoidably with his wedding band. Abby said never a word. I saw her a few minutes later groaning up the stairs with a mutton

sandwich, a wedge of apple pie, and a pitcher of iced tea with half
an inch of sugar boiling up from the bottom.

When Lizzie was excited her eyes seemed to grow larger and paler—
color and expression would drain away—she would stare hard, but
at something no one else could see. The effect was not pleasant,
though reporters at the trial found it "incandescent," "hypnotizing,"
and so on—descriptions she cherished. No one found the mottling
of her skin attractive. Even as a girl Lizzie did not blush in the usual
sense—blood rising in her face would not blend with the pallor of her
skin but fought an ugly battle all along her jaw and straggled out
in her cheeks. Often when these signs of inner emotion were most
evident her voice and manner would indicate total self-possession:
"I have received Mr. Robinson's bill. Twenty-five thousand dollars.
I will not pay it."

Noting the inner stress, I did not mention her new house on French
Street nor any of the other extravagances that had followed her
acquittal far more quickly than Mr. Robinson's fee.

"I thought he was my friend—he called me his little girl."

"He saved your life, Lizzie."

She stared. "I was innocent, was I not?"

"Mr. Robinson made the jury see it."

"You did not think it was self-evident?"

"It is not a matter of what I thought."

"Well, I won't pay it! I won't be robbed, I won't be blackmailed!"

"Blackmailed!"

"Don't you see the dilemma Mr. Robinson is trying to put me in?
No innocent person would be charged such a fee. If I pay, it will be
said that I bought an acquittal."

"And if you don't?"

"That I wasn't willing to pay for one."

I hardly knew where to begin. "Why would he create such a
dilemma?"

"You can't guess?"

"No."

"Mr. Robinson doesn't believe me innocent," she said flatly. "This
is his way of saying so. I will not pay it!"

Either then or later—for we went over and over every point—she
said: "You look so downcast, Emma. If it will make you feel better,
*you* may pay him."

"How could it make me feel better, unless you lacked the money?"

"True," she said. "And you've had enough expenses from the trial as it is."

"I? I have had no expenses."

"Yes," she said, staring hard, "it is common knowledge."

Either then or later, when I wearied of playing games, I asked bluntly: "Are you speaking of Bridget?"

"Yes—of the way she dressed at the trial—her ticket back to Ireland—the farm she bought there. She couldn't possibly have saved enough from the wages Father paid her."

"Servant-girls may believe she was bribed," I said sharply, "but no sensible person does."

"No sensible person believes that Bridget couldn't recall what dress I was wearing that morning, or whether I had changed from cotton to silk."

"If she remembered and chose not to tell, it was because she did not think the matter important. Her silence did not become an expense."

She opened her fan and looked at me over the edge. It was Mr. Robinson who persuaded her to carry a black fan during the trial. She had never used one before but so much attention was paid to it that she was never afterward without one. To my occasional annoyance: "Put that away. Coyness does not become either of us. I will tell you now that I made arrangements to help Bridget financially during the trial. She was, after all, unemployed for almost a year. She chose to spend the money on showy dresses—that was indiscreet, but I was not bribing her and therefore had no right to object. However it may have looked, my conscience was clear. When the trial was over she wanted to go home—that is natural—and Ireland is her home."

"It is all so easily explained, yet you have never explained it before."

"It was my own affair."

"Oh Emma," she suddenly said in a tone of peculiar satisfaction, "you are not a good liar! You believe I changed from the cotton to the silk that morning! You believe Bridget lied when she said she couldn't remember!"

"Lizzie, Lizzie! if you say you wore the silk all morning, I believe you. If Bridget lied when she said she could not remember anything to the contrary, she lied upon her own motion. The money I gave her was not a bribe!"

"It was a reward."

"It was neither—it was a simple gift!"


She would not pay Mr. Robinson but I found her at work on a gift for Mr. Moody. I thought at first she was adding to her own scrapbook of clippings and memorabilia of the trial. Then I saw two police photographs mounted opposite each other—Father—half sliding off the couch—profile streaked with blood—Mrs. Borden— wedged between the bed and bureau—feet awkwardly splayed. . . .

"Where—how—did you get these?"

"I asked for them. Oh, not for myself—" and she showed me the flyleaf: "For Mr. William Moody, as a memento of an interesting occasion."

"Lizzie, you cannot!"

"It's a duplicate of my own . . . except for those additions."

"Oh Lizzie, at the very least this is not in good taste!" For some reason the remark made her laugh out loud. I persisted: "It is . . . inappropriate—it will seem that you are taunting him."

"Not at all," she replied, fetching string and wrapping paper. "Mr. Moody is a young man on the threshold of his career. Even though he lost this case, his connection with it cannot but help him. He will be grateful."

The assistant prosecuting attorney!


That time the house was broken into—in broad daylight—about a year before the murders—the police questioned and questioned Bridget. A little gold watch and some jewelry were missing from Mrs. Borden's dressing table. She discovered the theft when she returned from one of her rare outings, a drive with Father to Swansea. The rest of us had been home all day—none of us heard any suspicious noises. It was Lizzie who discovered how the thief got in: someone had left the cellar door unbolted—the lock had been picked with a nail—Lizzie pointed to it still hanging in the keyhole.

The police came back next day to question Bridget further. Maybe she had opened the cellar door for an accomplice. . . . Lizzie had to be sent to her room—she could not stop talking and interfering. Father had already asked the police not to release news of the theft to the papers—now he asked them to drop the investigation altogether. "You will never catch the real thief. . . ." The word "real" struck me as odd at the time, but I believe he was trying to let the police know that he had no suspicion at all of Bridget.

That night he locked and bolted the door between Lizzie's bedroom and the one he and Mrs. Borden used. It had never been locked before, it was never unlocked again.

I knew Lizzie would forgive Father anything—I braced myself for an attack on Mrs. Borden for that silent accusation. Instead she seemed to put the matter completely out of her mind.

But a few weeks later, while Alice Russell was paying a visit, Lizzie suddenly began a rambling account of the theft. Alice had not heard of it before—after a few questions she fell tactfully silent. Lizzie said Father had been right to call off the investigation. Robberies so bold yet limited in scope (nothing taken but what belonged to Mrs. Borden!) could seldom be solved. Even the police said so. All we could do was try to prevent a repetition—as she had done by putting a lock on her side of the door. If a thief came up the backstairs again, he would no longer be able to pass from Father's room into hers and so to the front of the house. . . .

I heard this in startled silence. Later I checked. There indeed on Lizzie's side of the door was a shiny new lock.

Of the people who dropped away after the trial I missed Alice Russell most of all—she had been my best friend. Lizzie once made the astonishing suggestion that I exchange calls with her again.

"You know I cannot do that, Lizzie."

"Why not?—unless you have some quarrel I don't know about."

"We have not quarrelled, for we have not spoken since she testified against you."

She was toying with her fan. "She did not testify against me. She told what she saw. It could not hurt me."

I said warily, "I wonder that you can put it out of your memory so easily."

"Well," she said negligently, "what did she have to tell except that she saw me tearing up an old dress? But you saw me too—you knew the dress. When I told you I was going to burn it, you said, 'Yes, why don't you?' "

"In that," I said bitterly, "I had to contradict her."

"Is she angry about that? She can't be so petty!"

"I do not know how she feels."

"If she wanted her reputation for accuracy to go unchallenged she shouldn't have waited three months before telling her story."

I could have wept. "Out of fondness for me, Lizzie! When she could bear it no longer she sent to beg my forgiveness!"

"Ah, now I understand a little better your desire not to see her again," Lizzie said on that note of satisfaction I was learning to dread. "She needn't have implicated you."

"She did not implicate me."

"Forced you to contradict her, then."

"*You* did that! I told about the dress-burning the way *you* remembered it."

She rose and walked about the room, opening and shutting her fan. "Why did you let me burn it, Emma, when you still believed I had changed?"

According to Alice I had tried—I had not said, "Why don't you?" but "I would not do that if I were you!" She was coming back from church—on Sunday after the murders on Thursday—I let her in the back door—followed her through the entry into the kitchen—Lizzie was standing between the stove and the coal closet—she had a blue dress in her hand—with brown stains on the skirt. I knew she had stained a blue dress with brown paint several months earlier—several times she had mentioned throwing it away. I also knew the police were looking for a blue dress with blood stains on it. I could have said either "I would not do that if I were you" or "Why don't you?" Either.

"Alice may resent my contradicting her testimony," I said, "but she would never misinterpret my reasons for doing so."

"Do you think that I do?"

I would not answer.

She was never satisfied if I said I did not remember, or had not been paying attention, or had lost my way in the technicalities, contradictions, details. . . . Yet when Mr. Moody opened for the prosecution I remember thinking, "So there it all is—so *that's* their side," just as if nine months had not gone by, with an inquest and preliminary investigation. Mr. Robinson could bring tears to my eyes but I could seldom apply what he was saying to the point at hand. Mr. Moody was mercilessly clear and orderly. Watching Lizzie during his presentation, I thought, "Innocence alone can account for that detached expression."

Only when he came to the very end did her eyes and complexion show a change. The case against her, he said, had always had a weapon, a motive and an opportunity. The real puzzle had been the absence of a blood-stained dress. He promised to clear up this mystery—the prosecution would present new testimony by a witness who had seen Lizzie burning a bloody garment!

I felt my blood turn to ice—Alice was going to testify. Lizzie opened her fan—shut it. In later years, sensational journalism had her swooning virtually every day. In fact she did so only once. Just as Mr. Moody finished and started for his table she fainted dead away.

Mr. Moody's triumph was short-lived. In the days following, so many rulings from the bench favored the defense that he was rumored to have urged the District Attorney to withdraw from the case—throw the responsibility for freeing Lizzie upon the Court. There was much ugly comment upon the fact that the presiding judge was one of Mr. Robinson's appointees when Mr. Robinson was governor of the state. The District Attorney, however, did not withdraw. Apparently he did not feel as strongly as Mr. Moody that the trial was a mockery of justice.

Still, it was not to him that Lizzie sent her "memento of an interesting occasion."

Eventually she paid Mr. Robinson but announced that her door would be closed to him. Not that he had ever made any attempt to call. Neither had Mr. Jennings, her other lawyer, our family lawyer. After we moved up on the hill, he simply dropped away.

The house seemed far too large to me, but Lizzie said she planned to entertain extensively and would need room. She was no longer content with one maid—she engaged a "staff"—a housekeeper, a second maid, a cook, a Negro coachman. "What," I wondered silently, "will I do with myself all day?"

One afternoon I came back from shopping and found a workman carving the word "Maplecroft" on the front doorstep. I broke my silence.

"What is this?"—"The name I've given the house"—"What does it mean?"—"It doesn't 'mean' anything, I simply like the sound of it" —"You are making a mistake"—"In what way?"—"Naming a house will be thought inappropriate, in bad taste"—"By whom?"—"Everyone, and especially those whom you would least like to think it."

"Dearest Emma," she said, "you can only mean yourself. And while I value your opinion, you're too close to me to realize that I can't be what I was before."

"No, you cannot. More is now expected."

"Well, that is my point," she said, and would discuss it no further.

But people who accuse Lizzie of "social climbing" because she bought the house on French Street do not understand that Father could have moved up on the hill at any time—he would only have been taking his place among his peers. But he was not concerned with external signs of his standing. Lizzie's hints and pleas fell on deaf ears.

It was the only thing he would not do for her—he sent her on the Grand Tour—paid dressmakers' bills without complaint—stretched her allowance with gifts of money. . . . This generosity somewhat contradicted his basic nature but I never resented it. In such things as property and stocks he treated us equally, and he praised me where he could never have praised her—for wise management. He took both of us into his business confidence, however. I can recall only one time when he did not—and that was when he put a house in Mrs. Borden's name without telling us. We learned of it only by accident.

Lizzie was extraordinarily agitated: "She has persuaded him to go behind our backs! He would never have done this by himself!"

I agreed it was unlike him.

"What shall we do?"

I said we could do nothing except hope it would not happen again. That was not enough for Lizzie: "I shall let her know what I think of her!" She ceased to call her Mother. She went further—she would speak if they met but would not talk. Her silences were brooding—palpable—disquieting even to me. Mrs. Borden was clearly miserable, though her appetite was unaffected.

Father found a rental duplex and put it in our names. It was worth to each of us exactly what Mrs. Borden's house was worth. I was astounded by the crudeness of this attempt to atone for his secrecy and favoritism. Lizzie responded by refusing to take any more meals with him and Mrs. Borden. The house was heavy with tension.

He came to me for help. I had always had the room adjoining his and Mrs. Borden's. It was larger than Lizzie's, better furnished, and cheerier with two windows on the south. It fell to me when we first moved to Second Street only because I was the older. Now Father asked if I would exchange with Lizzie.

I said, "Yes, if you think it will raise her spirits."

But he would not directly admit his motive: "She has to go through your room to reach the hall closet. She shouldn't always be disturbing you."

True, eighteen or twenty of her dresses hung in the hall closet—her own would not hold them all. I said, "It is a considerate suggestion."

"I want you to offer it as your own," he said in his driest voice.

I thought for a moment. "She will not be deceived."

"Will you do it?"

"Well, I will say that the subject came up and that we agreed on the idea."

As I did. But he did not profit much from the exchange. Close on its heels came the daylight robbery. By then I was taking my meals with Lizzie and had ceased to call Mrs. Borden by her first name.

I had nothing to do the livelong day—I began to occupy myself at Central Congregational. Lizzie was scathing: "You've become a regular pew-warmer, Emma. You never were before. Why this sudden compulsion?"

"I am under no compulsion. I go freely."

"But you can't stay away freely, that's the point!"

I did not answer. She leaned her cheek on her fan and gazed at me poignantly: "Perhaps Miss Jubb is your reason. If so, why not say it? I know you need someone besides me."

I ached to hold her in my arms at that moment, comfort her, as when she was a child and had no mother but Emma. I had never cultivated the people who rallied round her during her trouble—I did not feel neglected when they dropped away. She seethed as if from an injustice.

For ten months the people we now lived among but seldom saw had made her their special care. They extolled her in the press as a person of the highest character and most delicate sensibilities—charged that she was being sacrificed to inept police performance and indifferent law enforcement—called her a martyr to low-bred envy or political opportunism—the scapegoat periodically demanded by the moneyless and propertyless. Mrs. Holmes, Mrs. Brayton, Mrs. Almy and their like kept her cell filled with fresh flowers. Only persons with influence obtained seats in the courtroom—and how many of them female! What a murmur of feminine admiration went up when she entered the first day in her dress of severest black but latest fashion—great leg-of-mutton sleeves—ruching of black lace—a black lace hat to set off the pallor of her face. And from one hand (the other lay on Reverend Buck's arm) drooped the quickly-famous long black fan.

When the words "Not guilty" were at last pronounced these same admirers wept, fainted, sank to their knees in prayers of thanksgiving. Mrs. Holmes gave a splendid reception. All the people Lizzie had always admired were there to admire her. How could she escape the conclusion that she had done something for them?

We returned to Second Street next day. While we waited for the housekeeper to answer the bell Lizzie kept glancing about. Only yesterday forty reporters or more were vying for her attention, people were holding up children for her to kiss. . . . Now the street was deserted.

We went in. I made a move toward the parlor but Lizzie walked straight ahead to the sitting room. She did not seem to notice the bare space along the wall—left by the couch where Father had been hacked to death. She was taking the pins out of her hat. "Do take another peek outside, Emma. Someone may be there."

I refused. "It is over," I said.

Gradually she saw that it was, though in more ways than the one I meant. She did not ask why—she retaliated. Formerly she had been a mainstay of Central Congregational—now she said spitefully, "Let Mariana Holmes find someone else to cook and serve dinners for newsboys!"

Reverend Buck tried without much enthusiasm to reconcile her, then turned the task over to his assistant. Reverend Jubb was more solicitous, going so far as to bring his sister with him each time. But after two visits Lizzie refused to come downstairs. I was their only catch.

"Aren't you afraid someone will think you are trying to atone for something?" Lizzie asked with a disagreeable smile.

Her other guess, about Miss Jubb, was closer. If I helped with the Christmas dinner for newsboys or kept accounts for the Fruit-and-Flower Mission, the reason was Miss Jubb's friendship. That and the fact that I had nothing to do all day long—except think.

Their clothing lay in a heap in the cellar for three days, then the police gave me permission to bury it—behind the stable—with an

officer watching. Then I scrubbed the blood off the doorjamb downstairs—the baseboard upstairs—thinking, "So little here, so much
on their clothes. . . ." Father's had spurted forward—only one splash
hit the doorjamb by his head—the murderer might have entirely
escaped being spattered. But he had straddled Mrs. Borden's body,
they said, after felling her with the first blow—he could scarcely have
avoided stains below the knees. Yet her blood shot forward too—
onto the baseboard—so possibly he could have walked along the
street without attracting attention—once he got out of the
house. . . .

It was *their* clothing that was soaked—pools of blood had spread
out on the floor. Lizzie's shoes and stockings were spotless—so was
her blue silk dress. There had been no cries or sounds of struggle
to alert her. Both died with the very first blow, medical examiners
said. The senseless hacking that followed was . . . just that.

I had been at the seashore. Alice met me at the station, all in tears.
Lizzie was waiting at home, dry-eyed. I do not know why she sent
for Alice instead of one of her own friends upon discovering Father's
body. It was poor Alice who went upstairs and found Mrs. Borden.

In the carriage she said: "Lizzie came to see me last night—burst
in, really. I felt quite concerned—she looked, well, distraught. She
said she was depressed and wanted to talk to someone—she said she
couldn't shake off the feeling that something terrible was going to
happen—she felt as if she should sleep with her eyes open. . . . Shall
I mention all this, Emma?"

"It will come out."

I never asked, never hinted that Alice should either speak or be
silent on any matter. She stayed with us the entire week following
the murders. So much of what she told me before Lizzie was arrested
is mixed up in my mind with what she told afterward in court. Was it
when she met me at the station, or later, that she mentioned a bundle
on the floor of my closet? Detectives had been searching for a murder
weapon, she said, but they had been very considerate—they had not
turned things completely upside down. In my room they had not even
disturbed the bundled-up blanket in the closet. . . . I could not
think what she meant—I left no such bundle—I found none when
I got home.

Mrs. Borden had received twenty blows, all from behind—Father ten. He had been taking a nap—one side of his face had been sliced away—the eye sliced in half. In the coffin, that side was pressed into the pillow. Lizzie bent down and kissed the upturned cheek. Her ring was still on his little finger.

Crowds lined the route to the cemetery. The hush was eerie. When Lizzie stepped out of the carriage at the gate it was possible to hear someone whisper, "She's not wearing black!"

It was like a portent of the future. I asked her if the printer had made an error when I saw "Lisbeth Borden" on her new calling cards. She had never been called anything but Lizzie.

"It's not an error. Lisbeth is my name now, and you must call me by it"—"I cannot do that"—"You mean you will not"—"Is it a legal change?"—"You know it isn't"—"Then of what use is it?"—"Oh, use!"—"Very well, for what reason at all do you wish to take a different name?"

She was silent, then with a curious little smile she said, "I'll tell you—if you'll tell me why you've taken to wearing nothing but black."

"There is no mystery in that."

"Surely you're not still in mourning."

"Not mourning exactly. I have never cared much for clothes. You know that. These now seem appropriate."

"That is becoming your favorite word."

"I am a limited person."

"Then this is a permanent change in your dress?"

"I have not thought of it that way—it may be."

"Well, and I'm changing my name!"

"The two things are not the same."

"True . . . they aren't. You must take care that your black doesn't begin to look like penance," said Lisbeth of Maplecroft.

She purchased one of the first automobiles in Fall River. I had only Miss Jubb's description of it—"long, black, like the undertaker's limousine." The Negro who had been her coachman, or perhaps another, became her chauffeur. She could be seen every day going for a drive, looking neither left nor right but staring straight ahead. By then her ostracism was complete. All too appropriately had "Maplecroft" been carved on her doorstep by a man from the tombstone works.

I went to her coachman after the unpleasantness over the book and asked him bluntly if he had been a party to it. A certain journalist had compiled an account of the case from his daily reports, court transcripts and so forth, and was giving it the sensational title *Fall River Tragedy*. It was supposed to clear up some "doubts" that Lizzie herself had stonily refused to clear up. Fall River was agog with anticipation—the outside world too, it was said, though the printing was being done locally. Lizzie was several times observed entering and leaving the shop. It was assumed that she was threatening legal action. But on publication day the printer announced that Miss Borden had bought up the entire printing and had it carted away the night before.

"Did you help her?"—"She say I help her?"—"The printer said she came with some Negro assistants—he couldn't identify them"—"Miss Lisbeth know what she doin' if she get colored mens. . . ."

I caught the note of admiration—it was Bridget all over again. "If she changed her dress you must tell Mr. Jennings," I said.

"Lizzie may be foolishly afraid that innocent stains will incriminate her," Mr. Jennings patiently explained. "But to a jury a perfectly clean dress may seem even more suspicious."

"A silk dress, Bridget!—heavy silk for house wear!—on the hottest day of the year!"

"If she changed from her cotton and don't want to tell, I daresay she has her reasons," Bridget said, addressing Mr. Jennings. "'Twouldn't be foolishness—not her."

"A pool of blood had dripped from the sofa when she discovered her father," said Mr. Jennings, "yet not even her hem was stained. It might be *very* foolish to maintain that."

"I can't see how me backin' up her own statement can harm her," Bridget said stubbornly. "Besides, all I'm really sayin' is, I don't *remember* what she was wearin'."

Mr. Jennings was still not easy in his mind—he went to Lizzie and pleaded with her not to conceal anything that might damage her case later. He was explicit.

She retaliated by replacing him with Mr. Robinson—but blamed me for undermining his faith in her innocence. She was lying on a cot when the matron let me in after their interview. "You have given me away, Emma"—"I only told him what I thought he ought to know for your defense"—"Bridget's word wasn't enough?"—"Bridget did not say you hadn't changed, only that she could not remember"—

"And you persuaded Mr. Jennings that that wasn't enough! upon what grounds? upon what grounds?"—"Upon grounds of common sense."

She turned her face to the wall: "I will never give in one inch—never!"

Nor did Bridget, though subjected to great pressure on the witness stand. Lizzie was wearing a blue dress but whether it was cotton or silk she did not remember. Her steadfastness deserved our gratitude, I thought, but as for bribing her, I might as well be accused of buying the coachman's silence! "Were the books destroyed?"—"Miss Lisbeth know best about that"—"Did any escape? were any saved back?"—"She know best about that."

After Alice testified that she saw Lizzie pulling a blue dress out of the coal closet that Sunday morning, Mr. Moody asked me if we usually kept our ragbag there. The question was excluded. I could easily have answered: no, we kept the ragbag in the pantry, for cleaning cloths and such. Lizzie probably got the dress out and tossed it into the coal closet, next to the stove, while she made a fire. Mr. Moody asked why Lizzie was burning the dress at all if we kept a ragbag. Excluded. I could have said: well, we didn't save every scrap! He asked if Lizzie usually disposed of old clothes by burning them in sweltering August heat. Excluded.

When I saw her there by the stove I didn't really think of *how* she was disposing of the dress, only of the fact that she was *doing* it, and that it might look suspicious. I might very well have said, "I wouldn't do that if I were you!" And yet I knew she had a blue cotton dress she had been planning to throw away. She was holding the dress so that the paint-stains didn't show, but it was the same one. For all I knew it had been in the ragbag for weeks! I could just as easily have said, "Yes, why don't you?"

Under siege, as it were, we pulled the blinds and spoke to no one but each other.

"Where are the books? Have they been destroyed?"

"You needn't worry. I paid well."

"It was the worst thing you could have done!"

"Yes—to the hypocritical."

"How could the book have hurt you? It could only show your innocence."

"Oh," she said with an ugly smile, "people are no longer interested in that . . . if they ever were."

"Then this latest act will give them comfort."

"This *latest* act!" she mocked.

"Why do you torture yourself!"

"Why have you stopped sitting on the porch in the evening?"

I did not answer. She recited coldly:

> Lizzie Borden took an axe,
> Gave her mother forty whacks.
> When she saw what she had done,
> She gave her father forty-one.

I shuddered. "You have heard the singing from the shrubbery," she said with her peculiar relish. "You have heard the taunts."

"Urchins . . . from under the hill."

"All the hill listens."

"What has this to do with the book!" I cried.

Her eyes had gone pale. "The book—why, if they want that, they must come to me"—"You saved copies then?"—"They must admit they are fascinated."

Over and over every point! Twelve years of it! What she would not tolerate from outsiders, she required of me: "Do you think Father really planned to give Swansea to her?"

"I do not know."

"He knew how much it meant to us—all the summers we spent there, from childhood on—until she came along and spoiled it."

"I should be surprised if he made the same mistake twice. He had already seen the consequences of one such secret transaction."

"If you *had* known, though, or even suspected, you'd have told me, wouldn't you? You wouldn't let me learn by accident?"

I would not answer. About two weeks before the murders I had heard some such rumor, but I was preparing to leave for the seaside and had no desire to upset her with anything so vague.

Either then or later (for she could not be satisfied) she said: "Suppose *I* had discovered such a plot—overheard them discussing it, say—if I had come to you, what would you have done?"

"Done?"

"Or suggested."

"I would have said what I said before: we can do nothing."

"Nothing. . . ," she echoed restlessly.

"I mean, we could not undo Father's decision."

"We could have shown our displeasure again—more strongly! We could have moved away, left them—left *her*, with her everlasting gorging and grasping!"

"I had no wish to leave Father."

"He had driven the wedge."

"I did not blame him. He could not have foreseen her unsuitability."

"But dwelling with such an impasse! Surely there were times when you felt you could bear it no longer!"

"I was more content then than I am now."

Yes, I said to the young man from the *Journal*, the lack of motive is puzzling, but no one who really knew Lizzie would believe that money or property could be *her* motive even if she were guilty. She was not acquisitive—that is a vulgar error.

How well I remember Mr. Moody's question after he had listened to an explanation of her break with Mrs. Borden: "A house put in her name? Is that all? There was no more to it than that?" Even he detected that property was insufficient as an explanation.

Perhaps it was unjust that a kind of obsession with Lizzie grew up right alongside the isolation of her. Perhaps she could not have prevented it. But from the day of her acquittal she adamantly refused to reassure her admirers. Questions they had been willing to suspend during her ordeal they must be willing to suspend forever. Of that, at least, she left them in no doubt. Not that anyone ever challenged her directly, she said irritably.

"Well, they are friends, not lawyers. They are waiting until you are ready."

"Ready? I should like to know one topic upon which you think I ought to set their minds at rest."

I had one on the tip of my tongue but suppressed it: "No, that is for you to decide."

And so the questions remained. "Where was your sister during the murders?" Thirty years later! The very question I had bitten back! The first one I asked when I returned from the seaside!

"Her whereabouts were established at the trial," I said to the reporter.

I could still see Mr. Moody exhibiting his plan of the house and yard. The front door was locked—the intruder had to come in the back—pass to the front—go upstairs to kill Mrs. Borden—come down to kill Father—escape out the back again—all without being seen or heard by either Lizzie or Bridget. And between the two deaths, an hour and a half gone by. . . .

He traced Bridget's movements with a pointer: working outside when Mrs. Borden died—taking a nap in her room in the garret when Father died. But where was Lizzie when Mrs. Borden died? Ironing in the kitchen? How did the murderer manage to slip past her? Somewhere else on the ground floor? How did he muffle the crash of a two-hundred pound body overhead? Why did she hear no cries, no sounds of struggle? Where did the murderer hide during that hour and a half before Father came home and lay down for a nap? And where was Lizzie when the second hacking to death took place? I could still hear Mr. Moody's relentless mockery of the defense: "Eating a pear!—in the loft of the barn!—where she had gone to find a piece of screenwire!—in a heavy silk dress!—in 100° heat!"

"There were contradictions at the trial," said the reporter. "I mean, did she ever explain to *your* satisfaction where she was?"

"My satisfaction was not the question."

The dress was immaculate when the police arrived. No blood on the hem, no dust from the loft.

She had a telephone installed at "Maplecroft." It was of little use to her and proved a trap to me. She had begun to take short trips out of town, staying for a day, sometimes overnight, in Boston or Providence. . . . On these occasions I would sometimes ring up Miss Jubb and invite her to bring her work over. One day while we were cozily occupied in my room, crocheting doilies for a church bazaar, Lizzie returned unexpectedly from Providence. I heard her speaking to the maid. I rose without haste and went to the head of the stairs. She had already started up. I remember her fur cape and her hat with the iridescent birds-wings. Her muff, oddly enough, was stuffed into her reticule.

"Miss Jubb is here, Lizzie," I said firmly. "Won't you come say hello?"

She brushed past me—she seemed distracted, breathless: "In a moment. . . ."

"She is taking off her things," I told Miss Jubb, but my face betrayed me. She started to put away her work: "Perhaps she does not feel well. . . ."

At that moment Lizzie swept into the room—color high—eyes luminous—both hands extended. "Dear Miss Jubb, how very nice to see you! I've been hoping you'd call!" For the next five minutes she chattered torrentially. Miss Jubb sent me so many gratified glances that I was forced to bend my eyes upon my crocheting. "You came back early. Did you finish all your shopping?"

"Oh yes—or rather, no. After Tilden's I let the rest go."

"Tilden's have such lovely things," sighed Miss Jubb, who could not afford any of them.

"Shall I show you what I bought there?" cried Lizzie. She hurried out and returned with two porcelain paintings. One was called "Love's Dream," the other "Love's Awakening." Miss Jubb went into raptures over them. Lizzie said effusively: "I meant them for my wall but now I have a different plan. One will be yours, the other Emma's, as a reminder to you of your friendship. You shall not refuse me!"

Miss Jubb burst into tears. For some time she had been hinting that I kept her away from Lizzie unnecessarily. I was unpleasantly reminded of other times when Lizzie pressed gifts on people, but, reproaching myself, I said that if Miss Jubb would accept her porcelain, I would accept mine. Blushing, she chose "Love's Dream" as more appropriate for herself. Lizzie laughed heartily: "Well, Emma, appropriate or not, that leaves 'Love's Awakening' to you!"

Not that it mattered. Miss Jubb broke hers while fastening it to the wall. Too embarrassed to say anything, even to me, she made a trip to Providence to have it repaired. At Tilden's the manager was summoned. When had she purchased this painting? "It was a gift." From whom? "Why, Lizzie Borden. . . ." Then she learned that the two porcelains had disappeared, unpaid-for, on the day of Lizzie's shopping trip.

Fall River woke to the headline "Lizzie Borden Again!"

Tilden's sent a detective with a warrant. Lizzie talked agitatedly with him, then came upstairs to me and said—so great was her confusion, "We must call Mr. Jennings right away!"

"An attorney is not necessary," I said. "Tilden's will not prosecute you if you go talk the matter over with them. You have been a good customer for many years."

"They have no grounds!" she began, then broke off. In a moment she said, "Well then, I shall go to Providence. I couldn't have taken the paintings without paying for them, but who will believe me?"

"Are you certain you have no receipt?"

"Yes. I seldom pay cash at Tilden's—I forgot all about a receipt."

"The clerk will have a record, a duplicate."

"No," she said, staring, "if anything it was the clerk who perpetrated this fraud—by slipping the paintings into my reticule."

"But Lizzie, you remember paying for them!"

"I mean he slipped them in to make me overlook the receipt."

He slipped them inside your muff, I thought, suddenly weary of trying to believe her.

Her jaw had mottled slightly: "And Miss Jubb played right into his hands."

"Miss Jubb is not to blame," I said angrily. "Miss Jubb has been greatly mortified!"

"I'm only saying that she gave the clerk his chance to raise a hue-and-cry against me."

"He would have done that the first day," I said with a cruelty I could not control, "if all he wanted was to have his name linked with that of Lizzie Borden."

She fell silent for a moment. "You're not coming with me, then? I must settle with Tilden's alone?"

"The purchase was yours alone."

"When I come back," she said, "the paintings will still be yours and Miss Jubb's."

As soon as she left the house I found a hammer—I broke "Love's Awakening" to bits.

In the spring before that terrible August, Father went out to the stable with a hatchet. Lizzie's pigeons had been attracting mischievous boys. Tools—feed—pieces of harness had been disappearing. To discourage marauders, Father beheaded the pigeons.

I began to think of leaving her.

The nurse asked today if there was anyone I wanted to get in touch with—just for company, she said, now that the doctor has decided I must not leave the hospital—"not for a while."

I said there was no one but asked to see the doctor as soon as he was free. I knew what her question really meant.

And yet I procrastinated . . . for I knew that if I ever left Fall River I would not come back. Lizzie could not stay away. Her trips became more frequent, more prolonged—not only Boston and Providence but New York—Philadelphia—Washington. But after a week, or two weeks, or a month away, she would return—Lizzie Borden would be seen again in Fall River.

Playbills showed how she occupied herself when her shopping was done. She did not discuss this new interest with me—I learned about her friendship with Nance O'Neil from the newspaper—inexorably "Lizzie Borden Again" arrived.

A lawsuit against Miss O'Neil would have been news in any case, a popular actress sued by her manager to recover advances and loans. But add that Lizzie Borden appeared every day in court as her champion—that Lizzie Borden hired the lawyer who was defending her— that Lizzie Borden had given her the little gold watch that was pinned to her bosom!

She came home during a recess in the case. I had not seen her for a month. She had been at a resort hotel near Boston. According to the newspapers she had met Miss O'Neil there, taking refuge from the cupidity of her manager. She warned me in provocative words not to tamper with Miss O'Neil's portrait of herself as a woman wronged, misunderstood, persecuted—just the kind of woman, in effect, that she was best known for portraying on the stage. "She is a gifted and sadly maligned young woman. The manager has used her ruthlessly. I will not desert her!"

"I have not suggested that you should. I know nothing about her, the case, or your friendship—except what anyone can know."

She opened and shut her fan. "As for the newspapers, she is not ashamed to have her name linked with Lizzie Borden's."

"To which of you is that a compliment?"

"When we first met she knew me by the name I use at hotels for the sake of privacy. I merely presented myself as an admirer, someone who had seen all her plays. Later I had to tell her that the person who wished to befriend her was not Lisabeth Andrews but Lizzie Borden. She said, 'But my dear, I've known that all along! It makes no difference to me.'"

I said nothing. She toyed with her fan. "The remark doesn't dispose you in her favor?"

"Why should it? Such professions cost her nothing but you a great deal."

"Oh, *cost!*" she said harshly. Then her tone softened: "Poor Emma! Some things are worth paying for, others aren't. You've never learned the difference."

"I have not had good teachers," I said.

After the suit was settled Lizzie continued to rescue her from small debts and indulge her taste for trinkets and jewelry. Miss O'Neil repaid her by introducing her to "artistic" people and consulting her (or pretending to) on personal and professional matters. I accused myself of small-mindedness. I still had Miss Jubb, she had not deserted me—why should I begrudge Lizzie this friendship, sorely in need as she was?

So when she announced that Miss O'Neil's company had been engaged for a performance in Fall River and that she was entertaining them afterward, I said briskly, "Then I'm to meet Miss O'Neil at last!"

"There's time for you to make other plans," she said. "I know you don't approve of artists—"

"I do not *know* any artists," I interrupted. "If I did I would judge them on individual merits, not as a group."

"Dearest Emma," she said, "I've always been able to count on you. . . ."

I felt a familiar dread.

Caterers, florists, musicians came and went. "Maplecroft" was finally going to serve its function. Only, from my window, there was not a soul to be seen on the street unless someone delivering ice— potted palms—a grand piano. . . . Not even any children hanging around the front gate in a spirit of anticipation—their mothers had swept them out of sight.

I tried to help—once I went downstairs in time to collide with a delivery of wine. "Oh, don't look so stricken, Emma! It's champagne, not gin!" I thought of all those years she'd worked for the Temperance Union—how they had held prayer meetings for her during the trial. She read my mind: "Don't worry, I'm not going to break my pledge. Only my guests aren't used to lemonade and iced tea!"

Long before the guests arrived, I had decided to keep to my room. Anything, I thought, would be better than appearing with my feelings on my sleeve. I had prepared an excuse I hoped would placate

Lizzie. I awaited her knock momentarily. But only the sounds of the party increasingly assaulted my door.

Shortly before eleven I crept down the backstairs and phoned Miss Jubb. She could hear the din in the background—the music, the strident laughter, the crashing of glass: "I'll be waiting in a carriage down the block."

I hurriedly began to pack an overnight bag, but now that I hoped to escape undetected, there came a knock. I opened the door on Nance O'Neil.

She glided in, casting a glance all about, as if to say, "What a charming room!"—then, turning, clasped her hands entreatingly: "It *is* Emma, isn't it? I've so wanted to meet you! I'm naughty to force myself on you this way, but Lisbeth told me the beautiful thing you said about artists—I knew you wouldn't turn me away!"

She was extraordinarily pretty—I could understand Lizzie's infatuation with her—that delicacy of face and figure did not run in the Borden family. But her effusiveness left me ill-at-ease. I thought at first that it was inspired by wine, but soon saw that it was only one of many poses she could summon up with instant ease. Her eyes fell on my traveling bag: "You're taking a trip? Lisbeth didn't say why you hadn't come down."

"Yes . . . I'm sorry I cannot spend time with you."

"But you're not leaving tonight surely!" she cried. "Won't you come downstairs for a while? Lisbeth would be so pleased—she's very proud of you!"

"No, I cannot. I am sorry she has sent you on a futile errand."

"No, no, no! I came of my own free will! Oh, I'm too impulsive—it's my greatest fault!—you *do* think me naughty!" Here she pouted charmingly.

"You have not been naughty," I replied, "only misused. You may tell my sister I said so."

She ceased magically to convey childlike sincerity—her bearing and expression shed an atmosphere of injured pride and reproachful forgiveness. I returned to my packing, not wanting to furnish her with further opportunities to display her art.

Five minutes later I stood at the door with my bag. I turned out the light and listened. Just as I was ready to slip out, I heard voices hurrying along the hall—then a sharp rapping—then the door was flung open. I had just time to shrink into the darkness behind it.

"She's not here," Lizzie said.

"Her suitcase was on the bed. . . ."—a shaft of light fell where it had been.

"It's gone—she's gone."

"Perhaps you can overtake her," Miss O'Neil murmured plaintively.

"You don't know her," Lizzie said in a hoarse voice. She closed the door but they did not move away. "I wonder what you said to precipitate her flight?"

"I?" Miss O'Neil fairly shrieked. "I said nothing! Her flight, if that's what it was, was already planned!"

"She would never have left at this time of night—she dreads scandal too much."

"Perhaps *you* are the one who doesn't know her," Miss O'Neil unwisely remarked.

"She is my sister!" Lizzie said harshly.

"But you've often said how different you are."

"We're two sides of the same coin."

"Don't let's stand here arguing," Miss O'Neil said placatingly. "She'll come back."

"Is that what you want?" Lizzie asked in a strange tone.

"Why, what do you mean?"

"It isn't what *I* want—*I* don't want her to come back."

"Well then, neither do I!"

"I thought not," Lizzie said with satisfaction.

"I don't know what you're trying to prove," Miss O'Neil said in a disturbed voice. "I assure you I did nothing to cause her to leave—I came to her at your request. . . . She said you had misused me," she ended with some heat. "I'm beginning to think she was right!"

Then Lizzie became placating: "I haven't misused you—Emma spoke out of jealousy—because I feel closer to you than I ever did to her—and because you understand me better."

"I don't like that kind of jealousy, Lizzie. You must go after her and explain—Why, what is the matter?"

"You called me *Lizzie*."

"Did I? Well, talking to your sister—hearing her—you know how I simply absorb things—"

"It is not my name. But perhaps there are those who make jokes about it in private," Lizzie said grimly.

Poor Miss O'Neil! "This is beside the point! We were talking about your sister!"

"I cannot go after Emma, I cannot bring her back. She left me long before tonight. I've lived with her door locked against me for twelve years. I'll hardly know she's gone."

"Don't talk about it, Lisbeth dear!"

"No, I won't burden you," said Lizzie. "And yet . . . I can't help feeling that somehow you took my side when you were with her—perhaps not even knowing it."

Miss O'Neil's voice, already at a distance, faded rapidly: "Come now! quickly! No, I won't listen to any more. . . ."

After the scandal at Tyngsboro, she apparently did not. Lizzie was sadly in error if she imagined that her connection with drunkenness and misconduct would go unnoticed simply because it did not occur in Fall River but in a house she rented for a week somewhere else. Miss Jubb learned a great deal more than I would allow her to tell me—"If you are fascinated with her," I said snappishly, "you must not use me as an excuse." There need not even have been the bitter climactic quarrel that Miss Jubb got wind of. Those butterfly wings could not in any case have supported the burden of Lizzie Borden for long.

The doctor came. I said, "I want my body taken to Fall River—we have a family plot in Oak Grove cemetery."

"I've already promised to see to that, Miss Borden, and your other requests will be honored too."

His choice of words roused my attention: "I have asked before?"—"Yes"—"And made other requests?"—"Yes, but when you weren't quite yourself perhaps"—"What did I say?"—"You asked to be buried the same way your sister was"—"That is correct, I do not want a ceremony"—"I mean, you asked to be buried at night"—"Did I?"—"You asked for Negro pallbearers only. . . ."

I fell to thinking. "Well, I will go halfway with you," I said. "I don't mind the Negro pallbearers but I don't want the other part."

"I'm not surprised," she said. "Do you remember the day you changed rooms with Alice Russell? It was Saturday, after the police told us not to leave the house."

"You asked if someone in the house was suspected—you demanded to know who it was!"

"That night you asked Alice to sleep in your room. You took the one she'd been using, Father's and Mrs. Borden's. You put their lock and bolt between us. We never again had rooms opening freely into each other."

"Yes, I knew what you meant, even if poor Miss O'Neil did not."

"You have given me away, Emma."

"If you changed your dress you must say so."

"I will never give in."

"*I have no reason to wish to be buried at night!*"

"Now that's more like it." The doctor's voice startled me. "Let's have less talk about dying and more about getting well. You have a long time to live!"

Well, that is not true. In the very course of nature I cannot live *much* longer. If I die quite soon, though—say within seven days of your death, or ten days, some such noticeable number—remember, I am seventy-seven!—it will be a coincidence! I hope you will not try to make any more of it than that.

# ALTERNATIVES

## ALICE ADAMS

Alice Adams grew up in Chapel Hill, North Carolina, and graduated from Radcliffe. Since then she has lived mainly in San Francisco. This is her fourth appearance in the O. Henry Prize Stories. Her second novel, *Families and Survivors*, will be published this year by Alfred A. Knopf.

It is the summer of 1935, and there are two people sitting at the end of a porch. The house is in Maine, at the edge of a high bluff that overlooks a large and for the moment peaceful lake. Tom Todd and Barbara Rutherford. They have recently met (she and her husband are houseguests of the Todds). They laugh a lot, they are excited about each other, and they have no idea what to do with what they feel. She is a very blond, bright-eyed girl in her twenties, wearing very short white shorts, swinging long thin legs below the high hammock on which she is perched, looking down at Tom. He is a fair, slender man with sad lines beside his mouth, but (not now!) now he is laughing with Babs. Some ten years older than she, he is a professor, writing a book on Shelley (Oh wild West Wind!) but the Depression has had unhappy effects on his university (Hilton, in the Middle South): 10 percent salary cuts, cancellation of sabbaticals. He is unable to finish his book (no promotion); they rely more and more on his wife's small income from her bookstore. And he himself has been depressed—but not now. What a girl, this Babs!

The house itself is old, with weathered shingles that once were green, and its shape is peculiar; it used to be the central lodge for a camp for underprivileged girls that Jessica Todd owned and ran before her marriage to Tom. The large, high living room is still full of souvenirs from that era: group pictures of girls in bloomers and middies, who danced or rather posed in discreet Greek tunics, and wore headbands; and over the fireplace, just below a moldering deer's head, there is a mouse-nibbled triangular felt banner, once dark green, that announced the name of the camp: Wabuwana. Why does Jessica keep all those things around, as though those were her happiest days? No one ever asked. Since there were no bedrooms Tom and Jessica sleep in a curtained-off alcove, with not much privacy; two very small rooms that once were storage closets are bedrooms for their children, Avery and Devlin. Babs and her husband, Wilfred Rutherford, have been put in a tent down the path, on one of a row of gray plank tent floors where all the camper girls used to sleep. Babs said, "How absolutely divine—I've never slept in a tent." "You haven't?" Jessica asked. "I think I sleep best in tents."

A narrow screened-in porch runs the length of the house, and there is a long table out there—too long for just the four Todds, better (less lonely) with even two guests. The porch widens at its end, making a sort of round room, where Tom and Babs now are, not looking at the view.

Around the house there are clumps of hemlocks, tall Norway pines, white pines, and birches that bend out from the high bank. Across the smooth bright lake are the White Mountains, the Presidential Range—sharp blue Mount Adams and farther back, in the exceptionally clear days of early fall, such as this day is, you can see Mount Washington silhouetted. Lesser, gentler slopes take up the foreground: Mount Pleasant, Douglas Hill.

Beside Babs in the hammock lies a ukelele—hers, which Tom wants her to play.

"Oh, but I'm no good at *all*," she protests. "Wilfred can't stand it when I play!"

"I'll be able to stand it, I can promise you that, my dear."

Her accent is very Bostonian, his Southern; both tendencies seem to intensify as they talk together.

She picks up the instrument, plucks the four strings as she sings, "My dog has fleas."

"So does Louise," he sings mockingly, an echo. Tom is fond of simple ridiculous jokes but he feels it necessary always to deliver them as though someone else were talking. In fact, he says almost everything indirectly.

They both laugh, looking at each other.

They are still laughing when Jessica comes out from the living room where she has been reading (every summer she rereads Jane

Austen) and walks down the length of the porch to where they are, and says, "Oh, a ukelele, how nice, Barbara. Some of our girls used to play."

Chivalrous Tom gets up to offer his chair—"Here you are, old dear." She did not want to sit so close to the hammock but does anyway, a small shapeless woman on the edge of her chair.

Jessica is only a few years older than Tom but she looks considerably more so, with graying hair and sad brown eyes, a tightly compressed mouth. She has strong and definite Anglo-Saxon notions about good behavior (they all do, this helpless group of American Protestants, Tom and Jessica, Barbara and Wilfred) which they try and almost succeed in passing on to their children. Jessica wears no makeup and is dressed in what she calls "camp clothes," meaning things that are old and shabby (what she thinks she deserves). "Won't you play something for us?" she asks Babs.

"Perhaps you will succeed in persuasion where I have failed," says Tom. As he sees it, his chief duty toward his wife is to be unfailingly polite, and he always is, although sometimes it comes across a little heavily.

Of course Jessica feels the currents between Babs and Tom but she accepts what she senses with melancholy resignation. There is a woman at home whom Tom likes too, small, blond Irene McGinnis, and Irene is crazy about Tom—that's clear—but nothing happens. Sometimes they kiss; Jessica has noticed that Verlie, the maid, always hides Tom's handkerchiefs. Verlie also likes Tom. Nothing more will happen with Babs. (But she is wrong.) It is only mildly depressing for Jessica, a further reminder that she is an aging, not physically attractive woman, and that her excellent mind is not compelling to Tom. But she is used to all that. She sighs, and says, "I think there's going to be a very beautiful sunset," and she looks across the lake to the mountains. "There's Mount Washington," she says.

Then the porch door bangs open and Wilfred walks toward them, a heavy, dark young man with sleeves rolled up over big hairy arms; he has been washing and polishing his new Ford. He is a distant cousin of Jessica's. "Babs, you're not going to play that thing, are you?"

"No, darling, I absolutely promise."

"Well," Tom says, "surely it's time for a drink?"

"It surely is," says Babs, giggling, mocking him.

He gestures as though to slap at the calf of her long leg, but of course he does not; his hand stops some inches away.

Down a wide pine-needled path, some distance from the lodge, there is a decaying birchbark canoe, inside which white Indian pipes grow. They were planted years back by the camper girls. Around the canoe stands a grove of pines with knotted roots, risen up from the ground, in which chipmunks live. Feeding the chipmunks is what Jessica and Tom's children do when they aren't swimming or playing on the beach. Skinny, dark Avery and smaller, fairer Devlin—in their skimpy shorts they sit cross-legged on the pine needles, making clucking noises to bring out the chipmunks.

A small chipmunk comes out, bright-eyed, switching his tail back and forth, looking at the children, but then he scurries off.

Devlin asks, "Do you like Babs?" He underlines the name, meaning that he thinks it's silly.

"She's OK." Avery's voice is tight; she is confused by Babs. She doesn't know whether to think, as her mother probably does, that Babs's white shorts are too short, that she is too dressed up in her pink silk shirt for camp, or to be pleased at the novel sort of attention she gets from Babs, who said last night at dinner, "You know, Avery, when you're a little older you should have an evening dress this color," and pointed to the flame-gold gladioli on the table, in a gray stone crock.

"Her shorts are too short," says Devlin.

"What do you know about clothes? They're supposed to be short —*shorts*." Saying this, for a moment Avery feels that she *is* Babs, who wears lipstick and anything she wants to, whom everyone looks at.

"Mother doesn't wear shorts, ever."

"So what? You think she's well dressed?"

Devlin is appalled; he has no idea what to make of what she has said. "I'll tell!" He is desperate. "I'll tell her what you said."

"Just try, you silly little sissy. Come on, I'll race you to the lodge."

Both children scramble up, Avery first, of course, and run across the slippery pines, their skinny brown legs flashing between the trees, and arrive at the house together and slam open the screen door and tear down the length of the porch to the cluster of grown-ups.

"Mother, do you know what Avery said?"

"No, darling, but please don't tell me unless it was something very amusing." This is out of character for Jessica, and Devlin stares at his mother, who strokes his light hair, and says, "Now, let's all be quiet. Barbara is going to play a song."

Babs picks up her ukelele and looks down at it as she begins her song, which turns out to be a long ballad about a lonely cowboy and a pretty city girl. She has an attractive, controlled alto voice. She becomes more and more sure of herself as she goes along, and sometimes looks up and smiles around at the group—at Tom—as she sings.

Tom has an exceptional ear, as well as a memory for words; somewhere, sometime, he has heard that ballad before, so that by the time she reaches the end he is singing with her, and they reach the last line together, looking into each other's eyes with a great stagy show of exaggeration; they sing together, "And they loved forever more."

But they are not, that night, lying hotly together on the cold beach, furiously kissing, wildly touching everywhere. That happens only in Tom's mind, as he lies next to Jessica and hears her soft sad snores. In her cot, in the tent, Babs sleeps very soundly, as she always does, and she dreams of the first boy she ever kissed, whose name was not Tom.

In the late forties, almost the same group gathers for dinner around a large white restaurant table, the Buon Gusto, in San Francisco. There are Tom and Jessica, and Babs, but she is without Wilfred, whom she has just divorced in Reno. Devlin is there, Devlin grown plump and sleek, smug with his new job of supervising window display at the City of Paris. Avery is there, with her second husband, fat, intellectual Stanley. (Her first marriage, to Paul Blue, the black trumpet player, was annulled; Paul was already married, and his first wife had lied about the divorce.)

Tom and Barbara have spent the afternoon in bed together, in her hotel room—that old love finally consummated. They are both violently aware of the afternoon behind them; they are partly still there, together in the tangled sea-smelling sheets. Barbara presses her legs close. Tom wonders if there is any smell of her on him that anyone could notice.

No one notices anything; they all have problems of their own.

In the more than ten years since they were all in Maine Jessica has sunk further into her own painful and very private despair. She is not fatter, but her body has lost all definition, and her clothes are deliberately middle-aged, as though she were eager to be done with being a sexual woman. Her melancholy eyes are large, darkly shadowed; below them her cheeks sag, and the corners of her mouth have a small sad downward turn. Tom is always carrying on—the phrase she uses to herself—with someone or other; she has little energy left with which to care. But sometimes, still, a lively rebellious voice within her cries out that it is all cruelly unfair; she has done everything that she was taught a wife is expected to do; she has kept house and cared for children and listened to Tom, laughed at his jokes and never said no when he felt like making love—done all those things, been a faithful and quiet wife when often she didn't want to at all, and there he is, unable to keep his eyes off Babs, laughing at all *her* jokes.

Tom has promised Barbara that he will leave Jessica; this winter they will get a divorce, and he will apply for a teaching job at Stanford or U.C., and he and Babs will live in San Francisco; they are both in love with the city.

Avery has recently begun psychoanalysis with a very orthodox Freudian; he says nothing, and she becomes more and more hysterical—she is lost! And now this untimely visit from her parents; agonized, she questions them about events of her early childhood, as though to get her bearings. "Was I nine or ten when I had whooping cough?"

"What?" says Jessica, who had daringly been embarked on an alternate version of her own life, in which she did not marry Tom but instead went on to graduate school herself, and took a doctorate in Classics. (But who would have hired a woman professor in the twenties?) "Tom, I'd love another drink," she says. "Barbara? you too?" Late in her life Jessica has discovered the numbing effects of drink—you can sleep!

"Oh, yes, divine."

Sipping what is still his first vermouth, Devlin repeats to himself that most women are disgusting. He excepts his mother. He is sitting next to Babs, and he cannot stand her perfume, which is Joy.

Looking at Jessica, whom, curiously, she has always liked, Barbara feels a chill in her heart. Are they doing the right thing, she and Tom? He says they are; he says Jessica has her bookstore and her student poet friends ("Fairies, most of them, from the look of them," Tom says), and that living with him does not make her happy at all; he has never made her happy. Is he only talking to himself, rationalizing? Barbara doesn't know.

All these people, so many of them Southern, make Avery's husband, Stanley, feel quite lost; in fact, he finds it hard to understand anything they say. Tom is especially opaque: the heavy Southern accent and heavier irony combine to create confusion, which is perhaps what Tom intends. Stanley thinks Tom is a little crazy, and feels great sympathy for Jessica, whom he admires. And he thinks: poor Avery, growing up in all that—no wonder Devlin's queer and Avery has to go to a shrink. Stanley feels an awful guilt toward Avery, for not supplying all that Tom and Jessica failed to give her, and for his persistent "premature ejaculations"—and putting the phrase in quotes is not much help.

"I remember your whooping cough very well indeed," says Tom, pulling in his chin so that the back of his head jerks up; it is a characteristic gesture, an odd combination of self-mockery and self-congratulation. "It was the same summer you pushed Harry McGinnis into the swimming pool." He turns to Stanley, who is as incomprehensible to him as he is to Stanley, but he tries. "Odd gesture, that. Her mother and I thought she had a sort of 'crush' on young Harry, and then she went and pushed him into the pool." He chuckles. "Don't try to tell me that ladies aren't creatures of whim, even twelve-year-old girls."

"I was nine," says Avery, and does not add: you had a crush on Harry's mother, you were crazy about Irene that summer.

Jessica thinks the same thing, and she and Avery are both looking at Tom, so that he feels the thought.

"I remember teasing Irene about the bathing suit she wore that day," he says recklessly, staring about with his clear blue eyes at the unfamiliar room.

"What was it like?" asks Barbara, very interested.

"Oh, some sort of ruffled thing. You know how those Southern gals are," he says, clearly not meaning either his wife or his daughter.

"I must have thought the whooping cough was a sort of punishment," Avery says. "For having a crush on Harry, as you put it."

"Yes, probably," Jessica agrees, being herself familiar with many varieties of guilt. "You were awful sick—it was terrible. There was nothing we could do."

"When was the first summer you came to Maine?" Devlin asks Babs, coldly curious, nearly rude. It is clear that he wishes she never had.

"1935. In September. In fact September ninth," she says, and then blushes for the accuracy of her recall, and looks at Tom.

"Verlie took care of me," says Avery, still involved with her whooping cough.

Jessica sighs deeply. "Yes, I suppose she did."

Almost ten years later, in the middle fifties, Tom and Barbara are married. In the chapel of the little church, the Swedenborgian, in San Francisco, both their faces stream with tears as the minister says those words.

In her forties, Barbara is a striking woman still, with her small disdainful nose, her sleekly knotted pale hair, and her beautiful way of walking, holding herself forward like a present. She has aged softly, as very fine-skinned very blond women sometimes do. And Tom is handsome still; they make a handsome couple (they always have).

Avery is there; she reflects that she is now older than Barbara was in 1935, that summer in Maine. She is almost thirty, divorced from Stanley, and disturbingly in love with two men at once. Has Barbara never loved anyone but Tom? (Has she?) Avery sees their tears as highly romantic.

She herself is a nervy, attractive girl with emphatic dark eyebrows, large dark eyes, and a friendly soft mouth, heavy breasts on an otherwise slender body. She wishes she had not worn her black silk suit, despite its chic; two friends have assured her that no one thought about wearing black to weddings anymore, but now it seems a thing not to have done. "I wore black to my father's wedding"—thank God she is not still seeing Dr. Gunderscheim, and will use that sentence only as a joke. Mainly, Avery is wondering which of the two men to marry, Charles or Christopher. (The slight similarity of the names seems ominous—what does it mean?) This wondering is a heavy obsessive worry to her; it drags at her mind, pulling it down. Now for the first time, in the small dim chapel, candlelit, it wildly occurs to her that perhaps she should marry neither of them, perhaps she should not marry at all, and she stares about the chapel, terrified.

"I pronounce you man and wife," says the minister, who is kindly, thin, white-haired. He is very old; in fact he quietly dies the following year.

And then, almost as though nothing had happened, they have all left the chapel: Tom and Barbara, Avery and Devlin, who was Tom's best man. ("I gave my father away," is another of Avery's new post-wedding jokes.) But something has happened: Tom and Barbara are married. They don't believe it either. He gives her a deep and prolonged kiss (why does it look so awkward?) which embarrasses Devlin, so that he stares up and down the pretty, tree-lined street. He is thinking of Jessica, who is dead.

And he passionately wishes that she had not died, savagely blames Tom and Barbara for that death. Trivial, entirely selfish people—so he sees them; he compares the frivolity of their connection with Jessica's heavy suffering. Since Jessica's death Devlin has been in a sort of voluntary retreat. He left his window-display job and most of his friends; he stays at home on the wrong side of Telegraph Hill, without a view. He reads a lot and listens to music and does an occasional watercolor. He rarely sees Avery, and disapproves of what he understands to be her life. ("You don't think it's dykey, the way you sleep around?" was the terrible sentence he spoke to her, on the eve of Jessica's funeral, and it has never been retracted.) Sometimes in his fantasies it is ten years back, and Tom and Jessica get a divorce and she comes out to live in San Francisco. He finds her a pretty apartment on Telegraph Hill and her hair grows beautifully white and she wears nice tweeds and entertains at tea. And Tom and Barbara move to hell—Los Angeles or Mexico or somewhere. Most people who know him assume Devlin to be homosexual; asexual is actually the more accurate description.

They stand there, that quite striking group, all blinking in a brilliant October sun that instantly dries all tears; for several moments they are all transfixed there, unable to walk, all together, to their separate cars, to continue to the friend's house where there is to be the wedding reception. (Why this hesitation? do none of them believe in the wedding? what is a marriage?)

Five years later, in the early sixties, Avery drives up to Maine from Hilton, for various reasons which do not include a strong desire to see Tom and Barbara. She has been married to Christopher for four years, and she came out from San Francisco to Hilton to see how it was away from him. Away from him she fell wildly in love with a man in Hilton named Jason Valentine, and now (for various reasons) she has decided that she needs some time away from Jason.

She drives smoothly, quietly, along the pine-needled road in her Corvair to find no one there. No car.

But the screen door is unlatched, and she goes in, stepping up from the old stone step onto the long narrow porch, from which the long table has been removed, replaced with a new one that is small and round. (But where did they put the old one?) And there are some bright yellow canvas chairs, new and somehow shocking against the weathered shingled wall.

Inside the house are more violent changes, more bright new fabrics: curtains, bandanna-red, and a bandanna bedspread on the conspicuous wide bed. Beside the fireplace is a white wicker sofa (new) with chintz cushions—more red. So much red and so much newness make Avery dizzy; almost angrily she wonders where the old things are, the decaying banners and sepia photographs of girls in Greek costumes. She goes into the kitchen and it is all painted yellow, into what was the large closet where she used to sleep—but a wall has been knocked out between her room and Devlin's; it is all one room now, a new room, entirely strange, with a new iron bed, a crocheted bedspread, which is white. Is that where they will expect her to sleep? She wishes there were a phone. Tomorrow she will have to drive into town to call Jason at his studio.

Needing a drink, Avery goes back into the kitchen, and finds a bottle of an unfamiliar brand of bourbon. She gets ice from the refrigerator (terrifyingly new—so white!), water from the tap—thank God, the same old sink. With her clutched drink she walks quickly through the living room to the porch, down to the end. She looks out across the lake with sentimentally teared eyes, noting that it is clear but not quite clear enough to see Mount Washington.

Being in love with Jason, who is a nonpracticing architect (he would rather paint), who worries about his work (his nonwork), who loves her but is elusive (she has no idea when they will see each other again), has tightened all Avery's nerves: she is taut, cries easily, and is all concentrated on being in love with Jason.

A car drives up, a Mustang—Barbara is faithful to Fords. And there they are saying, "Avery, but we didn't ex*pect* you, we went into *Port*land, for *lob*sters. Oh, dear, how awful, we only bought *two!*" Embracing, laughing. Tears (why?) in everyone's eyes.

They settle down, after packages are put away, Avery's bags in the new guest room, and they watch the sunset: a disappointing pale pastel. And they drink a lot.

Barbara is nervous, both because of this shift in schedule and because of Avery, whom she regards as an intellectual, like Tom. She is always afraid of what Avery will say—a not-unfounded fear. Also, she is upset about the prospect of two lobsters for three people.

What he considers her untimely arrival permits Tom's usual am-

bivalence about Avery to yield to a single emotion: extreme irrita-
tion. How inconsiderate she is—always has been! Besides, he was
looking forward to his lobster.

Avery chooses this unpropitious moment to announce that she is
leaving Christopher. "We've been making each other miserable,"
she says. "We have been, for a long time." She trails off.

Tom brightens. "Well, old dear, I always think incompatibility is a
good reason not to live together." He has no notion of his own pruri-
ence in regard to his daughter.

She does. She says, "Oh, Christ."

Barbara goes into the kitchen to divide up the lobster; a skilled
hostess, she does quite well, and she makes a good mayonnaise, as
she listens to the jagged sounds of the quarrel on the porch. Avery
and Tom. She sighs.

Now darkness surrounds the house, and silence, except for a faint
soft lapping of small waves on the shore, and tiny noises from the
woods: small animals shifting weight on the leaves, a bird moving on
a branch.

"Although I have what I suppose is an old-fashioned prejudice
against divorce," Tom unfortunately says.

"Christ, is that why you stayed married to mother and made her
as miserable as you could? Christ, I have a prejudice against misery!"
Avery feels her voice (and herself) getting out of control.

Barbara announces dinner, and they go to the pretty new table,
where places are set, candles lit. Barbara distributes the lobster, giving Tom the major share, but he scowls down at his plate.

As Avery does at hers—in Hilton, with Jason, she was generally
too overstimulated, too "in love" to eat; now she is exhausted and
very hungry. She turns to Barbara, as though for help. "Don't you ever
wish you'd got married before you did? What a waste those years
were. That time in San Francisco, why not then?"

Startled, Barbara has no idea what to answer. She has never allowed herself to think in these terms, imaginatively to revise her life.
"I feel lucky we've had these years we have had," she says—which,
for her, is the truth. She loves Tom; she feels that she is lucky to be
his wife.

"But those last years were horrible for mother," Avery says. "You
might have spared her that time."

"I think I might be in a better position than you to be the judge
of that." Enraged, Tom takes a characteristic stance: his chin trust

out, he is everyone's superior—he is especially superior to women and children, particularly his own.

"Oh, yeah?" In her childhood, this was considered the rudest remark one could make; then Avery would never have said it to Tom. "You think she just plain died of a heart attack, don't you? Well, her room was full of empty sherry bottles. All over. Everywhere those drab brown empty bottles, smelling sweet. Julia told me, when she cleaned it out."

This information (which is new) is so shocking (and so absolutely credible) to Tom that he must dismiss it at once. His desperate and hopeless guilts toward Jessica have forced him to take a sanctimonious tone in speaking of her. He must dismiss this charge at once. "As a matter of fact, Julia is quite unreliable, as Verlie was," he says.

Avery explodes. "Julia is unreliable! Verlie was! Christ—why? because they're black? because they're women?"

Barbara has begun to cry. "You've got to stop this," she says. "Why quarrel about the past? It's over—"

Tom and Avery stare at each other, in terrible pain; they would like to weep, to embrace, but they are unable to do either.

Tom draws himself up stiffly—stiffly he turns to Barbara. "You're quite right, old dear," he says.

Several things attack Avery's mind at once: one, that she would like to say, goddam you both, or something obscene, and take off down the turnpike, back to Boston; two, she is too drunk for the turnpike; and three, she has just noticed that Tom speaks to Barbara exactly as though she were Jessica, as though neither of them were people but something generic named Wife.

And so the moment goes, the awful emotions subside, and they all retreat to trivia. Although Avery's hands still shake, she comments on the mayonnaise (she is not excruciatingly Southern Jessica's daughter for nothing), which Barbara gratefully takes up.

"I'm never sure it will come out right," she says. "I've had the most embarrassing failures, but of course tonight, just for family—" She is unable to finish the sentence, or to remember what she meant.

Later, during the next few years before Tom's death, Avery looks back and thinks that yes, she should have left then, drunk or not. She could have found a motel. That would have been a strong gesture, a refusal to put up with any more of what she saw as Tom's male imperialism, his vast selfishness. (But poor Avery was constantly plagued with alternatives; she constantly rewrote her life into new versions in which she did not marry Stanley. Or Christopher. Sometimes she thought she should have stayed with Paul Blue; in that version, of course, he was not married.) After Tom died she thought that perhaps it was just as well she hadn't left, but she was never quite sure.

Against everyone's advice, early in the summer after Tom died, Barbara drove alone to Maine. Even Devlin had called to dissuade her (in fact ever since Tom's funeral, to which Avery did not even come—Tom had died while she was in Mount Zion Hospital being treated for depression—a new and warm connection had been established between Barbara and Devlin; they wrote back and forth; she phoned him for various pieces of advice—she had begun to rely on him as she was used to relying on Tom).

Devlin said, "Darling Barbara, do you see it as an exercise in masochism? I wouldn't have thought it of you."

"Angel, you don't understand. I love that house. I've been extremely happy there."

"Barbara, let me be blunt: don't you think you'll be fantastically lonely?"

"No, I don't."

And so, after visits with friends and relatives in Boston, Barbara drives on to Maine in her newest Ford, and arrives in a twilight of early July. She parks near the house, gets out, pausing only briefly to observe the weather, which is clear, and to smile at the warm familiar smell of pines. Then she walks briskly over to the porch and opens the padlock on the screen door.

Her first reaction, stepping up onto the porch, could be considered odd: she decides that those yellow chairs are wrong for the porch. This pleases her: changing them for something else will give her something to do. She enters the living room, sniffs at the musty, airless space, and goes into the kitchen, where last summer she hid a bottle of bourbon in the flour bin. (Sometimes stray hunters or fishermen break into the house and take things.) No one has taken it, and she makes herself a good stiff drink, and goes to the rounded end of the porch, to sit and rest.

And much more clearly than she can remember anything that happened last month, last winter or fall, she sees that scene of over thirty years ago, sees Tom (how young he was, how handsome), as he urged her to play her ukelele (play what? did he name a song?), and she sees Jessica come out to where they are (making some reference to the girls who used to come to camp—poor Jessica), and Wilfred, as always angrily serious, puffing although not yet fat, and then wild, skinny Avery (why did she and Jason Valentine not marry?) and frightened Devlin, holding his mother's arm. She sees all those people, and herself among them, and for an instant she has a sense that she *is* all of them—that she is Jessica as well as Barbara, is Wilfred, Avery, Devlin, and Tom.

But this is an unfamiliar mood, or sense, for her, and she shakes it off, literally shaking her head and lifting her chin. She remembers then that she put the old chairs and the table in the shed next to the kitchen.

Three days later Barbara has restored the lodge to what (to herself) she calls its "old look." The old chairs and old long table are back. She has even put up some of Jessica's old pictures in the living room.

She has no idea why she made such an effort, except that she firmly believes (always has) in the efficacy of physical work; she was driven by a strong, controlling instinct, and she also believes in her instincts. She even laughs to herself at what could seem a whim, and in writing a note to Devlin she says, "You'd have thought I was restoring Williamsburg, and you should see my blisters!"

And so at the end of her day she is seated there at the end of the porch, and everything but herself looks just as it did when she first saw it. She drinks the two stiff highballs that she allows herself before dinner, and she remembers all the best times with Tom, San Francisco hotels and Paris honeymoon, the big parties in Hilton, and she sheds a few tears, but she does not try to change anything that happened. She does not imagine an altered, better life that she might have had.

# OUT IN THE GARAGE

### RICHARD HILL

Richard Hill is thirty-one and is temporarily living on the Gulf near St. Petersburg, Florida, where he was born. Since teaching English at the University of South Florida at Tampa three years ago, he has traveled and lived in New York, Hollywood, and New Orleans. He has published a novel, *Ghost Story*, and has written fiction and journalism for *Harper's*, *Rolling Stone*, *Oui*, the *Village Voice*, and other periodicals as well as *American Review*.

He looked young. The cancer had eaten age as well as life, as though to compensate somewhat for what it was doing by making him a little like the slick, suntanned dude in two-toned shoes of my earliest memories. He was embarrassed as well as frightened at this point. We had learned of the cancer when I was home last and he had gone through the terror then. He had visited all the car dealerships where he'd worked and said, "Boys, you're looking at a dead man." He had called old friends and enemies, dug out photos of beloved cars and boats and motorcycles, had even spoken of the possibility of an afterlife. Now he was a little tired of the business and, as I say, embarrassed. He was tired of being carcinoma's Willy Loman. He and I have always overreacted, but we've usually had the sense to be embarrassed later.

Since the news that it was inoperable, he had puttered in the garage, making Briggs and Stratton-powered go-carts for my absent sons, trying to get a 125 cc Benelli motorcycle to start, recycling the enormous variety of bolts, belts, pulleys, solid rubber wheels, aluminum tubing, canvas, and other materials from one project into another. I had always considered him a mechanical genius, wondered under what weight of music lessons, literary ambitions, great hopes, those genes had been smothered in me. Somehow I had never even been able to find the right tool when he called from beneath one of his projects.

We sat in the kitchen for a while. "Did the doctor tell you to come home?" he asked.

"No, I just ran out of options again, and money."

"You should get another teaching job, stop screwing around letting people dump on you. If you got a salary, you can tell 'em all to go shit in their hats."

I tried to change the subject. "You know what I remember more than anything else? Coming back from the theater in Highlands after a Johnny Mack Brown movie, through the mountains, falling asleep in the car. You and Mom carrying Sister and me into the cabin, putting us into pajamas. The sound of that river and the cold sheets."

He was pleased. "Kids in pajamas. Believe me, that's the only thing. The rest of it isn't worth a noseful. You know I couldn't handle much of you after you grew up."

We wept for a while at the loss of innocence, then went out to the garage where he showed me the Benelli. "Can't get the sonofabitch started," he said. "It's getting gas, spark, everything, but it won't start." This was another of the challenges he'd thrown at me all these years. He knows I ride motorcycles, but I take them to the shop when they need it. I didn't care about this one, but I cranked on it until sweat ran grainy on my glasses and finally it sputtered. He was delighted, and adjusted the carburetor until it coughed out. He knew the quitter was going to quit again, and this time he had to quit too. He went in for his Demerol injection and a nap and I went out to get drunk. His disappointment in me was as obvious as ever.

I stayed at my sister's nearby, in one of those wonderland apartment complexes with pools, saunas, divorcees. But I'd lost any sexual interest, so I drank and read and sat by the pool in the strange November Florida sun. Mother was giving him massive injections now, along with the tranquilizers and sleeping pills. He wanted the shots every four hours at least and she was exhausted. When I did visit, he was either unconscious or demanding another shot, and mother spent most of her conversation on the difficulties she faced. I resent stories about heroic families and dignified deaths. We raged and bitched, wept and accused, summoned pleasant memories and vomited old grudges. He didn't look young any more and was no longer able to go to the garage. For the most part, I stayed away and drunk.

The Blue Room is where the hustlers go in that town. It's where you see your used-car and new-car bums in white shoes and wide white belts. Conversation there is mostly "Laugh-In" clichés. The room is so dark they have taken off their shades, and you can see the flaws the sunglasses have made in their tans as they blink at the banana-breasted, pot-bellied, topless dancer from West Virginia. Many of the insurance peddlers and manufacturer's reps go there too. It's a tough life, no shit, they say, but I wouldn't be in anything else.

Three Dog Night are singing "Joy to the World" on the jukebox. A dude next to me is drinking a vodka and tonic and talking about selling Cadillacs. I've come here with a vague notion of getting into a fight. I haven't been in one in a long time and I have a feeling it would help. I ask the dude if he ever knew my father; for some reason I'm trembling.

"Jesus," he says. "I'll say I knew your father. Everybody who ever sold cars in this town knew him. Funniest man in the world, great storyteller. Sorry to hear about him. Christ he floored us when he came by that day and told us he was going to die. Nobody said much around there for days. I'm Ted Telshow."

I'm wilting. It doesn't look as if the fight is going to work. Then he says, "God, it just hit me. You must be the fucking kid."

"What did you say?"

He's so enthusiastic that he misses my threatening tone. "The fucking kid. Christ, you're a legend. Your father made you famous. Every car salesman in town knows about you."

"Like what?" He's got me now.

"Like—Oh Jesus this is beautiful—the time you kept Spicola's daughter out all night in a trailer." At the name Spicola, Telshow gets attention all around the bar. "And at two in the morning this big black Caddy pulls up to your parents' house and Spicola's boys get out in those dark business suits and politely ring the doorbell. Your dad is mad until he sees who it is, then he's terrified. He gets dressed and tries to find you before Spicola's boys do and break your legs. And when he gets to the trailer at four A.M. it's still rocking!"

"Hey, guys," Telshow says expansively, beaming pride, "this is the fucking kid." At least half the hustlers in the bar seem to know what that means. "You're the kid used to drink grain alcohol," says one. "You ran a brand-new Ford demonstrator into the Wine House restaurant," says another. "I thought you were in Hollywood, writing movies." "Hey, what's it like on a waterbed?"

Suddenly the anger is gone and I'm telling stories, some true, some not, making excuses, spinning myth, entertaining, as my father did, the troops. Like him I rise above them, pull myself up on a thread of narrative. I drink free, until my excesses choke themselves. I have done it again. I stop in the middle of something, gulp the rest of my drink through a throat dried by lies, excuse myself. They protest, offering me more booze. But I'm not prepared to perform for it. "You're as good as he was," says Telshow. "He was really proud of you."

Mother couldn't take care of him any longer and he was in the hospital. He was bitter, claimed he'd been thrown out. When I came to see him he said, "God it's good to see a friendly face again. Your mother has sent me here to die. I never thought she'd be capable of it." He looked tiny, mummified. I tried to explain how mother just couldn't do it anymore, how she loved him and was there in the hospital every day. "OK," he said, "you sell me out too." I wondered at the meanness of his look until I understood suddenly that he was now a junkie. The nurses here weren't giving him half the drugs my mother had.

"You know what Doctor Bell said," he reminded me sullenly. "He said I wouldn't have any pain. I got plenty pain now. And you know what *you* said. . . ." I had promised, in the initial terror and resentment at the news he would die, to help him. Whenever he asked, whenever he decided that he'd had enough, I would get him enough Seconal or Nembutal or Tuinal to do the job. If he really wanted, I had gushed, I would get him enough acid so that he could go out, as he put it, "with a smile on my face and fuck Jack Webb." Drugs were the only pleasure, perhaps the only meaning left for him, and he wasn't getting enough. This was the last thing he would challenge me to do.

Bell's office was across the street. I remembered him as an arrogant, brusque man with a *cum laude* from Harvard and a big reputation. He seemed to think that only an M.D. degree permitted one to talk about the mysteries of the body, yet he felt at home discussing literature, had recommended books to me and borrowed from Dad a huge, expensive book on the movies that my sister had bought him. It had been three weeks now and he hadn't returned it.

I asked the receptionist if I could see him briefly and soon she took me into his office. He was friendly enough, asked me how things were going in Hollywood. "Fine," I lied. "Dad says he's not getting enough drugs."

"Your father is like you. He wants to practice medicine."

"I'm just asking if there's anything you can do to make him more comfortable. I don't want you to do anything unethical."

"I don't know why people can't just trust the doctor, why they all seem to think they know as much—"

"Hey, nobody said he knows as much as you. I'm just asking you to share some of it. It's my old man over there rotting and degrading himself begging the nurses for shots you haven't authorized."

"Now just a minute. I'm the doctor. You and your father never got along anyway, the way I hear it."

"O.K., that tears it. What the fuck does that crack have to do with medicine, you pompous bastard? You stay away from that, you understand. And if you don't or if I hear one more time that I don't have an M.D., I'm going to deck you and walk out of here. I'm not here to threaten or gratify your ego. I want more drugs for my dad, and if you can do it, fine. If you can't, there's nothing more I can say, except that you better have that book back in his room tomorrow or you're going to need a bone doctor, doctor."

Several beats. I'm trembling and so is he. Finally: "Look, don't walk out of here mad. Surely we can discuss this like intelligent people."

"If you'll stop insulting my intelligence and remember why I'm here, maybe we can."

He started to react again, then stopped. I had him, he knew, because I was not playing by his rules and was willing to be a lot more disorderly in his office than he was.

"OK," he said. "I guarantee that your father is comfortable and reasonably alert."

"I'll accept that. The thing is, he doesn't want to be alert anymore. What does he have to do with his time but beg for drugs?"

"He's an addict already, you know. And he's almost as willful as you are. He just isn't getting as much as your mother gave him."

"I know that, but you promised he wouldn't suffer, and he's suffering in a real way now. He's degrading himself. Why not give him all you can, within your ethical bounds. That's what I'm asking. Is that possible?"

"His functions will deteriorate faster. He's only got one kidney working now. He won't live long."

"He doesn't want to. Please, just think about it."

"I'll think about it."

That night my ex-wife, the Dragon Lady, called to say she was sending the kids for Christmas. "Christmas, you deranged bitch, my father is dying. You want them around for that?"

"I don't have anyplace else to send them," she said. Then she told me the flight number and time and hung up. The next day Dr. Bell put my father on a heavy morphine schedule and he was rarely conscious after that.

My sons arrived, one of them covered with chicken pox. For several days I bathed him and gave him tranquilizers against his anxiety about the pox and his most recent dislocation. Their life began to smooth out, as it became apparent their mother wasn't going to want them back. I registered them for school near my mother's house, where we were all staying.

Since there was little else to do I started working. I planed sticking doors. I repaired doorknobs and put a lock on the bathroom door. I put all the engines on their original mountings—lawnmowers, edgers, etcetera—and got them all running. I mowed and edged the lawn. I was wearing one of my father's old T-shirts which had been many times soaked in grease and gas and fish juices and which now and then gave me delicious ambiguous primal odors. The boys watched me curiously, cautiously. I sent the older one for a wrench and he came back with a pair of pliers. The fucking kid, I thought; we're running it by again. And would this kid honor me too late some day with a patience, tolerance, maybe a love of something I had loved?

Time slowed out there. I learned patience with the tools and with myself. I touched what my father had touched, in many cases finished his work. And I saw how weak he had been. Sometimes I would sit in that midden heap he had made and reflect on a stripped bolt. Had he not seen it was threaded wrong? How could *he* have forced the nut so far down its shaft against the protesting metal? The garage was filled with apparent successes, machines that worked, but there was always something subtly wrong. I could see better ways of doing them, but then I was playing critic to his creator, as perhaps all children must.

My muscles ached pleasantly now and the tips of my fingers were raw and sensitive from trying so many nuts and bolts and screws and clips and cables. I had never felt so useful. Things, tools, materials were working for me as they never had before. I talked to them, sat and wondered about their mysteries until I understood. Why had he done this? Should I change it? Why is this handle taped? What was he trying to do? I loved the smell of gasoline and oil and sweat. For weeks I had been driving my friends crazy, vibrating like a struck tuning fork. I had realized that my life now was too revolutionary in its impatience with time for them to tolerate and had stopped seeing them. But now . . . I had never felt less like a revolutionary and more like a man.

When there was nothing left to fix but the motorcycle, I went to work on it. The saddest lessons were there because he'd worked on it last. First the brakes. Unbelievably botched, jury-rigged, bent from impatience or misunderstanding into a shape less functional than its original. How was it supposed to work? I studied it quietly for hours, trying to see somehow its original form and function, gripping and releasing handles, watching cables convulse, levers move, until suddenly a small revelation. My mother brought me sandwiches which I ate without looking up. I think she was pleased to see me there.

One day it ran and I sat astride it, laughing. The clutch worked, the brakes worked, the carburetor adjustment seemed all right. God, what satisfaction. I thought of the friend in graduate school who had slipped me a note during a seminar in Milton which read: "Fuck this. I have a chance to be a Honda mechanic." And he did, just walked out and I never saw him again. I imagine he's happy, having exchanged meter for cubic centimeter.

I rode it all that afternoon, until I got a ticket for having no license tag. Then, feeling completely loony and macho, I went looking for a fight.

In the Stick and Rudder satisfaction is almost guaranteed. There is a violent fight there almost every night, a cutting on the average of once a week. It is a dark, ugly beer bar down near the airport and the harbor where men go when they must either hurt someone or be hurt and want it done in the simplest terms. People with hair like mine *never* go there, even if they are wearing a sweaty, greasy T-shirt.

The bartender's eyes glaze momentarily and conversation along the bar dies. I order a Sneaky Pete, two of which I know will make me murderous. Port wine mixed with draught beer. Jesus, I'll probably get killed here. But I'm smiling, and nobody knows what to make of that. Like Indians, they are in awe of insanity. For a while it appears nobody will try. I order my second, try to catch their eyes in the mirror and get it started before I'm too drunk to swing.

Finally the wiry guy next to me asks my opinion of Nixon. I answer that it's a good thing we didn't elect him. Other questions from other drinkers. They're not rude; they're trying to pin me first, find out if I'm crazy; so we have this lunatic press conference and I'm trying to give the best Zen answers I can. "What do you do?" the wiry guy asks.

"I've been earning a living as a writer, but I'm really a motorcycle and small-engine mechanic." They still haven't got enough to go on.

"What the hell do you people want out of life?" Somebody had to ask that. This is it. I stand up.

"Well, I've always wanted to fuck Juliet Jones, in the heart. Her sister Eve too."

Oh Christ, I've done it. Everybody is looking to the other end of the bar where my man has gotten up and is walking toward me. He's in his forties, built like a troll, big red hands. Probably a fisherman, this guy who's going to kill me. I decide to kick him, then I realize I can't move. I can't fight anymore. Then he takes from his pocket a pair of spoons and begins to play them against his callused palm, doing a little jig and singing. I am paralyzed.

He dances up and down the bar, playing the spoons on drinkers' heads. Nobody protests. He plays them on my head, having to dance on tiptoe to reach me. "Don't do that," I say numbly.

"I like you, lad," he says. "I like the cut of your jib." This becomes a general announcement, as he dances and plays on other heads. "This lad's all right. Nobody fucks with him. He's under my protection. You know, lad, I always wanted a son with your salt. I'm going to adopt you, take you home to meet the missus. We'll fish together. By God, I'm going to do it."

My ears are burning. Is this old man crazier than I am? Is he serious? Nobody is laughing, even with him talking like Jack Hawkins from *Treasure Island*.

"How about it, lad?"

"I don't need another father."

He seems surprised. "Well, think it over. Have another of those crazyman drinks and we'll talk about it."

I lurch to the men's room, where I vomit the beer and wine into a clogged toilet. Then I open the window and climb through, trembling from the threat of adoption, and drive home.

At three in the morning the phone rings and I reach it first. My father is dead. Mother and I cry. Then she makes coffee and I take a Tuinal and a Thorazine. We will handle it differently, this night. When I'm sleepy I crawl into his bed, in his bedroom, where I've been sleeping in Oedipal confusion all this time.

I'm almost asleep or maybe I am asleep when I hear his footsteps, the old, heavy footsteps from when he was well, come down the hall into the bedroom, and something cold falls on me. I want to call my mother, as I did when I was a child, but I don't. I lie there until the cold passes and I am no longer afraid and think: all right, old man, cold man, what do I do now?

# IS ANYONE LEFT THIS
# TIME OF YEAR?

FREDERICK BUSCH

Frederick Busch was born in Brooklyn, New York, in
1941. He received his A.B. from Muhlenberg College and
M.A. from Columbia. He lives in Poolville, New York,
with his wife and two sons, and teaches literature at Col-
gate, where he is an associate professor. His novel, *I
Wanted a Year Without Fall*, and collection of stories,
*Breathing Trouble*, have been published in England, and
his critical study *Hawkes: A Guide to His Fiction* was published by Syracuse University Press in America. His stories
have appeared in *Fiction*, *New American Review*, *Quarterly Review of Literature*, *Carleton Miscellany*, *New Directions*, *Iowa Review*, *Stand*, and other magazines. Mr.
Busch has just completed a new novel.

Not in Wexford, not in Cork. Not in Limerick, nor Nenagh, Killalo,
Tulla, Gort. Nor Galway, under the Spanish arch on slimy cobbles
near the bay where gypsy children beg. And not in Oughterard,
the clap of crowding Galway gone, the smell of so many hungry
breaths. And then there is Clifden. You can drive yourself deeper
into the west if you want. You can get yourself nearly into the sea,
rip the oil pan out on rocks and scours down to Aughrus More or
Kill. But Clifden is far enough, coming in at dusk past the Twelve
Bens and the autumn bogs of purple and burnt-brown that go like
tideflats away from the cracked road's edge. You keep on west at the
low red sun and fall into Clifden like a suitcase loaded with stones
that falls in the sea.

The Dromaneen is closed. The Ivy Manor is closed. Salt House is
closed. Keogh's is closed. The long street of Clifden is dark that runs

First published in *The Fiddlehead*. Reprinted by permission of John Cushman
Associates, Inc.

to the other long street: they meet at a very sharp angle and point down the hill, over brick and mortar ruins of the Old Town, over moss-grown steps and a broken paving, into the bay. Paper and cans swept from bins by the wind are in the streets, moving. Light from the car shows where on the streets the car, swept in from the east, is moving too. Empty metal kegs of Harp and Guinness crowd the curbings every three doorways and then there is light from the Metropolitan, open, and the light falls onto the street and MAU-MEEN'S—HIGH CLASS VICTUALLER. UNDERTAKER, closed. The Alcock and Brown is open too; this is tinted glass and white stone and Connemara marble labeled CONNEMARA MARBLE, this is where the red and brown tour buses come, where the lobby is rich with Irish Coffee and genuine Irish wool and the booklets on Alcock and Brown, who ended their transatlantic airplane race by landing at Lough Fadda in a bog at an angle of forty-five degrees, sinking.

I land at the Inishturk Hotel, which is always open in the early fall, though most of the tourists are home or at the Alcock and Brown. I came from the dark clenched street past the foyer, where they still have not covered the red and black circuits and switches and fusebox plates that crawl on the high left-hand wall like a network of nerves. And there is the white urn of umbrellas, the bright brass handle on the door to the fireplace room, the Irish china and African hangings and red-flowered wall-paper, hundred-year old wood of steps and bannister that go up to three floors of rooms. There is the dark carpet that goes past the desk with Gary Merrill's signature under glass into the empty cavernous unlit lounge—vases and candlestands and feathers on lampshades, the wood of dried arrangements, ebony, Waterford crystal, ugly prints in golden frames. The emptiness, silence, absorption of light: what you drive at the sun for, fall to from lichenous mountains, Clifden (An Clochan, The Stepping Stones).

If I didn't come at the dusk of a Sunday past silent men who curl forever on donkey chaises, rocked, staring down their cigarettes at the road, and then past only the black road and darkening bogs, I could go down the hill to a ramp where cattle graze above the sea and seem, at a distance and when the sun is bright on the water, to step on the ocean and eat. But at night, now, I can enter the empty hotel and be noticed in a while and fill in the form and give the registration code and passport number and forwarding address—write None—and wait for Sheila to look and smile with her angry nose, eyes with still too much of the dark silver makeup around them, and say "Oh, now so. Of course. You didn't come again yet. We wondered, weeks back. So now you're here. And I've given a single one to you! That's easy to change, this time of year."

And then I must tell her to leave it at a single room.

And she must say "Oh. A single, then."

And I must say a single, then.

She must look away, to Gary Merrill's modest hand. Then she: "Well I'll take you up myself, then, if you've no objections. You of all should know how there's nearly no one left this time of year. We do it all ourselves, you'll remember. Mother and me. We shall perish if we don't take care, I suppose. Overwork even in November, to listen to us."

I follow her dark short skirt, bright thighs, up the carpeted stairs to room eleven, its dense rich blankets and rug, the squat Victorian bureau, high wardrobe from some other time, the electric fire with ragged cord, the window over the street and the coastal perfume of mildew barely contained, and the usual slatted folding rack on which one lays his suitcase filled with stones.

She says "We're happy you're back and dinner is aways half-seven."

I tell her I'm happy I'm back, and dinner at half-seven.

She says "I remember now all your jokes about my marrying at thirty-three, you know. Well this year I'm thirty-four." She smiles her angry smile and holds her fingers out, like a child in school, for inspection. "Will you tell me this is the real lucky year?"

I tell her this is the real lucky year and dinner at half-seven, as ever, and there are smiles. Then there is the room and what is in it and the time to wait. Then, still waiting, there is the private bar downstairs, the light-stained wood, bright fabrics, low uncomfortable chairs against the walls, the round china ashtrays and white plastic lightshades and Sheila behind the bar, who draws the Guinness but this time doesn't smile.

Her mother in tinted glasses who is six feet tall is smoking short cigarettes on the customers' side of the bar, telling her stories again to the ladies. One, in an open raincoat, leans back low in her straight-back chair and watches her hands on the cocktail table snap a little lighter on and off. Smoke from a frayed butt goes up in a line from her ashtray out of sight. Another lady in her red plaid old tailored suit sits straight on a high square barstool and stares ahead, out of sight, and nods. The inside of her wrist leans on her collarbone and her fingers hold the cigarette near her lips and she squints inside of its smoke and stares. They have all together done their hair, which is knotted on the nape and parted in the middle, drawn back very tight, very blue.

Sheila's mother puffs and leans against the bar and tells her story of Murray who won a what-you-may-call-it, letter, in swimming in the States. Murray is about to dive from their drifting gondola into the reeking Venetian canal. And she is about to ask the gondolier if he can swim. Then she is going to hold her question, for what if he can't? When she can't either, and at her age and condition of life? And Murray is about to dive and slide, like a pale freckled porpoise, through the Italian waters, then climb back into the boat and shiver and grin. They are about to head back. She is about to learn that the gondolier cannot swim. She will come to say " 'Our sweet sacred Mother' is what I said. 'And that still don't make me your sister, you Roman' I said" she will say and they will laugh.

I go out to the dark still lobby, then, and leave them poised—the boy on the hired gunwale, the mother edging into fear at the Papist canal—and stand in the empty fireplace lounge, with its coal fire silent and stinking; everything metal or wooden is polished, and shapes come back from all around in the coal's low light.

When Sheila comes in there is only the hiss of coal and the falling of ash through the grate. You of all should know how there's nearly no one left this time of year. Then she puts the half-gone glass of stout on the imitation-ivory-inlaid table near the door and does not look away from what she does and is out of the writhing reflections and the sound of ash gone down. We do it all ourselves, you'll remember. We shall perish if we don't take care.

The small gold cymbal at the stairs first turning is rung, and lights are out in the dining-room entrance, and out where Gary Merrill's signature is under glass, out in the great lounge, in the fireplace room they are out, and now in the diningroom itself they mostly are out. Twenty-five tables covered with white are in the room, long and oval and sheeted and cold. Five long tables are covered with glassware and silver that crowds to every edge, and there are bright red paper napkins at each place, and lights above each loaded table, hot on the ceiling, cold and yellow below. One of the tables has napkins and glasses and plates at each place, but silverware for hands at only one, and Sheila sees me to the seat. She says "I thought it would make for more cheer. We haven't that many people, you know. Two others, only.

They're just married. They showed me how Hallowe'en is played in the States. We played Bob o' the Apple and we caught ghosts and lighted a squash. There's only one meal on the menu this time of year, you'll remember. Is that alright with you?"

I tell her only one meal on the menu is alright with me this time of year. The darkened rest of the room spins out from my table like the hall of a closed museum. Everything is cold to touch. No one tells the room to live.

Sheila brings what the meal is and takes the dishes away. I thank her after each course. She looks some other place. She says "Would you like any more? We have enough for more if you'd like." She pulls at the towel tucked into her apron and her hands caress one another as if there is comfort there.

I tell her no and thank her and she brings the bitter coffee and takes the cup away. She brings a cognac and goes away and the newly-married Americans come. She has hair the color of the red that is shiny on green pears, and he is bald and tall. His face reacts to everything she does and hers, all earnest frowns, reacts to what he says. They are happy with each other through the cheese and biscuits, and then he orders two sweet cherry liqueurs and she hesitates and shakes her head. Sheila brings me another cognac and he drinks the liqueur. She shakes her head again and he reaches for her glass. Sheila comes with one more cognac and he finishes her drink and orders one more. His wife says "No more?" She says to Sheila "We hardly ever drink."

His face goes red, I watch it change as the burn goes across it, but he shakes his head and finally grins, says "I didn't really want the first one. It tasted like cherry cough medicine at home. We hardly ever drink."

When they leave he moves her chair back from the table and helps her away. He leans a shoulder, an arm, toward her as if to shield her from something in ambush. She pulls on his sleeve and he nods, bending down to her, and straightens and turns to me and nods, says "Well, goodnight now." She smiles very widely as if she were trying to say something earnest and useful, something more helpful than only goodnight.

I say goodnight.

Sheila comes back when the children are gone and says "Could I bring you anything more? Aren't they gentle people? Pardon, of course, but especially for Americans. They have all that love on them like rain on a tree."

I ask her for a cognac and thank her.

She wipes her hands on the towel and says "You know we have to charge you five-and-three for every glass?"

I thank her for worrying.

"I don't mind worrying, then."

I cough and look at the table and wait.

She says "Did you enjoy the meal?"

I say that I enjoyed the meal. Then I look at the table and then I ask Sheila if she would like to drink a brandy with me.

She says "Not until you mean that, thank you just the same, and I haven't driven you to it in desperation. I'm sorry that you've felt so."

Her angry eyes are poised on my face, her hands are still. I tell her that I'm driven to nothing at all. I tell her not to worry and I smile. She leaves and returns with the cognac and I tell her maybe we can have a drink before I leave.

"And leaving already?" she says.

I tell her no. I tell her I don't know. I look at the brandy, which is colored in the dim cold light like the stiffened surface of the dying bogs I came through, burnt-away brown and gold all day underneath no sky. It was the color of ashes from the ground straight up in all directions, with no cloud and no color and no light reflected—dirty ash gone down on everything, and no sky. Through Maam Cross, Recess and Ballynahinch I came under no sky, and at Cashel Hill, among the Bens, the day was punctured by dusk, the sides collapsed in and ashen horizons leaked out, and there was the sun: red and swollen, grazing on the surface of the sea. You drive your car down the final hills and at the sun, to Clifden, where you drink the night's last cognac and see that she has gone, so leave the glass on the table and go to bed.

I go to bed. And later, in the dark, I sit up. I sit in the bay of the window and watch the town and sleep there, falling forward and coming out of sleep with my fingers clawing, my lips wide apart and dry, cracking, sounds coming up from my sleep which I don't want to hear. Barefoot and in pajamas, then, I go downstairs along the carpeting to stand, like a child at night in the big house, before the locked saloon bar door. There are no fires and no lights, the flesh of my feet shines phosphorescent, like fish belly-up in dark waters. I stand and I look at the door and shrug my shoulders and stand.

Sheila's mother says "Do you need a drink?"

She wears wide-legged white pajamas under a dark robe and she must have dark slippers on, for she looms above me and all I see to hold her up is an inch of whiteness a little over the floor. Her hair is still up, her brown-tinted glasses still on, a cigarette yet in her hand, its redness moving as she speaks. She says "Do you need a small something?"

I say I need something.

She says "I do myself. Almost always now."

Her keys ring as if they are huge, and she opens the door in, poised above the inch of whiteness that moves along the floor. She does not turn the bar lights on, but goes behind the counter—it smells like the closet of a dirty smoker, cigarettes and flesh combined —and she serves me something which I drink. She pours it for herself and then for me, and I wrestle up to a stool while she drinks and pours again.

"Isn't it a pity not to sleep?" she says. "I never knew what peace meant until I lost the power of sleep."

I say it is a great pity not to sleep.

"The rooms you leave at night lose their attraction in the morning somehow" she says. "As if they need your sleep to renew them as well as you yourself needing the sleep, sort of. Do you follow me?"

I say I've noticed it also, the rooms eroding away over many mornings.

"Do you pray at night?" she says. "Are you religious?"

I say that I'm not religious. I say I don't pray.

"Does that mean you have no hope?" she says. "Would you like another?"

I say I don't mind another.

"John Jameson" she says. "Not that Old Paddy—which is genuine Irish, right enough, but it's coarse like most of the genuine Irish. And a bad bargain, like the genuine Irish, costing as much as a good whiskey does. Have you tasted the difference?"

I say I've tasted them both and Paddy is coarse. I say I don't mind.

She says "Do you have feelings over the Belfast problems they're having?"

I say no.

She pours us each another then says "Is there anything you'd care to discuss, then?"

I say no.

She says "I'll leave you the bottle, then, and with our good wishes, and I will be off to my bed if not, Lord willing, my sleep."

I thank her and wish her sleep and she is gone. I leave my drink on the bar and walk around the room. Into my eyes, the pupils large enough by now, and focused, things like chairs and ashtrays come, and then they're out and I've gone around the room again. Soon I stop and finish my drink, leave the glass beside the bottle and go outside, closing the door very gently. On the carpeted steps, a blanket around her head and torso, like a gypsy woman sleeping at someone's door a while, squats Sheila; her feet are covered, her arms are in the blanket, so only the low brightness of her face shows up—unappeased eyes and angry beak and teeth.

"I see you're having a difficult night" she says. "Who teased me once about long nights."

I say yes.

"I'm sorry" she says.

I tell her not to be sorry.

"Oh I am" she says. "I'm lonely and sorry and confused and thirty-four."

I say who's not confused. I tell her I'm more than thirty-four. I tell her everyone's sad, it's the season.

She says "Couldn't people ever help each other with their lives?"

I tell her I wouldn't know.

"Shouldn't they do what they can?" she says. "Make the try for comfort's sake?"

I tell her no. I go up past her on the steps and from the back and the stairs' first turning she is vanished into her blanket, she is one of the Inishturk's dark fabrics in the slack season, waiting for another year.

I go to bed and fall asleep and my cracked lips wake me up and then I sleep again. Then it is morning and time for breakfast, which the children don't attend. Sheila has the electric fires on. She brings in coffee and sets it before me in that ballroom of silence, she folds her towel and says to it "What can I make you for breakfast?"

I ask her how she slept. She nods and I see the sockets of her eyes, silver shadow gone, flesh raw. I tell her some kind of juice and thank her.

She says "I made my decision last night. Would you like to hear it?"

I say yes.

She says "I've decided I'm marrying in the time between when we close and when we open in May. It means I'll be a missus if you come here again in the fall and notice me about, laughing and all."

I say good, getting married.

"Because it's time now not to live alone. And mothers don't count in such. It's time now not to be living alone anymore at my time and place."

I look at the table and then I say yes, that's good, marrying.

"Even if I have to find him in a Galway saloon" she says. "Because I will find a husband, I decided now."

I fold my red napkin in quarters and nod. I look at the dark brown sugar, tiny useless teaspoons, the stubs of my fingernails folding the fourths into eighths. I nod and keep nodding while she watches me and I tell her sausages, tomato, scrambled egg.

Then it is the Brandy and Soda Road, with a sky and sun today before lunch at the Inishturk, saxifrage in the heaths showing, cattle and sheep at the stone fences and in the bogs where the Atlantic pushes through the grass in long tidal pools, like the fingers of a mad lover in a lover's hair. After a while the bright fading grass is level with the narrow road, and the hills have rippled back to where the sea is. Sometimes there are cottages—thatched cement, slate on cement—they have no power lines and are alone, symmetrical and boring, ugly, strong, surrounded by fence and with cattle in the door-yard, always, cropping what is mostly stone and some grass, these pastures.

Past a settlement of three square grey cement houses, one of which has PROVISIONS neatly painted in black on the stone of its wall, an unpaved road curves off and goes behind the houses in a wide brown arc. The houses vanish and a hill comes up, high weeds blown by the wind from the sea. The road, grown rockier, heads for the hill and climbs it, toward three shapes outlined on the sky. A small diesel engine covered by tarps is throbbing, it is surrounded by empty jeep cans used for gasoline; wires from the engine run to a high dark van in which no one is sitting, and antennae on the van's roof jump in the steady hard winds. Nearby is a small blue caravan with padlocked door, the sides scratched deep, the windows covered with blinds. The engine pushes electricity out to the van where the radio is, and no one appears. Down the hill and on the other side is a lower hill, and then the Atlantic foaming in at the bleached-bone sand of the small bay. Out on the ocean there are boats that men here call to with their radio, if the men here call, if there are men to call now, warning of winds such as these that now drive the ocean in and rock the

trailer and my car and the untended antennae that the throbbing
engine feeds.

It is time to go there now, where the ocean never stops banging
onto the bone-white beach, The Shore of the Plover, where the sand
is made of tiny shells with nothing in them any more except the wind.
You of all should know how there's hardly anyone left this time of
year. We do it all ourselves.

The dirt road goes down to a narrow track with deep scours, and
the car's sides crush against low weeds and high rocks and the track
runs off to the right, away from the bay. There are no houses, there
is one long hill to the left, low and in between the ocean and the
track, and then the ground on the right rises up to another low hill,
and that comes up near the track soon, while the fields before the car
open out and just go on.

The car goes slower as the wheel pulls my hands back and forth
and the steel around me makes sounds of things shaking loose. The
light brown earth of the track is disappearing as the car falls farther
on. A man is very small with no face on the leftward hill as he lifts
from the ground and moves a few steps and then returns to where
he was before and stoops and lifts. There is nothing on the hill to
my right. And far ahead, down the rock-field, at the farthest point of
my sight, a small white pony bends to the ground, a brown pony
stands erect. They are totally still. And the car stops, for the track is
gone, and there is only rock and some grass. There is track that stops,
and a man who endlessly stoops on top of a hill, and two unmoving
ponies down the vast stony meadow, and the track ending, a gash or
two in the earth and nothing then: the tiny car, the tinier man inside
it, the hidden sea, the wind, the immensity coming down on it all
like a scream.

It is time to turn the car around and follow the track back, pick up
the suitcase, and pay them at the Inishturk and leave, to drive up
from Clifden back through the Bens and east it would look like
through Maam Cross and Oughterard, across the Corrib back to see
once more if there is some other place, this time in Galway, down at
the crowded small streets, where there is anyone left this time of
year.

# CAMBRIDGE IS SINKING!

JOHN J. CLAYTON

John J. Clayton was born and raised in New York City.
He received his B.A. from Columbia College, his Ph.D.
from Indiana University. He has published fiction in
*Massachusetts Review* and *Antioch Review*. His book on
Saul Bellow, now in paperback, won a *Choice* prize. He
teaches creative writing and modern fiction at the University of Massachusetts, Amherst.

The Sunday night telephone call from Steve's parents: his mother
sorrowed that such an educated boy couldn't find a job. She suggested kelp and brewer's yeast. His father told him, "What kind of
economics did you study, so when I ask for the names of some stocks,
which ones should I buy, you can't tell me?"

"It's true, Dad."

George rolled a joint and handed it to Steve. Steve shook his head.
"But thanks anyway," he said to George, hand covering the phone.

"Man, you're becoming a Puritan," George said.

"Stevie, you're getting to be practically a vagrant," his father
sighed.

Susan kissed him in a rush on the way out to her support meeting.
Where was *his* support meeting? He closed his eyes and floated
downstream. "Goodby, baby."

A one-eyed cat pounced from cushion to cushion along the floor.
He hooked his claws into the Indian bedspreads that were the flowing walls of the livingroom. The cat floated, purring, until Steve
yelled—

"Che! For Christsakes!"—and Che leaped off a gold flower into
the lifeboat. It wasn't a lifeboat; really an inflated surplus raft of rub-

berized canvas; it floated in the lagoon of a Cambridge livingroom. It was Steve who nicknamed it the Lifeboat and christened it with a quart of beer.

Steve scratched the cat's ears and seduced him into his lap under Section 4 of the Sunday New York *Times:* The Week in Review. Burrowing underneath, Che bulged out Nixon's smiling face into a mask. Che made a rough sea out of Wages and Prices, Law and Order, Education. Steve stopped trying to read.

The *Times* on a Sunday! Travel and Resorts. V*oila!* A Guide to Gold in the Hills of France. Arts and Leisure. Business and Finance. Sports. Remember sports? My God. It was clear something was over.

All these years the New York *Times* was going on, not just a thing to clip articles from for a movement newspaper, but a thing people read. Truly, there were people who went to Broadway shows on the advice of Clive Barnes and Walter Kerr, who examined the rise and fall of mutual funds, who attended and supported the college and church of their choice, who visited Bermuda on an eight-day package plan, who discussed cybernetics and school architecture. People who had never had a second-hand millennial notion of where we were heading—only a vague anger and uneasiness.

Steve tried to telepathize all this to Che under the newspaper blanket: Che, it's over. Hey. John is making films, Fred lives with eight other people on a farm. But it isn't a *commune,* whatever that was. The experiment is over.

Look: when Nancy cleared out of the apartment with her stash of acid and peyote and speed and hash after being released from Mass Mental, cleared out and went home to Connecticut; when trippy Phil decided to campaign for George McGovern and nobody laughed; when the *Rolling Stone* subscription ran out; when Steve himself stopped buying the *Liberated Guardian* or worrying about its differences from the regular *Guardian;* when George—when George—stopped doing acid and got into a heavy wordless depression that he dulled with bottle after bottle of Tavola—and said he'd stop drinking "soon—and maybe get into yoga or a school thing"— something was finished, over.

Che purred.

The lifeboat floated like a bright orange H.M.S. Queen Elizabeth sofa in the middle of the sunset floor. Steve sat in the lifeboat on one of the inflated cushions reading Arts and Leisure and listening to

Ray Charles through the wall of George's room. As long as it was Ray Charles he didn't bother to drown it out with the livingroom stereo. As if he had the energy. He sipped cranberry juice out of an Ocean Spray bottle and looked through this newspaper of strange science fiction planet aha.

Ray Charles whined to dead stop in mid-song. George stood in the doorway and stood there with something to say and stood there and waited.

"Come aboard. I'm liking this old boat better and better."

George: hippo body, leonine face with a wild red mane. He ignored the boat. "Steve, I'm going back to school."

"School? To do what?"

"Get a masters."

"What in?"

"I haven't got that far yet. I'll let you know." The door closed. Ray Charles started up from where he left off.

Steve smiled. He stretched out in the lifeboat and let it float him downstream. They came to a rapids, he and Che and the New York *Times*, and he began negotiating the white water. George. George: school? Well why not.

George. One day last year when George was tripping he found his Harvard diploma in the trunk under his bed: he ripped it into a lot of pieces and burned—or began to burn—the pieces one by one. But halfway through he chickened out and spent the rest of his trip on his knees staring into the jigsaw fragments as if they were the entrails of Homeric birds, *telling him something*. Yesterday, when Steve went into his room to retrieve his bathrobe, he found the fragments glued onto oak tag: half a B.A. on the wall. Nothing else was any different: unmade bed, unread books, undressed George, sacked out in the bathrobe. Steve burned a wooden match and with the cooled char wrote R.I.P. on George's forehead. George did.

Susan was gone for hours. Sunday night. Steve sat crosslegged in his lifeboat and made up lists on 3 x 5 cards.

It was a joke that began when he was doing his honors thesis at Harvard. On the backs of throwaway 3 x 5's he'd write

B-214:
Steve Kalman cites Marx—18th Brumaire—
"Peasants shld be led into socialism
by being asked to do housecleaning once a week."

He'd tape that to the bathroom mirror so the early morning peasants, recovering from dope and alcohol and speed, could hate him and get some adrenalin working. It was therapeutic.

Now the lists were different:

B-307:
Steve Kalman tells us in his definitive
work on Engels' late period:

a) learn karate
b) practice abdominal breathing while making love
c) read Marx' *Grundrisse*
d) read something through to the last page
e) "Be modest and prudent, guard against arrogance
   and rashness, and serve the . . . people heart and soul" (Mao)
f) specifically: fight racism, sexism, exploitation
   (whew!)
g) practice revolution

When he felt it might be necessary to do something about an item on the list, he closed his eyes and meditated. Words sneaked in: what he might have said to Susan, what was the shortest route to Harvard Square, would he see his guru face to face the way Sam said he had, how many gallons would it take to do the kitchen. Aach, you should just get into the waiting, into this time without political meetings or leafletting at factory gates. Get into something.

In his mind's eye Steve saw Susan's face. All right, she wasn't Beatrice or Shri Krishna. But who was, nowadays?

She came in late from her support group; Steve was in a gloomy half-sleep. She curled up behind him and touched her lips to the baby hairs on his back. He grunted and turned around: "And that's another thing—" he kissed her cheek, her nipple.

"What's another thing?"

"Your other nipple." Which he addressed himself to. "Listen. You come home after an exciting day at work while I've just swept the floors and wiped up the children's doodoo. Then you, you want to make love."

She held the cheeks of his ass and pressed him against her. They kissed. "Stephen, I don't have what you just said quite figured out, but I think you're making a sexist comment."

"Sexist? What sexist? I envy you your support group. You leave me nothing but the lifeboat and Chairman Mao."

"And a couple of years ago you'd have been up all night hammering out a 'position.' I think you're better off."

"We make love more, for sure."

"Let's make love, Steve."

And they did.

"Let's get out of Cambridge before it sinks. Cambridge is sinking."

Susan played with his curly black hair and beard, a Cambridge Dionysus. "You're silly. Cambridge is built on money. There are new banks all over the place."

"Then it's *us* who are sinking. We've got a lifeboat, let's go."

"Go where?"

"How about British Columbia? They need teachers. Or northern Ontario?"

"You'll get a lot of political thinking done up there."

"In exile? Look at Ho Chi Minh. Look at Lenin."

"Oh, baby. They were connected to a party."

"I love you. You're right. Let's go to Quebec and get away from politics."

"Away from politics? Quebec?"

"To Ontario."

"But baby, you're away from 'politics' right here. That's what you're complaining about."

"But Cambridge is sinking."

At night in bed it was funny and they had each other. But daytime after they breakfasted and kissed goodby and Susan would go off to teach her fourth grade class and Steve would go off to the library to read Trotsky or Ian Fleming or he'd sub at a Cambridge junior high and sit dully in the faculty lounge waiting for his class to begin, then he'd think again, like the words of an irritating jingle that wouldn't stay quiet, about whether to go on for his doctorate in sociology so he could be unemployed as a PhD instead of unemployed as an MA.

Susan was off at work. Steve washed the dishes this morning. MA. PhD. The dishes. If you called it karma yoga it was better than dishwashing. But he envied Susan her nine-year olds, even if she were being paid to socialize them into a society with no meaningful work, a society which—*watch it:* do the dishes and stop the words.

He did the dishes—then spent the rest of the morning at Widener Library reading Mao's "On Contradictions."

He was to meet George for lunch. On his way Jeff Segal passed him a leaflet without looking up.

> The press loves to boast that the student move-
> ment is dead. It's alive and fighting back. And
> SDS is in the forefront of that fight. . . .

My God—SDS. (Which meant, in fact, PL) Well, Steve felt happy that somebody considered themselves a Movement, even a handful of people using the rhetoric of 1950's ad men.

Steve passed through Harvard Square—past the straight-looking Jesus freaks and the bald Krishna freaks dancing in their saffron or white sheets and their insulated rubber boots. In the corner news store, across from the kiosk (Steve remembered when they "took" the Square and people got up on the kiosk and the cops came. So the freaks charged off in all directions busting windows—called *liberating the Square*—while he, Steve, who'd helped organize the march and rally, walked quietly a-way.)—in the corner news and magazine store there was George reading the sex books at the rear of the store.

"Hey George!"

They got out into the street and stood blinking at the noon light like a couple of junkies oozing out of a basement. George took out from his army coat lining the copy of *Fusion* he'd ripped off. He thumbed through the record reviews and he headed down Boylston to Minute Man Radio. "You stay here, Steve. I know what you think about my ripping off."

Steve watched the young women of Cambridge pass. A lot of fine lunchtime arrogance that he delighted in; but, he considered, not a hell of a lot in their eyes to back it up. One blonde on the other side of Boylston, tall, with a strong walk and no-bullshit eyes: Steve fell in love with her right away and they started living together but she had kids and he didn't get it on with them and she had perverse tastes in bed and didn't understand politics so by the time she actually crossed the street and passed by they'd separated it was too bad but anyway there was Susan to think of and so on. But they smiled at each other. Then George came out with Bob Dylan—*Greatest Hits Volume II* and showed it to Steve when they'd sat down for lunch.

They ate in the Française under the painted pipes, ate their good quiche and drank French coffee. "George, I think this is a Hemingway memoir. I'm feeling nostalgia for this place while I'm still here. That's bad.

"I wonder where I'm going, George. . . .

"I can't be Raskolnikov, George, as long as I can afford quiche for lunch. But it's the direction things are moving."

George ran his thick fingers through his wild red mane. "Not me. I decided. I don't want to be a casualty. I'm getting my MA in English and moving into a publishing house. I've got an uncle."

"Could you get your uncle to help you get your room cleaned up?"

"It's a pretty hip publishing house."

"I bet, George, that they make their profits off only the most freaky books."

"What's wrong with you, anyway?"

Steve bought George an espresso. "Here. Forgive me. This is so I can take our lunch off my taxes. I'm organizing you into our new revolutionary party."

"You couldn't organize your ass, lately."

Steve agreed. "I'm into getting my internal organs to communicate. I'm establishing dialogue at all levels."

After lunch Steve called Susan in the teachers' lounge at her school. "Hello, baby? Cambridge is collapsing."

"Love, I can't do anything about that. 31 kids is all I can handle."

"Pretend I'm a reporter from the *Times* and you're a terrific genius. 'Tell me, Miss French, how did you get to be such a terrific genius? I mean, here the city is falling down and nobody can stop snorting coke long enough to shore up a building, and here you are helping 31 human kids to survive. How, how, how, Miss French?' "

"Steve, you know better, you nut."

"Steve knows what he knows; me, I'm a reporter."

"Well," she cleared her throat, "I take vitamins, and I make love a lot with my friend Steve. And I ask his advice—"

"Ha! Fat chance!"

"—and I owe it to my sisters in the women's movement."

Steve didn't laugh. "It's true, it's true. Ah, anyway, love, I miss you."

Steve went up to the raised desk at the Booksmith on Brattle Street to ask the manager whether the one volume reduction of Marx' *Grundrisse* was out in paper. The "manager"—long mustachios and shaggy hair like a riverboat gambler, $50 boots up on the desk where they could make a *statement*—aha, it turned out to be Phil. Hey, Phil.

Phil looked down from the counter, stopped picking his Mississippi teeth and grinned. "I've been meaning to stop by, Steve. You didn't know I had this gig, huh?"

"It's good to see you."

"Sure. I watch the motherfuckers on my closed circuit swivel-eye TV set-up, dig it, and I check out the Square when things are slow. It's okay. I'm learning. In a couple of months I'm going out to Brattleboro, open a bookstore. A hip, a very hip bookstore."

"In Vermont?"

"There's a whole lot of freaks in Vermont."

"You doing a movement bookstore?"

Phil began picking his teeth like waiting to look at his hole card. Grinned his riverboat grin. "My uncle's setting me up, Steve. I want to make bread, man. As much as I can make in two, three years, and then I'll sell and split for someplace."

"Where?" Steve played at *naif* to Phil's heavy hipoisie.

"Lots of time to work that one out."

Steve forgot to ask about Marx. But Marx was all right. He found a *Capital* and when the camera had swiveled away, he slipped it into his bookbag. Then a Debray. A Che. Mao's *Quotations*. A Kropotkin. Into the lining of his Air Force parka. If Phil noticed, he didn't say. They grinned hip gambler grins at one another and Phil said, "Later, Steve."

Marx, Mao, Che, Debray, and Kropotkin. A complete infield, including catcher.

Steve pitched his winnings out of his lining, into the lifeboat.

"*You*, Steve?"

"Everybody's got an uncle, George. Wow. I remember Phil when we took the administration building. He was up on a car that night doing a Mario Savio. And now—" Steve told George about the *very* hip bookstore in Brattleboro.

"Everybody's got an uncle, huh?" George grunted. "And you're pure, huh?" He assimilated it into his computer; it fit. He swallowed once, then his massive moon face framed by red solar fire, his face relaxed. He went back to his room. Steve considered tacking up a 3 x 5 sign over the doorway: The Bestiary. Today he was a wall-eyed computer. Yesterday George was a griffin. Tomorrow he could expect a drunken red-haired cyclops.

What animal was Steve? Steve was *existentialops meshugenah.* Nearly extinct, thank God. Little survival value. Never looked down at the ground. Every bush a metaphor. Can't go for a picnic on a hillside without watching for a lion, a wolf, and a leopard.

He shrugged. Ask Chairman Mao. He opened the *Red Book* at random:

> We should rid our ranks of all impotent
> thinking. All views that overestimate the
> strength of the enemy and underestimate
> the strength of the people are wrong.

Good advice. But, plagued by impotent thinking, he climbed into the lifeboat and hugged his knees and sulked. He sat there till George, hammering up another picture on his wall, got to him. "George, will you cool it? Cool it, George. I'm miserable. The sky's falling down."

He tossed Mao aft in the boat, fitted real oars to the real oarlocks, and began to row in the imaginary water. It was smoother and easier than in real water—there was no struggle, and so, no forward motion. All things proceed by contraries. Blake or Heraclitus or Hegel or Marx. He rowed.

He rowed. Aha! It began to make sense. He was expressing precisely the "contraries" he felt in this year of the Nixon: him pushing, nothing pushing back but hot air from the radiators.

So. He closed his eyes. There was a forest on both sides. Tactical Police were utterly lost in the woods. Maybe it was a beer commercial. Inside his head Steve did up a joint and floated, eyes closed. The Tactical Police were stoned. Then he turned inside out and floated into a deep jungle world. There was a fat parrot with iridescent yellow and green, red and blue wing feathers. It was as big as a tiger.

George had a real parrot in his room, and it was the only thing George took care of. Including George. It wasn't very beautiful, certainly not iridescent or big as a tiger. It liked dope, ice cream, and Cream of Wheat. Like George. But now Steve floated while a very different bird floated overhead like a bubble or helium-filled crystal ball. He watched for the Good Witch of the West. Or for the Wizard of the East. But before any such visitation, he fell asleep.

Cambridge is a lie. Doesn't exist never existed. I am in my cups. The moon a cracked saucer. We are hardly acquainted.

In the graveyard of the Unitarian Church, sixteen-year old run-aways slept, dreaming of breasts with amphetamine nipples. They are all the time tired. Cats prowl the graveyard lean and angry. They suck blood and fly moon-wards. The Unitarians under ground are coughing uneasily. They are pressed down by the weight.

He woke up. He pretended it was a Caribbean cruise, this was the ship's boat, his jeans were a dinner jacket and tuxedo trousers. Susan was off to the captain's table getting champagne cocktails.

When she came back they walked through the Square arm in arm with champagne glasses and a bottle of Mumm's. It was spring, they kissed in front of a Bogart poster and poured more champagne for a toast. The Beatles were on again at the Brattle. There was no-body else in the theatre. All the psychedelic flowers were fading, wilting dingy, like the murals on WPA post office walls. The sub-marine had faded to a rusty chartreuse. Steve remembered when it was bright yellow and Lucy looked just like an acid lady. You used to get stoned or drop acid and get into the colors.

The lifeboat was getting full. Harpo was asleep on a raccoon coat, and George and his girl, very stoned, were examining a wind-up see-through clock they'd ripped off at DR. Steve could hardly spread out his newspaper. It was a rush-hour subway except everybody had suitcases and guitars with them. "Is this the way to Charles Street?" The sign over the door said DORCHESTER.

They held on and on, the subway was behaving like a bad little boy they were disappointed and wrote a strong note home but his government didn't reply. They floated through Cambridge trying to find the exit. They shouted FIRE! but it wasn't a crowded theatre, and so they were stuck, everyone with their own suitcase and their own piece of the action.

Susan's key turned in the lock.

"Susan—hey, Susan! Let's go get dinner!"


The neighborhood food cooperative operated out of Ellen's apart-ment. Her twins crawled among the market boxes and noshed grapes.

"Stop noshing grapes!" Ellen warned. Susan put an Angela Davis defense petition on the table for coop members to sign. Chairman Mao sat crosslegged on a cushion slicing a California avocado with his pocket knife. He ate slice after slice of the creamy green fruit.

Coop members started arriving to pick up their orders. 23 member households came in; only five ordered Angela Davis. Steve threw up his hands: "Dare to struggle, dare to win!" Chairman Mao shrugged sympathetically. He'd had trouble of his own with Cambridge intellectual types. Ellen hugged her twins and said, "But it's people that count, not politics." She put a Paul Klee on the stereo and recited W. B. Yeats.

Early spring. Cambridge. Torpor, confusion, scattered energies. A return to sanity was advertised in *Life* and in the little magazines. Aha, you mean sanity's *in* again. Okay! The art show Steve and Susan took in after dinner so they could drink free wine and hold hands, it was all giant realistic figures and giant, colorful geometrics. He could imagine them in the lobby of the new, sane, John Hancock Building. They said EXPENSIVE, CAREFUL, INTELLIGENT, PURPOSEFUL, SERIOUS; but HIP. And look at the long hair on the doctors and PR men at the opening. Everyone was hip.

"They're into patchouli oil on their genitalia for sure!"

"Who're you kidding?" Susan laughed. "You don't want to see paintings, you came to kvetch. You're a silly man. I want a Baskin & Robbins ice cream cone. And I'm willing to buy one for you, too."

"You're throwing your wealth up to me."

"Well," Susan sighed, and took his arm like a lady, "some of us have firm positions in the world. Only Harvard Square trash does substitute teaching. This is a free country. Anyone with a little guts and brains and in-i-sha-tiff—"

"All right, I want an ice cream cone." He stopped and right there on Mass Avenue kissed her, because she was so fine, because her tight jeans made him want to rub her thighs, because she kept him going through the foolishness.

They walked by the Charles River with their bridges burned behind them. There was nothing but to shrug. An invisible demonstration passed them from 1969 waving red and black flags and shouting old slogans. So they marched too. Steve lifted a revolutionary fist and shouted, "Take Harvard!" Susan said he sounded like a Princeton fan from the 50's.

"In the 50's I was a kid waiting for someone to push a button and end my having to go to school. I wouldn't blow up: just my school. The walls. Then in the 60's I expected us to tear down the walls."

"Well?"

"Now? Ah, Susan, where will we end up?"

"In a clock factory?"

On the other side of the river the business students stood by the bank with almost long hair and fat empty pockets. They bought and sold dope and sincere greeting cards with pictures of couples walking almost naked by the edge of the sea. Since the bridges were burned, Steve could yell, "You think you smell any sweeter, baby?" The business majors at the bank ignored them. When they had their stock options, where would Susan and Steve be? In the bathtub making love? In their lifeboat on a stream in British Columbia trying to locate the Source?

They wanted to make love, so they went back to their lifeboat and opened a bottle of cheap champagne. "What should we toast?" she asked.

"The river that gets us out of here?"

Steve made love with Susan on a quilt in the bottom of the rubber boat, a raft made for saving downed fliers.

Tuesday at lunch George and Steve spent a bottle of beer mourning the casualties.

"I decided again this morning," George said. "Not to be a casualty."

"Terrific."

"It's been a war of attrition. You know, 'I have seen the best minds of my generation . . .'"

"And some of the worst," Steve said.

"Sure. But like last night. Lynne came in to crash at 2 A.M. She didn't want to ball, just have a place. I think Paul kicked her out. This morning I woke up to the smell of dope, and she was getting sexed up and so we balled, but she didn't even know I was here. I can't get into that sickness anymore."

"Well," Steve said, "afterwards Lynne came into the kitchen, you were still in bed, Susan was off at work. We had coffee. I asked about her children. Her mother is still taking care of them. 'But I'm really together, Steve.' She's told me that about three times this past year. 'I couldn't stay in that hospital; nobody knew anything about where I was coming from. My *supposed* therapist had never done acid, but he's telling me about drugs. But anyway, they detoxified me. Cleaned me out.'

"I asked her how much she'd been doing. 'Wow, too much,' she said. 'I was exploring heavy things, I was deep into myself. But back-to-back acid trips . . . Too much. I think the hospital was good. But this psychiatrist with long hair, you know? . . . About my father.' Her voice started fading out. 'I had to split. I had to get back to my kids. . . .' So she signed herself out.

"I reminisced about her kids—one day Susan and I took Lynne and the kids out to the Children's Zoo. So I was blabbing and fixing coffee, I turned around, and Lynne was doing up a joint, and her clear blue eyes were really spaced out. She was fingering Nancy's old flute, recorder really, and she was talking to it: 'This side is blue, is Hegel, and the lower register is red, is Marx. The point is to listen down into the tone of God. Otherwise you're condemned to repeat the cycle.'

"I gave her a kiss on the cheek and went back to my lifeboat to read. I understand you about casualties, George."

The casualties. And what about Lynne's two little girls? Today Nixon was on TV from Mars. He toasted a new "long march" of the American and Martian people. Two years ago we thought it was all set to autodestruct: General Murders and Lying Johnson and Noxious Trixter and Spirococcus Agony and the Chase Banana Bank. Now we're out looking for jobs. Peter, who put me down for getting a degree. Offered a job at Michigan if he'd finish his dissertation. He refused, lived on welfare and organized at factory gates. Now he's still on welfare, but there's hardly a movement to support him. Two years ago he was right. Now he's another kind of casualty.

The bridge is burning while we stand in the middle. Our long hair is burning, wild and beautiful. We are the work of art we never had time to make.

I don't want to be a casualty.

Feeling restless, uneasy, he sat crosslegged on a pillow in the orange boat. He tried paddling down a magic river of umbrella trees, giraffes with french horn necks, a translucent lady with hummingbirds flying out of her third eye. But the film kept breaking. To placate him or perhaps to make things more difficult, the projectionist flashed a scene out of his childhood: floating on a black rubber tube, a towel wrapped around the valve like the bathing suit that sheltered his own penis. He floated safe and self-sufficiently past the breaker rocks. Where nobody could touch him. Meanwhile his mother stood by the edge of the ocean waving a red kerchief she pulled out of the cleft between her heavy breasts. She called and called, she tried to interest the lifeguard in his case. Steve's lips and ears were sealed.

Steve opened his eyes. They burned a little from salt water although he was 24 years old, although this was a make-believe boat, a livingroom prop. He felt like a shmuck. Chairman Mao's face was red.

He didn't close his eyes again. "Hey, George? George!"

"I'm doing up a joint," George said from the other room. Then he came in and lit up. "Want a toke?"

"Listen, George—"

"I'm gonna get stoned and then get my room clean. Clean."

"George, first, come with me for a couple of hours. We'll wash our sins away in the tide."


They lifted the inflated rubber boat onto their heads like dislocated duck hunters. Through the french doors to the balcony, then by rope to the back yard. Steve lashed it to the top of George's '59 Cadillac. He wore a red blanket pinned at the collar, Indian style.

At the Harvard crew house they put the boat in the water and pushed off into the Charles. Metaphor of Indian so long ago no Prudential Center or Georgian architecture of Harvard. Nice to push off into the river wrapped in such a metaphor. But today there was oil and dirt on the surface of the Charles; perch, hypnotized or drugged, maintained freedom of consciousness by meditating on their own motion. Even the fish with hooks in their mouths were contemplating their Being and harking to a different drummer. That's all more metaphor, too, for who would go fishing in the Charles? Steve played a rinky-dink tune to the fish on Nancy's recorder, but they turned belly up and became free of their bodies and of the river. The smell was nasty.

George said he felt like Huck Finn. Steve thought that was possible. They floated under the Harvard footbridge and past the site of the future water purification plant to the River Street Bridge. Stench of traffic and COCA-COLA in two-story letters. The river curved. "I can see myself as Tom Sawyer," Steve said. "For me it wasn't quite real, getting Jim out of slavery. I always figured on Aunt Sally's investment firm to settle down into. But for you, George, it was a real plunge. You almost didn't come back out. You were almost a shaman who didn't return."

"What are you saying, you crazy fool?"

"We must steer the boat. Susan's school is by the left bank. She'll be getting out in fifteen minutes."

Kids in the playground on the other side of Memorial Drive waved at the young man in the bright red blanket. Steve leaned over the chain link fence: "Peace to white and black brothers," he said, spreading his arms. "Tell Princess Afterglow we have come." George and a small boy tossed a ball back and forth over the fence.

"You're silly," a little boy told the Indian.

"Call Miss French. Ask Miss French to come down to the fence."

Miss French came down to the fence. Two little girls held her hands as they led her to the fence. She laughed and laughed and gestured *ten minutes* with her fingers.

George took up the recorder. It squeaked. "Steve. Those kids. That's where it's at."

"George, I don't believe you said that. Listen, George. I may dig being crazy or playing at being a child, but I can tell you that won't save me. Or being a freak. Or being an Indian. Metaphor won't save me. I got to save my own ass, so to speak. I mean, it's not any kind of revolution to float down the Charles in an orange boat."

"It was your idea. And who's talking about revolution? You're getting incredibly straight."

"And there—see—you can't make it on categories like straight. It's all over—the time you could think of *them* as bread and wine. So everything turns to shit in your mouth. Is bound to." He tugged at George's matted hair. "Except I don't feel like that this afternoon. I feel pretty manic and joyful."

Susan leaned against her bookbag in the stern and stretched back, her face parallel to the sky, and took it all in.

"Just smell this water. Don't let's fall in, friends," Susan said. "We'd be pickled in a minute."

They paddled upstream towards Harvard. Downstream, upstream. Circle-line sightseeing: on your right is Stop and Cop, and the Robert Hall Big Man Shop. Fer you, George. Harvard crews raced each other towards the lifeboat; alongside was the coach's motor launch. The coach, in trenchcoat, scarf trailing crimson in the wind, stood droning into a bullhorn. For a second, Married Students' Housing was upside down in the water; then a gust of wind shattered it into an impressionist canvas.

The shells raced by and the orange lifeboat rocked in their wake

and in the wake of the launch. They shared an apple left over from
Susan's lunch and didn't fight the rocking.

They rowed. They were rowing home. Home because

> The cat has to be fed.
> And the parrot.
> Because we are hungry and
>    the place needs to be cleaned up bad.
>    There are lots of books at home, and a telephone.
>    Home doesn't smell as bad as this river.

No wild crowds on shore cheered this. From the footbridge no Radcliffe girls dropped white roses on their heads. Farther on, even
more to the point, no marchers cheered them with raised fists, with
red flags in the spring breeze, with a bullhorn dropped down off
the Anderson Bridge so that Steve and Susan and George could
address the crowd:

"Well, it's been a terrific five years. We've all learned how to make
love and posters. We can really get into the here and now at times
and we've learned to respect our fantasies. Yum yum. We're glad to
be going home. We hope to see all the old faces tomorrow right after
the revolution is over so we can clean up the paper we dropped."

After this didn't happen they paddled up Memorial Drive some
more. The gulls were fishing. The shells raced past them going the
other way and they rocked and bobbed, like a floater for fish. They
sang,

> Fish on a line
> all strung out
> If I cry the moon will go away.
> Are you with me?
> Plenty of conditions
> Sold by the millions
> Nice to tell you
> can't hold water.

They drew pictures of fish in the water like invisible ink to be recovered later and read.

"We can't get anywhere this way," Steve said.

"Just float, man. The trouble with you is you never learned to
float." George shrugged and reversed his oar, so the boat circled
after itself like a dog after tail, like Paolo and Francesca. Infinite
longing unsatisfied. But this was merely parody. George knew better

than to long. The river stank but he had a cold. Steve and Susan were kissing on the bottom of the boat. Who knows how this fairy tale goes?

Why are the bridges all falling down? Why are the boats floating against bars of ivory soap and turning over? It doesn't matter how the words go. They wound me up and didn't give me directions, Steve groaned, playing wind-up toy. But when he finished kissing his friend Susan, he took up paddle and coaxed George into rowing upstream past Harvard to the boathouse.


Steve—oh God Steve you've got to stop torchereeng yrself, Steve decided painfully. CHINA WASN'T BUILT IN A DAY. Steve closed his eyes and meditated, crosslegged in the wet lifeboat, on the career of Mao Tse Tung.

Susan and George carried in a brass tray with what was left of the champagne. But Steve was meditating.

"Join us, why don't you? We've got some heavy pazoola here on a fancy gold tray," George like a six foot three red-haired genie wheedled. "Cut the meditating."

"Who's meditating? I'm telephoning Mao Tse Tung in Peking. *Hello, Peking?*"

"Well, tell us what he says."

Chairman Mao, Chairman Mao, Steve said inside his head. Tell us what we can do in this year of the Nixon.

Ah, yes, Mister Nixon. . . .

It's been a long winter, Chairman Mao.

With no leaves on the trees, the wind shrieks; when leaves fill the branches, the wind rustles.

I think, Steve said, inside his head, I get what you mean.

The important thing, Chairman Mao said, is to get outside your head. Open your eyes. What do you see?

The rubberized canvas sides of my orange raft and a print of Primavera on my wall. My friends are offering me champagne on a gold tray. A brass tray to be exact.

Chairman Mao supposed a difficulty in translation. You, you behave like a blind man groping for fish. Open your eyes. Study conditions conscientiously. Proceed from objective reality and not from subjective wishes. Conclusions invariably come after investigation, and not before. Open your eyes.

"Open your eyes and your mouth," Susan said. "Here it comes."
She tilted a glass of champagne to his lips.

"Well, nobody can say those are elitist grapes. Those are the people's grapes," Steve said, pursing his mouth.

"Connoisseur! Drink up!"

Picking up the pieces. Picking up the check. Somebody got to pay
before we split and all them lights go out. Ah, well, but it's time to
clean up and start almost from scratch.

Susan and Steve helped George clean up his room: Two green
plastic trash bags full of wine bottles and dustballs, moulding plates
of spaghetti, old *Rolling Stones*, socks with cat spray, insulating felt
strips chewed up by the parrot, Kleenex and Tampax and a cracked
copy of Bob Dylan's *Greatest Hits Volume I* and a few cracked
*ands* that broke open like milkweed pods and had to be vacuumed
up in a search and destroy operation.

When George's room was swept and scrubbed, George decided
to wash away the Charles River effluvium in the bathtub. So Steve
and Susan sat crosslegged in the bottom of the lifeboat. Wiped out.

Then Steve pulled the plug. The boat hissed disapproval, deflated,
expired. They were sitting in their own space, for better or worse.

# THE THINGS

### JOHN GARDNER

John Gardner was born in 1933. He lives with his wife
and two children on a farm in Illinois, and teaches at
Southern Illinois University. He has written five novels, including, most recently, *Nickel Mountain,* and the poem
*Jason and Medeia.*

Henry and Callie came out on the porch to watch him down the
driveway. Callie was holding the baby, wrapped up in its yellow
blanket, she herself in one of her own tricolor afghans, three shades
of green, waving with her free hand, and Henry was close beside her,
a little behind her, like a balding upright bear with one paw on her
shoulder, waving too. The dog was at her other side. The porch
light was on—cheap imitation of a carriage lamp—and beyond that
there was the light in the livingroom windows, giving the figures on
the porch a kind of aura, their faces not as light as their outlines. On
the yard, in the dewy new-mown grass to their left and in front of
them, there were rectangular splays of light from the windows and
the open door, and there was faint light on the sharp little crocuses
below the windows and still fainter light on the carious trunks and
lower boughs of the tamaracks at the edge of the driveway, beyond
the painted rocks. The tops of the trees were dark silhouettes, as
black as the mountain or the gable of the house; on the other side
of the silhouettes was the abyss of sky dotted with stars. It was all
like a picture for a life insurance ad in the *Saturday Evening Post.*
He could envy them.

When he came to the highway he stopped and waited, the only
hand he had leaving the steering wheel to shift down to low, his foot
on the brake, the truck nosing sharply downward. There were headlights coming from the south. He looked back and saw Henry and

Callie going into the house, the dog standing up now, neither friendly nor unfriendly, merely official, the way Shepherds were supposed to be, watching. The porch lights flicked on and off—Callie saying one more goodbye—then stayed off. Almost the same instant, the headlights on the highway veered toward him crazily, then teetered away again, the last possible second. The car's inside lights were on and he had a fleeting glimpse of drunken kids leering out at him as their car burned past. "Crazy sons of bitches!" he thought. His heart was pounding, and he was still hearing, as though time had snagged, the sudden howl of motor and the rushing wind and the scream of bad tappets. They shot away down the level space in front of Henry's, then up the further hill. In a matter of seconds they were over the hill and gone, and the night was empty. He pulled out onto the highway, his right leg shaky on the accelerator. And now—the whole beautiful night gone sour—he was thinking again of the murder.

Henry had told him about it. He'd heard it on the radio. "It was up on the Nickel Mountain, not ten miles from here," he said. "Some old man. They said his name was—I forget. I guess when he came home they were already inside the house. They hit him on the head with some kind of a pipe. The way they had it on the radio, he was a mess."

Callie was sitting with the baby on her lap. The light from the lamp over her head gave her hair a sheen. The baby was asleep, its fingers curled around one of hers, but she was still singing to it.

George had said, "They know yet who did it?" The picture in his mind was of his own house, as isolated as any to be found and one that would no doubt be attractive to vandals or thieves—a high old brick house with balustered porches, round-arched windows, lightning rods, cupolas, and facing the road a victorian tower like a square old-fashioned silo. "They don't know yet," he said. "Could've been anybody. Those lonely old houses, it's a wonder things like that don't happen more often."

("Sit," Callie said. The dog lowered himself again slowly, like a gray-black lion at her feet, and lay his wide head on his front paws, ears raised, mournful eyes looking up at her. He sighed.)

George Loomis turned the spoon over idly in his hand while they talked. It was silver plate, one of their wedding presents. He was sorry they hadn't chosen something real—because they were his friends, and it disturbed him that friends of his should have junk in their house. She'd chosen it because it was "practical," no doubt; forgetting that plate would scratch and wear away and that anyhow when you married a man who'd been a bachelor all those years you didn't need to squeeze your pennies till Lincoln squeaked. But above all what was wrong was that it was light: in your hand it felt like nothing. With good things, you knew you had them when you had them. That was how it was with all their things—except the solid old sterling candlesticks (up on top of the player piano where they didn't belong, no candles in them) and maybe the antimacassars from Callie's Aunt Mae, and Callie's afghans. But if it didn't matter to you then it didn't, that was it. Except that he knew it did matter to Henry. Why did he let her do it? He said abruptly, "Maybe it was thieves."

Henry shrugged. "They don't know yet. Could be thieves. Then again could be kids, or some tramp."

"Jesus," George said. He'd thought often of the possibility of thieves breaking in. He was not a worrier by nature, but it was a fact that he had a lot of good things in his house, some of them things that had been in the family for two hundred years— God only knew how much those might be worth—and some of them things he'd picked up himself from time to time, in junk shops up in Utica, at auctions here and there, in used book shops. Bill Kelsey had told him he should open a store.

("You got more old stuff than any twenty people," he'd said.

"There's a lot of it, all right," George had admitted, "and more in the other rooms; even some in the woodshed. I walled it up with insulation, so it's dry." He opened the door to what had been his mother's bedroom and stepped back so Bill could look in.

"Christ in a crock," Bill Kelsey said, "what's all that?"

"*National Geographics*," he said, grinning. "Whole file of them. The rolls in the corner are maps. Thirty-seven in all. Engraved." There were various other magazines too—*Linn's Weekly Stamp News, Texas Gun Collector, American Rifleman.*

"What in hell do you use them for?" Kelsey was amazed. Impressed, too, but mostly amazed. He stood tipped forward, looking, his thumbs hooked inside the bib of his overalls.

George had said ironically, closing the door again, "*Use* them for? Sometimes I go in and touch them" and he winked. But it was true. It was the richest pleasure in his life, just picking them up, knowing they were his, safe from the destroyers who cut the woodcuts from great old editions like his illustrated Goethe, or saw down hand-crafted Kentucky pistols and weld on modern sights. In the pear-wood breakfront he'd found at the Goodwill at Oneonta he had nine original Hohner mouth-harps, in wooden cases as solemn and ele-gant as coffins. They'd cost plenty, once. Every stroke of the infi-nitely elaborate design was cut in by hand by some nearsighted old German silversmith, dead now for more than a century.

"Man, you'll collect anything!" Bill Kelsey said.

George nodded, serious.

Bill Kelsey cocked his head, looking down at the newel post, saying, "I wonder if a person could get anything for that junk in my attic."

"Could be," George had said, excitement in his chest. "Why don't we take a look some time?")

He set down the spoon with finality. "It must have been kids," he said.

Henry opened his hands. Nobody knew.


It was a warm night, for May. He drove slowly, as always, his left foot riding the slack in the clutch, the ankle stiff in its metal brace. Fog lay white as snow in the valley bottom, the trees at the sides of the valley dark and gloomy. Here away from the lights of Henry's house, no lights in sight but the stars and the moon and the flicker-ing headlights of his own truck, the night seemed less dim than it had before. If he wanted to, he could drive with his headlights turned off. Might have to if that wire was to jiggle any looser. He ought to have fixed it weeks ago, but he'd put it off. He put off more and more, these days. The accident was nine, ten months ago now; ac-cording to Doc Cathey he was as fit as he was ever going to be, the remaining left arm grown unnaturally muscular, the wrist conspicu-ously larger now that it took the whole beating of stripping out the cows. He could do pretty much what he'd done before, if he wanted to. It just took him longer. But he'd lost his drive, the whole thing had made him older. He'd skipped the cultipacking this year—the disking had left the ground level enough, and the rain was pretty good, the ground would likely hold in enough moisture to get by. Lou Millet was putting in the soybeans for him—labor Lou owed him from two years ago—that would take care of seven acres, and the soil bank would take care of ten more. The alfalfa took care of itself. If the sky fell in he could live all right on the disability pension from

the army. So he let things slide. He'd get up in the morning and milk
the cows and clean up the barn, and after that he'd work for a couple
of hours at the plowing, already so far behind schedule it didn't much
matter. (*Corn knee high by the fourth of July.* He'd be lucky if he
had the stuff planted.) Around noon he'd come in and quit till five-
o'clock choretime, spend his time pasting stamps in, or silver-
polishing the two ceremonial Scottish swords (he'd gotten them
both for $70), or just sitting in front of the television, half asleep.
Plowing had been a pleasure once—the smell of new turned sillion,
the blue-black sheen of the cut earth rolling off straight as an arrow,
dark under the pines at the top of the hill (the ginger-water jug
showing dull silver in the burdocks under the trees), the plowed
ground richer and warmer where the sunlight struck. He'd be conscious of both the past and the future—riding side-saddle on the
tractor seat, one hand on the steering wheel, the other on the
plow: he would remember intensely, as if still inside them, other
springs, plowing with that same F-20 or riding the gastank while his
father plowed, rear end growling as if running on chains and the air
sad-sweet with the scent of new buds and pinesap running and new-
turned ground, and in the same flow of intense sensation he would
see his crop growing and ripening, field-corn towering over your
head, the stalks oozing sweeter than honey when the blade bit
through. Even after he'd come back from Korea, one foot smashed
and his breathing bad from the mess-up in his chest, the plowing
was good, he could handle it. But now it was changed. He plowed
one-handed now, fighting the steering-wheel lefthanded, jerked off
balance whenever the front wheels climbed over a rock, his right
hand no longer there to anchor him; and when he saw a big rock
coming at him he could no longer raise the plow on the run but had
to throw in the clutch with his gimpy foot, reach back for the lever,
and drive no-handed for a minute. More often than not, it seemed
to him, he saw the rock coming in under too late, and before he
could shove in the clutch he was hearing the crack of steel like a rifle
shot and the point was gone, half the mollboard with it, and the
plow was skidding along one wheel in the air, like a crippled duck.
One of these days, as sure as anything, he'd break the one fist he
had left, hitting the tractor tire in his rage. The accident had left
him hard up as hell (let alone the way his picking things up was
beginning to cost him), yet he'd seen no choice but to get a new
plow, a trip-spring rubber-tired son of a bitch the F-20 wasn't horse

enough to pull, which meant getting the big DC. They'd pretty
near laughed in his face at the bank. But they'd loaned him the
money, finally. Because the house was worth plenty, never mind
the land. ("Business is business," the man had said. He poked his
moustache with his pen, feeling guilty. George Loomis had said,
"Sometimes," sarcastically, meaning that sometimes it was more, a
way of staying alive, but he hadn't bothered to explain what he
meant, had merely signed where the man made the x with his ballpoint pen.) If he ever did get the corn in the ground he'd need a
new outfit to get it up into the silo. It was the fucking antique corn-
binder that had taken off his arm. (A long time ago, it seemed by
now. As if in a different life.)

It would be something, he thought then, walking into your house
one night and finding a couple of nuts there, standing in the
kitchen with big lead pipes, or pistols.

He turned up the dirt road that wound up Crow Mountain to his
house. The lights were all off at the Shaffer place. Walt's jeep was
parked by the mailbox as usual, under the limbs of the beech tree, in
case it should rain. The green and white plastic lawn furniture sat as
always in the bare dirt yard among metal toy trucks and plastic blocks
and pieces of dolls. The thought of their oldest girl, Mary Jane,
passed briefly through his mind. He would see her bringing in eggs
in a wire basket sometimes as he was driving past. She would wave,
and he would wave back. She looked Polish, like her mother. Light
brown hair, thick ankles. Somebody'd told him she had a cedar chest
full of things for her marriage. Be too late pretty soon. She was getting close to her thirties now.

At Sylvester's there were no lights but the flicker of the television.
Sylvester would be sitting with his shoes off and no shirt on, his
wife ironing in the barren back room. The kids would be sitting
around more or less naked, invisible as the overstuffed chairs they
sat in in the darkened room, or invisible except for their eyes and
their dirty underwear. That was the last house for more than two
miles, as the road went—the last house on this side of the mountain
except for his own and the Ritchie place, abandoned now for ten
years and gone to ruin.

The headlights jiggled out and he leaned forward. They came on
again.

Then he remembered the man he'd met down in Slater, at Bittner's. He couldn't say at first why the trifling memory made him

uneasy, or why he should happen to remember it at all—except, maybe, that the man's disappearing went with the general uneasiness he'd been feeling ever since that car had come barrelling straight at him.

Bittner had been sitting ritched back on two legs of his red wooden chair, squarely facing his open front door, a little ways back from it, where he could look out into the street. George had been in town for a couple of errands at Salway's, and he'd decided to drop by the old man's shop on the chance he had stumbled onto something he didn't know the worth of. When he went in the old man said, "Odd do," as usual, lifting his eyebrows, looking over his glasses, and George nodded, standing in the doorway a moment, getting his eyes adjusted to the darkness and clutter—rickety tables, fairgrounds-glass vases, clocks, featherdusters, crocks, baskets, chairs, firedogs, scuttles, birdcages, pictures in ornately machine-carved broken frames, maple spindles, chests of drawers, hundreds of dusty, disintegrating books (*The Ladies' Repository*, Volume 24, *Ideal Suggestion, Elsie Venner*). He started along the nearer wall of bookshelves, not reading the titles or even looking at particular books, gazing vaguely, like a hunter taking in acres at once, waiting for a good binding to separate itself from the surrounding trash. When he was halfway down the aisle, Bittner said, "Here's the man you should talk to. He must have a spinning wheel or two." He turned and saw that the old man was not talking to him but to another man, standing in the darkest part of the room, reaching down into one of the bins of odds and ends. The man looked around, not slowly but somehow too cautiously, and George knew the man was blind. "How do you do?" the man said. He had dark glasses on and a touring cap. In one hand he held a pair of carved ivory chopsticks, in the other, his cane. George nodded, realizing only later that a nod did no good.

Bittner said, "George is a collector. I don't know what-all he's got."

"You don't say," the man said. He wasn't from the Catskills. Vermont, maybe.

"He's got old records, magazines, stamps, I don't know what-all."

"I'm not really much of a collector," George said.

Bittner said, waving, "Boot-jacks, arrowheads, antique furniture, picture frames, china, paperweights—"

Again, thoughtfully, the blind man said, "You don't say." He came toward him down the aisle, smiling vaguely, moving the cane almost casually back and forth across the aisle like a witching rod. When he was within three feet of George he knew it, and held out his hand. "My name's Glore," he said. They shook hands. "George Loomis," George said. The man's skin was pale and flaccid, as if he'd spent years in the darkest corners of junkstores. "Do you really collect antique paperweights?" he said.

George said, "I've got a few. Nothing valuable." After a moment he added, "A couple of them were family things, and I happened to run across some more that looked good with them. I don't really collect."

Bittner laughed scornfully, behind him. "What he means is, he ain't letting anything go. Regular miser. He-he-he!"

The blind man's interest was sharper now. He inclined his head very slightly, his left hand groping out toward the bookshelf. He said, "I'd be interested to *see* your things some time."

"Anytime you say," George said, not as heartily as he might have. He liked nothing better than showing off his things, but Bittner was right, he was a miser about them.

The blind man said, "Where do you live?"

George told him, and the man listened carefully, as if taking it down in his mind. When he had it, he said, "You expect to be home this afternoon?"

"I expect so," George said.

That was the last he'd seen of the man. When he'd asked Bittner about him, later, Bittner said he didn't know who the man was. "Glore," George said, and Bittner remembered that that was the name he'd said, yes, but that was all he knew. He'd come into town in an old Lincoln, Bittner remembered then. A young black-headed fellow driving for him. They'd come and they'd gone. "That's business," Bittner said. George had nodded, thinking.

He wondered now, for the first time, if Glore had really been blind. He put the thought out of his mind at once, sensibly, but he still felt jumpy. He carried the idea of the murder on Nickel Mountain like a weight on his chest, that and the teasing contrast of Callie and Henry waving in the warmth of the yellow porchlight, behind him, ahead of him a carload of teen-agers burning toward him, brainless and deadly.

He'd come to his own driveway now. He could look down to his left and see the whole valley, the willows and the creek cutting through the middle, and directly below him the gleaming rails of the New York Central tracks curving onto the trestle. He let go of the wheel to grab the gearshift and shift down to second, then caught hold of the wheel again. He pulled up past the overgrown lawn in front—his headlights sweeping across the weeds and treetrunks—and turned sharply at the fence and backed into the shed. When he switched the ignition off the stillness dropped around him like a trap. He'd noticed the same thing once before, tonight, when he'd first come out of the Soames' house onto the porch. Callie had noticed it too and had said, "It's quiet tonight. Must be rain coming."

The headlights—staring ahead and a little upward, because of the pitch of the shed's dirt floor—made the weeds around the hand-crank gaspump look pocked-gray as old bone. Every line of the American-wire fence stood out, unnaturally distinct, like the chipping sign on the pump: *Warning. Contains Lead.* Far beyond the fence the headlights eerily lighted just the top of the gambrel peak of the haybarn roof.

He turned out the lights, got out of the truck, and slammed the door behind him. It was then he knew, with a certainty that made him go cold as ice, that somebody was watching from the house.

He knew that very possibly it was nothing but nerves. Even probably. The story of the murder, the car swerving at him, the odd encounter (as it seemed to him now) two weeks ago at Bittner's—all that together might naturally give you the jitters. But he didn't for one minute believe it to be nerves. There was somebody there. He knew it as surely as he'd known it that night when they started up the quiet looking valley in Korea: it was as though a sense keener than the ordinary five had caught some unmistakable signal. He'd kept on walking, that night, cautious but not giving in to the feeling that there were rifles trained on him; and then suddenly, crazily, he was staring into lights, and McBrearty was falling back against him, dead already, and he felt the hit, and next minute he was coughing blood and couldn't breathe and knew for certain he was dying, thinking (he would never forget): *Now I'll find out if this horseshit about heaven's really true.* But he'd lived, and now he was no kid any more, he knew what he couldn't have imagined then: if they wanted to kill him, they could do it—he was mortal. Everything on earth was destructible, old books, guns, clocks, even bookholders of bronze.

He stood out of sight against the wall of the shed and tried to make his mind work. (The truck smelled of gas and heated belts and alcohol in the radiator. The motor was clicking. He could smell the dirt floor of the shed and the lighter, delicately acrid scent of moulding burlap. *I meant to patch the bags,* he thought. *It must've slipped my mind.* He had to get calm.) The obvious thing to do, he knew the next instant, was climb into the truck again and get out of there; go get help. It would take him ten minutes to get to Sylvester's and call up the sheriff, ten minutes more for the sheriff and his men to get to Sylvester's, another ten minutes to get back. And then *they* could go in; it was what they were paid for. By that time maybe whoever was there might be gone.—Gone, if they were thieves, with maybe fifteen thousand dollars worth of his things.—And if they were kids?

He saw them again, far more sharply than he'd seen them at the time, leering out at him as the car roared past. What if they were to set fire to the house? His heart was beating so hard it ached, and he pressed his fist to his chest, unable to breathe. He could no more get rid of the ache than the image in his head, fire churning behind the round-arched windows of all three stories, the burning furniture not even visible in all that hell, flames licking the balustered porch, crawling out the eaves to the great carved dentils, then walls falling down like a landslide inside the brick shell, the fire going suddenly white. He'd seen ordinary houses burn. It would be something.

He got hold of himself. The house stood silent and severe as ever; inside, no sign of movement. For an instant he was certain there was a figure at the middle livingroom window, but the next instant he no longer knew for sure. Then he remembered the rifle in the woodshed.

He'd left it there—on the cloth-draped cherry dresser he was storing there—months ago, at the time of the bobcat scare. Somebody had found tracks by his cowbarn door, and he'd called the troopers and the troopers had said they were bobcat. The word got around quickly, and pretty soon bobcats were showing up everywhere— flitting across a mountain road just in front of a car, prowling in the bushes beside some outhouse, standing stock still on a moonlit, snowy lawn. Sylvester's wife had been scared, and when George Loomis had seen she couldn't be kidded out of it he'd told her he'd bring her the rifle. He'd gotten it out and cleaned it up and loaded some bullets and thrown them in a paper sack, and he'd taken it out to the woodshed to loan Sylvester when he came for the milk. When

Sylvester got there, the cat had been shot already, the other side of Athensville, so he didn't take it. ("There may be more," George had said. Sylvester had grinned. "'Ere's always more," he said. "'Ose old woods is somethin' else.")

The driveway was white in the moonlight, but he hopped across it fast, gimp foot swinging, and dove into the weeds on the far side. Nothing happened. He lay perfectly still with his forearm pushing into the soft, gritty earth, the damp weeds touching his face rotten smelling and sappy smelling at the same time, and he waited. Then he started crawling, circling three quarters of the way around the house to get to the woodshed without crossing an open space. When he got the walnut tree at the edge of where the garden had been last year—grown up in weeds now, the same as the rest—he stopped again and raised his head to look up at the house. Still no sign. He thought: *What if it really is all just nerves?* The minute he allowed himself to ask the question, he knew, secretly, the truth: there was no one there. If he weren't crazy he'd stand up right now and walk on into the house. But he was. Or he was gutless, more like: the very thought of standing up made his legs go weak.

The ground was mucky, this side of the house. It squeezed between his fingers when he leaned on his hand, and it clogged the brace on his hand, and it clogged the brace on his ankle, making his foot as heavy as it would be in a cast. His sweater was damp and smelling of wool from the dew he'd come through, and his pantlegs were as soaked as if he'd fallen in the pasture brook. He reached the brick wall and got up, pressing close to it, and in five seconds he was in the woodshed, leaning against the toolbench, getting his breath.

When he jerked the door open ("ridiculous? Jesus!" he would tell them all later) plunging in with the rifle leveled, the kitchen was empty. The door to the livingroom stood open, as always, and he knew before he reached it that there was no one there. There was no one in the dining room, the library, the pantry, or the downstairs bedroom—he went through each room, turning on the lights—and no one on either the front or back stairs, no one on either the second floor or the third. There was nothing, no one in the house but himself and his things.

And now, rational at last, he recognized with terrible clarity the hollowness of his life. He saw, as if it had burned itself into his mind, the image of Callie, Henry, the baby, and the dog, grouped in the warm yellow light of the porch. If Henry Soames had crept through wet grass and mud that way to protect what was his, it would have meant something. Even if it had been all delusion, the mock-heroics of a helmeted clown, it would have counted.

"Fool!" he whispered, humiliated and hot from head to foot with anger, meeting his eyes in the mirror, ready to cry.

The rifle crooked in his arm was heavy, and he glanced down at it. It was old as the hills—a .45-70 Springfield from 1873, an officer's model, according to the chart in *Shotgun News*—yet there was still blue on the barrel, beautiful and cool against the mellow brown of the walnut stock. It was a rare thing to find one that old that still had the blue. Most people wouldn't notice or think it was important, but just the same, it was a rare find; a thing that should be preserved. And then he thought, feeling a flurry of excitement, as though he were about to discover something: *I was never more scared in my life. My God. Right from the first minute, I thought I'd had it.* He went back into the kitchen to hunt up a polishing rag and some whiskey. He figured he'd earned it.

# VIA NEGATIVA

JAMES SALTER

James Salter has had stories in the O. Henry Collections
of 1970 and 1972. He is published in *The Paris Review*.
The best known of his novels is A *Sport and a Pastime*.
He was born in 1926.

There is a kind of minor writer who is found in a room of the library
signing his novel. His index finger is the color of tea, his smile filled
with bad teeth. He knows literature, however. His sad bones are made
of it. He knows what was written and where writers died. His opinions are cold but accurate. They are pure, at least there is that.

He's unknown, though not without a few admirers. They are really
like marriage, uninteresting, but what else is there? His life is his
journals. In them somewhere is a line from the astrologer: your natural companions are women. Occasionally, perhaps. No more than
that. His hair is thin. His clothes are a little out of style. He is aware,
however, that there is a great, a final glory which falls on certain figures barely noticed in their time, touches them in obscurity and re-
creates their lives. His heroes are Musil and, of course, Gerard
Manley Hopkins. Bunin.

There are writers like P. in an expensive suit and fine, English
shoes who come walking down the street in eye-splintering sunlight,
the crowd seeming to part for them, to leave an opening like the eye
of a storm.

"I hear you got a fortune for your book."

"What? Don't believe it," they say, though everyone knows.

On close examination, the shoes are even handmade. Their owner
has a rich head of hair. His face is powerful, his brow, his long nose.
A suffering face, strong as a door. He recognizes his questioner as
someone who has published several stories. He only has a moment to
talk.

First appeared in issue No. 55, Fall 1972, of *The Paris Review*.

"Money doesn't mean anything," he says. "Look at me. I can't even get a decent haircut."

He's serious. He doesn't smile. When he came back from London and was asked to endorse a novel by a young acquaintance he said, let him do it the way I did, on his own. They all want something, he said.

And there are old writers who owe their eminence to the *New Yorker* and travel in wealthy circles like W, who was famous at twenty. Some critics now feel his work is shallow and too derivative —he had been a friend of the greatest writer of our time, a writer who inspired countless imitators, perhaps it would be better to say one of the great writers, not everyone is in agreement, and I don't want to get into arguments. They broke up later anyway, W didn't like to say why.

His first, much-published story—everyone knows it—brought him at least fifty women over the years, he used to say. His wife was aware of it. In the end he broke with her, too. He was not a man who kept his looks. Small veins began to appear in his cheeks. His eyes became red. He insulted people, even waiters in restaurants. Still, in his youth he was said to have been very generous, very brave. He was against injustice. He gave money to the Loyalists in Spain.

Morning. The dentists are laying out their picks. In the doorways, as the sun hits them, the bums begin to groan. Nile went on the bus to visit his mother, the words of Victor Hugo about *all the armies in the world being unable to stop an idea whose time has come* on an advertisement above his head. His hair was uncombed. His face had the arrogance, the bruised lips of someone determined to live without money. His mother met him at the door and took this pale face in her hands. She stepped back to see better. She was trembling slightly with a steady, rhythmic movement.

"Your teeth," she said.

He covered them with his tongue. His aunt came from the kitchen to embrace him.

"Where have you been?" she cried. "Guess what we're having for lunch."

Like many fat women, she liked to laugh. She was twice a widow, but one drink was enough to make her dance. She went to set the table. Passing the window, she glanced out. There was a movie house across the street.

"Degenerates," she said.

Nile sat between them, pulling his chair close to the table with little scrapes. They had not bothered to dress. The warmth of family lunches when the only interest is food. He was always hungry when he came. He ate a slice of bread heavy with butter as he talked. There was scrod and sauteed onions on a huge dish. Voices everywhere—the television was going, the radio in the kitchen. His mouth was full as he answered their questions.

"It's a little flat," his mother announced. "Did you cook it the same way?"

"Exactly the same," his aunt said. She tasted it herself. "It may need salt."

"You don't put salt on seafood," his mother said.

Nile kept eating. The fish fell apart beneath his fork, moist and white, he could taste the faint iodine of the sea. He knew the very market where it had been displayed on ice, the Jewish owner who did not shave. His aunt was watching him.

"Do you know something?" she said.

"What?"

She was not speaking to him. She had made a discovery.

"For a minute then, while he was eating, he looked just like his father."

A sudden, sweet pause opened in the room, a depth that had not been there when they were talking only of immorality and the danger of the blacks. His mother looked at him reverently.

"Did you hear that?" she asked. Her voice was hushed, she longed for the myths of the past. Her eyes had darkness around them, her flesh was old.

"How do you look like him?" She wanted to hear it recited.

"I don't," he said.

They did not hear him. They were arguing about his childhood, various details of it, poems he had memorized, his beautiful hair. What a good student he had been. How grown-up when he ate, the fork too large for his hand. His chin was like his father's, they said. The shape of his head.

"In the back," his aunt said.

"A beautiful head," his mother confirmed. "You have a perfect head, did you know that?"

Afterwards he lay on the couch and listened as they cleared the dishes. He closed his eyes. Everything was familiar to him, phrases he had heard before, quarrels about the past, even the smell of the cushions beneath his head. In the bedroom was a collection of photographs in ill-fitting frames. In them, if one traced the progression, was a face growing older and older, more and more unpromising. Had he really written all those earnest letters preserved in shoe boxes together with school books and folded programs? He was sleeping in the museum of his life.

He left at four. The doorman was reading the newspaper, his collar unbuttoned, the air surrounding him rich with odors of cooking. He didn't bother to look up as Nile went out. He was absorbed in a description of two young women whose bound bodies had been found on the bank of a canal. There were no pictures, only those from a high-school yearbook. It was June. The street was lined with cars, the gutters melting.

The shops were closed. In their windows, abandoned to afternoon, were displays of books, cosmetics, leather clothes. He lingered before them. A great longing for money, a thirst rose in him, a desire to be recognized. He was walking for the hundredth time on streets which in no way acknowledged him, past endless apartments, consulates— in one of them worked the French girl who had been the model for Anne-Marie Costallat—banks. He came to the fifties, behind the great hotels. The streets seemed dank, like servants' quarters. Paper lay everywhere, envelopes, empty packages of cigarettes.

In Jeanine's apartment it was better. The floor was polished. Her breath was sweet.

"Have you been out?" he asked her.

"No, not yet."

"The streets are melting," he said. "You weren't working, were you?"

"I was reading."

From her windows one could see the deep salon in the rear of the Plaza in which hairdressers worked. It was red, with mirrors that multiplied its secrets. Naked, on certain afternoons, they had watched its silent acts.

"What are you reading?" he asked.

"Gogol."

"Gogol . . ." He closed his eyes and began to recite, almost mechanically, "*In the carriage sat a gentleman, not handsome but not bad-looking, not too stout and not too thin, not old, but not so very young . . .*"

"What a memory you have."

"Listen, what novel is this? *For a long time I used to go to bed early . . .*"

"That's too easy," she said.

She was sitting on the couch, her legs drawn up beneath her, the book near her hand.

"I guess it is," he said. "Did you know this about Gogol? He died a virgin."

"Is that true?"

"The Russians are a little curious that way," he said. "Chekhov himself thought once a year was sufficient for a writer."

She smiled. He had told her that before, he realized.

"Not everyone agrees with that," he murmured. "You know who I saw on the street yesterday? Dressed like a banker. Even his shoes."

"Who?"

Nile described him. After a moment she knew who he must be talking about.

"He's written a new book," she said.

"So I hear. I thought he was going to hold out his ring for me to kiss. I said, listen, tell me one thing, honestly: all the money, the attention . . ."

"You didn't."

Nile smiled. The teeth his mother wept over were revealed.

"He was terrified. He knew what I was going to say. He had everything, everybody was talking about him, and all I had was a pin. A needle. If I pushed, it would go straight to his heart."

She had a boy's face and arms with a faint trace of muscle. Her fingernails were bitten clean. The afternoon light which had somehow found its way into the room gleamed from her knees. She was from Montana. When they first met, Nile had seen her as complaisant, which excited him, even stupid, but he discovered it was only a vast distance, perhaps of childhood, which surrounded her. She revealed herself in simple, unexpected acts, like a farmboy undressing. As she sat on the couch, one arm was exposed beside her. Within its elbow he could see the long, rich artery curved down to her wrist. It was full. It lay without beating.

She had been married. Her past astonished him. Her body bore no mark of it, not even a memory, it seemed. All she had learned was how to live alone. In the bathroom were soaps with the name printed on them, soaps that had never been wet. There were fresh towels, flowers in a blue glass. The bed was flat and smooth. There were books, fruit, announcements stuck in the edge of the mirror.

"What did you ask him?" she said.

"Do you have any wine?" Nile said. While she was gone, he continued in a louder voice, "He's afraid of me. He's afraid of me because I've accomplished nothing."

He looked up. Plaster was flaking from the ceiling.

"You know what Cocteau said," he called. "There's a fame worse than failure. I asked him if he thought he really deserved it all."

"And what did he say?"

"I don't remember. What's this?" He took the bottle of sea-colored glass she carried. The label was slightly stained. "A Pauillac. I don't remember this. Did I buy it?"

"No."

"I didn't think so." He smelled it. "Very good. Someone gave it to you," he suggested.

She filled his glass.

"Do you want to go to a film?" he asked.

"I don't think so."

He looked at the wine.

"No?" he said.

She was silent. After a moment she said,

"I can't."

He began to inspect titles in the bookcase near him, many he had never read.

"How's your mother?" he asked. "I like your mother." He opened one of the books. "Do you write to her?"

"Sometimes."

"You know, Viking is interested in me," he said abruptly. "They're interested in my stories. They want me to expand *Lovenights*."

"I've always liked that story," she said.

"I'm already working. I'm getting up very early. They want me to have a photograph made."

"Who did you see at Viking?"

"I forget his name. He's a . . . dark hair, he's about my size. I should know his name. Well, what's the difference?"

She went into the bedroom to change her clothes. He wanted to follow her.

"Don't," she said.

He sat down again. He could hear occasional, ordinary sounds, drawers opening and being shut, periods of silence. It was as if she were packing.

"Where are you going?" he called.

She was brushing her hair. He could hear the swift, rhythmic strokes. She was facing herself in the mirror, not even aware of him. He was like a letter lying on the table, the half-read Gogol, like the wine. When she emerged, he could not look at her. He sat slouched, like a passionate child.

"Jeanine," he said, "I know I've disappointed you. But it's true about Viking."

"Of course, it's true."

"I'll be very busy . . . Do you have to go just now?"

"I'm a bit late."

"No, you're not," he said. "Please."

She could not answer.

"Anyway, I have to go home and work," he said. "Where are you going?"

"I'll be back by eleven," she said. "Why don't you call me?"

She tried to touch his hair.

"There's more wine," she said. She no longer believed in him. In things he might say, yes, but not in him. She had lost her faith.

"Jeanine . . ."

"Goodbye, Nile," she said. It was the way she ended telephone calls.

She was going to the nineties, to dinner in an apartment she had not seen. Her arms were bare. Her face seemed very young.

When the door closed, panic seized him. He was suddenly desperate. His thoughts seemed to fly away, to scatter like birds. It was a deathlike hour. On television, the journalists were answering complex questions. The streets were still. He began to go through her things. First the closets. The drawers. He found her letters. He sat down to read them, letters from her brother, her lawyer, people he did not know. He began pulling forth everything, shirts, underclothes, long clinging weeds which were stockings. He kicked her shoes away, spilled open boxes. He broke her necklaces, pieces rained to the floor. The wildness, the release of a murderer filled him. As she sat smoking, sometimes with a smile, the men nearby uncertain, seeking to hold her glance, he whipped her like a yelping dog from room to room, pushing her into walls, tearing her clothes. She was stumbling, crying, he felt the horror of his acts. He had no right to them—why did this justify everything?

He was bathed in sweat, breathless, afraid to stay. He closed the door softly. There were old newspapers piled in the hall, the faint sounds from other apartments, children returning from errands to the store.

In the street he saw on every side, in darkening windows, in reflections, as if suddenly it were visible to him, a kind of chaos. It welcomed, it acclaimed him. The huge tires of buses roared past. It was the last hour of light. He felt the solitude of crime. He stopped, like an addict, in a phone booth. His legs were weak. No, beneath the weakness was something else. For a moment he saw unknown depths to himself, he glittered with images. It seemed he was attracting the glances of women who passed. They recognize me, he thought, they smell me in the dark like mares. He smiled at them with the cracked lips of an incorrigible. He cared nothing for them, only for the power to disturb. He was bending their love towards him, a stupid love, a love without which he could not breathe.

It was late when he arrived home. He closed the door. Darkness. He turned on the light. He had no sense of belonging there. He looked at himself in the bathroom mirror. There was a skylight over his head, the panes were black. He sat beneath the small, nude photograph of a girl he had lived with, the edges were curled, and began to play, the G was sticking, the piano was out of tune. In Bach there was not only order and coherence but more, a code, a repetition which everything depended on. After a while he felt a pounding beneath his feet, the broom of the idiot on the floor below. He continued to play. The pounding grew louder. If he had a car . . . Suddenly the idea broke over him as if it were the one thing he had been trying to think of: a car. He would be speeding from the city to find himself at dawn on long, country roads. Vermont, no, further, Newfoundland, where the coast was still deserted. That was it, a car, he saw it plainly. He saw it parked in the gentle light of daybreak, its body stained from the journey, a faintly battered body that had survived some terrible, early crash.

All is chance or nothing is chance. At dinner Jeanine met a man who longed, he said, to perform an act of great and unending generosity, like Genet's in giving his house to a former lover.

"Did he do that?" she asked.

"They say."

It was P. The room was filled with people, and he was speaking to her, quite naturally, as if they had met before. She did not wonder what to say to him, she did not have to say anything. He was quite near. The fine wrinkles in his brow were visible, wrinkles not yet deepened.

"Generosity purifies," he said. He was later to tell her that words were no accident, their arrangement and choice was like another voice speaking, a voice which revealed everything. Vocabulary was like fingerprints, he said, like handwriting, like the body which revealed the invisible soul, which expressed it.

His face was dark, his features deep. He was part of another, a mysterious race. She was aware of how different her own face was with its wide mouth, its grey eyes, slow, curious, clear as a stream. She was aware also that the dress which concealed her breasts, the depth of the chairs, the dimensions of this room afloat now in evening, all of these were part of her immersion into the flow of a great life. Her heart was beating slowly but hard. She had never felt so sure of herself, so bewildered by the ease with which it all was opening.

"I'm suspicious and grasping," he said. He was beginning his confessions. "I recognize that." Later he told her that in his entire life he had only been free for an hour, and that hour was always with her.

She asked no questions. She recognized him. In her own apartment the lights were burning. The air of the city, bitter as acid, was absolutely still. She did not breathe it. She was breathing another air. She had not smiled once as yet. He later told her that this was the most powerful thing of all that had attracted him. Her breasts, he said, were like those of black slave girls in the *National Geographic*.

# BAKTI'S HAND

## BLAIR FULLER

Blair Fuller was born in New York in 1927 and has lived
for the past dozen years in San Francisco. His novel, A *Far
Place*, was published by Harper & Row in the late fifties
and a short novel, A *Butterfly Net and a Kingdom*, was
included in a Random House book, *Three Short Novels*,
in the early sixties. "Bakti's Hand" is one of a dozen or so
published stories. He has been an editor of *The Paris Review* for a number of years and has taught at Barnard
College, Stanford, California State University at Hayward
and, on a Fulbright, at the University of Oran, Algeria. He
is a Director of the Squaw Valley Community of Writers,
a bookstore owner, married, and the father of three
children.

Bakti's briefcase was heavy in his hand but he did not glance at the
cars passing in his direction. He stamped along the muddy kilometer
from his barren apartment to the University's gate watching ahead
to avoid the puddles, looking across the flat fields at the olive-oil factory with its now abandoned stork's nest still perched on its shorter
chimney, and at the shepherds, hidden under the hoods of their
*djellabahs,* tending their dirty flocks. No disgrace not to own a car
in socialist Algeria, yet he did not want to see a colleague's brake-
lights and be forced to trot over and accept the lift. *Any* of his colleagues—Algerian, French, or the solitary American, Sledd, whose
largest, newest model Mercedes was something of a shock. Most
especially Bakti did not want to see Benslimane who was chauffeur-
ing the distinguished visitor from Lyon, Le Professeur Carrère, Docteur d'État, on the highest rung of the French academic ladder.

Bakti need not have been concerned. He reached the gate a few
minutes before nine, the appointed hour, but no Oran faculty meet-

ing had ever begun within a half hour of schedule. As the gatekeeper, whose face had been crushed by shrapnel around the left eye, opened the grill for him, Bakti could see through the lines of palms that there were no cars parked by the Faculté des Lettres.

He opened the conference room and by putting the two tables together to make one, aligning the metal folding chairs around it, and straightening the few stacks of supplies in the shelves, made it look as formal as possible. The campus had been a French Aviation Base, built in a colonial "moorish" style with high ceilings and tall windows, so that formality was both natural to it and absurd. Given the tinniness of the furniture, the bad light and the flaking of the gray wall paint, not much could be done. Bakti went outside and smoked a cigarette, sitting on a bench near the doors of the auditorium that had been a mess hall. It was very quiet. The examinations had been given ten days before and most of the students had vanished to return on the day the results would be announced. In the distance he could hear a solitary light plane taking off, circling and coming down, then taking off again.

His colleagues arrived separately, the first one eighteen minutes late. They were apologetic to Bakti for their tardiness, and courteous, each in his own way. The French teachers of Spanish bowed slightly as they shook hands. Mlle. Arnaud, young and radical, briefly surrendered the ends of her fingers. The stout Englishwoman, married to an Algerian engineer, forgot to extend her hand and blushed. Sledd neither offered his hand nor blushed, but drawled out "Bonjour," making two words of it. Aidouni was jumpy with correctness, as finally was Benslimane, the other French University trained Algerian. All of them were overshadowed in graciousness by Professor Carrère who was extremely happy to be among them, cocking his cameo head this way and that and savoring the introductions. His pink cheeks gave off a sharp cologne, while his blazer, hard white collar, and the green and white striped ribbon in his buttonhole radiated those reasons for which he had been imported for a few days at such expense to the government—his unquestionable qualifications, his eminently sound judgment. To Bakti's surprise he and Carrère were equally short, but they weighed quite differently on the earth.

Bakti led the way inside. They seated themselves, and Bakti standing, eyes on the table, said a few words about procedure. During this meeting they would arrive at final grades for all the upperclassmen taking certificates in English and Spanish. Since there were so few in Spanish they would be dealt with first, but the Spanish faculty was asked not to leave when their section had been completed. It was hoped that today with the collaboration of Professor Carrère precedents could be set for the judgment of all the language sections in future. For this reason the Arabic section, Benslimane and Aidouni, was present although no certificates would be offered in Arabic until next year.

Bakti took his seat and the "Spaniards" got quickly to their business, a formality, for they had had only four students and had certainly made their decisions in advance. Carrère followed their dialogue alertly but did not speak. Because he was a Professor of English rather than of Spanish? Because the two "Spaniards" were French? When three students had been passed and the fourth invited to take a remedial exam in October, Bakti asked for comments. There were none. "Mlle. Arnaud, will you please begin with the first candidate in English."

"Benabadji, Abdelkader, 8.4 in Translation." And the name went around the table. He had achieved 6.8 in British History and Institutions, 11.8, his high, in American Literature. Bakti had given him 10.0, the passing grade, in his course in American Civilisation. Having announced it and then, like the others, having averaged Benabadji's failing score, he glanced up along the table and waited for Carrère's approval. Carrère gave it, faintly and gravely nodding his head, and Bakti ducked down to his grades-ledger in sudden embarrassment. His colleagues all knew how bitterly he had opposed the invitation to Carrère, that he had offered his resignation when the Dean had overruled him. The Department of Languages did not need an antique from Lyons to legitimize its degrees! he had protested, and they must all have heard him say it. Bakti the party member, the committed revolutionary! So that now it must seem that he was playing "petit negre."

Bakti hunched his shoulders, feeling the uneasiness around him, no help to his own discomfort. How had he so wrongly calculated? When a prisoner of the French twelve years ago, his tactful discretion had not saved him from torture—his left hand now holding the grades-ledger was scarred on its back where one electrode had been implanted. But after stubbornness and terror of his own comrades had combined to keep his mouth shut until fainting once, then deference had freed him of suspicion. He had supposed, since he had been welcomed out the prison doors by the triumphant FLN while the French were scrambling for the boats, that now Carrère would take his deference as irony, an irony which would act as a cement between himself and the others. But Carrère evidently sensed no irony. He indeed seemed ready to be helpful to a teacher so lacking in authority!

"Perhaps," Carrère was saying, "I might facilitate matters by averaging the grades as they are read out?" And not waiting for an answer he took a fat pen from an inside pocket and a sheet of paper from Benslimane's notebook. Then he looked gravely around the table; he was at their service.

Bakti nodded to Mlle. Arnaud that she should start the second round. She glared at him a moment, then putting her elbows on the table and joining her hands under her chin, her ultimate in dignified gestures, she read off "Benmiloud, Mohammed, 7.8 in Translation."

Since Carrère was dutifully recording the numbers, acting like the secretary the Department could not afford, it should have been possible to forget his position and potential power, to think of him simply as a functionary in a routine. On the contrary his unique elevation was emphasized. That a Docteur d'État should be doing clerical work for such a crew of people! Bakti glanced at Mlle. Arnaud, so prim and icy, and saw the sad little brownish stone in the ring on her little finger and the plainness of her blouse and sweater, and they made him feel the tremors in the shaky table and the dankness of the walls around them. Images of a conference room at Leeds —masked fluorescent lights, a solid blond wood table with ashtrays the size of soup bowls for English pipesmokers, and notepaper laid meticulously before each seat—crossed his mind. And then the industrial-looking campus of New York State University at Fredonia, not pretty because there was so much equipment—laboratories, gymnasiums, auditoriums—that the exteriors of the buildings were ungainly, like dust covers over office machines. Why hadn't they sent him to some poorer, gloomier places for study outside Algeria?

Now Carrère was saying, "Why don't we average the first two essays and then the first mid-term. . . ?"

And Bakti found himself saying that yes, that sounded to be a very good idea, let's do it that way, not consulting the others. He turned crisply on them, prompting scores and demanding repetitions, and their expressions changed. Sledd cocked his head a bit quizzically; the Englishwoman's upper lip beaded; Benslimane's mouth had gone disparagingly slack. Never mind; Bakti had got himself back in hand and working, and he saw that the lids of Carrère's eyes had raised. Carrère's voice had a new, clearer tone. Together they would be able to get the work done now, without a lot of unnecessary sensitivity. Carrère was a professional, so was he, and they needed to understand no more than that about one another.

"—At Lyons it is our habit to give extra weight to the second essay, on the ground, needless to say, that improvement should be recognized and rewarded."

What could Bakti do but agree to the principle involved?

"In general in the Department at Lyons we find . . ."

No doubt it was so found everywhere.

"At Leeds . . . ," said Bakti *à propos* a student's being unable to take an examination and unavailable for its makeup. Carrère's lids came slowly down as Bakti painstakingly explained the Leeds formula. Of course, Bakti realized in mid-development, only French procedures would count for Carrère. He reached the end of the outline and brief pros and cons and looked coolly at Carrère for comment. None came. "The Leeds formula seems fair enough to me," Bakti said, looking elsewhere around the table.

Carrère's silence had released them and several wished to talk, but Carrère cut them off by a clearing of his throat. "At Lyons—" he began. What Bakti had wished to believe was a common professionalism had simply been an aspect of the old colonial game. Let the cooperative Algerian speak first to make way for the colonial fiat! Bakti had ignored and silenced the colleagues with whom his entire future lay! O smart Bakti, shrewd, double-thinking fellow! He ground the blunt end of his ballpoint against the table top and a zinging vibration made Carrère's lids flutter and his glance shoot down. Bakti stopped his hand and glared at it. He had been a fellow professional in Carrère's eyes until the moment he had had something to contribute. How could he have imagined that Carrère would want to find the best solution, rather than the one he could impose! Bakti, idiot!

. . . It seemed that at Lyons there were some half dozen categories of acceptable excuses for missing an examination, all of them *verified*, attested to by competent authorities which equally, of course, did not exist in Algeria and would not exist for a generation to come. "This has the advantage, needless to say . . . on the whole it seems satisfactory to all concerned." Carrère's complicated and monotone discourse had softened the others to doughy speechlessness. The spectacle of their unsettled mouths put the lash to Bakti.

"Professor Carrère, we do not have those agencies here, those means of supervision. Our situation is quite different and I am sure you will understand that we are looking for an Algerian solution, that we cannot borrow our solutions any longer from abroad. . ." The absolute hush pleased him; so did Carrère's eyes.

Carrère said, "If you do not want to know what I know of such matters, I wonder why you asked me here?"

"We are happy to have your advice, but we are anxious to find an Algerian Solution."

Benslimane rushed to rescue the moment. "We were extremely gratified that you could accept our invitation, Monsieur le Professeur. While Bakti is quite right in saying we seek an Algerian solution, these solutions must of course be made up of others antecedent to our own. It is precisely for this reason . . ." And this was worse than "petit negre." Benslimane, Bakti's equal as head of the Arabic section, Benslimane, a leader of the "Cadets of the Revolution!" Apparently his wish was to gloss things over until there would seem to have been no conflict at all! His eyes darted around the table as he spoke and he was watched in silence. When he had finished, Carrère could be gracious again.

"I feel quite certain, my dear friends, that we can resolve all our problems with patience, with mutual understanding. Certainly there is no necessity for comment on the sad political history between our two nations; I feel we would do well to ignore politics, that politics can only be disruptive to deliberations on strictly academic matters."

And Bakti could see he was getting away with this, that the others would now prefer to remove politics from the room, that is to say, remove Bakti's anger, and they would happily ignore the fact that it was Carrère who had been playing politics and so cleverly that he had produced the classic colonial situation: the colonized split and angry at one another while the colonial power coasts on serenely to its goals. Of course they would be happy enough to forget contentious politics! Bakti raised his left hand against his chest and turned the back of it toward Benslimane who appeared so mistily pleased by Carrère's reaction that he could see nothing. Benslimane knew the scar's significance, after all!

You despicable winner, Carrère! Bakti could see him walking immaculately through the cold rains of Lyons. His trousers would never lose their press, the collar of his raincoat would never wrinkle. Nothing a student could say or do would surprise him. Their names would be dots on a list, their faces shapes in a mass—except the pretty ones. Carrère had an eye for those all right, had an eye for Mlle. Arnaud right here at the table, and probably could have her. Would, quite likely. He would fix her with those pale eyes under the arched brows, never smiling, never being ingratiating or apparently trying to charm, and talk about her future when she returned to teach in France. Where had she in mind to teach? Ah, perhaps he could be of some assistance, one of his oldest colleagues happened to be. . . . If she would give him some particulars about herself he could write a note on her behalf. Why didn't she come by the hotel. . . ? Bakti visualized her, the bony Marxist spreading herself on the shoddy hotel sheets, her soul kept pristine by the pretense that this was happening to her because she was a member of a certain class, trapped in certain circumstances. Historical inevitability! Bakti would like to present her with a few inevitabilities! Any Algerian girl would give ten years to be as free as the continually martyred Mlle. Arnaud.

He shook his head, trying to concentrate on the ledger. *What* were they arguing about? Borderline cases. Those one might be kind to for one reason or another and pass, or be strict with and fail. Let them jabber at it; Bakti had no wish to contribute. The expected viewpoints came forth: that one must not be too easy, the certificates must have genuine value, especially since the University was new, but that many students had been disadvantaged in language study because of the prohibition against almost all travel outside the country and the virtual absence of foreigners within it; that others were still more severely disadvantaged since they already were teachers at primary or secondary school level and could only come one day a week to class—almost half of the students were in this category. While the Oran certificates should be as difficult to obtain and as prestigious as those of the Sorbonne, Oxford, and Harvard, still, it must be understood that the students had been ill-favored and that we must certainly graduate some of them.

The Englishwoman now tried to help by telling an opaque anecdote about the Red Brick Universities when they had first opened; Mlle. Arnaud wanted to help too; she had witnessed the salutary effect on others of having failed examinations. They re-prepared them so well. She could not speak from her own experience, but. . . . Benslimane nodded eagerly. Up to this moment more than half the students had failed and would either waste months preparing for a retake of their examinations or would drop out of the University. Quite likely some of the girls who failed would be summarily married off by their impatient fathers. But Benslimane was apparently pleased that any kind of consensus could be reached.

Sledd now spoke up, his words in French struggled over separately, like the formations of a mechanical voice box. What he said, however, was sharply human. "If we failed this proportion of our students in America, we'd conclude that we hadn't taught them well enough."

"That is your point of view?" Carrère said, very coolly, apparently sincere.

And Sledd went right into it with statistics on intelligence and achievement which were virtually untranslatable from the American to any other culture, as Bakti knew. Then some philosophy, pertinent enough, about the necessity of training people for useful purposes, and the social disservice of keeping them overlong in schools. This, of course, was unpalatable to most of those in the room for whom staying-power had been the principal ingredient of academic success.

In fact Carrère's coolness had already cued their attitudes so that when Carrère said, "Our point of view, on the other hand . . . ," it was a genuine *our*, Bakti excepted. "Our point of view, on the other hand, is that it is the responsibility of the student to learn. We present the material; that is our responsibility. It is not our responsibility that the student succeed."

Sledd said, "Do you consider that you have no social responsibility?"

Crazy! An American, the lone "imperialist," for God knew how many bloody miles, talking social responsibility to a group of people everyone of whom call himself a socialist! And here came the Cadet of the Revolution to gloss it all over.

"Perhaps," said the Cadet, "it is more responsible to discourage students sometimes, rather than give rise to false hopes."

"And too," said Carrère, "there is the question of equivalence." After a brief silence. "There is no point in granting certificates and degrees which are not acceptable elsewhere."

The sweet reason of this statement, so casually and certainly pronounced, shot a jet of hysteria into Bakti's brain. What "elsewhere?" There was only one elsewhere so far as Carrère was concerned: the Universities of France! Intellectual and cultural imperialism pure and simple! Trap Algerian students into a system which would lead them inevitably to France. No wonder Lyons had been happy to grant him leave to come here.

"Most students will not go elsewhere," Sledd said, apparently wishing honestly to enlighten Carrère. "Most will finish their education here and go directly into professional life. Shouldn't they be our first concern?"

Carrère said, "They most assuredly should be our first concern," subtly emphasizing the "our," "—most assuredly, and my concern is that they should be able to continue to higher studies."

Bakti said loudly, "In France, you mean."

After a second, Carrère said, "In France," and raised his shoulders. "French standards are accepted throughout the . . . world."

Bakti knew that Carrère had almost said "*civilized* world." He said, "Perhaps *our* standards will be acceptable elsewhere too. In fact, to have what you call 'equivalence,' our curriculum would have to be identical with that of a French University. We did not fight the Revolution for that."

A "Spaniard" said sharply, "Bakti!"

"And further I would say it would be unwise of us in the extreme to model our curriculum on one which has been considered in all quarters obsolete and socially valueless! The English section, at least, will not do so." The Englishwoman's cheeks were brilliant red; all eyes were downcast. "Now," Bakti said. "Let us go through the individual cases and be as just as we can. Mlle. Arnaud." He nodded to her. She cleared her voice and they started again around the circle.

Either opinions had been more polarized than Bakti had suspected or Sledd and Carrère had polarized them. The Carrère-side grades were all failing or barely passing while the Sledd-side's were all generous, some of them fatuously so. Clearly the grades were being changed as they were being read out! Naturally, Bakti thought, Carrère would want all but a tiny tame elite of Algerian students to fail! And of course Sledd would be easy! One had but to see him stooping down to a student for a consultation, helpfully taking the girls' elbows in his hand, always *agreeing* with them initially—miracles though that might require—until he spoke his own piece. More important, the American point of view would find a large Algerian elite of mediocre education desirable. Algeria should become a kind of new midwestern bread-and-oil basket to be manipulated by Washington and New York! Since there were no official diplomatic relations, who had allowed Sledd into the country?

Bakti slowed the proceedings to be certain that the grades were being shaded and became doubly convinced that they were. It did not take that long to read a figure from a column! He heard an absurdly low grade for Chiali, Ahmed, and hiked Chiali's grade in American Civilisation two points when it came his turn, scribbling a note to himself to rectify his ledger. The American gave Djezzar, Sidi Mohamed, a grade worthy of a genius and Bakti dropped him three points. So it went through the entire list.

When the final candidate, Tayeb, Fatiha, had been averaged and there had been no objections or amendments, Bakti said, "We have done our work." Carrère was smiling at him with wide, luminous eyes. Carrère had nothing but contempt for what he had seen, for what Bakti had done. Yet if *they* could play that game, why not Bakti? He was no longer the boy that every adult Frenchman had known was a thief and scoundrel, guilty of whatever they claimed he was. He should no longer know that breathless state in which it was impossible, treasonous to oneself, to attempt an explanation or make a case, or even shout if he wanted.

"We have finished," he said. "Let us break up."

He rose as did the others, all of them busily collecting their things as the chairs scraped. He delayed, wishing that they would get out the door ahead of him, but their haste and the arrogant tilt of Carrère's chin goaded, and he said, "Mlle. Arnaud, please." She waited clutching her notebooks to her bosom as the others filed out. She was sullen, her mouth fattening.

"Close the door," he said.

"No, I shall not."

"This University is not a French University."

Silence.

"We have no reason to accept French standards."

"What are your standards then?"

"We will develop them." He was rubbing his scar with his thumb. "So long as you are on the faculty you would do well to remember it."

"That's what you wished to say to me?"

"The past is not entirely forgotten, Mlle. Arnaud."

"You like to be reminded of it, perhaps." This was sarcastic but in a different tone. She was very pale now.

"Everything today reminds me of it. Professor Carrère—"

"Oh, well," she interrupted. "You know he is very old school, conservative. You mustn't believe that every influence from France . . ."

and so on, suddenly rather girlish, chattering away, worried about her job, he supposed. ". . . in any case that is over and done with now."

He said quietly, "I wish some things were over and done with."

Which silenced her. Her lips twitched and her fingers worked the edges of her notebooks. He could spread her out on *his* grubby sheets. Perhaps he should tie her ankles to the bed frame.

He said, "Our next meeting is tomorrow at nine. First year students."

"Yes." Pretending blindly to look at her watch.

"I will lock up."

She left. He heard her going quickly down the hall, heels not touching, chasing Carrère. He snapped his briefcase shut, closed the window, and locked the door behind him. The hall was partially flooded from the women's toilets. He picked his way out to the quadrangle where fires of uprooted weeds were smoldering between the lines of palms. The smoke plumes drifted upward, yellow in the sunlight, making the birds scold.

A girl appeared at his elbow. "Please, sir, can you tell me if I passed?" He could not for the moment think of her name, although she had been in his course. She smiled her plea, a thin, gray-skinned girl with mottled gums.

"No results available." His brusqueness rocked her backwards and clamped her mouth shut. Rather than softening him, the gesture annoyed. "The grades are given to everyone at the same time."

"Yes, sir."

"There are no special cases."

"Yes, sir."

"You will have to wait." He nodded, dismissing her.

"Goodbye, sir." She turned awkwardly, stumbled off the single low step, then hurried away.

He could see Carrère and the others perhaps one hundred yards ahead of him, near the highway, neither strolling nor striding, walking clumsily together. He stepped down and scuffed his heel into the gravel roadway. He remembered the girl's name, Hassani, Rachida. I've done it to her, he thought.

He started walking, closing his mouth against the bitter smoke and squinting at the half-renovated buildings whose stucco walls were veined with white plaster repairs. The Faculté des Sciences on his left was an almost empty shell; there were chairs to sit on but almost no laboratory equipment. The Faculté de Médecine next it, which had been established longer, was better organized but less than half-staffed, and the General Hospital in the city was a chaos of overwork and incompetence.

There was everything to be done here, all new and to be accomplished.

Starting with himself.

# TROY STREET

ROBERT HEMENWAY

Robert Hemenway was born in South Haven, Michigan,
in 1921. He went to school there and in Ann Arbor, and
then to the University of Chicago. He has been a teacher
and an editor. He is now living in Austria and writing
stories.

In his dream Laurence MacLean was home, back in Michigan, walking slowly down Troy Street in Geneva with a woman he thought,
on waking, must be his wife, although he did not see her face. They
went past the fieldstone public library, on the corner opposite the
Methodist church, and past the first few of the small frame houses
that backed on the ravine. It was late winter. Snow lay on the ground,
though the walks were clear—old snow, stained at the base of the
trees, crusted, pockmarked by rain. He seemed to be showing the
town to the woman walking beside him. He pointed out a large
house on the other side of the street. "That's the Hall place," he
said. "A girl named Prince lived there. She lives in New York City
now." It was in fact the Hall place, but the rest of what he said
was dream. They kept on walking past low gray houses along the way
he had often taken going to and coming from school, and then he
got down on his knees in the snow beside the walk and bent over
to kiss the ground. Soot-blackened snow, crusted and rough after
thaws and freezes, stubbled patches of earth showing through. The
sense that he had come home to the center of his world. MacLean
sobbed aloud, a single cry, and woke up alone in his Manhattan
apartment, oppressed with unfamiliar nostalgia.

Straightforward expression of homesickness and longing though
it seemed, the dream puzzled him and remained with him. The
crusted snow, the hard earth, the woman standing there. She was

wearing a black evening gown, he thought, and over it a long white hooded cape. Perhaps not his wife, after all. She was his second wife. They had been divorced for three years, and in his dreams she and other women were often confused. MacLean had read somewhere that to dream of a specific, clearly identified spot on the earth's surface meant you belonged there; it was the place where you should go if you were, finally, to comprehend your own nature, to become yourself. Then, was he being told to return home—back to the shores of Lake Michigan, back to Geneva? In memory, surely, and not in actuality; *his* Geneva, after a third of a century, was no longer there. Back to his childhood, then? To where the map of his self had been drawn, its cardinal points fixed. He supposed so. He supposed that was what the dream "said"—telling him what he already knew. He was fifty now, and had for some time been trying to understand himself, trying to recall his first years. Well, he would go on trying. There was something in the dream that had the urgency of a command.

But the full meaning of the dream eluded him. That overwhelming sense in it of coming back home, back to where he belonged, was clear enough. But why precisely there—on Troy Street, blocks from where he lived? Blocks? No, not as far as that sounded. Not as far as it had seemed when on a dusty afternoon not long after his fourth birthday he had set out alone from the Doctor's house— Dr. Read and Mother Read, his maternal grandparents—to visit his Grandma and Grandpa MacLean alone. The spot where he knelt in the dream was about two blocks from the Read house one way, two blocks from the MacLean house the other. There on Troy Street, he was midway between them. Where, on his way to visit the MacLeans, the attraction of their house began to increase as that of the Read house began to wane. Where their forces were equally strong. At his magnetic center. Though the power of the Read house, where he and his parents stayed when they came from Detroit to visit and where he was brought up after his mother's death, was the stronger of the two.

But was that how he had gone from the Reads' to the MacLeans'? Not often. Not by himself. He usually took a shortcut through the ravine that ran down the center of the block. Going that way, he escaped the part of Troy Street that figured in his dream, where the trees were low and close together and cast thick shade, and where no one he knew lived but old Mrs. Hall and, a little farther on, Tom

Corey. Ah, but it had been *there,* hadn't it, right in front of Tom Corey's place, that he had knelt in the dream? In front of that small low-eaved rough-shingled house, its front porch no more than a step above the ground?

Remembering that much, he began to remember Tom. "Don't you ever talk to that man," his Grandmother Read would say when Tom passed their house, walking swiftly, eyes straight ahead, his heels clicking—looking as if he meant to talk to no one at all before he got where he wanted to go. Tom was touched in the head. He dressed like a pirate out of "Treasure Island," and even from the Read porch, high and set far back from the sidewalk, you could smell the patchouli on him. Or Mother Read could. "Don't you ever let him *give* you anything," she would say. "If he ever tries to speak to you, I want you to run right home as fast as your little legs will carry you, d'you understand?" MacLean must first have heard this when he was very young—four or five. But Tom had never approached him, or anyone MacLean knew. He was always busy on affairs of his own. And what clothes he wore! Knickers of gray corduroy, strapped below the knee. White hose—women's stockings, it was said. Shiny black patent shoes like Pilgrims' shoes, silver buckles and all. Billowing shirts of white cotton, open wide at the neck when it was warm. A tight-sleeved waistcoat when it was cool. And in winter a long navy-blue cape lined in red, like the one George Washington wore when he knelt in the snow at Valley Forge. Tom Corey was a small man, old but with a show of power still in his arms and upper body, and he walked chest out, as if he knew exactly who he was and where he was going. He tied back his hair, long and black still, with a ribbon at the nape of his neck.

Tom had lived on Troy Street since well before the First World War. His house was across the ravine from the Read house, opposite their back lawn, and when MacLean was a child he often watched Tom working in his vegetable garden, down in the ravine. There and when he was gardening for people in the neighborhood he wore denim overalls and looked like any farmer. But he had once been a circus acrobat, it was said, and a sailor. He had been to Europe, to Africa. He came to Geneva one summer with the circus and stayed. He borrowed a rowboat and ferried people across the North River for a penny a ride, and before long he had saved enough to buy the boat. Tom's penny crossing, well below the bridge, was a quick, pleasant way to get from the town to the north beach. Grandfather Mac-

Lean, when he was managing summer cottages across the river in the early nineteen hundreds, rode over and back with him two or three times a week from July until September. It was about then that Tom took to wearing his sailor outfit, and he never gave it up. At first, he lived in a shack on the riverbank, summer and winter. During the cold months he made a few dollars working with the men who sawed up the river ice and stacked it between layers of straw in the icehouse next to the fruit-packing plant. Then he got a little money—inherited it or saved it—and bought the Troy Street house. He gave up the penny crossing. There was a motor bus to the beach by then. He lived on until he was well up into his eighties, doing odd jobs around town. People tolerated him, but they warned their children away. There were stories. . . . Of what? MacLean could only guess. In Tom's last days, the stories were a good half century old.

How could a child not be in awe of Tom Corey—of Tom the Pirate, as the children called him? How could one not admire him? There were others that MacLean was not allowed to speak to—boys who were "bad," a neighbor who had been to prison, the riverbend Fergusons, who had married their own first cousins, Mother Read said, and worse. MacLean half admired them all, but never approached Tom or the others whose company was forbidden him. He seldom flouted restrictions, even when he knew they were unfair. He had wanted rules and boundaries then. He needed rules, needed to think them reasonable and right.

But the ground MacLean had knelt to kiss in his dream was in Tom Corey's front yard, and that was neither reasonable nor right. It made no sense at all. *There* had never been the center of his world. No. It was the edge of the forbidden for him when he was a child—of mystery, of something to be feared. Not Tom Corey alone—and he hadn't feared Tom, not exactly—but something about that street, that gloomy street where the poor lived. He was still uneasy walking down Troy Street. Was it no more than a lingering fear of the dark?

MacLean had had all a child's ordinary fears, he supposed, but what he feared most when he was young was nothing in his experience, nothing in Geneva. It was the Great War, which had come to an end before he was born. He would lie in bed at night, even into his early teens, and thank God quite simply that he had been spared that war, that he had been born after it into a time of peace, and in America, a peaceful and prosperous land. In western Michigan, where there had never even *been* war, where the Indians had signed away their lands and moved peaceably to reservations without a fight. He felt the Great War there back of him, threatening him still. His father had been in it, in the front lines, and had been lucky (MacLean overheard someone say this when he was very young) to get back alive. His father never talked about the war, except in a joking, guarded way. His voice rose in pitch when the subject came up, as it did when he spoke of MacLean's mother, for many years after her death. The war, like sex and death, was something of which no one in MacLean's family would speak directly, and he read anything about the war that he could find in the Read house and the public library: Remarque and Hemingway, Pershing's memoirs, Dos Passos, Henri Barbusse, Guy Empey, C. E. Montague, "Her Privates We." He would try to place his father in the scenes of which he read—to dress him in military uniform, put him among rats and the bodies of the dead in a muddy shell crater, see him firing his Colt .45 or lobbing a Mills grenade, hear him singing with his fellow-officers, "Here's to the dead who've left us, and here's to the next to die." But he had no success.

For his father (in fedora, dark business suit and vest now, with white shirt and watch chain and figured tie) *had* come back alive! He *had* been lucky! MacLean would recite this, too, as he lay in bed. His father, Captain Charles C. MacLean ("Howdy, Cap'n," the old-timers sitting on the railing in front of the Geneva Bank always said), had come back without a scratch, wearing a French Croix de Guerre and the double silver bars of his field commission, and married his mother, Jeannie Read, and they had had him, their son Larry. Laurence Read MacLean. Their little Larry. Their Schnickelfritz. Their Stick-in-the-Mud. How lucky he was! How lucky he was to have been *born!* For what if his father had not come back? There would be no Laurence Read MacLean at all.

That persistent sense throughout his childhood of the war behind him, and ahead of him a future shining bright. He saw his life then as a path of light that led away from the blackness of the war, was clouded for a time by his mother's death, and then went straight on, glowing, toward a future that would look like the drawings in *Popular Science*—tall hexagonal towers, their tops in the clouds, with dirigibles overhead and, lower down, Autogiros like dragonflies shuttling between landing platforms half a mile up in the sky.

He had never for more than a day found himself without hope, although he had rarely for as much as a day been without fear. And here in the city, working on Park Avenue in one of its shining towers at a job he enjoyed as often as not, wasn't he alive in a future much like the one he had imagined? Had he been wrong to hope? Had he been wrong to be afraid?

His mother taught him to pray, and his prayers ended "God bless all of us, and *God bless me!*" He would shout it sometimes, bouncing on his bed after the formal bedside prayer was done—laughing, his mother laughing with him.

His God was not a punishing God. MacLean had been told only of Heaven. The place of Hell was taken in his imagination by nothingness, by senselessness, by what was at the heart of nearly everything he feared—dissolution. (Feared and sometimes sought for.) That was what had terrified him about the Great War—men blown to bits by the thousands, senselessly. Utterly destroyed. . . . Senselessness. Meaninglessness. The dissolution of meaning. He feared these as he feared losing consciousness, losing control—something that he already knew by the time he was eight or nine. He had tantrums, and he fainted sometimes, and his nosebleeds took a long while to stop, and he wet his bed, and he was knocked unconscious once or twice. By the time he was eight, he had been skipped two grades, and there were boys in his class, though he was strong enough for his age, who could knock him down. He avoided fights. He shied from physical contact. He gave up rather than go on with a fight, even if he was winning—especially when he was winning. There came to be so little point in fighting with him that he was usually left alone.

What self-confidence he had been given! Always, in luck for the moment or out, that preserving sense of his luck in the long run. He knew that he had been born at the right time and in the right place, though he knew no more of his vocation or of his destiny than that his future was bright.

And so he would lie there in his bed in the back upstairs room of the Read house, sure of his future and of his good fortune, as indolent at nine as he was to be at twenty-nine—lie there congratulating himself. How lucky he was to live in Geneva! There was no safer place to be. He would lie between the stiff muslin sheets, imagining earthquakes, hurricanes, tornadoes, fires—all of them somewhere else. Or he would see before his eyes the great world, spherical (nearly) and immense, serenely moving on its course about the sun, spinning away, spinning away, enclosed and cushioned by its atmosphere, its surface scarred and troubled by disasters and wars, while he, Larry MacLean, lay safe and sound in his bed.

"God's in his heaven—all's right with the world." Alas, he felt still in his bones that this was true. He had been given no subtler belief than that. "God is good, and has a care of us." Like St. Augustine, he had never come to believe less. "In joy the universe was created, in joy it is sustained, in joy it will be dissolved." That, too? Yes, perhaps. But what did he know of these things? He seldom prayed. He fled the Church—any church—as if it were the Enemy. And there was no humility in him. Only that blasted blind American confidence. Nothing deprived him of it for long.

The confidence came from his mother. His father had less of it; an ironic last-ditch courage took its place. MacLean had found a notebook in the Read attic not long before the house was torn down in the late fifties. In it, along with a record of his intellectual progress for his first six years, he discovered his mother's lecture notes. She had taken a course on child development. *He* was the child. There he read, in his mother's hand, his own instinctive, anachronistic belief—what everyone, he supposed, had been taught in American schools in the early years of the century:

> Nature keeps things in order. We are divinely given a mind and curiosity to try and understand the divine mind and its divine plan. The more we study the law and plan of all living things, the more humble we should feel. . . . We try to figure out scientific laws to understand the divine plan of life. . . . Scientists are men of divine insight, for after all we are no more than Servants or Helpers of God.

Geneva had two famous sons that MacLean knew of. One a botanist, the other a geologist. They both were scientists in the old way—classifiers, discoverers of the natural order, the divine plan. In the same notebook he read:

> God started the seed growing. He started the ball rolling, and it follows its own laws. Nature keeps things in order. The young of horse not zebra. Wolves never foxes. Thistle seeds never grow sunflowers. . . .

That sanguine belief in the world's rightness! Taught in school and church, where they sang:

> This is my Father's world
> And to my listening ears
> All nature sings and 'round me rings
> The music of the spheres.

Lying on the Reads' broad lawn one night, MacLean had heard the music of the spheres.

An ordered world, of which he learned in civics class as well as science class. The rightness of the civil order, springing from the twin fountains of law, the Declaration of Independence and the Constitution! Those geometric charts he had been required to copy until he knew them by heart, in which were displayed, boxed neatly, the departments of government on the federal, the state, the county, the township, and the municipal level. All those tables of organization, and not a word about power! He was in the eleventh grade before a history teacher suggested that the legal order and the political order might not be the same.

Yet no matter what he was taught he felt always, behind him and beneath him and within him, hints of darkness. No one in his family, neither Read nor MacLean, would acknowledge the dark. Indeed, their energy—pioneer's energy, still—was turned entirely toward denying it, toward overcoming the wilderness. The Reads, especially. His grandfather, a school principal who had gone to college at thirty, with a wife and two children, in order to be a doctor. His grandmother and his mother, teachers. His uncle, too, a doctor. The Read house, with its edifying books and magazines. The compendiums of useful information and gems of literature. The sets of Tennyson and Thackeray and Scott and "Great Events by Famous Historians." The *Golden Book* and *Delineator* and the *Review of Reviews*. The Reads had tried to do so much—beyond their capacities. They had gone too far from the farm. But were the MacLeans, who had expected less and who achieved less, any more aware of the dark? His father, perhaps, but it was something he did not care to go into. For MacLean, the dark was never far away. The ravines in the town, most of them uncultivated tangles of brush, unlike Tom Corey's garden. The nights of storm, when the electric light would fail. The North River, deep and opaque between the two piers. The North River near the bridge, where there was ice-skating in winter and you could buy roasted sweet potatoes and eat them out of your hand. Children drowned there if the ice broke, Mother Read said—ice that was thick enough to be sawn out in blocks two feet square! He was not allowed to skate on the river. And the darkness of the inland lakes, bordered by pines, where men fished through the ice in winter as they sat in sheds beside coal stoves. If they forgot to move the sheds, MacLean had believed, the ice would slowly, slowly melt, and they would slip quietly, chairs and hissing stove and all, into the depths below. And the darkness of the grave. And the dark of nothingness, the absolute black of never having been at all. For if his father had been blown to bits, then he, Larry MacLean, could not have been born. He would lie in bed sometimes trying to imagine the unimaginable, his own nonbeing. But then, when he was seven or eight, he would begin to imagine something else—himself in another body. Could he already have known of the transmigration of souls? And whenever he tried to imagine himself in another body, it was that of a young girl. Thinking of it in those first years after his mother's death, he would slip into languorous fantasies. He had already read the story of the boy Tip and his friends (Jack Pumpkinhead, the Tin Woodman, and Mr. Woggle-Bug among them) in which Tip, long under the wicked witch Mombi's evil spell, is transformed at the end into what he has always been, the Princess Ozma of Oz. How MacLean had longed to become that princess, fresh and beautiful as a May morning, her eyes as sparkling as two diamonds and her lips tinted like a tourmaline, with her robes of silken gauze floating about her like a cloud, and dainty satin slippers on her feet! For a time he persuaded himself that he was indeed a princess, trapped in the ordinary body of a boy.

But he was a boy, and his father's son, and he knew it. People told him he was the spit 'n' image, and teased him about his ears, which stuck out as far as his dad's and his Grandfather MacLean's. Like a taxicab going down the street with both doors open, his father said. The porter on the train from Detroit to Kalamazoo once remarked, looking down at the two of them, "My, my, Mister, you *sure* left your mark on him." MacLean's father never tired of that story. By the time he was thirteen, MacLean had forgotten his fear of the Great War and forgotten the Princess Ozma of Oz. He was determined to get into West Point.

How much, though, he had once wanted to be a girl! Less was expected of girls, and so much was expected of him. Could he ever become all that the Reads and his father wanted him to be? He lacked something, he didn't know what—in spite of that sense of rightness he had, that sense of his luck. He did not know that others, older than he, might have the same feeling of incompleteness. The people in his world were as solid as statues, all of a piece. Including Tom Corey.

Before long, voices and images would begin to tempt him away from Geneva, but when he was not yet more than a child he knew where he belonged. The world outside was a spectacle, no more—a picture show that played in his mind while he thought or read. He had no real desire to be elsewhere than he was, much as he wanted sometimes to be other than he was. Years would pass before the great world found its power over him. Years more would pass before its power began to wane.

All along, emissaries were coming to Geneva from that alien world. Summer excursion boats from Chicago that brought poor Jews from the West Side for a few days' stay at one of the resorts in the woods far from the lake shore, from which they would be brought to the north beach in old trucks and buses—even a horse-drawn charabanc —on which were painted letters in a strange script and curious consonantal names. And there were the rich, the Gentiles, families from Cincinnati and Memphis and St. Louis who came to live beside the lake in their summer houses. And the one-ring circus that pitched its tent in August across the river. And the travelling tent theatre that performed its melodramas and its barnyard farces in late September each year, after the summer people had gone. The sideshows that came to town on flatcars—medical wonders and freaks of nature that he was not permitted to see, and an evil-smelling, embalmed, eroded carcass of a whale that he was. And the stunt fliers. And the slave ship that anchored below the bridge one summer, rusty shackles and fetters still in its hold. The sweetish smell of the stockyards that came from Chicago now and then on a strong, hot wind. The light from the Lindbergh beacon on the Palmolive Building far across the lake, flashing every sixty seconds, reflected off the clouds. Once, Chicago's skyline, pink and shimmering, upside down—a mirage! It lasted for hours, and he watched it from the beach all one afternoon. And the ships from England and Norway carrying white clay and bales of wood pulp for the Kalamazoo paper mills. And the Scotch whiskey and sharp English cigarettes that the ship's officers would bring to the Read house when they came to dinner with his

Aunt Betsy and her boyfriend, the shipping agent in Geneva. Mac-
Lean's first cigarette had been a Senior Service, his first taste of
hard liquor Vat 69. And the movies. Those stiff Bible dramas, tinted
rose or blue, that were shown in the church on Tuesday nights, and
the science movies in the school assembly, and on Saturday and Sunday the talkies in the Michigan Theatre downtown. And Tom Corey.

All the unknown, slowly becoming the familiar, which would soon
begin to elicit his fears and his desires.

MacLean had worked for Tom Corey once. Not for long. He had
nearly forgotten. It didn't last for more than a fall and winter. He
was twelve, already in the ninth grade, and busy, his time after classes
taken up with orchestra practice, band practice, the brass choir, the
Scouts. At lunch one day, his grandfather had asked him to stop by
the hospital after school, and in the Doctor's office there, with the
thick green and blue obstetrics and surgery books that MacLean was
not allowed to look at, though he could read Gray's "Anatomy" if
he wanted, and the essays of Osler, and the *Journal of the American
Medical Association*, his grandfather said, "I know how much you
have to do, but I want you to help Tom Corey out with his chores.
He turned his ankle this morning and broke it, and he's upstairs with
a brand-new cast on one foot. He'll be going home tomorrow."

"Grandma says I'm not allowed to even *talk* to Tom Corey," Mac-
Lean said. He played his grandparents off against each other when
he had the chance.

The Doctor went on. "Poor Tom is old and frail now," he said.
"He's as gentle as a lamb, and he's a neighbor." Then he showed
MacLean where the fracture was, drawing a line on MacLean's own
ankle with his finger and twisting the ankle enough for him to feel
the stress that would break the bone. It could have been no more
than a hairline fracture, for Tom, old as he was, wasn't laid up for
long. MacLean took care of his fires—the four-lid cookstove in the
kitchen and the potbellied stove with the isinglass window in the
living room. Tom slept in an alcove off the living room. There was
a pantry next to the kitchen, and a back room full of junk, and an
inside toilet but no bathtub, and that was all. MacLean went over
there in the morning on the way to school and in the evening, before
or after dinner. And on Saturdays, Sundays, and holidays. He shook
the stoves down, took out the ashes, and kept the scuttles filled from
the coalbin outside. And took out the garbage, and ran errands if

he had to. The old man fed the fires himself, and fixed his own meals, and washed up. A clerk from the IGA store who lived down the block brought his vittles, as Tom called them, though MacLean remembered taking something from the Reads' dinner table to him now and then.

How MacLean begrudged the time it cost him! And he wasn't paid a cent.

Old Tom didn't think much of the arrangement, either. "Never had to be taken care of before," he'd say. "I can fend for myself." But he couldn't. The ankle pained him. MacLean would find him in bed at first, with a stocking cap on. And once with it off. He was nearly bald. That black hair of his was a wig.

Tom's temper improved as the ankle hurt less and he grew used to having someone around, and MacLean would find him sitting at the living-room table by the window, or out in the kitchen doing the dishes. He could stand, using an armpit crutch. So long as he wore the cast, he dressed in robe and nightgown, with a cloth slipper on his good foot.

MacLean thought him ungrateful. Never more than "Hello, boy" out of him at first. Much of the time, he was reading the Geneva *Journal*. MacLean brought him the family copy, one or two days old, after everyone in the Read household was finished with it. Tom pored over the paper with a magnifying glass. He had no attention to spare for MacLean at all.

MacLean told his father, over from Detroit on one of his weekend visits, that he was working for Tom Corey. "Sailor Tom?" his father said, anxiety in his voice. Then he laughed his barking laugh, almost a cough—not unkind. "Tom used to be quite a character," he said. "Don't get him going on Africa. He could be a holy terror once he got started, back when I was a kid." Dr. Read said that Tom had changed since then, and was an old, old man.

But Tom wouldn't talk about Africa when MacLean asked him. He parried his questions the way MacLean's father did questions about the war.

There were mementos of Africa in the house: A small, cracked tusk, its point broken off, stood in one corner. On a wall hung a framed map of the continent with legends in a foreign language and with neat ranges of mountains crisscrossing the Sahara. Near it was a brown photograph of Teddy Roosevelt in khakis and sun helmet, gun under his arm and a dead lion lying at his side. The picture had

been carefully cut from a magazine and tacked up. A pair of curved
antelope horns, cracked and broken, hung over the door to the living
room. In the alcove was a wooden mask in which hair and beard were
formed by rusted nails driven into the face and skull.

And then MacLean began playing cards with Tom Corey—black-
jack, with burnt matchsticks for money. Tom taught him the game.
"Hit me! Hit me again! No more!" they would cry. The old man, looking at his cards, would open his eyes wide. He had one short-sighted
eye, and would bring his head down close to the table to make sure
of his hand. MacLean learned how to flip out the cards smartly. During Christmas vacation, they played by the hour in the afternoon.
The living room was full of light then, when the trees were bare and
when, outside the three small-paned windows, there was fresh snow.
MacLean remembered Tom's eyes, a clouded bluish gray with yellowed whites. There was no depth to them—or, rather, no complexity, no human complexity. The eyes of a man wearing a mask that he
could not remove. But the eyes of an old creature, utterly spent,
with nothing left in him to draw one to him at all.

One evening when MacLean went over to shake down the fires,
Tom greeted him at the door, back in his sailor outfit again but
propped up still by his crutch. "Surprised you, hey?" he said, grinning, pleased as Punch. Looking like Punch. His black wig was on his
head, his face was shaved and powdered, and the Pilgrim shoes were
on his feet.

"I'm back in my shoes," he said happily, sitting down in his chair
behind the round table and looking at MacLean with wide-open eyes.
"I polished 'em this afternoon." He held out first one and then the
other white-stockinged leg for MacLean to see. "Your granddad
took off that cast this morning," he said. "I told him not to tell you."
He grinned. "The Doctor made me as good as new," he said. Tom's
twangy voice rang clearly now in MacLean's head. He went on.
"I've always had very small feet," he said confidentially. "Not easy to
fit. Size 6 Double A. Wimmin's 6 Double A. These are wimmin's
shoes. They fit beautiful again, left and right. You'll see. Next week,
I'll be dancing a jig."

It may have been on that night that Tom began to tell him of his
life in Africa. MacLean remembered little of it—of stories heard
once nearly forty years ago. How much, he wondered, was he making
up in trying to remember? How much had Tom made up, speaking of
a time more than fifty years before? The young boy from western

Connecticut fresh off the farm—a handsome lad in those days!—who was cabin boy on a steamer to Liverpool in the early seventies, then shipped with a friend on a sailing vessel headed down the African coast. Meeting hunters somewhere (on the ship? in one of those African ports, Luanda or Cape Town or Lourenço Marques?) and going along with them, after ivory and ostrich feathers and skins, into country (could it have been around the Zambezi?) that hadn't yet been hunted out. Two big Dutchmen, with Tom and his friend, and two Kaffirs who had hunted with the Dutchmen before, and the guns and dogs and horses. Only four pack-horses. Few supplies. They traded meat from their kills to the natives for fruit and grain.

Had Tom shot many animals, MacLean asked. "They did," Tom said flatly. "We boys never fired a gun from June to December. *We* were there for work and entertainment." MacLean had the picture in his mind still that he'd had then—the two boys in the campfire's flickering light, their chores done, Tom's friend playing his banjo while young Tom Corey dances a jig.

Tom had shown him a copy of their kill list on ruled paper that had been folded and unfolded many times, written with a nib pen in ink rusted with age. MacLean could remember nothing more of it, but he had seen enough such lists since reprinted in the back pages of hunters' memoirs, for Tom had driven him to read of the white hunters as his father had driven him to read of the Great War. How terrible those kill lists were! "LIST OF GAME SHOT," they were headed, and under that the dates—say, "June 7–December 18, 1873." And then the accounting—a casualty report, with all victims neatly summed up and tallied in rank order, from the great beasts on down. Totals at the bottom of each column, neatly carried forward, and the grand total at the end. Elephant, 22. Rhinoceros (black), 2. Rhinoceros (white), 1. Hippopotamus, 4. Lion, 2. Giraffe, 5. Buffalo, 17. (That meant, probably, that the hunters, carrying their new-fangled breech-loading rifles, had come upon a great herd.) Zebra, 3. Wart hog, 2. Ostrich, 2. Spotted hyena, 1. And then would come the antelopes, the rank and file: Eland, 3. Sable antelope, 12. Roan antelope, 2. Kudu, 2. Gemsbok, 1. Waterbuck, 1. Lechwe, 1. Puku, 3. Blue wildebeest, 5. Hartebeest, 1. Tsessebe, 27. (Another rout.) Impala, 6. Steinbok, 2. Say one hundred and twenty-seven in all? An average kill for a long season in the eighteen-seventies. A few years earlier, the totals ran higher.

Tom told him of the wonders, usually, and not the destruction.

The hunters were made welcome in most villages, for there had been few white men where they went and they were bringers of meat. In one place they had been feasted by the chief in a spacious, cool building where young girls, naked except for their loincloths, knelt before each of them holding a round palm-grass tray, laden with meat and fresh fruits, off which the men, sitting on low stools, dined.

Of the elephant they always cut out the heart, Tom said, and of the buffalo the tongue.

The Bushmen—little yellow fellows—who joined them on one hunt opened a great flap in a dead elephant's side, as big as a barn door. Then they pulled out his organs and his entrails, Tom said, and bathed inside him, singing, in his blood. They believed the blood gave them long life and strength, the elephant's powers.

One day, Tom had come upon a great herd of elephants when, on horseback alone and well away from camp, he broke through a stand of trees to find a plain before him. There they all were, hundreds of them, moving slowly, their trunks swinging, grazing silently like cattle in a field.

Tom had told him of a wounded elephant's death. MacLean remembered that clearly. The ankle by then was quite strong, for Tom took both parts. On one side of the living room, the hunter firing his gun, loading and firing again and again. Across the room, finally, the great creature dying. Ten shots, a dozen in him. More. Blood pouring from his side. "And then—" Tom stood raised to his full height with clasped hands held straight out at arm's length before him. He raised his hands high, still tightly clasped, and he howled. "That elephant stood right before us," Tom said. "He trumpeted with his trunk and he kept on trumpeting until the hills rang, with the blood spouting from him, *spurting* from that trunk in great spurts like the fountains at the Fair!" He dropped his hands and sat down at the table, breathing heavily. "And then the creature fell, and the ground trembled beneath our feet, and he was dead."

They cut the heart out of that elephant, Tom said, and found three holes in it where the bullets had gone clean through and another ball still there. And a dozen holes in his lungs. But he took better than an hour to die! Why, at his shoulder he stood over ten feet tall! His tusk weighed ninety pounds!

When he told MacLean such tales, Tom's eyes would shine—dimly, for he was quite old—and his voice would grow light. Oh, that terrible look of knowing, savage glee in a man's eyes! MacLean had seen it since, that sidelong glance. Once or twice in his father. Once in a good college friend, a bookish man who had read "Moby Dick" fourteen times, who came back from the Second War an infantry captain (he, too!) and told MacLean of marching prisoners off a cliff into the sea. "Those Germans," he said, with an odd laugh. "Perfect discipline. I told them 'Forward, *march!*' and over they went." (But he was a sensitive man still, and no more than twenty-five. Who could measure the depth and complexity of *his* glance?)

Tom was by now quite at his ease. "I was a strong little bugger in those days," the old man said once. "Nothing ever fazed me. Why, I fell on a wild pig and wrassled it—killed him with my bare hands. . . ." He hesitated. "Not my *bare* hands," he said, looking at MacLean slyly. "With my Booie knife. But first I wrassled him down."

Then he had looked at MacLean in a way that nearly frightened him. "Why, I bet I could wrassle you down right now," he said. "You're a skinny sort of kid." But he stopped short, shaking his head, and told MacLean to go home.

They had Indian-wrestled, though. Arm against arm, seated at the round table in the living room, close enough to equal for it to be almost a contest. MacLean was strong for a skinny kid. The old man had muscles still. MacLean sat there, exerting almost all his strength and feeling what was left of the old man's, looking at his oddly smooth face, the thick eyebrows and hairy ears, the dulled eyes.

But they *had* wrestled once, hadn't they? No, it wasn't wrestling, exactly. Tom had been teasing MacLean about being skinny, and MacLean had suddenly picked him up, just to show him he could, and held him cradled in his arms like a child. He remembered standing there, legs spread, with Tom lying in his arms in those ancient sailor clothes and breathing quickly right into his face. How light he was! Mere skin and bones. Tiny Mother Read could have been no lighter. MacLean decided to show the old man how strong he really was, and stood there holding him, counting aloud slowly. Five . . . ten . . . twenty . . . Longer. What a fearsome smell the old man had up that close! Not patchouli at all, but sweet decay. God. But he had held him. How cold the old man's body was. He had held him until Tom asked to be put down. For a minute or more. MacLean shivered at the memory of it. He had never touched *anyone* for so long then—not like that. Wrestling in gym was not like that. The

sense of some current flowing back and forth between them scared
him blue. But how it pleased Tom, being held! MacLean knew it,
and went on holding him, while Tom began crooning softly. It was
horrible, as if he were nursing Death in his arms, but he went on
holding him. "Now rock me," Tom said, closing his eyes, and for a
moment MacLean rocked him, and then Tom asked to be set down.

His duties at Tom's ended shortly after that. Tom no longer really
needed help, and after stopping over for a few more games of black-
jack MacLean found himself busy with other things. Old Tom was
still alive when MacLean left Geneva to go to college, and he did not
die until sometime toward the end of the Second War.

What more could there be to remember of Tom Corey? His house
had long since been torn down. Most of the ravine had been filled
in. All but one or two of the old houses on Troy Street that dated
back to before the Civil War were gone. Ranch houses had taken their
place.

And MacLean went on wondering, still, why he had kissed the
ground just there, on Troy Street before Tom Corey's, until it came
to him suddenly that he hadn't kissed the ground. He had knelt, but
he hadn't kissed the ground. What if the place wasn't the point—or
not all of it? What if it was the woman? What if she were the key to
the dream? He had turned his back to Tom Corey's when he knelt,
and he had knelt before her, the woman with him, the woman in the
white cape. He had knelt before her as if in homage. But who was
she? Not his wife, he felt certain now, or his mother, or any figure
out of his conscious world. Familiar though she seemed, she was a
stranger, with all the power over him of the strange, and he had
gone to his knees in submission or in supplication before her. Who
was she? The cape was hooded. She was half turned away from him,
and her head was bowed. He had not seen her face.

# WHAT KIND OF A MAN
# CUTS HIS FINGER OFF?

<small>Rolaine Hochstein (a native of Yonkers, New York) is a
graduate of Syracuse University School of Journalism, and
attended Columbia University School of the Arts. She
lives with her husband and three children in Tenafly, New
Jersey. Her work has appeared in numerous magazines,
among them *McCall's*, *MS*, and the *Antioch Review*.</small>

They were in France. In Paris. On the Left Bank crowded close to
the Seine. Or else high on the Right Bank in, say, an Algerian neighborhood. A scrapbox of an apartment, up noisy wooden stairs. There
is a toilet down the hall. Cracks in the blue painted toilet seat reveal
its original brown finish. The linoleum floor once had a pattern in
it; now it has the look and feel of gravel. The bathtub, yard-high
porcelain cemented on three sides into an alcove under the stairs, is
on the second floor, the *premier étage*, as the concierge insists, her
pancake lips distended in disapproval of this frowzy, overwrought
couple of Americans who have no time or taste for civilities. They
have to go down two flights to take a bath. The concierge turns on
the water taps. It costs them two francs. Still, Nicola takes a bath
every day. *Every* day. She is fastidious, though distraught. Her personal cleanliness is a thread that attaches her to the white sheet of
sanity. Evan never takes a bath. Sometimes he splashes himself with
water from the yellowed kitchen sink or from the bidet in the bedroom. "Jesus!" he yells at Nicola as she wraps a wilted dressing gown
around her skinny bones and takes up a limp rag of a towel.
"Jesus!" he seethes as she feels with sensitive finger tips the perfo-
rated patterns of the tinny wall along the landing. "Cheese-us!" he
hollers after her as she flaps down the stairs in splayed huaraches.

"Can't you use the fucking bidet?" Maybe it was during one of Nicola's baths that he yanked a kitchen drawer out from over a shelf with pots in it, snatched a bread knife with his right hand, spread his left hand on the enamel table top and cut off a finger.

*Cut his finger off?* Really, I can't imagine it. I am a small, dark, assertive woman. People tend to check their buttons when I enter a room. I am high up in a market research firm. I make up surveys and after analyzing the results, I can tell a manufacturer that his cranberry juice cocktail sales will rise if he changes his packaging to pink and yellow spotted containers. If I am unmarried—and I am—it is not because I have had no offers. Nicola, on the other hand, needed attachments. I could understand her running off with Evan. It was the cutting off of the finger that stamped itself into my convolutions and I cannot smooth it out. I work up to that point—or, rather, the cutting edge—using details from here and there: a bathtub from a stop on a student tour, a toilet from a pause during a downtown bridge game, a dressing gown from an alcoholic neighbor, kitchens and bedrooms from various apartments of aged relatives in the Bronx. But when it comes to the operation, the actual removal of a finger, my construction pops and fades out.

They were married. The fact of this marriage was a fourth color, superimposed on my earlier picture of torn and fighting lovers. Only after the divorce did Nicola tell me they had been married. It filled out some empty outlines and deepened the whole picture. She arrived at work one day with her hair sleek and glinting in the steely light of the office we shared. She entered through a glass door, high heels clacking against terrazzo tiles. She was wearing a new red suit, pinched at the waist, pointed at the bust. She sat poised on the edge of her desk chair framed by depths of windows high over Madison Avenue, Manhattan, her eyes and earrings gleaming. Even her ears were beautiful: cockle shells clipped with gold, and her voice a silver bell as she told me. She had been changing slowly ever since she started on the job, but on this day she had reached a summit. I was of course very jealous; I felt coarse beside her delicacy. But she had changed so gradually that there had been no discrete moment for me to stop liking her. "I am so happy today," she said. "My divorce came through."

Divorce? Divorce? I tried to cover confusion. "I thought you had it a long time already." The diction of defensive humor.

"No," she said, petting me, a terrier. "This is the divorce from Evan." She was around thirty-two, maybe seven years older than I. But she had lived squares and cubes of my life. I had a divorced aunt. It was a family scandal. "You were married to Evan?" I asked, blinking in the sharp light.

Let me try to get this into focus. Let's go back some years, maybe about four years before I met her. Nicola Masonet is at a faculty party. She is pale and loose and she doesn't know who to talk to. The math and science wives have crisp hair in efficient, tight waves. The English and arts wives have buns carelessly pinned in place. Nicola's tan hair hangs to her narrow shoulders and she is agreeable but lost. It is the apartment of an assistant professor, the first floor of a rented white frame house that rises righteously from its plinth of grass. The living room is large, poorly lit, cluttered and at present filled with standing, sitting, talking, smoking, lounging people. On a card table two kitchen plates are lined with just enough thinly-sliced bologna, liverwurst, spiced ham to cover. Also some saltines and American cheese. Bottles of house-brand booze are crowded on top of a small-screen TV set, among negligible furnishings and under conflicting smells of tobacco, pot, liquorous breath and—emanating inescapably from the kitchen—catshit and baby spit-up. (The hostility here is mine; Nicola's was deeper and beyond words. What she felt, I bet, was depression.) The math wives are chatting about where they buy shoes and what their husbands make out of wood in the back shed. The art wives sit on the floor at their husbands' feet, occasionally hauling themselves up to run for their masters' refills. Nicola will not sit at the feet of her husband nor hang over his shoulder. She is still young and she yearns for excitement, there among women she doesn't like and men whose hands she must avoid. She is alone among turtle-neck shirts and pipes and early wrinkles and insinuating gallantry. Paul Masonet, her husband—a painter who teaches turning into a teacher who paints—is contentedly occupied. I see him large and solid and definitely a clinker under the covers. And none of that bare stuff either! Perhaps his father was a minister or he had a very close best friend. His face adheres to regularity. He is older and protective and all his students adore him. A rock of a man except for that marshmallow part, he is balanced between the arms of a mammoth stuffed chair. There are females all around him: science wives, somebody's friend, an unmarried sister. They perch on the back and arms of the kicked-in, cat-hairy chair and listen to him while Nicola—though it is really me—is dying amid the shoes and the colic and the hands and the disgruntled accounts about deans who play favorites and she hates luncheon meat and she doesn't like to get drunk. In comes this visiting writer, this guest lecturer or newly-instated poet-in-residence.

Evan Pardon is a short man with a powerful motor who moves on little cat feet and has eyes like double-consommé, a livid and petulant mouth. I happen to know—from outside the context of this story—that girls who never do it, do it for him. He has had many wives, three or four, and they all look like Nicola. Not the Nicola who was led into my office, introduced as my new assistant, straining to produce a smile, wearing a kind of crepe housedress without sleeves, her hands flaking with eczema, scraped fingers fluttering at her neckline and a scrawny neck under a drawn deer face with crinkles of sad hair. And not the Nicola, accomplished and elegant, who told me with a brilliant smile that she was now divorced from Evan Pardon. All of his wives—all of the women that he felt he had to bind to him—looked at first like Nicola must have looked at that faculty party.

If I were there, doggy as I was when I assigned tabulations to Nicola, he would have passed me over. Introduced to him, I would be honored, titillated. We shake hands. Mine is grubby, a paw. His is bony, threatening, with black hairs on the knuckles. His hands are warm and moist with ten, long, nervous fingers. He says something civil in a low, uninterested voice but he has already got his sulky glance speculatively settled on the slender, fragile, leaf-of-a-woman off by the bookshelves beside the fireplace, handling a piece of jade. He leaves me and goes to her.

But say that I too have the coloring of an autumn maple tree, cheeks honed to a dark apple polish and a sharp, valiant little chin and that you could take one look at me in my tweedy skirt and sweater and know that I have pale, polished round legs that are as nice all the way up as the fine calves and ankles and the narrow feet in the pretty buckled shoes. And I move with the unconscious grace instilled by a mother who was once a ballet dancer in White Russia before she came to the States and married a man who ended up a janitor in a San Francisco apartment building. I have this negligent grace plus breasts full and fruity, accepted though outstanding in proportion to the rest of my body, which is lean. My mother told me I was beautiful so I have lived with it and accepted it calmly and this man approaches, an exotic among the ruddy middle-Americans and he says something about the piece of jade I am holding as if I were doing it a favor. He looks into my eyes, not frankly, and he says, "You're Paul's wife?"

I say a tentative "yes" and, because I am Nicola—and not me— I do not launch a recital of my campus activities and my political opinions and my taste in art objects. Oblique firelight plays on my face and I look, probably, wistful and he speaks, familiarly, as if we had met before, about gatherings at the homes of faculty members, an observation with which I agree, one side of my lips stretched about a quarter of an inch. Most men are attracted to me, so I don't have to talk much. He talks. I am interested.

On the day she learned that she was no longer legally married to Evan Pardon, Nicola told me that she had not, after all, been his mistress in Paris. The admission changed my view of her. It was a view that had made me uncomfortable. In the house where I grew up—my father no janitor, but a professional man—it was felt and often said outright that a woman who sleeps with a man who is not her husband is a tramp. I could not consider Nicola a tramp; she was very classy, I thought. Intelligent, too. She had a voice like frosted trees in the wind. Fine bones and, after the eczema cleared up and she grew nails again, which were shaped and buffed but not lacquered, a musical way of moving her hands. Yet, when I knew they had been married, it made a difference. I felt both relieved and disappointed. "No. We were not living in sin," she said, amused at me. Her eyes were brown and rather small, tapering to long points at the outer edges, and she was near-sighted. She said this with a sarcastic narrowing of those long points. "I would rather people thought that," she added with an anger that I felt in my own blunt bones.

"I hate him so much. I couldn't stand for anyone to think I was married to him. Now I'm not and it doesn't matter anymore." She took a sheaf of survey forms and a tally sheet. She worked close because she didn't like to wear her glasses.

I could work twice as fast as she could. I had time to think. I tried to feel how she and Evan had got together.

"You like stone carving?" he asks her.

"Only when it's not refined. I like the shape rough with no unnecessary details. Spare, you see. Just the strong line to suggest the object represented because. . . ."

But that is me talking and Evan would soon have excused himself to get a drink and never come near me again if he could avoid it. Nicola says something altogether different, something feminine, itself suggestive, so that very soon he insists on taking her to a museum he knows or a rock quarry someplace and she accepts.

Evan is an artist and an intellectual. That means he gets his rewards by being recognized by other intellectual artists. It also means he can make excuses in his mind for any enormity of behavior. He lays somebody's wife and he says it's his responsibility to himself to experience beauty, to force his emotions out of their frame. I don't know. His stories and poems appear in little literary magazines. I bought one of his novels once. Half the words were in italics and I couldn't follow his story though I am sure one of his characters was based on Nicola. She was holy because beautiful and she was destructive. The hero found her alone in a park and she was drifting, drowning in mediocrity, it seemed, and he felt helplessly drawn by her need for life and breath. I could hardly make it out because the language was so dreamy and the words unfamiliar and all mixed in with some philosophy about not talking or touching but communicating through essences of maleness and femaleness. It was beyond me. But if the few facts I could extract were accurate and it *was* Nicola he was writing about, she was so hungry for sex that it didn't take him long to make out.

After one of their expeditions, she came to his rooms. Evan was divorced, separated, temporarily womanless anyway. A wallful of books. A stereo set someplace unexpected. Did he play Haydn or Wagner? Records, books, typewritten sheets of paper were strewn about the floor, prints of woodcuts tacked over his landlady's landscapes. A hot plate on top of a dresser. A night table for a bar. He made drinks, getting ice from the landlady's kitchen.

Nicola was a winter leaf, touching points of the room. She read the titles of his books, turned over a record jacket, peered at last year's Christmas cards stuck on a bulletin board on the wall over his typewriter. Slowly she unwound the long, thickly knit scarf she had wrapped around her head. There were sparkles of snow in her hair. He touched them with his fingertips and they disappeared. From a pile of records, she took up a new release of *Petrouchka*. He set it on the turntable above the stop, over the Mozart or the Debussy, to play later. She smiled at him with her lips closed. He touched her cheek which was burning from the cold outside and the booze within. She began to unbutton her coat, still moving among the crumpled papers on the floor, the open books, the socks, the pajamas. It was a point of honor with him; he removed nothing nor apologized for the mess. After she knew the room, felt herself a part of it, and Evan had made her another drink, Nicola slipped into a little maple arm-chair with a calico cushion.

"No," Evan said, a film director. "Not there. I want you by the window where the light hits your hair."

She obeys, taking her drink, leaving the scarf and coat—her flowing bark—hollowed out on the back and arms of the calico chair. She lowers herself into a leathery cushioned lounge chair. He follows dreamily, steers himself to the leather chair arm, his own arm encased in beige cashmere (brown wool?) sliding along the back, a half-inch of lit air between it and her sloping shoulders. If she relaxes and leans back, her shoulder will press against his arm (in flannel shirting?).

Nicola bolts to her feet. "Who did that woodcut? It looks like one of Paul's." Or she leans forward and aims a wicked smile at Evan: "You know? This reminds me of a scene from a French movie I saw just last week. Guess what comes next." Or, in a schoolgirl pipe: "I think I should go home now."

Ah, but these are *my* variations. Nicola stays, either from daring or desperation. She has a small, black mole below her left shoulder blade. Her shoulder blades are prominent, the most vulnerable part of her, physically speaking. One day after we had become friends, after I had seen that she did not want my job, after she saw that I admired her, we went out for dinner together, first stopping at her apartment while she changed clothes. It was a shabby walk-up in the Chelsea section, made her own by a hand-woven Mexican tablecloth, a few flowers in a shapely vase, some interesting paintings by Paul Masonet and other artists she had known, a stuffed toy koala, whimsical reminders to herself stuck in the dresser mirror. A parasol hung from the overhead light. It was a one-room apartment and she took off her dress in front of me. This is not an unusual thing, yet Nicola's undressing embarrassed me. She wore white cotton underpants, the kind that show from under the dresses of kindergarten girls, and a very plain white bra. Her stockings, which sometimes bagged around the ankles, were held up by a thin strip of garter belt. The skin around her ribs seemed almost transparent and her belly was flat as a boy's. I knew about her and men—she had already mentioned the elopement to Paris; it was part of the reason for my embarrassment —but I saw no signs of dissipation. No scars or bruises on her body, no swellings of voluptuous flesh. And in the apartment, no sleeping pills, dirty books, cheap cosmetics, accumulation of liquor bottles. There was one green glass decanter of port wine, from which she served me. She might have been a frolicsome nun. On the spare body —David or Diana going slightly flaccid toward maturity—the only blemish was a tiny black mole under a shoulder blade.

Evan noticed the mole on that cold, bleak afternoon when Nicola came to his apartment. Subsequently he decorated it with water colors, centrifugal designs intricately looping around the ribs and across the shoulder. Nicola, enlivened, avidly experimental, might have worked this affair into a reasonable schedule. But Evan couldn't have enough. He groaned when she broke away to cook her husband's dinner, wash her husband's socks, open the door for her husband's guests. Jealousy metastasized. It took him over and he took her over. "If you love me, you'll come away."

An intellectual knows how to build up a case. An artist can present it. A man like Evan can move a woman. What moved Nicola was—I am sure—his art.

Evan: "I can't stay here. I can't work. I need you for my work. Come away with me so that I can write again." The intellectual designs a syllogism. The artist rides it with a whip in his hand and kicking heels. Evan's eyes boil. His blood bubbles. He wallops himself into a howling hollow. Nicola is sucked in. Besides, I think she had a muse complex. In any case, she left Paul to his students and his pipe and his academic paintings that could be produced anywhere as long as there was somebody around who would wash socks and open doors.

So that's how an elopement happens. But then what? In one or two or three years, what sets of mood and circumstance change animal to mineral? What interplays brought Nicola to the state she was in when she crossed the ocean alone with a sprung mind, on a ship she never saw, and landed washed up, at the desk next to mine? And why—not to ask how—did Evan cut off his finger?

I couldn't read his novel but I studied all the pages that had words about Carol—who was Nicola though Evan's Nicola was certainly not my Nicola. There was no reference to self-mutilation. There was a time in Paris, however, with Carol selfish, Carol wanting, Carol compulsively middle-class and drawing the fluids of creation out of the martyred hero.

If he had deigned to write in plain English, I might have read a passage like this: "Her nose was shaped for rejecting the smells of life. She fretted about dirt and arose at dawn to begin daily battle with imagined vermin. She had a breakfast fetish, snuffing out my waking impulses under a weight of oatmeal and a wash of orange juice. I heaved myself from eating table to writing table but she assaulted the atmosphere with detergent, bug-killer, aerosol spray. Always, under my legs there was a broom."

Somehow the muse failed to amuse. But Evan Pardon would never admit, let alone put into writing, such ordinary annoyances. He had to curl them into psychic disturbances on a very high plane. Likewise, Nicola might have felt simply that she had got entangled with an egotistical slob, but that would be hard to face up to after she had dumped a steady husband for him. Whatever it was that unstuck her had to be awful. The day she came to my office she had to press her palms together to hold a question sheet steady between them. No decent employment agency would have sent the old Nicola, the grassy faculty wife, to such a lowly job. Even Joe Seigel, our playfully lecherous boss, did not stir—an oversight he later repaired by falling all over her with compliments and gallantries that she took like Titania accepting homage from Bottom the Weaver.

She had begun to recover by the time she told me that her ex-boyfriend had lopped his finger off, on purpose. I liked her enough by then for her to have confidence in me. She did her share of the work, managed to respect my seniority on the job without conceding her edge in years and experience. "You city guys really plow into it," she said, disarming me with a wry smile. "I won't always be this awkward," she promised, regarding her scabbed hands as if they belonged to somebody else. She laughed like the courageous dying; but with her first paycheck she had her hair done, bought a cheap plain dress that looked good on her. She had no friends in the city and must have been lonely. I didn't think about that. I was flattered by her confidence.

"I guess you've gathered that I come from hard times." I was no gatherer; I worked with facts. "This man I lived with, a brute." Humphrey Bogart, I thought. "The bastard I went to Europe with." Jean-Paul Belmondo. "A writer. . . ." Norman Mailer. Already, I could hardly remember the papery, pointed face she had come with. "Evan thought he loved paintings, but he only loved having them." Evan? "Evan Pardon, the beast I lived with. You've heard of him?" I was impressed that she had held off so long from mentioning the name. Knowing that she was very sore, I blurred my recognition under a mumble about back pages of book review sections. Factually, Pardon had been employed years earlier in an editorial office, working beside a girl I knew. She had described him as "sneakily sexy." She told me he had seduced an East Indian cookbook writer. Fascinating story. This must have been before he ran away with Nicola. "But my dear," I or my friend might have told her, "he tries to lay *all* the girls." If she had been here or we there and time recirculated, we could have warned her. But Nicola would have gone anyway. Consider the outrage at that college. Consider her husband and her conscience. She withstood all this. She would not have listened to us. "He needs me," she would have said.

After the collision and the corrosion, while she was recuperating above Madison Avenue, she told me, "He turned into a madman." He hated himself? He hated Nicola for loving him? Is it possible? "We had violent fights," she said. She had been promoted from poll-taker to my assistant. She was smooth by the time she told me this, leaning across her desk. "He had fits of insanity. One night he took a knife and cut off his finger."

I didn't believe it. I haven't seen Nicola for a long time. She is married to a violinist and doesn't return my calls. I did, however, run across Evan Pardon once, not very long ago. He showed up at a cocktail party I was at, had a drink, talked to a few people and left. We were not introduced. But I got a good look. On his left hand where his ring finger used to be, there is a stump.

"Why? Why?" I asked Nicola.

"He was jealous and wanted to punish me."

I still can't believe it. Paris again. They stand in that kitchen. It smells of flower-spray over cooked vegetables. There are coffee stains on the table, a set mousetrap on the floor which no polish helps. Wishful white curtains set off the grimy walls. A typewriter is on a shelf under a tall, almost empty cupboard, a lettuce basket suspended from a hook, old magazines piled in a corner on top of a suitcase never opened, two pots on the two-burner stove, a box of cigars (his) and a three-way mirror (hers). Nicola is crying, fox eyes spilling tears. She cries in hollow gasps and is so thin that the line of her gums shows through the skin around her mouth.

"I wasn't flirting." She gasps and whoops. "I was only glad for someone to talk to. You never talk to me."

He snorts.

"Don't you see what I look like? Would I dare flirt looking the way I do? Can I be charming in stockings with runs? My dress hangs. Who would want me?"

He says, "Shut up."

She chokes. "Do you have any idea what you've done?"

"Stop it!" He makes as if to hit her across the skeletal mouth. He is wearing loafers without socks. His ankles are swollen because he drinks too much. No. He doesn't drink that much but he suffers from stomach pains, migraine headaches. His bouclé pullover hangs far below his belt. He is built like a garage mechanic, wide in the shoulder and chest. The pants on his short legs sag and are stained. Under the pullover or the velour sweatshirt, his fly is half open. He does not wear underwear. Sometimes hair gets caught in his zipper and he howls with pain. Now he howls at Nicola because she is in his way. Intrusion is the villain of his life. Nicola wants to be with other people. She wants to go to cafés at night when he wants to work. He cannot write and he blames his block on her. He stays in the kitchen battling his typewriter—two keys are stuck, on top of everything else, and he has to stop to pull back the keys. He can't bear to have her in the room with him. She can't bear another night in the bedroom, crowded with the brass bed and the potbellied dresser and the one broken chair beside the idiot leer of the bidet. He will not let her out of the house without him. He even watches her go down the stairs to take a bath, makes sure she wears nothing but a dressing gown, rails at her because he thinks she takes baths to get away from him. She is afraid he will leave her alone in Paris. She has dreams that he wants to leave her, dreams that reverse the truth and freeze her with fear. Her French is primitive and she has no money. She knows no one. In the bedroom in her boredom, her energy scuttles inward and attacks her. She feels the guilt of having deserted Paul, poor Paul who loved her as a father. Her writer does not write. There is nothing to share and she feels guilty for this, too. She hates Evan for mak-

ing her guilty and she hates the demands that—in his frustration
—he makes on her perishable body.

"Stop it!" he howls and snatches a knife from a wooden drawer
that does not close properly.

"Kill me," Nicola dares him. "You may as well finish it."

He raises the knife—or maybe it's a butcher's cleaver. Can a knife
cut through bone? He hefts the chopper over his shoulder and drives
it down on his hand. Because he knows that he wants to kill her.

But if that were the case, he would have amputated a thumb or
the index finger. Even a pinky would have to be meticulously,
strenuously sawed off. I have worked it out on my own kitchen table.
There is no way for such a swing to come down on only a middle
finger. Perhaps he put it into a paper cutter and guillotined it. Could
he have hacked at it with a penknife?

I just don't know. It's beyond me. If Nicola, who left us soon after
her divorce from Evan for a more suitable job with a dealer in
European antiques and rare books, had explained it to me; even if
I met Evan again and this time we talked and got around to Paris
kitchens, I would not be able to feel my way to understanding.
With details from her, an account from him, a thorough reading of
his novel, observations from mutual friends, a long letter from Paul
Masonet, I could possibly put it all together. But it would turn out,
I think, like an argument between an insurance man and his wife in
their two-family house someplace on Long Island.

# THE FISH TRAP

### PETER LEACH

Peter Leach is a native of St. Louis, Missouri. His story "Black Jesus" won the *Panache* Frances Steloff award and was reprinted in *Best Little Magazine Fiction 1971*, NYU Press.

When the wardens come to dynamite us, Pappa hid in the coal mine. All the people was standing around cussing and chaffing the wardens, but not one of them helped out.

Pappa come up the path just kind of walking fast right by the house and the dump. I tried to follow him. "Where you going, Pappa?"

"Don't talk to me," he said.

He went on through the trees up the hollow to the coal mine not running just walking fast. Sometimes he done that when he was constipated, but he had a gun.

It was a half hour later the Warden come to the house and said, "You . . . boy . . . where's old Mann?"

I called Mamma.

He said, "I am the fish and game warden, and that trap is going for all time to come."

Mamma come out then, and he said the same thing to her. She never buttoned her dress right and was all sweaty and hanging out in front at him. She said, "My husband run off the other game wardens, and he will run you off too."

"I know about those other fellows," he said.

"They tried to mess with my husband, and went home sadder and wiser."

"That was in the Clemens administration."

Mamma looked off between the sycamore and cottonwood trees

down the path to the river where the trap was. "It's a vested right," she said, "that was handed down." They was always harassing us about the fish trap. All it is is a dam the Indians built acrost the narrow east channel of the Gasconade River with a six foot gap in the middle with a slat-sided chute box that lets all the water through but keeps the fish.

"It is a violation of the game laws of the State of Missouri that has gone unchecked for more than thirty years."

"The big stones in the dam was laid there by Indians."

"I understand your feeling, Mrs. Mann. When I first come up to this picturesque spot, I stood and gazed for ten minutes at the dam and your trap. It was like I had stumbled into a scene from a hundred years ago."

"The Missouri Indians had a village on the terrace under the bluff," Mamma said. "The boy finds arrowheads and scrapers there yet."

"It seemed I was far from all civilization in the Ozark hollows and woods instead of central Missouri."

Mamma said, "They fought a battle in eighteen hundred and fourteen when the Sac and Fox come and tried to drive them off from the fish trap of their ancestors. They killed eleven of the Sac and Fox and scalped and gutted them and buried the guts in the corn mounds for fertilizer. It's all in the records at the court house. Missouris deeded the land to Antoine Soulard."

"I was at the court house last week," said the Warden. "The District Attorney and I were looking at those records, purely for interest."

"In eighteen hundred and sixty-two, Soulard sold out to Simeon Barker," said Mamma. "He sold to Black, and in eighteen and eighty-nine Black sold to my husband, and we fixed up the dam with ironwood logs."

"You don't own the land."

"My husband and I own the rights."

"What rights?"

"To work the trap."

"The law don't recognize the purchase of an illegal right," the Warden said.

"It was handed down and paid for."

"It's against the game laws to catch fish in a trap."

"The game laws are for the rich man."

"The game laws are to protect the wild creatures, for everybody."

"This here trap was before the laws. We run it to live, not for sport like some city fellow. You are taking the bread out of the mouth of this boy and his little brothers and sisters."

"From what I heard you live pretty good off of this trap, to the tune of about three thousand dollars a year cash money. Everywhere I go I hear about the fish trap. It is talked on all the trains. They ask me why I don't tear it out, and how can I expect the farmers not to trap? The merchants in Chouteau are just fed up. They try to build a grocery business, and you sell your fish at five cents a pound year in and year out. It's un-American, and I am going to enforce the law. Where's your husband?"

"The merchants in Chouteau?" Mamma said. "I thought it." She spat pretty near the Warden's boot and pulled out her snuff can like the finest lady you ever saw and took a pinch with her little finger curled and put it up there real dainty between her lip and her gum. She wasn't scared of no game warden.

"Where is your husband?" he said.

"For all you know," Mamma said, "he might be up a tree with his thirty-thirty taking a bead on the back of your head."

The Warden turned around real quick, and Mamma laughed the way she done when she talks about putting poison in our food and makes the hair stand up on the back of my neck. "Boy," she said, "run find your pappa and tell him there's another one of them game wardens here that wants to be run off the place."

The Warden was cursing and looking around kind of nervous, and I cut down the path and up into the hollow where the old mine was.

I went in as far as the light and called, "Pappa . . . ? Pappa . . . it's me."

His voice come from behind me tight and hissing like a snake. He was hid up above the entrance squatting on the ledge with his thirty-thirty across his knees. "I *told* you to get." He was kind of runty and yellow faced.

"Pappa, you scared me."

"Get on out, before—"

"Mamma *said*. There's another warden here says he's going to dynamite the fish trap into kingdom come. He can't do that. He can't, Pappa, can he?"

"I know who's here."

I argued and begged him, trying to make him come out and be a man. You could smell the tubs of mash back in the tunnel and it made me almost sick. I told him it was our right since the Indians, how it was fought over, and about the guts of the Sac and Fox in the corn mounds, and about the Warden arguing and trying to insult Mamma.

He groaned and cursed, perched up there rocking back and forth and cursing the law and cursing me for my lip, but the Warden insulting Mamma, that done it, and he climbed down.

He went a few steps down the path and stopped, holding his thirty-thirty deer rifle like he was hunting birds with it. I tried to go on past him but he put up his hand for me to stop, and when I started to ask why he slapped me all of a sudden up the side of the head so hard that I went down and sat there seeing stars.

By the time I woke up, my brother-in-law Charley that works the night shift was running down from the house to the river in just his shirt and Pappa running, and I took off after them.

When I come out of the trees all the people waiting to buy fish was down on the far bank and some up on the dam shouting at the Warden and the two fellows with him and Pappa and Charley running out from the near bank onto the gravel bar cursing and yelling trying to get at the Warden but the fellows that come with him with shotguns, and the Warden's team and wagon the wheels wrapped in burlap so he could sneak up on us through the bottoms, and the Warden kneeling by the chute fooling around, then he stands up and fires his shotgun once into the air and screams, *"Dynamite!"* and you could see it then the fuses sputtering like snakes of fire, and you never saw folks clear off so fast falling over each other to get up that muddy bank, and their horses and teams jumping around, and one team and wagon spooked and went running away back the graded road to Chouteau.

Only Pappa and Charley didn't know what to do. Pappa stopped, dropped the thirty-thirty, Charley run back and Pappa after him, then Pappa stopped again and run back like he was going to try to snuff them fuses only it was too late, then he went toward his gun, and stopped and cut back for the bank, all quivering and shaking, running with his knees high as if the ground was red hot, and his eyes bugged out like a horse in a barn fire.

Then it went, the whole earth shook and a giant hand like Pappa knocking me down, it blew the wind out of me and a lightning flash in broad daylight the sound a half second later inside your head, and rocks, logs, boards, and mud and water rose in the air like a flower, slow, up near as high as the tall flaking sycamore trees, and there was fish hanging in the air, then it all come down thump and splattering, water, fish, gravel, and mud still splashing down after, and there was a long time with no sound at all, not even a locust or a bird, and then all them folks scrambling and scurrying for the horses and wagons to get away afraid to have our misfortune rub off or the Warden give them a summons.

The river ran strong twenty foot wide where the dam was blowed out and over parts of the gravel bar that was dry before, and the pool emptied, and a couple of worthless big old gar fish lay flopping and clicking their bony scales stranded in a mud hole near me. I saw Pappa's thirty-thirty laying where the water just went down again, and I went and got it and slipped back into the willow thicket under the bank and shook off the water and dried it on my shirt.

The Warden and his men come out and they helped him up into his wagon and sidled off in different directions, quick but like they didn't want to let on how much of a hurry they was in.

I followed along through the willows then by a trail I know. The other two wasn't with the Warden now. He went along pretty quiet, the sacking on his wheels all muddy. Sometimes I was close to him, sometimes a ways off. Then he stopped and got out and started pulling at something, a net, and he just pulled it out of the water and chopped it up with his axe. I lay there behind a tangle of old roots not fifty foot away drawing a bead on him and gnats whining around trying to crawl inside my ears and my eyes and up my nose. I would have then, but it was too close up.

Further on he done it again, and inside of a half hour he chopped up three more nets and a trot line, and there ain't nothing illegal anywhere about a trot line. I almost let him have it then. I could see the cloud of gnats around his head too.

At Haun's Mill he caught a fellow in the act of sitting in his boat doing nothing and he called him over to the bank and he give him such a cursing and a chewing up and down that he said if he would let him go he would tell the names of some other fellows that was seining, and he done it, and the Warden took down his name for a witness. After that he come on a johnboat tied on the bank and a net in it, and he chopped up the net and the boat too so it broke in the middle and the parts floated away. I knew then that I would do it.

I slipped on ahead about a half mile to a place where the bottoms narrows to between two bluffs and I could do it from the downstream side, then maybe I could go down to the Katy Railroad. I found a place about sixty feet up the bluff, a ledge that run around to the side and some thick cedars. He would have to pass right below on a shelf like not twenty feet wide between the limestone clift and the water. I heard his horse, and then him, whistling.

I worked the lever part way and checked the cartridge in the chamber. I cocked back the hammer, and lined up the bead in the V on where he would come.

His bay horse was shaking its head at the cloud of gnats and deer flies, walking, but wet with sweat in the heat, then the Warden in his trooper's hat with a badge and a revolver on his hip, and behind his seat on the new green painted wagon a pump shotgun and a axe and spade. I could have spit on him, he was passing that close below, then he was moving away, and there is something about the back of a man's head and his neck that you feel sorry for him.

I had to squirm sideways to keep the bead on his head, and I must have kicked loose a rock, and it rolled down and bounced on the roadway and into the water just behind the wagon. Well, you'd have thought a panther jumped on that horse. It reared back all wild-eyed in the traces and screamed like a man. It must have been half crazy anyhow from the deer flies. The Warden spun around, and right off he saw me, then he was beating the horse on the head with his whip handle until it settled down, and I wasn't even aiming at them when I pulled the trigger. I wasn't afraid. It was more like I come this far figuring to do it, I at least had to hear the gun go off once, like after a day out hunting when you are skunked.

The horse jerked like you shocked him with electric but didn't rear or try again to run off. He just stood still, kind of shaking. I didn't shoot nowhere near that horse either. The Warden sat there on the seat of the wagon looking up at me. I almost could have spit on him. "Did you try to kill me?" he said.

I looked back not quite in his eyes but off to one side. I didn't even work the lever to put another cartridge in. The gun was still pointing at him though. ". . . No . . ." I said.

"What were you trying to do?"

I lied, because I knew I could not do it now unless he committed something else like chopping up that good boat. ". . . Trying to scare your horse."

"Well, it don't take much to do that," he said, "with all this heat and insects."

". . . No, sir."

"Empty your gun." He said it in a different way, quiet.

I looked at him, the horse bent down eating grass now, the reins loose. I turned the gun over and worked the lever five times, catching the dull brass cartridges in my hand.

"One more," he said.

I worked it again, the sixth, and the brass from the shot I fired made seven.

"Now, come down here. . . . Take your time. Don't fall."

He made me give him the cartridges, and he put them in his pocket.

"You are the boy from the fish trap."

"Yes, sir."

He looked at me a while, him up on the seat of the wagon and me down beside the road. "Then your name is Mann . . ."

I looked down at my feet.

Well, he give me a talking to like I never heard. You can imagine, even if I didn't actually mean to hit him when I fired the gun.

Then he said climb up, and he would ride me a ways, so I did, and he set the horse to plodding on, and we talked a while. He said he was filing complaints at Chouteau about Pappa and the seiners, and they would pay fines, but nobody was going to prison, yet, and the main thing was for this illegal fish taking and market hunting to stop before all the wildlife was killed off, because when that happened it would not be long before mankind died off too, starving in the barren land and choking on its own filth in the septic rivers. I could not follow all that, but I acted like I did.

I told him about the Indians and the big fish we took in the trap, one that its tail dragged the ground when the man that bought it tied it by the gills to his saddle horn, and many times fish that their tails hung out over the gate of a flat bed wagon.

He said that was truly remarkable, but it was finished for all time to come.

Then he said come visit at the hatchery some time, and in the spring they maybe could use a stout boy. He let me off at the Katy Railroad bridge where our river run into the Missouri. The last thing he said was he supposed I knew that for what I done I could be sent to the Booneville reformatory, and worse than that for what I was thinking about doing.

"I know," I said. I was down in the road. He let me take Pappa's gun.

He reached in his pocket and handed down the cartridges. "If you tell your old man," he said, "will you get a whipping?"

". . . Not from him."

"From your Mamma?"

I didn't know what to say.

"Will you?"

"Not for what you think."

"How's that?"

"For missing."

His eyes blazed up and his lips pressed and went white but not at me exactly.

"Will you damned people ever learn?" he said. "You live like the Indians."

He shook the reins of his tired horse and went rolling along the gravel road by the tracks to Westphalia. "Well, what does that make you?" I said.

I never told Pappa, or her, anything, and I just took the whipping for going off a long time without saying I would miss dinner. That was the last time though. I have not took a whipping since, and I am not about to. I did not have to kill that warden to know I could if I wanted to, and I may yet. Nights, Pappa and me and Charley been working a little at a time repairing the trap.

The stones the Indians laid was mostly still there, and we hauled in more stone and ironwood logs and built the dam to just above the high water line, and the six foot gap in the center, then the beams and slats for the bottom of the trap itself to let all the water through and hold the eating size fish, and boards along the sides like a cattle chute. Pappa says this place was meant by nature to be a fish trap.

# THE WRONG MAN

## NORMA KLEIN

Norma Klein was born in New York City where she has lived all her life. She has published about sixty short stories in magazines such as *Sewanee Review, Mademoiselle* and *Descant* and in the *Prize Stories 1963 and 1968* and *Best American Short Stories 1969.* She has published a collection of short fiction, *Love and Other Euphemisms,* and two novels for young people, *Mom, the Wolfman and Me* and *It's Not What You Expect,* both serialized in MS. Her first adult novel, *Give Me One Good Reason,* was published last fall. She is married to a biochemist and has two young daughters.

"How do you like it?"

"Great."

"No—*seriously.*"

Max Robish veered around in his office desk chair to stare at his fourteen-year-old stepdaughter, Mandy, who framed the doorway, the miniskirt, or whatever it was, revealing two freckled lengths of preadolescent flab.

"Really want to know?" he said.

Her face became uncertain. She giggled. "Not if it's something *mean.*"

He raised one eyebrow.

She blushed, hesitated. "Everyone wears them short," she said.

"I know."

One leg was wound, stork-like, around the other. "Well . . . I just thought I'd ask you."

"Sure, Mandy, any time." He veered back to regard once again the stack of pre-Christmas exams piled to one side of the desk. "The reign of William IV was marked by civil disorder. Could you discuss in 300 words or less the causes of this unrest?" High school history was so beautifully simple-minded. He often had had cause, in his usual deprecatory reflections on his profession, to observe this. Cause and then effect. It was lovely. He glanced at one paper. A pity about Mandy. He had often thought that the one thing that would lend a certain color to his marriage would be an intense, incestuous affair with his stepdaughter. The slyness, the mystery, the tears on all sides! But she was such a plump, dowdy little thing. Either her pubescence was being delayed or, more likely, it would never arrive. Yet sadly (for her) his sarcastic jibes which he tried, to some extent, to keep under wraps, served only to stimulate her puppyish adoration of him. If only she'd lose weight; maybe there was a tender little body under there—God knew . . . But who cared really? In ten years, maybe, he'd be ready for Lolitas, at fifty or sixty. Now they still reminded him uncomfortably of his own three sisters in their long gone girlhoods with their twisted pigtails and rubber-banded teeth, hardly an erotic vision.

He looked at the desk calendar in which a black card indicating the date had been placed. His wife did this, straightening up his "things," though he had warned her off a couple of times. But if it gave her pleasure. Which little enough did. December 21st. He had had a vague, premonitory anxiety all morning and now, staring at the date, he realized it had not been—as he had thought—the usual nausea at the arrival of the Christmas season and its related festivities. No, one year ago today Alice, his first wife, had committed suicide. They had been divorced five years already, though he still, sporadically, kept in touch with her. She had shown no special desire to see Timmy, of whom he had been awarded custody and who was, in any case, away most of the year at camp or boarding school. She was drunk a good deal of the time, not, as in the beginning, loudly and abusively so, but almost pleasant, vague, nostalgic, incoherent. He dreaded her sober a good deal more. Already, then, she had reminded him of her mother, who had lived to seventy-two as a quite contented, generally incoherent lush. And then the suicide which seemed extravagant. Her life was a mess, granted—but more so than anyone else's? To do it during Christmas had seemed so stagey—or had she been, quite genuinely, unaware of the season? What implications could Christmas have for a woman living alone and to all intents and purposes, liking it? Still, he stared at the date, as though the black, precise letters would serve up some key or illumination.

"Darling?"

It was Ginny, fresh from an orgy of shopping, eyes bright. "Are you almost done?"

"I haven't really begun," he said.

His wife had the illusion that he was always at work on some project of earth-shaking significance—or so she seemed to pretend.

"Because—well, I told the Murgitraughs we'd meet them at two."

"The who?"

"You remember—he did that portrait of Sean Olsen's wife. I had thought he might do Mandy. He's awfully talented."

"Umm." A vision of his stepdaughter, immortalized for the ages in some ten-by-twelve oily masterpiece, hanging over the nonexistent fireplace.

"So, anyway, if you're going to change. I mean, it isn't formal, but—"

"Where are we meeting them?"

"At the Whitney . . . They have some new things, Gwen said."

"Gwen?"

"His wife. You remember. The tall blond?"

He didn't. She flashed him a smile. "I'll just wash up."

"Right."

Not that he was especially loath to be torn from the exams. "Is Mandy coming?" he called in to the bedroom. Their bedroom was on the ground floor, Mandy's on the upper floor of the duplex apartment which was paid for out of his wife's ample inheritance of stocks.

"Why should *Mandy* go?" Ginny had the curious notion he "encouraged" Mandy in her furtive passion for himself. At first, when they had married, she had gone around beaming to friends over the change in her until then hostile little daughter. "She's just like a girl in love," she had chortled to Esther and Pam and the rest of them. And then, naturally enough, the tide had turned and the murky underside of the leaf revealed itself.

Ginny was in the bath. He "surprised" her there, submerged in sudsy water, a large bouffant cap on her head. She smiled up at him. It was vaguely reminiscent of various grade B movies he had seen and been bored by. Should he plunge his arms into the scalding water up to the elbow, seize her in his arms, and cry . . . Yet, Max pitied his wife, pitied her for the pleasant, attractive, but undeniably middleaged face that hovered between a smile and something sadder as she soaked in fragrant oils for his sake or, hopefully, for

some nonexistent lover. He pitied his wife, yes, but in the sense that
he pitied a dog with a rash on its behind, the pity never quite dif-
fusing into genuine compassion. She had made her bed—she was
lying in it. If not him—there would have been another bloodsucker,
possibly worse, more pernicious. His sins were overt, uncomplicated
ones. And—he prided himself on this point—he had never lied to
her. He had said, "I'm marrying you for your money. I'm sick of
poverty," and she had honored his refreshing candor.

Everyone had been glad at that time—his sisters with their large,
respectable suburban families, grown, in their forties, so alike he
scarcely distinguished them anymore, his brother, his parents still
venerably alive and active. Everyone was glad that he had chosen
"a woman of his own age." Or so it was discreetly said. Not some
wretched teeny bopper to foul up the family nest, nothing at all way
out, but instead a woman who, like him, had "been through a lot."
So she was rich. It couldn't hurt, could it?

"It's funny you don't remember the Murgitraughs," Ginny said,
toweling herself off.

"Should I? Were they distinctive in some way?"

"Yes! Well, I mean, he's very . . . unusual and she's very . . .
beautiful."

"Unusual" might mean the man was a raving madman. And "beautiful?" Well, that could be the simple truth. His wife had an accurate and unbiased eye for the attractions of her potential rivals.

"She's very tall," she said. "Oh six feet maybe."

"Good God."

"A very handsome woman."

So she was. Gwendolyn Murgitraugh, standing by her husband's
side, all of six feet at least, was a predictable, but stunning combination of cheekbones, elaborate hair, several pairs of eyes, a breathy
English accent that made her sound as though she'd just run around
the block several times.

"I knew your wife at Smith," she breathed to him as his wife and
Jim, the eccentric but successful portrait painter, were examining
some paintings up close.

"Did you?" Should he say, "Which one?"

"She was an extraordinary person."

"Ginny went to Radcliffe."

She smiled secretively. "Alice."

"Oh, Alice."

Gwendolyn Murgitraugh was fixing him with an uncomfortably intense, knowing look. "Alice and I were very close at one time . . ." Pause. "I was devastated to learn of her death."

The sculpture in the foreground at which his present wife and Gwendolyn M.'s present husband were staring was a jagged slash of metal, twisted into a no shape. Staring at it, Max permitted himself the luxury of hating this woman by his side, a comparative stranger, with the casual insidiousness of her prattle about death. But, of course, she must have tried it too. Sleeping pills, this or that. Before she'd met Jim, between lovers. When the $80,000 or whatever she was earning as model "wasn't enough." "How did you learn of her death?" he said.

"I read of it in the paper . . . But you were divorced then, weren't you?"

"Yes."

"Strange her doing it like that, with the plastic bag and the—"

"How did you hear of that?" The paper had printed "natural causes" which in a sense was true enough.

"From a friend . . . Henry Trent."

But he would not permit himself to be drawn further into this. Because Henry Trent, whom at one point he had hated—the first and, as it turned out, most respectable of Alice's lovers—was as unimportant to him now as that guard standing in the corner looking with boredom at the giant Wesselman nude on the opposite wall. Because his whole former life, when he thought about it at all, seemed as remote as though he had never lived it at all, but merely read of it in some book as a schoolboy. The person he was then—he had been a virgin when he had married Alice, she had worn her black hair parted in the middle, their naivete, both of them with their asthma and their families and their ambitions for each other and their life together—was something in which he no longer believed, even in retrospect.

"I haven't seen Henry Trent in a long time," he said. "How is he?"

"Well, not so well, really." You could see she devoured and loved these mournful details. "Those ulcers and then—Carolyn hasn't been well."

Wasn't his wife dead yet? Hadn't she had cancer supposedly? Which in some incredible way was supposed to justify his adulteries.

"I thought she'd be dead by now," he remarked as they passed on to the next room.

"Well, they've removed about *all* of her. But she goes on living."

"Remarkable."

"It is, isn't it? . . . Poor Henry has been through such a lot."

Suddenly Ginny beckoned. "Come here, you two! What are you gossiping about?"

"Old friends," Gwendolyn Murgitraugh said with a smile at Max. "We know some people in common."

"It's *you* I'd like to do, Virginia, sweetheart," Jim Murgitraugh was saying, grinning wildly at Ginny as she politely accepted a drink from him.

Is he for real? Max was thinking, slouched in the couch with his wild head of Negroid blondish curls and his wooden beads—one part hippy, one part homo, nine parts phony. He has a Jewish mother in the Bronx, no doubt, to whom he's little Bubela.

"Do you play an instrument?" Jim was saying.

"Me? No, I—" Ginny blushed. Even now, at forty-five with two bad marriages behind her and a third one going bad, she had that odd innocent blush which was so genuine and made her look so vulnerable, both calling attention to her age and defying it, that Max, watching it, often felt an inward cringe. "I've never had an ear for music," she said. "My sisters all took piano and—"

"Because I see you—somehow—" Eyes shut, dreamy, "with a cello—"

"*Playing* a cello?"

"Playing, maybe just holding it . . . you know, I love the tones of a cello—I mean the color tones—that rich red brown, like your hair. I'd see it all in those shades, like one of those photographs, mellow—"

"Mandy has red hair," Ginny said nervously.

"Does she? Yes, of course, I recall—"

The doorbell rang—another couple. Introductions. Shortly later—a few more. The noise quotient rose. More smoke. Max, who had given up smoking, began wandering restlessly around the oversized living room. How long was this to go on? Dinner too? Outside it was black as pitch.

"Do you like our house?" It was Gwendolyn, changed, at what point he couldn't recall, into a splashy purple and yellow Oriental print. Trousers? A skirt? It was hard to tell.

"Lovely."

"Jim all but designed it . . . Ripped down walls. He has this concept—"

In the background a discussion was ensuing about some pot brought to the gathering by a stoutish man in a goatee. "Great stuff," he was saying.

Ginny was always enthusiastic about pot. Part of the letting go bit, though until now she'd only gotten mild highs and had been very disappointed. He saw her intently watching the goateed man.

"Let me show you the rest of the house."

Blindly, tired, he followed her.

It seemed it was a duplex also. Gwendolyn M., like himself, had married into a duplex. Well, there were worse things to marry into. For some reason hard to fathom, the kitchen was on the top floor, a giant room, dazzling with pots and chrome fixtures. "Jim is a great cook."

Jim's talents seemed endless. "And what do *you* do?" he said.

She looked at him.

"Your husband's abilities seems so diversified."

"Oh no, it's just—" She looked defensive. "He really *is* good at all those things. He's not a fag or anything."

"I didn't assume—"

"Well, some people do. You know. I mean, his looks—"

"That's just part of the scene."

"Right!" She was relieved he understood. "When I met him, he was just a boy from the Bronx, a real square. Now he's loosened up a little. His analyst says that—"

She flung open another door. It was a narrow room with rows upon rows of cans in all sizes, rather like a giant Pop painting with all the bright labels glaring out. "The pantry," she said.

She evidently intended to be seduced in one of these many rooms. From the vague glaze that came over her expression, Max gathered this was the one. The "scene" downstairs was too uninviting for him to resist. Besides, though he had screwed women he disliked before, toward none could he remember such a pure, unadulterated (pun?) hatred as toward Gwendolyn Murgitraugh with her insect eyelashes and pouty English mouth. The very purity of his feeling was so sharp as to lend the moment of their coupling, otherwise undistinguished, a certain memorable quality. As for Gwendolyn, she was agile and professionally adept, as though there were another customer waiting outside the door. Even her cry of passion from the pseudo-Spanish linoleum floor seemed to him rehearsed, as though, in daily voice lessons, she had practiced to attain the right pitch and "tone."

When they were done, she withdrew, from behind a box of Aunt Jemima pancakes, a box of flowered Kleenex. Was this a regular routine? The pantry somehow aphrodisiac with its brightly colored labels?

"Why'd you marry Ginny?" Loose, slurred, her speech acquired the vulgarity he had sensed all along behind the acquired upperclass Englishness.

"Why not?"

"I'd of thought you went for—women of quality."

"Nope . . . I have catholic tastes."

She looked puzzled, evidently wondering if she should take this personally, then deciding to pass it by. "Don't you have a type or anything? I mean, Alice and Ginny are so different. Were." She stumbled over the tense.

"Are and were."

"Most people pick similar mates."

A truism? "Was the former Mr. Murgitraugh like the present one?"

"Well—well no, but Gene—we were very young."

He didn't want reminiscences of the early life and loves of G. M. "Jim's a swinger."

"Oh, not really . . . He's serious. Just because he's a success doesn't mean—"

"Far be it from me to sneer at success."

But she was melancholy, distracted by memories of Lonesome Gene. "He's married now. Has two kids. Sends me pictures sometimes."

"Cute little buggers?"

Gwendolyn smiled dreamily. "They are . . . really."

"So, have a couple."

"I can't."

"Oh?"

Rushing on, frantic, "I'd adopt one. I'd love a little Negro baby . . . Or a Vietnamese one . . . But Jim doesn't. He feels—"

"Oh, of course."

"I would die for a little baby," Gwendolyn Murgitraugh said, closing her eyes as though in orgasm.

Why were peoples' lives destroyed in such simple ways? A. wants an apple, but gets a banana. B. wants . . . He rose. "Come on, Gwenie . . . We better move."

She looked startled. "Gene used to call me that."

"Sorry."

"No, I like it."

So, he was being deprived of what had seemed the most genuine emotion he was likely to feel that evening—hatred. He was disappointed. Beneath the phony exterior of a Gwendolyn M. beats the heart of a . . .

Her hand rested on a can of Campbell's baked beans. "When I was at Smith, I admired Alice so much . . . I wanted to *be* her . . . She seemed to know just what she wanted out of life."

"She didn't."

"Her father used to come up and speak . . . Such a handsome man. Some of the girls had crushes on him . . . I never even *knew* my father."

"Shouldn't we go down?"

She was in a reverie. Maybe she'd had a little pot before. "Alice wrote poetry . . . She did *everything* . . . You know something?"

"What?"

"I made a pass at Alice's father once. He was so distinguished. He came to this party. He'd just lectured on—oh, I forget what. But Alice gave this party for him . . . I think we would've—only it was inconvenient."

"I'm sure he would have."

"He had a moustache . . . I didn't used to like men with moustaches. But on him it was different."

"Let's go down, Gwenie."

She was angry. "We'll go down, we'll go down . . . What's the big rush?"

"No rush."

"See them vomiting over each other. What's there to see?"

"Nothing." But he remained poised near the door.

She sprang up, pulling her swirls of Oriental silk around her. "What I can't figure out is—how come Alice married someone like you?" The hostility, if such it was, seemed so ingenuous it almost cleared the air.

"I don't know."

"Her father was so famous . . . I thought she'd marry some *famous* person."

"So did she."

"Maybe she thought *you'd* be famous, huh?"

"Maybe."

"Well—" Indifferent now. "You never know what you're marrying."

Ginny appeared to have had several small but intense visions which in the car on the way home she tried to convey to him. He listened and did not listen.

"How'd it go with Gwen?" she said suddenly.

"Okay."

"Nothing special?"

"No . . . She likes to do it in the pantry."

"She looked a little ill when you came down."

"I felt a little ill."

"Poor old thing. You're too much of a gentleman."

"Old-time chivalry."

She had the key. Max walked past her into the pleasantly crowded living room. This is a nice house. How does he afford it on a high school teacher's salary? Well, he has a talent for picking wives. You see, the first one had a famous father. And the second one had a lot of money.

"Max!"

The sound came from the other end of the house. "It's Timmy!"

"What about him?"

"The school called. He tried to run away."

"Where to?"

"I don't know. He's okay, though."

Mandy, in flowered pajamas, was puffy with tears. "They said— they'd call back."

But the call, an hour later, revealed nothing beyond the fact that he was in the dorm, had been caught "near the state line." More talk about "emotional upset," "adjusting to the strain of a broken home." Blah and more blah.

"That school is *crap*," Ginny said violently, drinking black coffee in the kitchen, ravenously picking at Chinese noodles left over from a takeout dinner. "We've *got* to take him out of it."

"Where to?"

"There are places . . . Let him stay home."

"He doesn't want to." His words had been: "This isn't my home."

"Maybe he's changed."

"Maybe."

The next morning he would set off for the school. Yet even now Max knew how he would feel. Not ready. Not ready for a six-hour drive, confrontations with headmasters and school psychologists, not ready most of all for Timmy who would say, "Look, Dad, lay *off*," who would be angry and hostile and not say why he had tried to do it, who would stare at him with the eyes of his dead first wife who had married the wrong man and only in death corrected her mistake.

# ROBOT

## GUY DAVENPORT

Guy Davenport was born in Anderson, South Carolina, in 1927. He teaches English at the University of Kentucky. He won the Blumenthal-Leviton Prize for Poetry in 1967. His books include: *The Intelligence of Louis Agassiz, Carmina Archilochi, Sappho: Songs and Fragments, Flowers and Leaves.*

Down there the ochre horse with black mane, black fetlocks, black tail, was prancing as if to a fanfare of Charpentier, though it would have been the music of shinbone fife and a drum that tickled her ears across the tall grass and chestnut forests along the Vézère.

Coencas, tousled haired, naked, and yawning, held Robot in his arms, dodging with lifted chin his wet nose and generous tongue. The campfire under its spit of forked sticks, its ashes ringed by rocks, looked abandoned in the woods light at morning. The crickets had begun again, and a single nightingale trilled through their wild chirr on the slopes beyond the trees.

The old priest was coming from Brive to look at the horses, the reindeer, and the red oxen. He knows more about them, Monsieur Laval had told them, than any man in Europe. More, *d'ailleurs*, than any man in the world.

Ravidat was awake, propped on his elbows in his sleeping bag. In one of the pup tents Agnel and Estreguil lay curled like cats. A leaf stuck to Estreguil's pink cheek. He had slept in a sweater, socks, and hat. Agnel's knees were near his chin.

Queroy and Marsal were asleep in the other tent under Ravidat's canvas jacket.

Since Thursday they had lived with the tarpans of the Dordogne in their eyes.

—Friday the thirteenth, Coencas said. *C'était par bonheur, la bonne chance.*

—We *felt* them on Thursday, Ravidat said, as when you know somebody's in the house without seeing or hearing them. They knew *we* were there.

—Scare me, Estreguil said, so I can scare Agnel.

Ravidat stretched kneeling, his open blue shirt that had bunched around his shoulders in sleep tumbling down his arched back like a crumpled piece of the September sky above them. He stood, naked but for his shirt, fell forward into ten brisk push-ups while Robot barked in his face, then rolled onto his back and pedalled his long legs spattered with leafshadow in the sharp morning air.

—Ravidat, Marsal said gloomily from his tent, is having a fit.

—Show me, Estreguil said.

—*Et alors, mes troglodytes,* Coencas hailed the tents, help me get a fire going.

Estreguil crawled out in silly haste. Agnel rolled behind him. Robot studied them anxiously, looking for signs of a game.

Ravidat had pointed on Thursday toward the slope across the Vézère.

—He is over there! he called through cupped hands.

The others were catching up. Coencas had whittled a staff and was whacking thistle and goldenrod with it. Marsal put two fingers in his mouth and whistled like a locomotive.

Ravidat was watching the shaken sedge across the river where Robot nosed his way. He was seventeen, long of jaw, summer brown. His eyes were glossy black discs set in elm-leaf outlines of boyish lashes. His new canvas jacket smelled of pipeclay and gunpowder. His corduroy trousers were speckled with beggar's lice and sticktights. Over his shoulder he carried his uncle Hector's old octagon-barreled breechloader.

The Vézère was low, for the summer had been dry, and the reeds along its bank were thick with dragonflies and quivering gnats.

Through a stand of scrub oak and plum bushes as yellow as butter the others filed toward him, Marsal with the other rabbit gun, Queroy with the sleeves of his sweater tied around his neck, Coencas in short blue pants, ribbed socks, a scab on one knee, brown cowlick over an eye, Estreguil sharp-nosed under a grey fedora, and little Agnel, who carried a frog.

The hum of an airplane had stopped them.

—Robot is over there on the slope, Ravidat said.

—A Messerschmidt, Coencas said. The Heinkels are much shriller.

—See my frog.

—When your hands are all warts where he's peed on you, Queroy said, we'll see your frog.

—The Stukas were so low we could hear them before we could see them, Coencas said. When a car stalled, or got hit, the people in the cars behind it would jump out and roll it in the ditch.

—They wouldn't roll *my* car in the ditch, Queroy said.

—They would, if you got kicked in the balls, like one man I saw. There were fights all the time. But when the Stukas came over the road, going down it with their machineguns *rat-a-tat, rat-a-tat*, everybody took to the fields, or woods if there were any. Afterwards, there were *burning* cars to get off the road.

Agnel watched Coencas' face with worried eyes.

—They are over there, Coencas said, pointing northwest.

Queroy spread his arms like a Stuka and ran in circles.

—Queroy is a Nazi, Estreguil said.

Estreguil was all dirty gold and inexplicably strange to look at. His hair was the brown of syrup, with eddies of rust spiralling in and out of the whorls of bright brass. His eyes were honey, his face apricot and wild pale rose over the cheeks. He had been to Paris, however, and had seen real Germans on the streets, had heard them pound on their drums. Coencas had only seen the bombers. Agnel didn't know what he had seen.

—You might have to live forever in Montignac, Marsal said. The Germans may never let you go back home.

—I'm glad, Queroy said.

—*Merde alors*, Ravidat said. Then he shouted across the river:

—*Bouge pas, Robot!*

—He's going up onto the *hectares* of the Rochefoucauld, Marsal said.

—We can cross down at the meadow ford, Ravidat said, leading the way. Marsal and Coencas joined him, and the three little boys came in a cluster behind, Agnel's frog puffing its throat and swimming with a free hind leg. Estreguil's large grey fedora was a gift from Madame Marsal, Jacques' mother.

Robot had met them halfway up the slope, splashing his tail from side to side. His feet were still too big and he still fell when he wheeled. He squeaked when he barked and he squatted to pee, like his mother, which he did with a laugh, lolling tongue, and idiot eyes. He had never in his life seen a rabbit.

He thrashed his tail while Ravidat tickled him behind the ears.

—Find us a rabbit, old boy, Ravidat said. Find us a rabbit.

Robot let out his tongue in an ecstasy and rolled his tail.

—When the Nazi tanks turn, Coencas was explaining, they don't do it like an auto. It comes, *bram! bram! bram!* to a corner. If it's turning right, the right tread stops, *clunk!* and the left keeps the same speed, spinning it right around.

He swung his left leg out.

—And when it's facing the street it's turning into, the right tread starts again. Sparks fly out of the cobbles. Keen.

Queroy turned like a tank, spraying leaves.

—Are the rabbits just *anywhere* around here? Estreguil asked. Are they hiding?

They entered the oak forest at the top of the hill. The silence inside made them aware of the cricket whirr in the fields they had left, and the cheep of finches in the tall September grass. They could no longer hear the drone of the airplane. Caterpillars had tented over the oleanders.

The hills of the Dordogne are worn down to easy slopes, and outcroppings with limestone facings slice across the barrows of the hills.

—*C'est bien ajusté le slip Kangourou?* Coencas slapped Ravidat on the behind.

—*Va à ravir,* Ravidat laughed. *Et marche aussi comme un coq en pâte.*

—*Capiteux, non?*

Ravidat leaned his gun carefully against an alder, unbuckled his belt, unbuttoned his fly, lowered his trousers, and raised his shirt tail. He was wearing a pair of Coencas' underpants cut like swimming briefs, trim, succinct, and minimal.

—They're the new style from Paris, Ravidat explained. They are called *Kangourous.*

—Because you jump in them! Agnel squealed.

—Because your *queue* sticks out of the pouch when you want it, Estreguil said. *Idiot!*

—Has your peter got bigger still? Queroy asked. His was as yet a little boy's, his testicles no bigger than a fig.

Marsal, like Coencas, was old enough to have his aureole of amber hair, but Ravidat was already a man, full bushed in black.

—Let us see, Queroy said.

They looked at the rose heft of its glans with professional curiosity, the twin testicles plump and tight, Marsal and Queroy with envy, Coencas more complacently, though he felt his mouth going dry. Ravidat admired himself with animal pride.

Agnel considered these mysteries briefly and held out his frog to a tangle of gnats dancing in the air.

—Don't hurt him, Estreguil said. Will he eat the gnats?

Coencas slid his hand down into his short pants, stuck out his tongue in sweet impudence, and bounced on his toes.

—*Attendez!* Marsal said quickly, his voice hushed.

Robot was crashing through leaves. His tenor bark piped down the slope.

Ravidat stuffed his cock back into his shorts and the frog leapt from Estreguil's hands.

Ravidat held his gun, which he had grabbed, against his chest with his chin while he did up his trousers. Marsal was already away among the trees. Then they all galloped down the hill, elbows out for balance.

—Up and around! Marsal shouted.

—Show me the rabbit! Agnel cried from behind them.

Ravidat and Marsal were out front, stalking to the top of the slope, sighting along their guns. Coencas, his stick at the ready, was at their backs with Estreguil and Queroy.

—Say if you see my frog, Agnel said.

—Everybody stop! Ravidat cried. Keep quiet.

The woods were wonderfully silent.

—He went down the slope, Marsal said quietly, and then across, down there, and up again, didn't he?

—If he catches it, will he eat it? Estreguil asked.

—Shut up.

Robot was barking again. They turned together.

—Show me the rabbit, Agnel said, falling backwards.

They ran around him.

—How did the dumb dog get *behind* us? Ravidat asked.

They plunged down the hill, looking, jumping for a better look, kneeling for a better look. The familiar oakwood as they ran through it became unfamiliar and directionless, as though it had suddenly lost its ordinariness.

Agnel tripped and fell, spewing up a dust of leaves. Ravidat and Coencas bounded over fallen trees, their mouths open like heroes in a battle. Marsal was more methodical, sprinting with his gun at port arms.

—Everybody still! he shouted.

Only Agnel kept padding on behind them.

—I hear Robot, Marsal said, but damned if I know where.

The woods were all at once quiet. The distances were deepening dark.

Then they heard Robot. His bark was vague and muted, as if down a well. It was beneath them.

—Holy God, Ravidat said.

—Quiet!

Marsal went on all fours and cocked his ear. Robot was howling like a chained puppy. Then he began to whimper.

—*Robot!* Ravidat called. Where *are* you? *Eh, mon bon bougre, où es tu, hein?*

Marsal began to move on hands and toes.

—He's under the ground, Ravidat. In a fox den or rabbit burrow.

—He'll come out, Ravidat said. I'll bet he has a rabbit.

—Show me, Agnel said.

Marsal was walking around the hill, signalling for the others to follow. They could hear Robot's howls more distinctly as they clambered over an ancient boulder, a great black knee of stone outcropping. They came to the upended roots of a fallen cedar.

—He's down there! Marsal said.

The cedar in falling had torn a ragged shellhole in the hillside, and the weather had melted it down in upon itself. There was a burrowmouth at the back of the cavity, down which Ravidat, lying on his stomach, shouted.

—Robot!

An echo gave back *bô! bô! bô!*

—Get out of there! Ravidat coaxed. Come up, old boy! Come up! Marsal gave a keen whistle.

—He's a hell of a long way down, Coencas said. You can tell.

Ravidat took off his canvas jacket, throwing it to Marsal.

—I'm going in after him.

—The hole's too small.

—Only the hole. You heard that echo. It's a cave.

—Sticks, Marsal ordered. Everybody find a good stick.

Agnel set to, arms over his head. Marsal drew his hunting knife and began to hack at the edges of the hole.

—It goes in level, he said. It must drop later on.

Estreguil came dragging a fallen limb as long as a horse. Ravidat brought a leafy length of white oak, stripping branches from it as he dragged it up to the hole.

—Let's get this up in there, he said, and walk it back and forth.

Ravidat and Coencas on one side, Marsal and Queroy on the other, like slaves at the oar of a trireme, they pushed and pulled, grinding the rim of the hole until Ravidat said that he thought he could crawl in.

—Go in backwards and feel with your feet, Marsal said. You can climb out then if you get stuck.

His legs in to the hips, he walked his elbows backwards, calling out, *Courage, Robot! Je viens!*

A half-circle of faces watched him: Marsal's big grey eyes and tousled brown hair, Queroy's long Spanish face with its eyes black as hornets, Coencas' flat-cheeked lean face, all olive and charcoal, Estreguil's long-nosed, buck-toothed blond face with its wet violet eyes, Agnel's taffy curls and open mouth full of uneven milk teeth.

Level light from the setting sun shone on Ravidat's face.

—We ought to have a rope, Marsal said.

—It goes down here, Ravidat's muffled voice came out. There's a ledge.

He lowered his feet, loose rotten stone crumbling as he found footholds. His elbows on the ledge, he struck a heap of scattering objects with his feet. They must lie on something. He dropped.

—I'm on another ledge! his distant voice rose, as if from behind closed doors several rooms away. I'm standing in a muck of bones. It's a graveyard down here!

Earth poured on him in rivulets. An ancient dust, mortuary and feral, lifted from the bones he had disturbed. Coencas was wriggling in head first, loosening pebbles and sliding loam.

—Matches, he said, reaching down into the dark.

Then he said:

—I'm coming down!

Ravidat caught him, shoulders and arms, so that the one, his feet still in daylight, hugged upside down the other standing in dark bones. They could hear Agnel saying:

—I'm next!

Coencas pivoted down, crashing onto the bones beside Ravidat.

—We're on a ledge, I think. Feel with your foot.

Coencas struck a match. White clay in striated marl beside them, utter blackness beyond and below, where Robot whined and yelped. Another match: the bones were large, bladed ribs in a heap, a long skull.

—Bourzat's ass!

—Queroy! Jacques! Ravidat shouted upwards. Last year, when old Bourzat's ass disappeared, you remember? Here it is!

—It was just about when that storm blew this old tree over, you're right, Marsal shouted down. You're right.

—Does it stink? Agnel hollered.

Another match showed that the ledge dropped at a fierce angle, but could be descended backwards, if there were footholds.

—Keep striking matches, Ravidat said. I'm going down.

Robot had found a rhythm, three yelps and a wail, and kept to it.

—There's no more ledge. I'm going to drop.

A slipping noise, cloth against stone, and then Coencas heard the *whomp* of feet on clay far below him in the dark.

—*Robot*, he heard, *ici, ici, vieux bougre.*

—I hear Robot's tongue and tail, Coencas said upward. Everybody come on down. It's a long drop after this ledge.

Coencas lowered himself from the ledge of bones and fell lightly onto soft clay.

—We're here, Ravidat said from solid dark.

Marsal and Queroy were inside, handing down Agnel and Estreguil.

—Can we get back *out*? Marsal asked.

—*Qui sait?* Coencas said in the voice of Frankenstein's monster, and his words, full of grunts and squeals, rolled around them.

—Is the rabbit down here, too? Estreguil said, panting.

—Can we *breathe*?

—Here's the far wall.

A match showed it to be calcined and bulbous, a white billow of stone. The floor was uneven, ribbed like river sand, pot-holed, an enormous round-bottomed gully.

—I've never been so dark before, Agnel said.

—You're *scared!* Estreguil said.

—So are you.

—It keeps going back, Ravidat's hollow voice boomed in a strange blur.

—I've got two more matches.

The hole through which they had entered was a dim wash of light above them.

—Agnel, Ravidat said beside them, take Robot. *Here!* Keep steady with one hand. Hold onto Robot with the other. Coencas is going to stand on my shoulders, and push you up to the ledge. *D'accord?*

—Good old Robot! Estreguil said.

Ravidat braced himself against the wall. Coencas, Estreguil and the dog under his arm, climbed onto his shoulders.

—Stand on your toes, Ravidat, Coencas said. I think we're just going to reach.

Estreguil pushed Robot onto the bone ledge. Then, skinning both knees, he clambered up himself. Agnel went up next, and had to come down again: he couldn't reach the ledge from Coencas' shoulders.

—You go up, Queroy, Ravidat said, and pull Agnel up when you get there.

Marsal went up next, showered them with dirt and pebbles, and hollered down:

—How are *you* going to get up?

—Get that long limb, Ravidat commanded. Poke it in, and you four bastards hold onto it for all you're worth.

Coencas climbed out first, using the limb as a rope, and Ravidat followed. The clarity of the long summer twilight still held. Robot was in Agnel's arms.

—We have, Ravidat said in a level voice, discovered a cave.

—Tell nobody, Marsal said. Estreguil! Agnel! You understand? *Nobody.* It's our cave.

—Find my frog, Agnel said.

—It's a damned *big* cave, Ravidat said. And Marsal and Queroy know what I'm thinking.

—What? asked Coencas. What is there to think about a cave?


At the ford Agnel fell into the Vézère. They dressed him in Queroy's sweater, and Ravidat carried him piggyback to the great spreading beech in Montignac.

—*Regardez les grands chasseurs!* the old men at their coffee sang out. Agnel had gone to sleep, Robot sat and let his tongue hang down, and Ravidat gave a confidential nod to the Catalan garage mechanic.

What he wanted, once they were leaning nonchalantly against the castle wall across the road from the beech and the elders, was grease. Old grease. And the use, for a day, of the old grease gun that had been retired since the new one arrived.

—Grease, my goose?

Precisely. The use to which it was to be put would be known in time. Meanwhile, could it be a matter among friends?

—*Seguramente*.

And he needed it first thing in the morning.

Queroy, Marsal, and Estreguil were to come out to the cave as soon as they were out of school. They could bring Agnel. Better to keep him in on it than have him pigeon.

—Meet me, Ravidat said to Coencas, at the flat rock on the river as soon as you're up. *Va bien?*

*Bien.* He heard the Heinkels in the night, and the cars of the refugees going through Montignac, headed south. He thought of the armies north and west, of white flares falling through the night sky, and of the long clanking rocking tanks that would most certainly come south. An old man under the great tree had said that the French battle flags had been taken to Marseille and had been paraded through the streets there. They were on their way, these flags, to the colonies in Africa.

By cockcrow he was up, making his own bowl of coffee, fetching the day's bread from the baker, as a surprise for his mother. He left a note for her saying that he would be back in the afternoon, and that he would be just south of town, in the Lascaux hills.

On the flat rock when he got there lay Ravidat's shoes and socks, trousers, canvas jacket, blue shirt and Kangourou underpants. Ravidat himself was swimming up the river toward him. He stripped and dove in, surfacing with a whoop. Ravidat heaved himself out of the river and sat on the flat rock, streaming. The day was a clear grey, the air sweet and cool. He walked in his lean brown nakedness to a plum bush from which he lifted a haversack that Coencas had not seen. Inside, as he showed the wet, grinning Coencas, was a long rope, the grease gun, and a thermos of coffee.

—A sip now, he said, the rest for later.

They dried in the sun. The coffee was laced with a dash of cognac.

—What do you think we're going to see? Coencas asked.

—You'll see when you see.

They secured the rope outside the cave, and let themselves down the shelved clay. Ravidat lit a match and fired the grease gun: the kind of torch with which he had gigged frogs at night. The flame was greenish yellow and large as a handkerchief. Ravidat held it high over his head.

Neither spoke.

Everywhere they looked there were animals. The vaulted ceiling was painted, the crinkled walls lime white and pale sulphur were painted with horses and cows, with high-antlered elk and animals they did not know. Between the animals were red dots and geometric designs.

—Did you know they were here?

—Yes, Ravidat said. They had to be.

The torch showed in its leaping flare a parade of Shetland ponies bounding like lambs. Above them jumped a disheveled cow like the one in *Mère Oie* over the moon. Handsome plump horses trotted one after the other, their tails arched like a cat's.

The cave branched into halls, corridors, tunnels.

They found long-necked reindeer, majestic bulls, lowing cows, great humped bison, mountain goats, plaited signs of quadrate lines, arrows, feathers, lozenges, circles, combs.

All the animals were in files and herds, flowing in long strides down some run of time through the silence of the mountain's hollow.

—They are *old*, Ravidat said.

—*Tout cela est grand*, Coencas said, *comme Victor Hugo.*

—They are prehistoric, like the painted caves of the Trois Frères and Combarelles. You have not been to them?

The cave was even larger than Ravidat had thought. It branched off three ways from where he had lit the torch, and two of these passages branched off in turn into narrow galleries where the floor was not clay but cleft rock. Their echoes rounded in remote darkness.

—It goes on and on.

They heard shouts outside: Marsal, Queroy, Estreguil, Agnel. They were out of school.

—Come look! Ravidat called up to them. It is Noah's Ark down here!

They told no one of the cave for three days. On the fourth they told their history teacher, Monsieur Laval, who had once taken them to the caves at Combarelles and Les Eyzies. He came out to the cave, trotting the last steep ten metres. When they held the torch for him, he gripped his hands and tears rimmed his eyes.

—Of all times! Of all times!

He found a lamp by which the painters had worked, the mortar in which the colors were ground, the palette.

Coencas found another lamp, a shallow dish in which a wick soaked in deer fat had lit the perpetual night of the cave.

They began to find, sunk in the clay of the floor, flint blades, though most of them were broken. They found most of these shattered stone knives, thirty-five of them in all, just beneath the buffalo and the herd of horses.

—Maurice Thaon! Monsieur Laval said. We must get Maurice Thaon. He will know who must be told.


Breuil, Thaon, who came the next day, bringing a block of drawing paper, told them, is just over at Brive-la-Gaillarde with Bouysonnie, would you believe it?

Ravidat held the torch while he drew.

—I had a note from him last week. He will be frantic. He will dance a dance in his soutane. He will hug us all. The war has driven us all together here, and we have found the most beautiful cave of them all.

—Lascaux, he said, as if to the horses that seemed to quiver in the torchlight. Lascaux.

The postman went to Brive on the nineteenth with Monsieur Laval's note addressed to L'Abbé Henri Breuil, whom he had the distinguished honor of informing that in a hillside on the estate of the Comtesse de la Rochefoucauld a prehistoric cave with extensive paintings had been discovered by some local boys. Knowing the eminent prehistorian would like to inspect this very interesting site, he awaited word from him and begged him to accept his most elevated sentiments.

Thaon arrived later the same day with drawings.

—A car! the Abbé shouted. Do we have the petrol? For myself, I can walk.

They drove up the next day at the Great Tree of Montignac in the Abbé Bouysonnie's wheezing Citroën. Laval mounted their run-ningboard and directed them to the Lascaux hills.

Robot barked them to a halt.

—Here we are! Monsieur Laval said, shifting from foot to foot and waving his arms as if he were conducting a band.

The six boys, all with uncombed hair, stood in front of the auto-mobile. L'Abbé Breuil herded them before him like so many geese.

—Brave boys, he cried, wonderful boys.

He stopped to look at their camp, shaking hands even with Estreguil and Agnel, who had never shaken hands with anybody before.

—I am decidedly prehistorical myself, is that what you're thinking, *mon gosse?*

Estreguil broke into a wide smile. He instantly liked the wide-backed old priest.

—Oh, I'm well beyond halfway to a hundred, and then some, he said to Agnel.

Then he turned to Ravidat, who stood with Robot in his arms.

—And that's the pooch to whom we're indebted, is it?

He patted the suspicious Robot, and mussed Ravidat's hair.

They promptly forgot that this was the man who knew more about prehistoric caves than anybody else in Europe. He was simply an easy old priest with a wounded eye. His face was long, rectangular, big-eared, with strong lines dropping to comfortable pendules and creases under his jaws. A silken wattle hung under his chin. The grey bristles of his thick eyebrows rose and fell as if part of the mecha-nism of his meticulous articulateness.

—My eye? Prehistory got it. We've been climbing around Les Eyzies all week, Bouysonnie and I, and one of your indestructible bushes, through which, mind you, I was making my way in clear for-getfulness of my age, whacked me in the eye. I see lights in it, rather beautiful.

—But I'm forgetting my manners. This is Dr. Cheynier, who has come to help me, he said to the boys as if uncovering a surprise, and this is Monsieur l'Abbé Bouysonnie, who is an expert in primitive religions. And we're all anxious to enter the cave, if you are ready.

The first thing the Abbé's electric lamp found inside the cave was a rabbit.

It sat chilled with fear in the cone of light, its sides shivering.

Marsal and Ravidat moved beside it just outside the beam, and the one chased it into the other's arms.

—We've not seen it the whole time we've been down here, Ravidat said.

—*He* was the first one in! Coencas said.

—Take him up, the Abbé said, and let him loose, and don't let the dog get him. He must be famished.

They heard Agnel shouting above.

—The rabbit! The bunny!

Light after light came on. A star trembled on the Abbé's horn-rimmed glasses. Silent, he looked. His weathered right hand was on Marsal's shoulder, as if he needed to touch the force that brought him here. A battery of lights shifted over their heads. Ravidat held the largest. Queroy aimed a long flashlight.

With his left hand the Abbé traced in the air the suave curves of a horse's back and belly.

—The colors! The tints! The gaiety of their movements! The wit of the drawing, the intelligence!

—They *are* old, are they not, Monsieur l'Abbé?

—Yes, *mon cher Laval*, no doubt at all of that.

He pointed higher, the lights climbing with his aim.

—They are as old as Altamira. Older, far older, than civilization.

A long cow faced her bull in the heart of the cave, the titan grandmother of Hathor and the cows of Africa upon whom the Nuer people still wait, burnishing their hair with her urine, imagining the female sun between her horns, replenishing the divine within human flesh with her holy blood.

With them run, as if pacing to the music of the first voice of the world, horses, elk, bears, and a spotted animal whose only portrait occurs here and whose bones have never been found. This first voice, the discourse of waters and rain, of wind in leaves and grass and upon mountain rocks, preceded the laugh of the jackal and the voices of the animals themselves, the rising wind of the cow's low, the water voice of the horse, the trumpet of the elk, bleat of the deer, growl of the bear.

In the Abbé's left eye trembled a jangle of red. He saw the prancing horse the color of crust through a snow of fireflies.

—Thaon brought me a drawing of this.

And of a line of reindeer:

—They are swimming a river. I have seen the motif before, carved on bone.

He worked the clay of the floor in his fingers.

—The bears were going when this cave was painted. Man could enter. The Aurignacian snow owl still drifted in at twilight, for the mice. One can imagine the sound of her wings in this stillness. The red rhinoceros was too blind to venture so much dark. The world belonged to the horse, the tarpan, the reindeer. Lion was terrible, but man could smoke him out of the caves, and lion, when the encounter came, was afraid of horse. The old elephants kept to themselves, eating trees.

They found the horse drawn upside down.

—Falling, do you suppose? Or weren't they oriented to the horizon, to the vertical? And these signs, these hieroglyphs! Are we ever going to read them, Bouysonnie?

They climbed out for lunch, cold chicken and mayonnaise and wine which Abbé Bouysonnie brought in two hampers, with Camembert and bread for dessert.

—It is a very great thing, is it not? Dr. Cheynier asked Abbé Breuil.

—So great that I sit here stunned. *Absolument bouleversé!* If there is a reason for my hanging on to such a disgraceful old age, it was to see this cave. A rabbit, a dog named—do I remember right?— Robot, these boys, a doctor's ration of petrol—he winked at Peyronie —and I suppose we must even give grudging thanks to the filthy *boches* for driving me from Paris. A veritable conspiracy of Providence!

Bouysonnie smiled.

—You've *always,* my dear Henri, been just around the corner from the discoveries, when, indeed, you weren't yourself the discoverer.

—I have, the Abbé said, I have.

He turned to the boys. Estreguil, who was sucking his fingers, was embarrassed.

—I have been around. Africa, oh yes, and China even. I was in China with a nephew of Voltaire who was quite close to his accomplished granduncle in spirit and brains. The church, in fact, thinks him too very much like his uncle, in a different sort of way. We went to China to look for the deep, the *very* deep, past of man. At Tcheou-kou-tien, a village some thirty-five kilometres below Peking, just under the lovely Fang Mountains—the Fang shan—*shan* is *mountain*

—we found a very old skull, four-hundred thousand, perhaps five-hundred thousand years old. Five hundred thousand years old! *Cinq cent mille ans!*

He looked at each boy in turn, to make certain that they were following.

—Pierre Teilhard de Chardin, that was my friend in China, the nephew of Voltaire. A tall man, all angles like a proper Jesuit. Me, I'm just a parish priest. They called us Don Quichote and Sancho Panza, our friends in those days. A man name of Pei made the actual discovery. We went to look at the tools. I was most interested in fire, and the ancient men of Peking definitely had that. As a matter of fact they cooked and ate each other.

—Ate each other!

It was Estroguil who interrupted, and Agnel looked at him as if he knew more about the subject than the old priest.

—Most prehistoric people did, Abbé Breuil said, rolling a cigarette.

—What *are* these caves? Dr. Cheynier asked.

—Arks for the spirits of animals, I think. The brain is inward, where one can see without looking, in the imagination. The caves were a kind of inward brain for the earth, the common body, and they put the animals there, so that Lascaux might dream forever of her animals, as man in the lust of their beauty and in need of their blood, venison, marrow, and hides, and in awe of their power and cunning, thought of them sleeping and waking.

He drank back the last of his wine and held his cup out for more.

—They were neither gods nor fetishes nor kinfolk nor demons nor mere food, but something of all.

An airplane buzzed in the distance.

—The animals themselves have sometimes confronted us, you know! I mean bones, and the mammoths found frozen in Siberia, I mean the beasts themselves in all their ruin, as distinct from paintings, engravings, carvings.

Coencas was trying to see the airplane.

—Listen carefully. In the Swiss Alps, up the side of the majestic Drachenberg, five thousand feet above the valley floor, you can find the entrance to a cave. It was in its day a hunters' cave. Inside it we have found all sorts of bones: wolf, lion, chamois, stag, even hare, who was a hefty alpine fellow in those times, before the last Ice Age locked all that world into a solid glacier and thousands of years of snow.

—Now the cave bear, an enormous creature now extinct, was a kind of god, or totem. They broke his bones and sucked out the marrow after they had eaten his flesh and rendered his grease and dressed themselves in his hide. But they placed his skull reverently on ledges in open caves, looking outward, sometimes as many as fifty, all looking outward with their eye sockets, formidable I assure you, especially when they are found, as in the cave of the Drachenberg, covered with ten thousand years of dust.

—Fine dust, not quite half an inch thick. It looks as if the skulls were sculpted of dust.

—The snouts of these dread cave bears are all pointed out toward the sunrise, each in its hump of dust, its mask of dust, and each with its pair of empty bear eyes under a brow of dust. The lower jaws have all been removed, so that the long yellow teeth hang more bearlike in the dark while the sun, morning after morning for twenty thousand years, found the skulls on their ledges. It was like a shop with nothing to sell on its shelves but skulls of bears.

Estreguil and Agnel put their arms around each other.

—You have, some of you, the Abbé said to the boys, been to Combarelles and Font-de-Gaume, Monsieur Laval has told me. It was I who discovered them, oh years and years ago, when your parents were infants. So you see, you have been in my caves and now I have been in yours. *Nous sommes confrères!*

—You are not, you know, the first boys to have discovered a paleolithic cave, though it seems that you have found the most beautiful of them all.

—Three strapping fine brothers discovered Le Tuc d'Audoubert and Les Trois Frères. They were in their teens when they found the Tuc, and soldiers home on leave from that other awful war when they found the cave that's named for them. Max, Louis, and Jacques de Bégouën they were. Their father is the Comte de Bégouën, Henri as he must always be to me, as I am Henri to him. He was retired after a lovely career of politics and owning a newspaper and such terrible things to a house in the Ariège, near St. Giron, though he has never really retired. He is, if I can put it euphemistically, a man who has never lost his taste, bless him, for the good things of this life.

—His dear wife died early, leaving him three sons to bring up. We may note that they were brought up very well indeed, if just a touch wild, young wolves even in their Sunday best. And the Count Bégouën, never stinting his love of good food, a splendid cellar, and a gracious lady with which to share them, is now in his eightieth year, as hale as a prime bull.

—But I'm getting off my subject as if I were eighty myself. On the Bégouën property, Montesquieu-Avantès, the little river Volp runs right through a largish hill, in one side, out the other. What else must a boy do, I need not tell you, but build a raft of oil-cans and wooden boxes, and paddle himself into that cave?

—That's what Max did, oh most decidedly. A farmer thereabouts, François Camel, had been as far up the Tuc d'Audoubert end of the mountain as where you can't go any farther unless you are a weasel, but that never stopped a boy, to my knowledge.

—They *all* went, of course, Jacques and Louis too. They got to a kind of beach and, what do you know, they came across an inscription scratched there in the eighteenth century. They had to turn back, but not for long. They came back and hacked the weasel hole until they could get into it. They found that it was a *gours,* a chimney in the rock, and up it they scampered, forty feet.

—When we turned the rabbit loose that Robot chased into the cave, Estreguil said, he ran as if the Germans were after him!

—*Taise-toi!* Ravidat said. *Où sont tes bonnes manières?*

The Abbé sighed, and smiled.

—And what did they find there? Sculpture! The very first prehistoric discoveries were of course sculpture, carved pebbles and bones, but this was modelled in clay, two bison, two bison moreover about to copulate. Close by they found the heelprints of children, such as Cartailhac would find later, also in the heart of a mountain, around the headless statue of a bear, with evidence that a real bear's head had been staked onto it. Both these sites seem to have been the occasion of a single ceremony. The animals were shaped by the light of a torch, who knows with what sacred dread, and children danced on their heels, and the cave was closed forever.

—The curious thing about this cave is that if you were to drill through the rock in the right direction you would come to the end of another cave, the Trois Frères, which the Bégouën boys found in 1916. At the uttermost recess of *it* is that strange sorcerer, or god, a man dancing in a mask with a beard. He wears antlers, a horse's tail, bear's paws. His sex is human, but it is placed where a cat's is, under the tail. He is our oldest portrait of God.

—The caves are the first draft of the book of Genesis, when man was a minor animal, not suspecting that the divine fire in his heart

was unique. He was thousands of years away from the domesticat-
ing of these animals. The dog was the first. He is man's oldest friend.

Abbé Breuil lit his pipe.

—Oh, Robot knew they were down there! He is one of them. I'm
afraid I've already scandalized the archbishop—he winked at Agnel
—with the heresy I can't get out of my head that animals most ob-
viously have souls, but unfallen ones, as they did not participate in
the sinful pride of our common parents. Ancient man must have
been in some measure envious of the animal, suspecting its supe-
riority.

—He was right, of course, he added.

A man in blue overalls had come up behind them.

—Ramón! Ravidat called out.

It was Ramón's grease gun that had first illumined the cave. But
he was signalling that he did not wish to be called to. He sat under
a tree some metres away and lit his pipe. He winked at Ravidat and
made himself comfortable.

—Abbé, are we going down again today?

—I think not, Thaon. I should rest my eye. It's full of lights again.
Will the boys keep their guard?

—You couldn't drive them away, Monsieur Laval said. They're
well set up in their camp. *Pour eux, c'est une aventure.*

—For us all, the Abbé smiled. We shall be at the Hôtel Commerce, he said to the boys, tweaking Agnel's ear and Estreguil's nose.

He shook hands with Ravidat, acknowledging his age and responsibility. His eyes indicated Ramón under the tree.

—Let no one into the cave, he said.

—That's an old friend, Ravidat explained. He is the mechanic in
Montignac.

—*Tiens. Jusqu'à demain.*

As the Citroën bounced down the hill, Monsieur Laval on the
runningboard, the Abbé Breuil waving his handkerchief from a window, Ramón walked toward them, his hands in his pockets.

—Madame Marsal, he said, will be sending up hot soup.

He approached Ravidat with a look that was both intimate and
inquisitive.

—Is it a big cave?

—It's a right good size, yes.

Ramón looked about him. He indicated with his eyes that he wanted a word apart. Ravidat followed him.

—Wait, Ramón said. *Marsal aussi.*

He put the flat of his hand out to the others. Then he stared at Coencas, who was looking at them from under his cowlick.

—You too, Ramón said. Come with us.

Queroy, Agnel, and Estreguil drew together, left out of a conspiracy.

—Why can't they come? Coencas asked.

Ramón's face showed that Coencas had jeopardized his own eligibility.

—What's it all about? Coencas was persistent.

Ramón saw his mistake. All or none, however dangerous that seemed. He stood in his indecision, pulling his nose.

—*Igual*, he said. Gather around.

He squatted, taking cigarette paper and a sack of tobacco from his pockets.

—This is a matter for *cojónes*, he said in a low voice. The priest will be through looking at the pictures in the cave in a few days. That's to be seen. I shall talk with him, too. And with the others. They're all French.

He sealed the cigarette with the tip of his tongue.

—The Germans are not here yet.

He looked at each of them in turn.

—They will be, in time. There are some of us who will be ready. Do you understand?

—I think I see, Ravidat said.

—We call ourselves the *Résistance*. We are all over France. Have you heard about us, Ravidat? No? Well, you have now. You and Marsal own guns. And you know your way about.

—You are a refugee, *hein?* he said to Coencas.

—From Charleville.

—And you and you, Ramón said to Estreguil and Agnel.

—They're old enough to understand, Ravidat said.

—I want you to swear, Ramón said. One hand on your balls, one on your heart. Swear!

—So help us God.

Ramón looked over his shoulder. It was only Robot jumping at a cricket. They sat quietly, listening to the trill of the nightingales and the wash of wind in the trees.

—The important thing at the moment, Ramón said, is a place to stash ammo. I can get straight off a consignment of Bren guns, if I can find a place to hide them. Is that cave big enough?

—You can hide anything in it, Ravidat said. It's as big as a castle down there.

—If you tell the priest, Coencas said, he won't let you. He'll be afraid you'll hurt the pictures.

—*Foutre les tableaux*, Ramón said. We won't tell him, then. We'll wait until he clears out.

—He's already said, Marsal put in, that he wants to keep the cave secret. That fits in. His secret and our secret will work out the same.

—Anybody who lets our secret out, Ramón said quietly, will have to answer to the *Résistance*. And we are many.

—When do we start? Coencas asked.

—I'll tell you when the time comes. The priest will be measuring the cave. Remember his figures. And tell me all his plans. When he's gone, we can begin to move.

He stood up.

—I'm going back down to the village.

He scooped Agnel up under the arms and held him above his head.

—You know about the Germans? he said. The war? If you tell anybody about this, we lose the war. If you don't, we win.

He set him down.

That goes for you too, he said to Estreguil, crooking his finger as if on a trigger.

—For all of us.

He set off, as casually as he came.

—*Ravidat*, he said, turning, *vous avez la plus longue verge. Soyez le capitaine de ces voyous!*

—*Nous sommes soldats!* Queroy said.

—*Agents, au moins*, Ravidat said.

—*Des espions!*

The moon when it rose was red and perfectly round. Robot gave it a perfunctory trombone howl, joined by Agnel, answered by an owl.

Queroy hinted that Marsal was afraid to be in the *Résistance*, that his mother wouldn't let him if she knew, and got his lip split in a pinwheel of a fight by the fire. Ravidat parted them with slaps and made them shake hands.

Estreguil fell asleep in his clothes beside Robot, who slept facing the fire.

Coencas standing in the red light pulled off his shorts and studied his dick:

—Mine's the next longest, he said to Ravidat.

—Mine is, Marsal said, crawling back out of his bedroll.

—No, Ravidat said. Robot, I think, is next in rank.

Next morning they found the figure of the hunter in the shaft at the back of the cave, a mere stick of a man, bird-headed, ithyphallic, childish. Beside him is a carved bird on a staff. His spear has gored a bison, whose bowels are spilling out. To the left of the hunter is a rhinoceros.

These signs, Thaon! *What* do they mean? These quartered squares on legs, are they houses on piles, as in the Swiss lake wattle houses, houses perhaps for souls? Are those feather shapes arrows, spears?

—Your *houses*, l'Abbé Bouysonnie said, have four legs. Could not they too be horses? Written horses beside the drawn horses?

We've got onto a wall of cats. Mountain lions, probably. One old tom has his tail up, testicles well drawn, spraying his territorial boundaries.

—The artist, Abbé Breuil added, has observed the whiplash curve you get in a stream of water coming from a shaking source. We have all seen a cat wiggle his behind when he's peeing.

Another cat has an arrow in its side, like the Sumerian lioness. These are engraved, not painted like the larger beasts.

Outside, over coffee, Abbé Breuil talked about the hunter, the disemboweled bison, and the rhinoceros.

—The rhinoceros trotting off to the left is in heat, you can tell that from her arched tail, even if you've only seen a cow or a cat ready for the male. It was the realism of the *chat qui pisse* that led me to see that. The rhythmic dots drawn under her tail are her delicious odor, I should think. She is ready to breed.

—To the Aurignacian hunter she is ready to die. Except that it is not death he brings with his spear. It is mating in another sense. Nor does this picture mean that she is to die while in heat. It means that in the painter's vocabulary of symbols to die by the spear and to receive the male are cognate female verbs.

—Reality is a fabric of many transparent films. That is the only way we can perceive anything. We think it up. Reality touches our intuition to the quick. We perceive *with* that intuition. Perhaps we perceive the intuition only, while reality remains forever beyond our grasp.

—Man is the javelin bearer, the penis bearer. Woman conceives through a wound that bleeds every lunar cycle, except when she holds the gift of the child, magically healed. The hieroglyphs of these cave painters for wound and vulva are probably the same.

Monsieur Thaon frowned.

—The hunter with arms outspread before the wounded bison is embracing the idea of death, which to him is the continuity of life. The spilling entrails are an ideogram of the vagina. The bison is life under the guise of death. Who knows what metamorphosis death was to these archaic minds?

—The hunter wears a bird mask exactly like the bird on his shaman's baton. He is therefore not a picture of a man but of that intuitive film over reality we call myth. He has assumed the character that the bird totem also represents. Together they have brought the bison down.


The terrace of the Hôtel Commerce, *cèpes paysannes*, Laval, Thaon, Breuil, Bouysonnie, *truite meunière*. Ravidat is in a chair apart, his fingers laced together. Coencas, slapping his beret on his thigh, has just come in.

—I was at Altamira, bless you, in the year 1902! the Abbé was saying. Eh! *It* was discovered by a dog, too. It was, it was! I have just now remembered the coincidence. It must have been Robot's Spanish grandfather.

—The cave, but not the paintings, which were discovered by a little girl. Her father, the owner of the property, had been going out to the cave for years, once his dog had found it, but he was looking for celts and flints. He had never once looked at the ceiling, if you can imagine. One day his little daughter came along with him, and walked in and looked up, first thing. *Papa*, she said, *los toros, los toros!*

—Cartailhac was convinced that those bulls were thousands and thousands of years old. I went down with him and began making drawings of them. I've been in the business ever since.

—One day at Altamira I was on my back drawing. They hadn't yet lowered the floor as they have now. I was working with crayons by candlelight, dabbed all over with dripping wax, drawing the great mural of bulls, when a very large-eyed young Spaniard came in on hands and knees. He had come from Barcelona, and his clothes were, I remember, of the Bohemian cut as they said in those days.

The Abbé's eyes became mischievous and knowing.

—He said *bon jour* and I said *bon jour*, odd as it was, *vous savez*, to be of a civility deep in a Magdalenian cave. And *bon jour* was precisely all the French he had. He lay on his back, looking, looking. *Hermoso*, he kept saying, *hermoso*. He was not interested in the age of the drawings, but, *ma foi*, in their beauty. He asked, as best I understood his Spanish, if he might touch them, and I explained that pigments that had adhered to limestone for twenty thousand years weren't likely to rub off now. But he didn't touch them. He took one of my candles and followed the bold lines of the beasts as if *he* were drawing them. There was a terrible look on his face, wonder and admiration, and a kind of worship.

—I got his name straight once we were outside. Picasso. It meant nothing to me then, of course. Such eyes.

—*Picasso*. He did not forget Altamira. His eye has never forgotten anything. The bison at Altamira were to him *très moderne*. I have always thought of him as a Cromagnon painter out of time.

—The painted caves in Spain are in the north, in the Cantabrian mountains. They are all across, from San Román in the west to Santimamiñe in the east, and this last is outside Guernica where the dive-bombers struck first in this awful war.

—And when Picasso painted his great symbolic picture of the bombing of Guernica, he made one of the bulls of Altamira dominate the design.

—But yes! said Abbé Bouysonnie. And I had never seen that at all.

—I like to think of that bull, whether at Altamira or in the angry and eloquent *Guernica*, as Being itself, in all its power and dumb presence.

And as if he suddenly found it more comfortable to change the subject, the Abbé Breuil turned to Monsieur Laval:

—What a beautiful old tree! he said of the Montignac beech that filled the *place* with its shade. They are cutting them down, you know, all over France, an obstruction to artillery sighting. A village without a tree is like a woman without hair. Some poet must write an elegy for the trees of the French villages, nay, for the trees of Europe. There was a venerable oak at Guernica, wasn't there? Some great pagan tree that burned when the divebombers came. I keep coming back, it seems, to Picasso.

—But, Bouysonnie said, Picasso does not allude to the Basque oak in his mural, does he?

—No, no, Breuil said. It is not in the prehistoric genius to depict trees. This man Picasso *is* a painter from the Reindeer Age. The *Guernica* with its wounded horse, its hieratic bull, its placing of images over images, is a prehistoric painting. It honors and grieves and stands in awe. I have copied hundreds and hundreds of these beasts until they file through my dreams. God will take me to them when I die, to the saucy Shetland tarpans whose jet manes run the length of their backs, to the long red ox and woolly rhinoceros. But perhaps the *Guernica* I see is not the one everybody sees. The painting I see is as old as Lascaux.

The Drachenberg bears, their jaws full of shadow: *We are Ursus, companions of the Pole Star, god of the Finnmark, brothers of Artemis Diktynna, lords of the forest. We are Bruin, Arkturus, Baloo. We are eaters of the honey of the bees of Han, the golden bees of Mykinai and Tiryns, the red bees of the Merovingians. Man with his gods fire and flint drove us from the caves but put our souls on the walls along with blind bison, shrill horse, slow cow, royal salmon, wizard elk, cruel puma, idiot jackal.*

In the forecourt of the chthonic granary of souls at Lascaux two long cows shamble toward three long cows, dewlapped Indus horned cattle lowing and prancing on stiff forelegs. They are not domestic and pied but wild and brown, still in their eland grazing age. Nor are these aurochs yet Hathor nor the royal herds of Harappa. They are, bulls and cows together, female to the Magdalenian mind, creatures of the realm of woman. So were bison, ox, and mammoth. The male domain was horse, ibex, stag.

Breuil leaned on his geologist's pick and gazed.

The bison transfixed by the hunter's spear at the back of the cave is new to us. In a kind of visual pun the spear is drawn from the sexual parts downward and emerges along the bison's belly like a penis in a ventral foreskin. Men have read languages before now without a dictionary.

How could he decipher what men had forgotten twenty thousand years ago?

His eye hurt. He was old. This place was holy. To know, to know. —No, *Breuil*, he said to himself aloud. *To see.*

Robot on his knees, the Abbé sat in the red rain of light that trembled through the shelved leaves of the great tree in the *place*. Ravidat sat at his feet in a seine of leafshadow. Monsieur le Maire in his high collar and the tricolor across his breast rolled the wine in his glass. Agnel and Estreguil stood on each side of Maurice Thaon, whose hands rested on their shoulders.

—You cannot imagine Africa, the Abbé was saying. Djibouti in the Somaliland, on the gulf of Aden, Nizan, is it not, who calls Aden the worst place in the world? Djibouti, then, is the next worst place. Admiral Scott, you remember, when he first saw Antarctica, said, *Mon Dieu! What an awful place!* and I wish I could have said something as fine about Djibouti but I was speechless.

The Mayor looked from Thaon to a concierge in black stockings who was standing at a respectable distance from the men. He nodded with deep appreciation of the Abbé's words.

—You have lived all your life in France, *mes gosses, messieurs et dames.*

He, too, nodded politely to the concierge, who dared not acknowledge the honor except by folding her arms.

—The Somaliland is a baked waste. My American friend Monsieur Kelley once said that France smells of wine, urine, and garlic, but Africa smells of carrion, of *merde* ripened by flies as big as hornets, of rotten water silver with filth and green with contagion.

—Indeed, said the Mayor.

—Djibouti is ravaged dirt streets, shacks with blinding tin roofs, whole buildings of rust and packing cases wired together.

—*Il est poète,* the Mayor whispered to Thaon, *l'Abbé!*

—And all of this steaming rot is surrounded by white mountains, sparkling mountains of salt. Imagine that. I was there with Père Teilhard de Chardin, as in China, and with an extraordinary man, a Catalan with an almost French name, Henri de Monfreid, from the Roussillon, the half-brother of Madame Agnès Huc de Monfreid. Their father fell out of a tree some twenty years ago, strange way to die. He was Georges-Daniel de Monfreid, a painter and friend of

Gauguin, whose paintings he used to buy under the pretense of selling them, to encourage him.

Maurice Thaon was laughing.

—Since when is a priest not a gossip? the Abbé asked. I'm putting
everybody to sleep.

Monsieur Thaon laughed the louder. The Mayor was confused
but smiled nevertheless, rolled the wine in his glass, and leaned for-
word attentively.

—*Et alors.* Where was I? The salt heaps of Djibouti. The stink of
Africa. *Ah!* That extraordinary man Henri de Monfreid. He has
been everywhere, everywhere that other people haven't been. He was
the man who took Père Teilhard to Abyssinia, its awful deserts. Harar,
where Rimbaud lived, Obok, Diredawa, Tajura. Prehistory is very
rich around there. They found rock paintings, lovely graceful animals, hunters with bows, geometric designs all dots and angles.

Marsal came closer, sitting behind Ravidat.

—I went with them a bit later, like going to the moon. At Obok
there is nothing alive. The old volcanoes are still in the week of
creation, black and wrinkled. The silence lifts the hair on the back
of your head.

—And then we got to Ganda-Biftu, where there are four-hundred
metres of paleolithic drawings across the face of a cliff. We climbed
up, having built a scaffold for the purpose. I drew and drew and drew,
as high up on the rock as the third story of a building. Sickle-horned
African buffalo, lions, antelope. And lithe men, far more realistically
drawn than in our European caves. And among the buffalo, quite
clearly, were long black oxen. You see what that implies. Domestica-
tion.

The Abbé stared before him, sipping his wine.

—We found more pictures, found them at Diredawa, and then
outside Harar. We went to the Porcupine Cave, as they have named
it, that Teilhard had seen earlier. But I saw something he had passed
over. It was a calcined protuberance, wonderfully suspicious, and with
no trouble at all I found a bone beneath. A human jawbone, but
not of man as we know him, but of the breed of men before us, the
apelike man Neanderthal. He had never been found in Africa before,
and it was not known that he was an artist. It was thought that he
could only arrange stones painted red ochre, and set the mountain
bears' skulls on ledges as in the cave at Drachenberg.

He drained his glass and set it on the table.
—But he could draw. *Mon Dieu,* he could draw.

The first boxes of ammunition were placed in the Shaft of The Hunter and the Bison late in October, when the moon was dark. Long cases of carbines packed in grease, grenades, flares, .45s rose in neat stacks to the black shins of the prancing horses.

At Drachenberg the bears' skulls sat on their ledges, hooded in dust older than Ur or Dilmun. Their muzzles all pointed to the rising sun, which fell upon them dimly in the depth of their cave in the cliff, lighting all but the sockets of their eyes.

*Historical Note*

The cave at Lascaux, on the estate of the Rochefoucaulds near Montignac in the Dordogne, was painted between 20,000 and 15,000 B.C. by men about whom we know nothing except that they hunted with arrowheads shaped like laurel leaves and were draughtsmen as accomplished as Hokusai and Carpaccio. The passage by which they entered the cave has never been discovered, but it is evident that they worked in darkness by torchlight. The animals they depicted all belonged to species now extinct. The outlines of the figures were engraved or brushed, and the pigment sprayed on.

Sealed for two hundred centuries, the cave was discovered on September 12, 1940, first by a rabbit, and immediately afterward by a dog named Robot, who was chasing it. Robot belonged to a boy from Montignac named Ravidat. Jacques Marsal, who was with Ravidat and Robot, is now a guide at Lascaux, though he only shows slides rather than leading visitors through the cave, which has been closed for over a decade and is expected to be closed indefinitely. The warmth of human breath had caused bacterial cultures to grow on the paintings.

M. André Leroi-Gourhan, whose work on the European prehistoric caves is the most brilliant and searching since that of the greatest of prehistorians, Abbé Henri Breuil (1877–1961), says in his monumental *Treasures of Prehistoric Art* that Lascaux "was discovered in 1940, quite accidentally, by two local boys, Ravidat and Marsal." Mlle. Annette Laming (now Mme. Laming-Emperaire) attributes the discovery to four boys. "Two of the boys," she says in her *Lascaux: Paintings and Engravings,* "Ravidat and Marsal, are natives of the Commune [Montignac in Périgord] and subsequently became guides to the cave—indeed they still fill this office. The third, Agnel, was on holiday in Montignac, and the fourth, Coencas, was a refugee there."

Mr. Glyn Daniel recognizes five discoverers, and is the sole historian of archeology to have recorded Robot's name. "On the morning of September 12, 1940," he says in his *Lascaux and Carnac*, "when the Battle of Britain was being fought out and France itself was divided into an occupied and unoccupied zone by a line that ran from Bordeaux north-east to Burgundy, five young men from Montignac went out rabbit-shooting. They were Ravidat, Marsal, Queroy, Coencas, and Estreguil. Ravidat, Marsal, and Queroy were local boys; the other two were refugees from occupied France. Ravidat, aged seventeen at the time, was the oldest of the five and the leader of the party. They had with them two guns and a dog—a famous dog to whom archeologists should erect a statue—the little dog Robot."

That Lascaux was used as a secret ammunition cache by the Résistance is recorded in André Malraux's *Anti-Memoirs*. The presence of Picasso at Altamira with the Abbé Breuil is affirmed by Alan Houghton Broderick's *Father of Prehistory: The Abbé Henri Breuil, His Life and Times*. The resemblance between the *Guernica* and the Sanctuary of the Bulls at Altamira is a perception which I assume occurred to Père Breuil. Other perceptions of the great prehistorian are actually ideas later worked out by M. Leroi-Gourhan, and some of them, such as the theory that the red dots at the rumps of the tarpans are graphs of sexual odor, are imaginary.

My story is an *assemblage* of facts insofar as they can be known. All the characters are real, including the Spanish mechanic, and the time scheme is as I have used it. The discovery of Lascaux was a pattern of coincidences which no professional story-teller would ask any reader to believe. It is slightly preposterous that the greatest living authority on prehistoric art was only a few miles away at the time of the discovery, though it is not surprising that schoolboys should be learned in the subject of painted prehistoric caves, as the region roundabout is rich in them, and their history teacher was an ardent amateur prehistorian.

M. Jacques Marsal told Daniel M. Madden in 1969 that he "and three other boys" discovered Lascaux [*New York Times*, 4 January 1970, "France Saves Lascaux Grotto, But Public Is Still Barred"]. The number of co-discoverers fell to two when M. Marsal talked with André Malraux earlier. Ravidat became a contractor, but holds with Marsal the honor of being an official guardian of the cave. The fortunes of Coencas, Estreguil, and Agnel I have failed to ascertain. Queroy was killed in the Résistance.

# PUT YOURSELF IN MY SHOES

RAYMOND CARVER

Raymond Carver was born in Clatskanie, Oregon, and grew up in Yakima, Washington. His stories have appeared in *Esquire, Harper's Bazaar, The Iowa Review, Perspective, North American Review, December, Best American Short Stories 1967, Best Little Magazine Fiction 1971 and 1972* and the anthology *The Secret Life of Our Times*. He has published two books of poetry: *Near Klamath* and *Winter Insomnia*. In 1970 he received a National Endowment for the Arts Grant, in 1971 the Joseph Henry Jackson Award and in 1972–73 was a Wallace Stegner Creative Writing Fellow at Stanford. Mr. Carver is presently a visiting lecturer in the graduate Writers' Workshop at the University of Iowa.

The telephone rang while he was running the vacuum cleaner. By this time he had worked his way through the apartment and was on the living room. He was using the brush attachment on the hose in order to get at cat hairs between the cushions. He could faintly hear the ringing. He stopped and listened, and then switched off the vacuum. He went to answer the telephone.

"Hello," he said. "Myers here."

"Myers, honey," she said. "How are you? What are you doing?"

"Nothing," he said. "Hello, Paula."

"There's an office party this afternoon," she said. "You're invited. Carl invited you."

"I don't think I can come," Myers said.

"Carl just this minute said get that old man of yours on the phone. Get him down here for a drink. Get him out of his ivory tower and back into the real world for a while. He's funny when he's drinking. Myers?"

"I heard you," Myers said. Myers used to work for Carl. Carl always talked of going to Paris and writing a novel. He had been sorry to see Myers quit. But Carl said he would watch for his name on the best-seller list. "I can't come now," Myers said.

"We found out some horrible news this morning," she continued, as if she hadn't heard him. "You remember Larry Gudinas. He was still here when you came to work. He helped out on science books for a while, and then they put him in the field, and then they canned him? We heard this morning he committed suicide. He shot himself in the mouth. Can you imagine? He lingered for three days, poor man. Think how his family must feel. Myers?"

"I heard you," Myers said. He tried to remember Larry Gudinas and recalled a tall, stooped man with wire frame glasses, bright ties, and a receding hairline. He could imagine the jolt, the head snapping back as the bullet tore into the open mouth. "Jesus," he said. "Well, I'm sorry to hear that."

"Come down to the office, honey, all right?" Paula said. "Everybody is just talking and having some drinks and listening to Christmas music. Come down," she said again.

He could hear the clink of glasses, loud voices, and then laughter at the other end of the line. "I don't want to come down," he said. "Paula?" A few snowflakes drifted past the window as he watched. He rubbed his finger across the glass, and then began to write his name on the glass as he waited.

"What? I heard," she said. "All right," she said. "Well, then, why don't we meet at Voyles for a drink? Myers?"

"Okay," he said. "Voyles, all right."

"Everybody here will be disappointed you didn't come," she said. "Carl especially. He admires you, you know. He does. He's told me so. He admires your nerve. He said if he had your nerve he would have quit years ago. It takes nerve to do what you did, he says. Myers?"

"I'm right here," Myers said. "I think I can get my car started. If I can't start it, I'll call you back."

"All right," she said. "I'll see you at Voyles. I'll leave here in a few minutes."

"Say hello to Carl for me," Myers said.

"I will," she said. "He's always talking about you."

He put the vacuum cleaner away. He shaved, put on another shirt, his shoes, and found his coat. He walked down the two flights and went to his car which was in the last stall and covered with snow.

He got in, worked the pedal a number of times, and tried the starter. It turned over, roared. He continued to press the pedal.

As he drove he looked at the people who hurried along the walks with shopping bags. He glanced at the gray sky, filled with flakes, and at the tall buildings with snow in the crevices and on the window ledges. He tried to see everything, save it for later. He was between stories, and he felt despicable. He found Voyles, a small bar on a corner next to a men's clothing store. He parked in back and went inside. He sat at the bar for a time and then carried a drink over to a little table near the door.

Paula came in then and said, "Merry Christmas, honey," and he got up and gave her a kiss on the cheek. He held a chair for her.

"What'll you have?" he said. "Scotch?"

"Scotch," she said. Then, "Scotch over ice," to the girl who came for her order.

Paula picked up his drink and drained the glass.

"I'll have another one too," Myers said to the girl. "I don't like this place," he said after the girl had moved away.

"What's wrong with it?" Paula said. "We used to come here. It's quiet, the drinks are good."

"I just don't like it," he said. "Let's have a drink and then go someplace else."

"Whatever you want," she said.

The girl arrived with the drinks, Myers paid her, and he and Paula touched glasses.

Paula's eyelids drooped slightly and her lips seemed puffed as she smiled. Myers stared. She could hold her drinks, but once in a while, if she had too much, she passed out.

"Carl says hello."

Myers nodded.

She sipped her drink. "How was your day today?"

He shrugged.

"What'd you do?" she said.

"Nothing," he said. "I vacuumed."

She touched his hand. "Everybody said to tell you hi."

They finished their drinks. "I have an idea," she said. "Why don't we stop and visit the Morgans for a few minutes? We've never met them, for God's sake. They've been back for months. We could just drop by and say 'Hello, we're the Myers.' Besides, they sent us a card. They asked us to stop during the holidays. They *invited* us. I don't want to go home," she added and fished in her purse for a cigarette.

Myers recalled setting the furnace and turning out all the lights that afternoon before he left for Voyles. He recalled the snow drifting past the window. "What about that insulting letter they sent telling us they heard we were keeping a cat in the house?" he said.

"They've forgotten about that by now," she said. "That wasn't anything serious anyway. Oh, let's do it, Myers! Let's go by."

"We should call first, if we're going to do anything like that," he said.

"No," she said. "That's part of it. Let's not call. Let's just go knock on the door and say 'Hello, we used to live here.' All right? Myers?"

"I think we should call," he said.

"It's the holidays," she said, getting up from her chair. "Come on, honey." She took his arm and they went outside.

He suggested they take her car and pick his car up later. Snow was falling. Most of the stores had closed. There were only a few people on the street. He opened the car door for her and then went around to the driver's side.

He pulled up in front of the house where they had lived for a year and turned the key off. Something took him as he saw the lighted windows, snow on the roof, and the station wagon in the drive. The curtains were open and Christmas tree lights blinked at them from behind the window.

They got out of the car. He took her elbow as they stepped over a pile of snow and started up the walk to the front porch. They had gone a few steps when a large bushy dog hurtled around the corner of the garage and headed straight for Myers.

"Oh, God," he said, hunching, stepping back and bringing his hands up. He slipped on the walk, his coat flapped, and he fell onto the frozen grass with the dread certainty that the dog would go for his throat. The dog growled once and then began to sniff Myers' coat.

Paula picked up a handful of snow and threw it at the dog. The porchlight came on, the door opened, and a man called, "Buzzy!" Myers got to his feet and began to brush himself off.

"What's going on?" the man in the doorway said. "Who is it? Buzzy, come here fellow. Come here."

"We're the Myers," Paula said with a nervous laugh. "We came to wish you a merry Christmas."

"The Myers?" the man in the doorway said, as if puzzled. "Get out! Get in the garage, Buzzy. Get, get! It's the Myers," he said to the woman who stood behind him trying to look past his shoulder.

"The Myers," she said. "Well, ask them in, ask them in, for heaven's sake." She stepped onto the porch and said, "Come in, please, it's freezing. I'm Hilda Morgan and this is Edgar. We're happy to meet you. Please come in."

They shook hands quickly on the front porch. Myers and Paula stepped inside and Edgar shut the door.

"Let me have your coats. Take off your coats," Edgar said. "You're all right?" he said to Myers, observing him closely, and Myers nodded. "I knew that dog was crazy, but he's never pulled anything like this. I saw it, I was looking out the window when it happened."

This remark seemed odd to Myers, and he looked at the man. Edgar was in his forties, nearly bald, and was dressed in slacks and a sweater and was wearing leather slippers.

"His name is Buzzy," Hilda announced and made a face. "It's Edgar's dog. I can't have an animal in the house myself, but Edgar bought this dog recently and promised to keep him outside at all times."

"He sleeps in the garage," Edgar said. "He begs to come in the house, but we can't allow it, you know. I think his frustration must have gotten the better of him tonight." He chuckled. "But sit down, sit down, if you can find a place with this clutter. Hilda, dear, move some of those things off the couch so Mr. and Mrs. Myers can sit down."

Hilda cleared the couch of packages, wrapping paper, scissors, a box of ribbons, and some loose bows. She put everything on the floor.

Myers noticed Edgar staring at him again, not smiling now. Paula said, "Myers, there's something in your hair, honey."

Myers put a hand up to the back of his head and found a dried leaf and a twig.

"That dog," Edgar said and chuckled again. "We were just having a hot drink and wrapping some last-minute gifts. Will you join us in a cup of holiday cheer? What would you like?"

"Anything is fine," Paula said.

"Anything," Myers said. "We shouldn't have interrupted."

"Nonsense," Edgar said. "We've been . . . very curious about the Myers. You'll have a hot drink, sir?"

"That's fine," Myers said.

"Mrs. Myers?" Edgar said.

Paula nodded.

"Two hot drinks coming up," Edgar said. "Dear, I think we're ready too, aren't we?" he said to his wife. "This is certainly an occasion." He took her cup and went out to the kitchen.

Myers heard the cupboard door bang and a muffled word that sounded like a curse. He blinked. He looked at Hilda Morgan who was settling herself into a chair at the end of the couch.

"Sit down over here, you two," Hilda said. She patted the arm of the couch. "Over here, by the fire. We'll have Mr. Morgan build it up again when he returns." They sat. Hilda clasped her hands in her lap and leaned forward slightly as if examining his face.

The living room was as he remembered it, except that on the wall behind Hilda's chair he saw three small framed prints. In one print a man in a vest and frock coat was tipping his hat to two ladies who held parasols. There were trees in the background, and a broad concourse with horses and carriages.

"How was Germany?" Paula said. She sat on the edge of the cushion and held her purse on her knees.

"We loved Germany," Edgar said, coming in from the kitchen with a small tray and four large cups.

Myers recognized the cups. He and Paula had used them when they lived here.

"Have you been to Germany, Mrs. Myers?" Edgar asked.

"We want to go," Paula said. "Don't we, Myers? Maybe next year, next summer. Or else the year after. As soon as we can afford it. Maybe as soon as Myers sells something. Myers writes."

"I should think a trip to Europe would be very beneficial to a writer," Edgar said. He put the cups into coasters. "Please help yourselves." He sat down in a chair across from his wife and gazed at Myers. "You said in your letter you were taking off work to write."

"That's true," Myers said and sipped his drink.

"He writes something almost every day," Paula said.

"Is that a fact?" Edgar said. "That's impressive. What did you write today, if I may ask?"

"Nothing," Myers said.

"It's the holidays," Paula said.

"You must be proud of him, Mrs. Myers," Hilda said.

"I am," Paula said.

"I'm happy for you," Hilda said.

"I heard something the other day that might interest you," Edgar said. He took out some tobacco and began to fill a pipe. Myers lighted a cigarette and looked around for an ashtray. He dropped the match behind the couch. "It's a horrible story really, but maybe you could use it, Mr. Myers." Edgar struck a flame and drew on the pipe. "Grist for the mill, you know, and all that," Edgar said and laughed and shook the match. "This fellow was about my age or so. He was a colleague for a couple of years. We knew each other a little, and we had good friends in common. Then he moved out, accepted a position at the university down the way. Well, you know how those things go sometimes, he began having an affair with one of his students."

Hilda made a disapproving noise with her tongue. She reached down for a small package that was wrapped in green paper and began to affix a red bow to the paper.

"According to all accounts, it was a torrid affair that lasted for some months," Edgar continued. "Right up until a short time ago, in fact. A week ago, to be exact. On that day, it was in the evening, he announced to his wife, they'd been married for twenty years, he announced to his wife that he wanted a divorce. You can imagine how his wife took it, coming out of the blue like that, so to speak. There was quite a row. The whole family got into it. She ordered him out of the house then and there. But just as he was leaving, his son, mark this, his *son*, who is seventeen and in high school, his son threw a can of tomato soup at his father and hit him in the forehead. It caused a concussion that sent the father to the hospital. His condition is quite serious." He drew on his pipe and gazed at Myers.

"I've never heard such a story," Hilda said. "Edgar, that's disgusting."

"Horrible," Paula said.

Myers grinned.

"Now there's a story for you, Mr. Myers," Edgar said, catching the grin and narrowing his eyes. "Think of the story if you could get inside that man's head."

"Or her head," Hilda said. "The wife's. Think of her story. To be betrayed in such fashion after twenty years. Think how she must feel."

"But imagine what that poor boy must be going through," Paula said. "Imagine, having almost killed his father."

"Yes, that's all true," Edgar said. "But here's something I don't think any of you has thought about. Think about this for a moment. Mr. Myers, are you listening? Tell me what you think of this. *Put yourself in the shoes of that eighteen year old coed who fell in love with a married man.* Think about her for a moment, and then you see the possibilities for your story." He nodded and leaned back in the chair with a satisfied expression.

"I'm afraid I don't have any sympathy for her," Hilda said. "I can imagine the sort she is. We all know what she's like. That kind preys on older men. I don't have any sympathy for him either, the man, the chaser, no I don't. No, I'm afraid my sympathies in this case are entirely with the wife and son."

"It would take a Tolstoy to tell it and tell it right," Edgar said. "No less than a Tolstoy. Mr. Myers, the water is still hot."

"Time to go," Myers said. He stood up and threw his cigarette into the fire.

"Stay," Hilda said. "We haven't got acquainted yet. You don't know how we have . . . speculated about you. Now that we're together at last, stay a little while. It's such a pleasant surprise."

"We appreciated the card and your note," Paula said.

"The card?" Hilda said.

Myers sat down again.

"We decided not to mail any cards this year," Paula said. "I didn't get around to it when I should have, and it seemed futile to do it at the last minute."

"You'll have another one, Mrs. Myers?" Edgar said, standing in front of her now with his hand on the cup. "You'll set an example for your husband?"

"It *was* good," Paula said. "It warms you."

"Right," Edgar said. "It warms you, that's right. Dear, did you hear Mrs. Myers? It warms you. That's very good."

"Mr. Myers?" he said and waited. "You'll join us?"

"All right," Myers said and let him take the cup.

The dog began to whine and scratch at the door.

"That dog. I don't know what's gotten into that dog tonight," Edgar said. He went to the kitchen and this time Myers distinctly heard him curse as he slammed the kettle onto a burner.

Hilda began to hum. She picked up a package half-wrapped, cut a piece of tape, and began sealing the paper.

Myers and Paula looked at each other. Myers lighted a cigarette. He dropped the match in his coaster. He looked at his watch.

In a moment, Hilda raised her head. "I believe I hear singing," she said. She listened. She rose from her chair and went to the front window. "It *is* singing. It's *carolers*. Carolers. Edgar!" she called. Myers and Paula went to the window. "I haven't seen carolers in years," Hilda said.

"What is it?" Edgar said. He had the tray and cups. "What is it? What's wrong?"

"Nothing's wrong, dear. It's carolers. There they are over there, across the street," Hilda said.

"Mrs. Myers," Edgar said, extending the tray. "Mr. Myers. Dear."

"Thank you," Paula said.

"Muchas gracias," Myers said.

Edgar put the tray down and came back to the window with his cup. There were nearly a dozen young people gathered on the walk in front of the house across the street. Boys and girls with an older, taller boy who wore a muffler and a topcoat. Myers could see the faces at the window across the way—the Ardreys—and when the carolers had finished, Jack Ardrey came to the door and gave something to the older boy. The group moved on down the walk, flashlights bobbing, and stopped in front of another house.

"They won't come here," Hilda said after a time.

"What? Why won't they come here?" Edgar said and turned to his wife. "What a Goddamned silly thing to say! Why won't they come here?"

"No, I just know they won't," Hilda said.

"And I say they will," Edgar said. In a minute, still watching, he said, "Mrs. Myers, are those carolers going to come here or not? What do you think? Will they return to bless this house? We'll leave it up to you."

Paula pressed closer to the window, but the carolers were far down the street now. Paula didn't answer. She continued looking out the window.

"Well, now that all the excitement is over," Edgar said, and went over to his chair. He sat down, frowned, and began to fill his pipe.

Myers and Paula went back to the couch. Hilda moved away from the window at last. She sat down. She smiled and gazed into her cup. Then she put the cup down and began to weep.

Edgar gave his handkerchief to his wife. He looked at Myers. Pres-

ently he began to drum on the arm of his chair. Myers moved his
feet. Paula looked into her purse for a cigarette. "See what you've
caused," Edgar said as he stared at something on the carpet near
Myers' shoes.

Myers couldn't believe he had heard him say this. Paula squeezed
his thigh, and Myers gathered himself to stand.

"Edgar, get them another drink," Hilda said as she dabbed her
eyes. She used the handkerchief on her nose. "I want them to hear
about Mrs. Attenborough. Mr. Myers writes. I think he might appre-
ciate this. We'll wait until you come back before we begin the story."

Edgar collected the cups without saying anything. He carried them
into the kitchen. Myers heard dishes clatter, cupboard doors bang.
Hilda seemed oblivious. She looked at Myers and smiled faintly.

"We have to go," Myers said. "We have to. Paula, get your coat."

"No, no, we insist, Mr. Myers," Hilda said. "We want you to hear
about Mrs. Attenborough, poor Mrs. Attenborough. You might ap-
preciate this story, too, Mrs. Myers. This is your chance to see how his
mind goes to work on raw material."

Edgar came back and passed out the hot drinks. He sat down
quickly.

"Tell them about Mrs. Attenborough, dear," Hilda said to her
husband.

"That dog almost tore my leg off," Myers said, and was at once
surprised at his words. He put his cup down.

"Oh, come, it wasn't that bad," Edgar said. "I saw it."

"You know writers," Hilda said to Paula. "They like to exaggerate."

"The power of the pen and all that," Edgar said.

"That's it," Hilda said. "Bend your pen into a plowshare, Mr.
Myers."

"We'll let Mrs. Morgan tell the story of Mrs. Attenborough,"
Edgar said, ignoring Myers who stood up at that moment. "Mrs.
Morgan was intimately connected with the affair. I've already told
you of the fellow who was knocked for a loop with a can of soup." He
chuckled. "We'll let Mrs. Morgan tell this one."

"You tell it, dear. And Mr. Myers, you listen closely," Hilda said.

"We have to go," Myers said. "Paula, let's go."

"Talk about honesty," Hilda said.

"Let's talk about it," Myers said. Then he said, "Paula, are you
coming?"

"I want you to hear this story," Edgar said, raising his voice. "You will insult Mrs. Morgan, you will insult us both, if you don't listen to this story." He clenched his pipe.

"Myers, please," Paula said anxiously. "I want to hear it, honest. Then we'll go. Myers? Please, honey, sit down for another minute."

Myers looked at her. She moved her fingers, as if signaling him. He hesitated, and then he sat next to her.

Hilda began. "One afternoon in Munich, Edgar and I went to the Dortmunder Museum. There was a Bauhaus exhibit that fall and Edgar said, the heck with it, let's take a day off—he was doing his research you see—the heck with it, let's take a day off. We caught a tram and rode across Munich to the museum. We spent several hours viewing the exhibit and revisiting some of the galleries to pay homage to a few of our favorites amongst the old masters. Just as we were to leave, I stepped into the ladies' room. I left my purse. In the purse was Edgar's monthly check from home that had come the day before, and a hundred and twenty dollars cash that I was going to deposit along with the check. I also had my identification cards in the purse. I did not miss it until we arrived home. Edgar immediately telephoned the museum authorities, but while he was talking I saw a taxi out front. A well-dressed woman with white hair got out. She was a stout woman and she was carrying two purses. I called for Edgar and went to the door. The woman introduced herself as Mrs. Attenborough, gave me my purse, and explained that she too had visited the museum that afternoon and while in the ladies' room had noticed a purse in the trash can. She of course opened the purse in an effort to trace the owner. There were the identification cards and such giving our local address. She immediately left the museum and took a taxi in order to deliver the purse herself. Edgar's check was there, but the money, the hundred and twenty dollars, was gone. Nevertheless, I was grateful the other things were intact. It was nearly four o'clock and we asked her to stay for tea. She sat down and after a little while began to tell us about herself. She had been born and reared in Australia, had married young, had three children, all sons, been widowed, and still lived in Australia with two of her sons. They raised sheep and had more than 20,000 acres of land for the sheep to run in, and many drovers and shearers and such who worked for them at certain times of the year. When she came to our home in Munich, she was then on her way home to Australia from England where she had been to visit her youngest son who was a barrister. She was returning to Australia when we met her," Hilda went on. "She was seeing some of the world in the process. She had many places yet to visit on her itinerary."

"Come to the point, dear," Edgar said.

"Yes. Here is what happened then. Mr. Myers, I'll go right to the climax, as you writers say. Suddenly, after we had had a very pleasant conversation for an hour, after she had told about herself and her adventurous life Down Under, she stood up to go. As she started to pass me her cup, her mouth flew open, the cup dropped, and she fell across our couch and died. Died, right in our living room. It was the most shocking moment in our lives."

Edgar nodded solemnly.

"God," Paula said.

"Fate sent her to die on the couch in our living room in Germany," Hilda said.

This struck Myers as funny and he began to laugh. "Fate–sent–her–to die–in–your–living–room?" he said between gasps.

"Is that funny, sir?" Edgar said. "Do you find that amusing?"

Myers nodded. He kept laughing. He wiped his eyes on his shirt sleeve. "I'm really sorry," he said. "I can't help it. That line, 'Fate sent her to die in our living room in Germany.' I'm sorry. Then what happened?" he managed to say. "I'd like to know how this ended."

"Mr. Myers, we didn't know what to do," Hilda said. "The shock was terrible. Edgar felt her pulse, but there was no sign of life. And she had begun to change color. Her face and hands were turning *gray*. Edgar went to the phone to call someone. Then he said, 'Open her purse, see if you can find where she's staying.' All the time averting my eyes from the poor thing there on the couch, I took up her purse. Imagine my complete surprise and bewilderment, my *utter* bewilderment, when the first thing I saw inside was my hundred and twenty dollars, still fastened with the paper clip. I was never so astonished."

"And disappointed," Edgar said. "Don't forget that. It was a keen disappointment."

Myers giggled.

"If you were a real writer, as you say you are, Mr. Myers, you wouldn't laugh," Edgar said as he got to his feet. "You wouldn't dare laugh! You'd try to understand. You'd plumb the depths of that poor soul's heart and try to understand. But you're no writer, sir!"

Myers kept laughing.

Edgar slammed the coffee table and the empty cups rattled in the coasters. "The real story lies right here, in this house, this very living room, and it's time it was told! The real story is here, Mr. Myers," Edgar said. He walked up and down over the shiny wrapping paper which had unrolled and now lay spread out across the carpet. He stopped to glare at Myers, who was by now holding his forehead and shaking with laughter. "Consider this for a possibility, Mr. Myers! Consider. A friend, let's call him Mr. X, is friends with, with Mr. and Mrs. Y, *as well as Mr. and Mrs. Z.* Mr. and Mrs. Y and Mr. and Mrs. Z do not know each other, unfortunately. I say unfortunately, because if they *had* known each other this story would not exist because it would never have taken place. Now Mr. X learns that Mr. and Mrs. Y are going away to Germany for a year and need someone to occupy their house during the time they are gone. Mr. and Mrs. Z are looking for suitable accommodations, and Mr. X tells them he knows of just the place. But before Mr. X can put Mr. and Mrs. Z in touch with Mr. and Mrs. Y, the Y's have to leave sooner than expected. Mr. X, being a friend, is left to rent the house at his discretion to anyone, including Mr. and Mrs. Y, I mean Z. Now Mr. and Mrs. . . .—Z move into the house and bring a cat with them that Mr. and Mrs. Y hear about later in a letter from Mr. X. Mr. and Mrs. Z bring a cat into the house *even though* the terms of the lease have expressly forbidden cats or other animals in the house because of Mrs. Y's asthma. The real story, Mr. Myers, lies in the situation I've just described. Mr. and Mrs. Z, I mean Mr. and Mrs. Y's moving into the Z's house, *invading* the Z's house, if the truth is to be told. Sleeping in the Z's bed is one thing, but unlocking the Z's private closet and using their linen, vandalizing the things found there, that was against the spirit and letter of the lease. And this same couple, the Z's, opened boxes of kitchen utensils marked Don't Open. And they broke dishes when it was spelled out, *spelled out* in that same lease, they were not to use the owners', that is the Z's *personal,* I emphasize personal, possessions." His lips were white. He continued to walk up and down on the paper, stopping every now and then to look at Myers and emit little puffing noises from his lips.

"And the bathroom things, dear, don't forget the bathroom things," Hilda said. "It's bad enough using the X's blankets and sheets, but when they also get into their bathroom things and go through the little private things stored in the attic, a line has to be drawn."

"That's the real story, Mr. Myers," Edgar said. He tried to fill his pipe. His hands trembled and tobacco spilled onto the carpet. "That's the real story that's waiting to be written."

"And it doesn't need Tolstoy to tell it," Hilda put in.

"It doesn't need Tolstoy," Edgar said.

Myers laughed. He and Paula got up from the couch at the same time and moved toward the door. "Good night," Myers said merrily.

Edgar was behind him. "If you were a real writer, sir, you'd put that story into words, and not pussyfoot around with it either."

Myers laughed again. He touched the doorknob. "One other thing," Edgar said. "I didn't intend to bring this up, but in light of your behavior here tonight, I wanted to tell you that I'm missing my two-volume set of *Jazz at the Philharmonic*. Those records are of great sentimental value. I bought them in 1955. And now I insist you tell me what happened to them."

"In all fairness, Edgar," Hilda said as she helped Paula with her coat, "after you took inventory of the records, you admitted you couldn't recall the last time you had seen those records."

"I'm sure of it now, though," Edgar said. "I'm positive I saw those records just before we left, and now, now I'd like this *writer* to tell me exactly what he knows of their whereabouts. Mr. Myers?"

But Myers was already out the door and, taking Paula by the hand, he hurried her down the walk to the car. They surprised Buzzy on the walk who yelped at them and then jumped to the side.

"I insist on knowing," Edgar called after them. "The nerve of some people!"

Myers got Paula into the car and then started the engine. He looked again at the couple on the porch. Hilda waved, and then she and Edgar went back inside and shut the door. They looked out at the car from behind the curtain.

Myers pulled away from the curb. "Those people are crazy," Paula said. This remark, too, struck Myers as funny. He patted her hand.

"They were scary," she said. In a minute, she leaned her head against his shoulder and said, "Honey, I'm going to fall asleep."

He didn't answer. Her voice seemed to come to him from a great distance. He kept driving. Snow rushed at the windshield. He was silent and watched the road. He was at the very end of a story.

# THE FAITHFUL

James Alan McPherson was born in Savannah, Georgia, in 1943. He attended college in Georgia, graduate school in Cambridge and in Iowa City. Since 1969 he has been a contributing editor for *The Atlantic Monthly*. This story represents his third appearance in this anthology.

There is John Butler, a barber, looking out his shop window on a slow Monday morning. Impeccable, as usual, in his starched white jacket, he stands and surveys the procession of colors blending into the avenue, a living advertisement of his profession. The colors are blurred; the window needs a cleaning; the red lettering has been allowed to fade, almost to a mere outline. Some of the passing faces he cannot recognize. But some recognize him behind the window and wave as they hurry past. Others, wanting to avoid all contact with the shop, pretend that he is not there. They ease out of view without acknowledging his nodding head. Still, he stands in his usual place between the edge of the window and the door; and when a familiar face moves by the window without glancing toward the shop, he shares the embarrassment and turns his own eyes away. In his mind he forgives the workers; but the shiftless, the workless, the timeless strollers up and down the avenue he does not spare.

"They still tryin' to starve us out," he says, turning to the members of his shop. Today it consists of Ray Powell, the second barber; Mickey Norris, who has again played hooky from school in order to earn a few dollars shining shoes; and two loafers, who have come in for a game of checkers and a chance to enjoy it. All wince to hear him start again.

"Maybe I'll go on down the block a minute," Mickey says, moving toward the door.

Copyright © 1973 by *The Atlantic Monthly* Company, Boston, Massachusetts. Reprinted with permission.

"Maybe you better go on to school," Butler tells him. "There ain't go'n be no work in here today."

Mickey, a sly boy, does not stray far from the green metal chair.

Butler gives him a severe look. "Not tomorrow either," he adds.

Mickey slinks back to the chair and sits, his hands going into his pockets for coins to toss.

Ray, a fat brown man who likes to give the impression of habitual efficiency, runs the edge of a hand towel between the teeth of his own black comb and puckers his lips in an exaggeration of effort. "It's just the first of the week, Reverend," he says. "Things are bound to pick up."

One of the loafers, Norm Tyson from the Projects, knows better: he allows his opponent an advantage on the board and, before the man can incorporate it, says: "Looks like it's yours."

And then the two of them leave.

Just after noon, when Ray has gone across the street for lunch and Mickey has wandered off until evening, a young man looks in the door. A massive black tiara of hair encircles his head; his matching light green shirt and bell-bottom trousers advertise his wealth. Butler flashes his most hospitable smile and rises from his chair.

"How much for a quick one?" the young man asks from the door.

"For all that, two-fifty, maybe three dollars," Butler says.

The young man snorts and throws back his arms in playful amazement. "Just for a *trim?* You wouldn't wanna mess up my vibrations, would you?"

Butler loosens the smile and lowers his voice. "No," he says. "Better go somewheres else. I got me some heavy hands."

The young man laughs. "A heavy hand make a rusty register in your business, don't it?" And backs out the door before the barber can form an answer.

At the end of the day some regulars do come in; but they are losing more hairs than Butler clips. Still, they lower their heads, more from respect than necessity, and allow him limited operations around the edges. These balding faithfuls—John Gilmore or Dick Kendricks or Willie Russell—the backbone of his Sunday congregation, fold their hands beneath the white sheet square and abide, in their turn, his wandering frustrations. "These whites have bull-shitted our young men," he says. "Now, me, I'm as proud as the next man. But our boys didn't stop gettin' haircuts until these white boys started that mess.

That's a fact. Wasn't no more than a couple years ago, they'd be lined up against that wall on a Saturday night laughin' at the white boys. But soon as they see these white kids runnin' round wild, all at once they hair ain't long enough no more."

John Gilmore keeps his head lowered, his lips tight, his eyes watching his hands work beneath the sheet.

Ray, sitting in his own chair, looks up from the paper he has been reading and says: "Hey, I see where they arrested a big shot for tax evasion. First of the year they bound to hamstring *one* for example." But no one picks it up. Ray rattles and folds the paper, and eases back into his reading.

"They know what they doin'," Butler continues. "Why, they tell me Miss Dawson's boy can't git into the university on that new free program because those folk up there think he's a Tom. As *smart* as that boy is, he can't git in. But you see old Buggsy Brooks goin' up there. They *took him out of jail*," he says, bending close to Gilmore's ear for emphasis. "You ought to see him struttin' around, hair on his head big as a basketball. Never read a book through in his life."

But no one, not even Gilmore who knows the true state of affairs, can muster the hardness of heart to take him on.

Once, there had been violent betting and spit-infested verbal battles and crowded-round checker games and hot clothes and numbers passing through; once, Butler would hum radio spirituals as he went about his work, or else trade righteous homilies with Ray, busy in the other chair. The men who remember those days—Gilmore, Kendricks, and the others—would like to have them back; but there is an unspoken fear of being too possessive about the past and a determination not to allow the present to slip out of focus. They recognize another world outside the shop door, and find it much easier to pay up and walk away when Butler is done with his work.

"If it wasn't for you belonging to his church," John Gilmore tells his wife after each visit, "I wouldn't go in there."

"Now don't you be no trouble to him," Marie Gilmore reminds her husband. "He ain't got much longer to go."

On Sundays Butler now converts his sermons. The themes still resemble something familiar to his congregation, but lately the images have been doing different work. The relative few who still come into the church to hear it are growing bored. Some have al-

ready visited Reverend Tarwell and his more magical thumpings
over on 138th. They like what they hear. There is talk that Tarwell
plans to have himself crucified next month at Easter Sunrise Service
and preach the entire sermon from the cross. Such resurrected rem-
nants of the South appeal to them; the oldest have ever been home-
sick. Besides, Butler seems to have an obsession with a single theme:

"I was walkin' down here this mornin', brothers and sisters," he
begins, his rising voice mellowing into a comfortable chant, "thinkin'
about the rift there is these days between father and son; thinkin'
about the breach there is between son and son and daughter and
daughter. I'm thinkin' this mornin' about old bloody Cain and his
guiltless brother; about old man Abraham castin' his son out into the
wilderness; about that old rascal, Saul, lettin' his *wine* turn him
against young David. I see little Joseph tossed in the dark pit, strip
naked of his garment by his brothers. And hungry Esau, just
a-droolin' at the mouth, sellin' his birthright for a mess of *pottage*.
There's old slick Jacob now, a-crawlin' in to blind Isaac's bedside
underneath the *fleece* of a wild and woolly animal; and Esau standin'
outside the door, just a-weepin' away. Next to him is old rebellious
Absalom, up in an *oak* tree, swingin' by his hair with Joab ridin'
*down* on him. Just look at that boy cuss. I want to cut him down,
Church, but I ain't got the strength. My arm is raised up to him, but
my *razor's* kind of rusty. So can I git an *a-men* over here . . . ?"

Some of the people on his left say a weak "a-men."

"Can I hear an *a-men* over there . . . ?"

Some few on the right say "a-men."

"My razor growin' *sharper* by the second . . ."


"You better lay off that stuff," Ella, his wife, tells him at Sunday
dinner. "The church done got tired of that one record you keep
playin'." They have not been invited out for Sunday dinner in over
five months.

"They ain't got no cause to complain," Butler tells her. "I give
them a good service. Besides, most of them don't even listen to
nothin' but the names."

"Just the same, you better lay off it for a while. It ain't their fault
you goin' out of business."

Butler looks over at her. She is chewing with a deliberation calculated to enrage him into an argument. "Whose fault you reckon it
is?" he demands.

She continues chewing, looking wise.

Butler looks at his own food. "All right," he says. "It's *my* fault."

"It ain't that you *have* to do Afros. Ray could do that and you could do your old customers. There ain't nothin' wrong with dividin' up the work thataway."

"Ray ain't go'n do fancy cuts in *my* place. First thing you know, these young fellows come hangin' round there and drive the old customers away."

She chews for a while, sips her coffee, and watches him. She takes her time in swallowing, smacks her lips, and then says: "Then you won't have a place for much longer."

He scrapes at his own plate, trying to avoid her eyes.

"And the way *you* goin'," she adds, "you won't be preachin' much longer either."

This thought he takes to bed with him while she lingers in the kitchen and sips, with irritating emphasis, another cup of coffee.

On another slow Monday morning, Ray, shaping his own moustache at the mirror, says: "You know, Reverend, I been thinking. Maybe we ought to go into processes. Nobody can say *now* that's imitating the white man. And there's guys on the block still wearing them."

Butler turns from the window, his face twitching. Images of winos and hustlers flash through his mind. "That's what you been thinkin', huh?" he says to Ray.

"Yeah, Reverend," Ray says, laughing to himself in the mirror. "Since the white folks always imitating us, maybe we could even process some of them."

"I don't process," Butler answers.

"It's work," Ray says, dropping the laugh and looking serious.

"It's devil's work," Butler says.

"Right now, I'd say we ain't got much of a choice."

Butler stands behind him. They exchange looks in the mirror. Ray works the scissors in his right hand, shaking off the hairs. Then he begins to clip his moustache again, drawing in his chin. Butler watches. After a while he says: "Ray, I know you think I'm a fool. I can't help that. But when you get to be my age change is just hard. You can shape a boy's life by what you do to his hair," he says, looking over at Mickey tossing coins against the wall. "Now everybody can't do that, but I'm proud to say I done it more than once in my lifetime. And I want to do it some more. But scrapin' a few loose hairs off every Tom, Dick, and Harry that come in here, just to get the money, why anybody can do that. You understand what I'm sayin'?"

Ray lowers the scissors but does not answer.

"You, Mickey? You understand?"

Mickey thinks it over, tossing another coin to the wall. After a while he says, "Naw, suh," and nods his head.

Butler walks back to the window. "That's what I figured," he finally says, looking out.

A little after one o'clock John Gilmore comes in for a quick shave during his lunch hour. Lying almost parallel in the chair, his rust-brown lips and eyelids showing through the lather, he makes careful conversation while Butler exercises the repressed magic in his hands. "Times being what they is in religion and all," he says, "I been wonderin' what you been plannin' to do."

"About what?" Butler says, not pausing in his work.

"Well," Gilmore begins, "Marie say Second Calvary ain't drawin' no stronger membership. In fact, a lot of folks thinkin' about plain quittin'."

"That's their business," he answers, holding back Gilmore's ear. "They git what they pay for."

Gilmore waits until his ear is allowed to fall back into place. Then he says: "I hear Reverend Tarwell thinkin' 'bout *you* for assistant pastor of his place. Times bein' good for the colored like they is, he thinkin' 'bout goin' into politics in a few years. When he step down, there sure go'n be a crowd over at his place for somebody."

Butler paused to wipe the razor. "Ain't most of his people from South Carolina?" he asks.

"Some."

"Well, most of mine from Alabama. There's two different styles."

Gilmore licks some lather off his lip with a delicate flicker of his tongue. He moistens both lips in the process. "That don't make a difference no more," he says. "People thinkin' 'bout *unity* these days. All of us in the same boat no matter where we from."

"Guess so," Butler says lightly. But after cleaning his razor again he says: "Where you from?"

"Alabama."

"Then why you worryin' about Tarwell's church? Why don't he bring his people over to *mine?*"

Gilmore tightens his lips.

"He's the one plannin' to leave the community, not me."

"I'll tell him that," Gilmore says, closing his eyes tight and easing into a resolved silence.


Late on Thursday afternoon, Ray, his eyes averted, says he has to go. "It was a good shop, Reverend," he says, "but I got me a family to support."

"Where you goin' to?" Butler asks.

"This new parlor over on 145th."

"It's all set up, huh?"

Ray says, "Yeah."

"Well," Butler says, forcing a smile, "maybe my luck will change some now with you gone."

Ray looks sad. His fat jaws break out in sweat. He wipes it away, turning up the edge of his moustache. Lately he has taken to wearing his hair long about his ears: a steady warning, but of unsuspected proportions. "It ain't nothing to do with *luck*, Reverend," he sighs. "God-*damn!* Everybody done switched over but *us*. Even the *barber schools* don't teach them old down-home cuts no more. You just *plain stubborn!*" Now he pauses, checking a great part of what has been building up in him. "Look, you want to get in on the money? It's easy as pie. There ain't no work involve in it. All you have to do is trim. *Trim!*" He sighs, smoothing down his ruffled moustache while stroking his face again. "You getting to be an old man, Reverend. You should be looking ahead. That's what I'm doing. That's *all* I'm doing."

"I'll take over your regulars."

"What regulars?" Ray says. "There ain't no regulars to divide. I cut your hair, you cut mine. Sometime Willie Russell or Jack Gilmore come in here out of guilt and let you burn their ears. What's gonna happen when they get tired? Who you go'n cut then, your*self?*"

"You can take your stuff with you," Butler tells him, oblivious of Ray's exasperation. "But mind you don't take the goodwill over there to 145th."

Ray, locking his mouth against more hot words, sprawls into his own chair, penitent and brooding. Mickey, smoking a cigarette and listening in the john, blows a stream of smoke into the air and thinks his own thoughts.

"Now old Isaac," he tells his people on another Sunday morning, "he's a-layin' down to die. He done followed out God's directions and now ain't worried about but one thing: makin' his dyin' bed comfortable. He done married to Rebekah, accordin' to his *father's* will; he done planted, in his old age, the *seed* of a great nation in her wombs. But now he's tired, Church, his eyesight is a-failin' and he's hungry for *red meat*. He's just about ready to lay his blessin' on anybody, just as long as he can get a taste of venison steak. But God, Glory Glory, is a-workin' against him, as he always works against the *unwise*. *He* can't run the risk of that blessin' fallin' on Esau, who is all covered with hair. So he has to make Rebekah his instrument, one more time, to see that his work git's done. I want you to picture old Isaac now, just layin' in his darkness pantin' for meat. And Jacob, God's beloved, sneakin' in to blind Isaac's bedside, a goatskin on his head, a service tray in his hand. But look here, Church: yonder, over there, runnin' up from the woods with his hair holdin' him down, here come old Esau just a-hustlin' home. It's gonna be a close one, Church; both these boys is *movin' fast*. Now who go'n put money down on Esau? I say who go'n *bet* on Jacob? Both these boys is hustlin' on in. Who go'n lay somethin' on Esau this mornin' now . . . ?"

No one responds.

". . . Well, then, who go'n *bet* on Jacob . . . ?"

Most of them are confused. But some of the oldest, and most faithful, lay uninspired "a-mens" on Jacob.

". . . The race is gettin' closer by the minute . . ."

Marie Gilmore, dressed in her best white usher's uniform, gets up and leaves the room.

There is John Butler, the barber, on another Monday morning; again loitering by the window, again considering the rhythm of the street. He has not housed a complete checker game for almost a month.

"How do you do one of these Afros?" he asks Mickey, turning from the window.

"Nothin' to it, Rev," says Mickey, a careful boy who bears the jokings of his buddies concerning his own close-cut hair in order to keep some steady work. "Nothin' to it," he repeats, anticipation in his wise eyes. "You just let it grow, put some stuff on it, and keep it even all the time."

"What kind of stuff? Sound like a process to me."

"Naw, Rev," Mickey says.

"What is this *stuff?*"

"It's just to keep dandruff out."

"You think I could do one?"

"Hell, Rev, *any*body can do it."

Butler thinks a bit. "Mickey, what does it do for these kids?"

Mickey looks up at him, his face suggesting the fire of deeply held knowledge. "What *don't* it do for you?" is his answer.

Butler considers this.


Just before closing time that same day John Gilmore comes in. He does not need a shave or even a trim. Nor does he offer much conversation. Butler waits. Finally Gilmore musters sufficient courage.

"Marie says she ain't comin' back to Second Calvary no more."

"Gone over to Tarwell, I bet."

Gilmore nods. His large hands dangle between his legs as he sits on the green metal chair across from Butler.

"She was a fine usher," Butler says. "Now Tarwell done beat me out of somethin' fine."

"You beat your*self*," Gilmore says. "She didn't no more want to go over there than I want to stop comin' in here."

Butler looks into him. Gilmore looks down at his hands.

"So that's how it is?"

Gilmore nods again.

"And you call yourself a *Alabama* boy."

"That's been over a long time ago. Things change."

"I suppose you fixin' to grow yourself an Afro too, with that bald spot on your head."

Gilmore grows irritated. He gets up and moves toward the door. "I ain't fixin' to do *nothin'*," he says. "But if I was you I'd be fixin' to close up shop for a while so's I could reread my Bible for a spell."

"I know the Good Book," Butler says. "Thank you kindly."

Gilmore turns at the door, his long right hand holding it open. "Or maybe give up the Good Book and go back down home where you can cut the kind of hair you want."

"Maybe *all* of us ought to go back," Butler calls after him. But John Gilmore has already closed the door.

Through the ebb of the afternoon he slumps in his chair, taking inventory of his situation. He is not a poor man: the title to the shop is clear; the upper floor of his duplex is rented out to a schoolteacher;

and there is, besides, a little money in the bank. But there is Mickey to consider if he should close up shop; his salary comes to three-fifty a week, regardless. He would not like to see Mickey leave too. He would not like to see Mickey over on 145th, picking up ideas which have always been alien to his shop. He thinks some more about Mickey. Then he thinks about the South. Closing time comes, and goes. Mickey, passing down the street, sees him there and comes in. Butler sends him for coffee and then leans back again and closes his eyes. He thinks about going home, but again he thinks about the South. His feet braced against the footrest, the chair swinging round on its own, he recalls the red dirt roads of Alabama.

"Gimmie a 'fro."

Having lost all sense of direction, he has to raise himself before the sound can be connected.

"Gimmie a 'fro, please?"

A boy is standing next to his chair. He is Tommy Gilmore, youngest son of his former customer. Butler once baptized him during the heat of a summer revival. Tommy's hair is gray-black and tightly curled, his mouth is open, his dungarees faded and torn at the knee; a dollar bill is held up to Butler in the edge of his fist.

"What you want?"

"A haircut."

"It's after closing time," Butler tells him. Then he sees the dollar. "And anyway, it's gonna cost you one-fifty. You got that much?"

The boy hands up the dollar.

"That ain't enough," Butler says, handing it back. "What else you got in your pocket? How much Marie give you?"

"Ain't got no more," the boy mumbles.

Greed lifts its thumb, but charity quickly waves it away. "You sure that's all you got?"

"Yes, sir."

Butler moves over to the hot-water heater and takes the board from behind it. He lays it across the armrests of his chair, takes a fresh cloth from the drawer and gives it a decisive snap. "Sit down, Mister," he tells the boy. "I'm gonna give you the nicest schoolboy you ever seen."

Tommy does not move. His fist tightens around the dollar. Part of it disappears into the vise. His eyes narrow cynically. "A schoolboy ain't no 'fro," he states.

"Git up on the board, son."

"You go'n *gimme* one?"

"I'm a barber, ain't I?"

The boy mounts.

Butler secures him, and then ties the cloth.

Mickey comes in with the coffee, surveys the room, and then sets the steaming cup on the counter below the mirror.

Butler fastens the safety pin in the knot behind the boy's neck. "Now look here, Mickey, and you'll learn something," he says as Mickey stands back to inspect the boy in the chair.

Mickey's eyes flicker over the scene, the curiosity in him slowly changing to doubt. "How you go'n do it, Rev? You ain't got no *comb*, you ain't got no *stuff*, and it ain't even *long* enough yet."

The boy begins to wiggle in the chair. The board shifts under him. "It is *too* long enough," he says.

"Naw it ain't," says Mickey, malice in his eyes, his eyes on the younger boy's face, his head solemnly swaggering. "You got to go four, five months before you get enough. And you ain't got but one or two yet."

"Shut your trap, Mickey," Butler orders. He straightens the board with one hand and places the other on the struggling boy's shoulder. "I'm goin' to work on it now," he says, pressing down.

"But it ain't go'n do no *good!*"

"Shut up or go on home!" Butler says.

Mickey struts over to his own green chair at the end of the row, his face beaming the aloofness of a protected bettor on a fixed poker game. He sits, watching with animal intensity. The boy sees him and begins to squirm again.

"Quiet down, now," the barber says, this time pressing down on the boy's head. "I know what I'm doin'."

The boy obeys, whimpering some. Butler begins to use his shears. The hair is hard and thick, tightly curled and matted; but, deep inside it, near the scalp, he sees red dust rising. He is furious in his work, a starved man: turning and clipping and holding and brushing and shaping and holding and looking and seeing, beyond it all, the red dust rising. In ten minutes it is done. He stands back for a final look, then opens the pin, undoes the knot. Again he shapes the white sheet-square; again he brushes. The boy steps down, still whimpering softly. The board goes back behind the hot-water tank. And Butler lifts him up to the long mirror. The last whiffs of steam curl out from the cooling coffee. Mickey tightens his mouth and reaches into his pocket for a coin to toss against the wall. The boy looks into the mirror.

There is the barber: under the single bulb which sends light out through the windows of his shop. Gesturing, mouthing, making swift movements with his hands in the face of the shouting John Gilmore, who stands between him and the window. The boy is clinging to the man, crying softly. There is Mickey, still in his green chair against the wall, his own eyes, his own mind deciding.

"If you didn't call yourself a minister of God, I'd *kick your ass!*" the tight-fisted John Gilmore is saying. His bottom lip is pushed far out from his face.

"Didn't you ever have a schoolboy when you was his age? Just answer me that."

"I went to a different school. But my son ain't no *plantation* Negro."

"He didn't have nothin' but a dollar anyhow."

"Then you should of send him somewheres else!"

Tommy's mouth is open. He is crying without sound.

"*Look* at him! You can't *tell* me he don't look better now."

"We go'n close you down, old man. You hear what I'm sayin'? We go'n close this joint down and your church *too!*"

"You go'n close us *all* down."

"We go'n run all you Toms from the community . . ."

Mickey slides his hand into his pocket, rattling the coins.

On still another Sunday morning he stands, tired now, old, facing the last few strays of a scattered flock. It is almost Easter. Word is going around that Tarwell has already nailed the cross together in the basement of his church. Some say they have seen it. Others, some of those who are sitting here, are still reserving judgment. Marie Gilmore is back; but she has not come for the sermon. She sits at the back of the room in a purple dress, her eyes cast down. Butler, looking fierce and defensive, stares at the six or so faces peering up at him. Some look sheepish; some impatient; some look numb as always, waiting to be moved. He stands before them, his two hands gripping the edges of the pulpit. They wait. Several plump ladies fan themselves, waiting. One, Betty Jessup, sitting on the front pew, leans forward and whispers: "You fixin' to preach, or what?"

He does not answer.

Now the people begin to murmur among themselves: "What's wrong with him?" "When's he gonna start?"

"We are a stiff-necked people," he begins, his voice unusually steady, the music gone. "Our heads turn thisaway and thataway, but only in one direction at a time." He pauses. "We'll be judged for it."

"Who go'n judge us?" Marie Gilmore suddenly fires from the back of the room. They all turn, their mouths hanging loose. Marie Gilmore rises. "Who's to say what's to be judged and what ain't?" she says through trembling lips. "Who's left to say for certain he knows the rules or can show us where they written down?" she says.

The people are amazed. Several of them wave their hands and nod their heads to quiet her. Marie Gilmore does not notice. Her eyes are fixed on Butler.

He stands behind the pulpit and does not say anything.

At Sunday dinner Ella says: "Well, what you go'n do *now?*"

"Send that truant officer after Mickey," he says quietly.

"What else?"

He shifts his eyes about the room, looking for something.

Ella sighs and strikes her chest. "Lord, why I had to marry a man with a *hard head?*"

Butler looks her in the face. "Because you couldn't do no better," he tells her.

# THE DEATH OF SUN

## WILLIAM EASTLAKE

William Eastlake is the author of five novels, a book of
poetry and essays, and numerous short stories. He lives in
Arizona where his avocations are working quarter horses
and trying to save mountain lions, coyotes, eagles, and
Indians from extinction.

The bird Sun was named Sun by the Indians because each day their
final eagle circled this part of the reservation like the clock of sun.
Sun, a grave and golden eagle-stream of light, sailed without movement as though propelled by some eternity, to orbit, to circumnavi-
gate this moon of earth, to alight upon his aerie from which he had
risen, and so Sun would sit with the same God dignity and decorous
finality with which he had emerged—then once more without seeming volition ride the crest of an updraft above Indian Country on
six-foot wings to settle again on his throne aerie in awful splendor,
admonitory, serene—regal and doomed. I have risen.

"Man, Fyodor Dostoevski said," the white teacher Mary-Forge
said, "without a sure idea of himself and the purpose of his life can-
not live and would sooner destroy himself than remain on earth."
"Who was Dostoevski?" the Navajo Indian Jesus Saves said.
"An Indian."
"What kind?"
"With that comment he could have been a Navajo," Mary-Forge
said.
"No way," Jesus Saves said.
"Why, no way could Dostoevski be an Indian?"
"I didn't say Dostoevski couldn't be an Indian, I said he couldn't
be a Navajo."
"Why is a Navajo different?"

"We are, that's all," Jesus Saves said. "In the words of Sören Kierkegaard—"

"Who was Sören Kierkegaard?"

"Another Russian," Jesus Saves said.

"Kierkegaard was a Dane."

"No, that was Hamlet," Jesus Saves said. "Remember?"

"You're peeved, Jesus Saves."

"No, I'm bugged," Jesus Saves said, "by people who start sentences with 'man.'"

"Dostoevski was accounting for the high suicide rate among Navajos. Since the white man invaded Navajo country the Navajo sees no hope or purpose to life."

"Then why didn't Dostoevski say that?"

"Because he never heard of the Navajo."

"Then I never heard of Dostoevski," Bull Who Looks Up said. "Two can play at this game."

"That's right," Jesus Saves said, sure of himself now and with purpose.

"What is the purpose of your life, Jesus Saves?"

"To get out of this school," Jesus Saves said.

Jesus Saves was named after a signboard erected by the Albuquerque First National Savings & Loan.

All of Mary-Forge's students were Navajos. When Mary-Forge was not ranching she was running this free school that taught the Indians about themselves and their country—Indian country.

"What has Dostoevski got to do with Indian country?"

"I'm getting to that," Mary-Forge said.

"Will you hurry up?"

"No," Mary-Forge said.

"Is that any way for a teacher to speak to a poor Indian?"

"Sigmund Freud," the Medicine Man said, "said—more in anguish I believe than in criticism—'What does the Indian want? My God, what does the Indian want?'"

"He said that about women."

"If he had lived longer, he would have said it about Indians."

"True."

"Why?"

"Because it sounds good, it sounds profound, it tends to make you take off and beat the hell out of the Indians."

"After we have finished off the women."

"The women were finished off a long time ago," the Medicine Man said.

"But like the Indians they can make a comeback."

"Who knows," the Medicine Man said, "we both may be a dying race."

"Who knows?"

"We both may have reached the point of no return, who knows?"

"If we don't want to find out, what the hell are we doing in school?"

"Who knows?"

"I know," Mary-Forge said, "I know all about the eagle."

"Tell us, Mary-Forge, all about the eagle."

"The eagle is being killed off."

"We know that, what do we do?"

"We get out of this school and find the people who are killing the eagle."

"Then?"

"Who knows?" Mary-Forge said.

Mary-Forge was a young woman—she was the youngest white woman the Navajos had ever seen. She was not a young girl, there are millions of young girls in America. In America young white girls suddenly become defeated women. A young white woman sure of herself and with a purpose in life such as Mary-Forge was unknown to the American Indian.

Mary-Forge had large wide-apart almond-shaped eyes, high full cheekbones, cocky let-us-all-give-thanks tipsy breasts, and good brains. The white American man is frightened by her brain. The Indian found it nice. They loved it. They tried to help Mary-Forge. Mary-Forge tried to help the Indians. They were both cripples. Both surrounded by the white reservation.

High on her right cheekbone Mary-Forge had a jagged two-inch scar caused by a stomping she got from high-heeled cowboy boots belonging to a sheep rancher from the Twin Slash Heart Ranch on the floor of the High Point Bar in Gallup.

Mary-Forge did not abruptly think of eagles in the little red schoolhouse filled with Indians. A helicopter had just flown over. The helicopter came to kill eagles. The only time the Indians ever saw or felt a helicopter on the red reservation was when the white ranchers came to kill eagles. Eagles killed sheep, they said, and several cases have been known, they said, where white babies have been plucked from playpens and dropped in the ocean, they said.

You could hear plain the whack-whack-whack of the huge rotor blades of the copter in the red schoolhouse. The yellow and blue copter was being flown by a flat-faced doctor-serious white rancher named Ira Osmun, who believed in conservation through predator control. Eagles were fine birds, but the sheep must be protected. Babies, too.

"Mr. Osmun," Wilson Drago, the shotgun-bearing sado-child-appearing co-pilot asked, "have the eagles got any white babies lately?"

"No."

"Then?"

"Because we are exercising predator control."

"When was the last white baby snatched by eagles and dropped into the ocean?"

"Not eagles, Drago, eagle, it only takes one. As long as there is one eagle there is always the possibility of your losing your child."

"I haven't any child."

"If you did."

"But I haven't."

"Someone does."

"No one in the area does."

"If they did, there would be the possibility of their losing them."

"No one can say nay to that," Wilson Drago said. "When was the last time a child was snatched?"

"It must have been a long time ago."

"Before living memory?"

"Yes, even then, Drago, I believe the stories to be apocryphal."

"What's that mean?"

"Lies."

"Then why are we shooting the eagles?"

"Because city people don't care about sheep. City people care about babies. You tell the people in Albuquerque that their babies have an outside chance, any chance that their baby will be snatched up and the possibility that it will be dropped in the ocean, kerplunk, and they will let you kill eagles."

"How far is the ocean?"

"People don't care how far the ocean is, they care about their babies."

"True."

"It's that simple."

"When was the last lamb that was snatched up?"

"Yesterday."

"That's serious."

"You better believe it, Drago."

"Why are we hovering over this red hogan?"

"Because before we kill an eagle we got to make sure what Mary-Forge is up to."

"What was she up to last time you heard?"

"Shooting down helicopters."

"All by herself?"

"It only takes one shot."

"You know, I bet that's right."

"You better believe it, Drago."

"Is this where she lives?"

"No—this is the little red schoolhouse she uses to get the Indians to attack the whites."

"What happened to your other co-pilots?"

"They got scared and quit."

"The last one?"

"Scared and quit."

"Just because of one woman?"

"Yes. You're not scared of a woman, are you, Drago?"

"No, I mean yes."

"Which is it, yes or no?"

"Yes," Wilson Drago said.

Below in the red hogan that was shaped like a beehive with a hole on top for the smoke to come out the Indians and Mary-Forge were getting ready to die on the spot.

"I'm not getting ready to die on the spot," Bull Who Looks Up said.

"You want to save the eagles, don't you?" Mary-Forge said.

"Let me think about that," Jesus Saves said.

"Pass me the gun," Mary-Forge said.

Now, from above in the copter the hogan below looked like a gun turret, a small fort defending the perimeter of Indian Country.

"Mary-Forge is an interesting problem," Ira Osmun said—shouted above the whack-whack-whack of the rotors.

"Every woman is."

"But every woman doesn't end up living with the Indians, with the eagles."

"What causes that?"

"We believe the Indians and the eagles become their surrogate children."

"What?"

"That they become a substitute for life."

"Oh? Why do you hate me?"

"What?"

"Why do you use such big words?"

"I'm sorry, Drago. Do you see any eagles?"

"No, but I see a gun."

"Where?"

"Coming out of the top of the hogan."

"Let Mary-Forge fire first."

"Why?"

"To establish a point of law. Then it's not between her eagles and my sheep."

"It becomes your ass or hers."

"Yes."

"But it could be my life."

"I've considered that, Drago."

"Thank you. Thank you very much," Wilson Drago said.

Sun, the golden eagle that was very carefully watching the two white animals that lived in the giant bird that went "Whack-whack-whack," was ready.

Today would be the day of death for Sun. His mate had been killed two days before. Without her the eaglets in the woven of yucca high basket nest would die. Today would be the day of death for Sun because without a sure idea of himself, without purpose in life, an eagle would sooner destroy himself than remain on earth. The last day of Sun.

"Because," Mary-Forge said, and taking the weapon and jerking in a shell, "because I know, even though the Indians and us and the eagle, even though we have no chance ever, we can go through the motions of courage, compassion, and concern. Because we are Sun and men, too. Hello, Sun."

"Stop talking and aim carefully."

"Did I say something?"

"You made a speech."

"I'm sorry," Mary-Forge said.

"Aim carefully."

Mary-Forge was standing on the wide shoulders of an Indian named When Someone Dies He Is Remembered. All the other Indians who belonged in the little red schoolhouse stood around and below her in the dim and alive dust watching Mary-Forge revolve like a gun turret with her lever-operated Marlin .30-30 pointing out of the smoke hatch high up on the slow turning and hard shoulders of When Someone Dies He Is Remembered.

"Why don't you shoot?" More Turquoise said. He almost whispered it as though the great noise of the copter did not exist.

"The thing keeps bobbling," Mary-Forge shouted down to the Indians.

Looking through the gunsights she had to go up and down up and down to try and get a shot. She did not want to hit the cowboys. It would be good enough to hit the engine or the rotor blades. Why not hit the cowboys? Because there are always more cowboys. There are not many eagles left on the planet earth, there are several million cowboys. There are more cowboys than there are Indians. That's for sure. But what is important now is that if we give one eagle for one cowboy soon all the eagles will have disappeared from the earth and cowboys will be standing in your bed. No, the helicopter is scarce. They will not give one helicopter for one eagle. A helicopter cost too much money. How much? A quarter million dollars, I bet. Hit them where their heart is. Hit them right in their helicopter.

But it danced. Now Mary-Forge noticed that although it was dancing it was going up and down with a rhythm. The thing to do is to wait until it hits bottom and then follow it up. She did and fired off a shot.

"Good girl," the Medicine Man said.

"That was close," Ira Osmun said to his shotgun, Wilson Drago. "Now that we know where Mary-Forge is we can chase the eagle."

Ira Osmun allowed the chopper to spurt up and away to tilt off at a weird angle so that it clawed its way sideways like a crab that flew, a piece of junk, of tin and chrome and gaudy paint, alien and obscene in the perfect pure blue New Mexican sky, an intruder in the path of sun. Now the chopper clawed its way to the aerie of Sun.

The eagle had watched it all happen. Sun had watched it happen many times now. Two days ago when they killed his mate was the last time. Sun looked down at his golden eagle chicks. The eaglets were absolute white, they would remain white and vulnerable for several months until the new feathers. But there was no more time. Sun watched the huge man junk bird clawing its way down the long valley that led to Mount Taylor. His home, his home and above all the homes of the Indians.

Like the Indians the ancestors of Sun had one time roamed a virgin continent abloom with the glory of life, alive with fresh flashing streams, a smogless sky, all the world a sweet poem of life where all was beginning. Nothing ever ended. Now it was all ending. The eagle, Sun, did not prepare to defend himself. He would not defend himself. There was nothing now to defend. The last hour of Sun.

"Catch me," Mary-Forge shouted from the top of the hogan and jumped. When she was caught by More Turquoise she continued to shout as the noise of the chopper was still there. "They've taken off for Mount Taylor to kill Sun. We've got to get on our horses and get our ass over there."

"Why?"

"To save Sun," Mary-Forge shouted. "Sun is the last eagle left in the county."

"But this is not a movie," the Medicine Man said. "We don't have to get on horses and gallop across the prairie. We can get in my pickup and drive there—quietly."

"On the road it will take two hours," Mary-Forge said. "And we'll need horses when we get there to follow the chopper."

"What would Dostoevski say about this?" the Medicine Man said.

"To hell with Dostoevski," Mary-Forge said.

Outside they slammed the saddles on the amazed Indian ponies, then threw themselves on and fled down the canyon a stream of dust and light a commingling of vivid flash and twirl so when they disappeared into the cottonwoods you held your breath until the phantoms, the abrupt magic of motion appeared again on the Cabrillo draw.

"Come on now, baby," Mary-Forge whispered to her horse Poco Mas. "What I said about Dostoevski I didn't mean. Poor Dostoevski. I meant seconds count. We didn't have time for a philosophical discussion. Come on now, baby, move good. Be good to me, baby, move good. Move good, baby. Move good. You can take that fence, baby. Take him! Good boy, baby. Good boy, Poco. Good boy. I'm sure the Medicine Man understands that when there are so few left, so few left Poco that there is not time for niceties. You'd think an Indian would understand that, wouldn't you? Still the Medicine Man is a strange Indian. A Freudian Medicine Man. But Bull Who Looks Up understands, look at him go. He's pulling ahead of us are you going to let him get away with that Poco?" Poco did not let the horse of Bull Who Looks Up stay ahead but passed him quickly, with Mary-Forge swinging her gun high and Bull Who Looks Up gesturing with his gun at the tin bird that crabbed across the sky.

"You see, Drago," Ira Osmun shouted to Wilson Drago, "we are the villains of the piece."

"What?"

"The bad guys."

"It's pretty hard to think of yourself as the bad guy, Mr. Osmun."

"Well, we are."

"Who are the good guys?"

"Mary-Forge."

"Screw me."

"No, she wouldn't do that because you're a bad guy. Because you kill eagles. People who never saw an eagle, never will see an eagle, never want to see an eagle, want eagles all over the place. Except the poor. The poor want sheep to eat. Did you ever hear of a poor person complaining about the lack of eagles? They have got an outfit of rich gentlemen called the Sierra Club. They egg on Indian-lovers like Mary-Forge to kill ranchers."

"Why?"

"They have nothing else to do."

"You think Mary-Forge actually has sex with the Indians?"

"Why else would she be on the reservation?"

"I never thought about that."

"Think about it."

"I guess you're right."

"Drago, what do you think about?"

"I don't think about eagles."

"What do you think about?"

"Ordinarily?"

"Yes."

"Like when I'm drinking?"

"Yes."

"Religion."

"Good, Drago, I like to hear you say that. Good. What religion?"

"They are all good. I guess Billy Graham is the best."

"Yes, if you're stupid."

"What?"

"Nothing, Drago. Keep your eye peeled for the eagle."

"You said I was stupid."

"I may have said the Sierra Club was stupid."

"Did you?"

"No, how could you be stupid and be that rich?"

"Why are they queer for eagles then?"

"They are for anything that is getting scarce. Indians, eagles, any-thing. Mary-Forge is against natural evolution, too."

"What's natural evolution mean?"

"When something is finished it's finished, forget it. We got a new evolution, the machine, this copter, a new bird."

"That makes sense."

"Remember we don't want to kill eagles."

"We have to."

"That's right."

The eagle that had to be killed, Sun, perched like an eagle on his aerie throne. A king, a keeper of one hundred square miles of Indian Country, an arbiter, a jury and judge, a shadow clock that had meas-ured time for two thousand years in slow shadow-circle and so now the earth, the Indians, the place, would be without reckoning, cer-tainly without the serene majesty of Sun, without, and this is what is our epitaph and harbinger, without the gold of silence the long lonely shadow beneath silent wing replaced now by the whack-whack-whack of tin, proceeding with crablike crippled crawl—the sweet song of man in awkward crazy metallic and cockeyed pounce, approached Sun.

Sun looked down on the eaglets in the nest. The thing to do would be to glide away from the whack-bird away from the nest. To fight it out somewhere else. If he could tangle himself in the wings of the whack-bird, that would be the end of whack-bird. The end of Sun. Sun jumped off his aerie without movement not abrupt or even peremptory but as though the reel of film had cut and then proceeded to a different scene. The bird Sun, the eagle, the great golden glider moving across the wilds of purple mesa in airfed steady no-beat, in hushed deadly amaze, seemed in funeral stateliness, mounting upward on invisible winds toward the other sun.

"If he climbs, we will climb with him, Drago. He is bound to run out of updrafts."

Wilson Drago slid open the door on his side and shifted the Harrington & Richardson pump gun into the ready position.

"How high will this thing climb, sir?"

"Ten thousand feet."

"The bird can climb higher than that."

"Yet he has to come down, Drago."

"How much fuel we got?"

"Fifty gallons."

"What are we consuming?"

"A gallon a minute."

"Shall I try a shot?"

"Yes."

Sun was spiraling upward in tight circles on a good rising current of air when the pellets of lead hit him. They hit like a gentle rain that gave him a quick lift. Sun was out of range. Both the copter and Sun were spiraling upward. The copter was gaining.

"Shall I try another shot?"

"Yes."

This time the lead pellets slammed into Sun like a hard rain and shoved him upward and crazy tilted him as a great ship will yaw in a sudden gust. Sun was still out of range.

Now the upward current of air ceased, collapsed under Sun abruptly and the copter closed the distance until Ira Osmun and Wilson Drago were alongside and looking into small yellow eyes as the great sailing ship of Sun coasted downward into deep sky.

"Shall I try a shot?"

"Yes."

Wilson Drago raised the Harrington & Richardson shotgun and pumped in a shell with a solid slam. He could almost touch Sun with the muzzle. The swift vessel of Sun sailed on as though expecting to take the broadside from the 12-gauge gun that would send him to the bottom—to the floor of earth.

"Now, Drago."

But the gliding ship of bird had already disappeared—folded its huge wing of sail and shot downward, down down down downward until just before earth it unleashed its enormous sail of wing and glided over the surface of earth—Indian Country. Down came the copter in quick chase.

There stood the Indians all in a row.

"Don't fire, men," Mary-Forge shouted, "until Sun has passed."

As Sun sailed toward the Indians the shadow of Sun came first, shading each Indian separately. Now came the swifting Sun and each mounted Indian raised his gun in salute. Again separately and in the order which Sun arrived and passed, now the Indians leveled their guns to kill the whack-bird.

"Oh, this is great, Drago," Ira Osmun shouted, "the Indians want to fight."

"What's great about that?"

"It's natural to fight Indians."

"It is?"

"Yes."

"Well I'll be."

"My grandfather would be proud of us now."

"Did he fight Indians?"

"He sure did. It's only a small part of the time the whites have been that they haven't fought Indians."

"Fighting has been hard on the Indians."

"That may well be, Drago, but it's natural."

"Why?"

"Because people naturally have a fear of strangers. It's called xenophobia. When you don't go along with nature you get into trouble. You suppress your natural instincts and that is dangerous. That's what's wrong with this country."

"It is? I wondered about that."

"There's nothing wrong with shooting Indians."

"I wondered about that."

"It's natural."

"No, Mr. Osmun there is something wrong."

"What's that?"

"Look. The Indians are shooting back."

Ira Osmun twisted the copter up and away. "Get out the rifle. We'll take care of the Indians."

"What about the eagle?"

"We've first got to take care of the Indians who are shooting at us and that girl who is shooting at us."

"Is she crazy?"

"Why else would she have intercourse with the Indians?"

"You mean screwing them?"

"Yes."

"She could have all sorts of reasons. We don't even know that she is screwing them. Maybe we are screwing the Indians."

"Drago, we discussed this before and decided that Mary-Forge was."

"What if she is?"

"Drago, you can't make up your mind about anything. You're being neurotic. When you don't understand why you do something you're being neurotic."

"I am?"

"Yes, get out the rifle."

"I still think it's her business if she is queer for Indians and eagles."

"But not if she shoots at us when she's doing it, that's neurotic."

"You're right there, Mr. Osmun."

"Get the rifle."

"O.K."

"You know, Drago, people, particularly people who love the Indians, are suppressing a need to kill them. It's called a love-hate relationship."

"It is? You can stop talking now, Mr. Osmun. I said I'd get the rifle."

Below the helicopter that circled in the brilliant, eye-hurting, New Mexican day, Mary-Forge told the Indians that the copter would be back, that the ranchers would not fight the eagle while being fired on by Indians. "The ranchers will not make the same mistake Custer did."

"What was that?"

"Fight on two fronts. Custer attacked the Sioux before he finished off Sitting Bull. We are the Sioux."

"We are? That's nice," the Navajo Bull Who Looks Up said. "When do we get out of this class?"

"We never do," Jesus Saves said.

"Get your ass behind the rocks!" the teacher Mary-Forge shouted. "Here they come!"

The copter flew over and sprayed the rocks with M-16 automatic rifle fire.

"That should teach the teacher that we outgun them, Drago," Ira Osmun said. "Now we can get the eagle!"

The golden eagle called Sun spiraled upward again, its wings steady, wild, sure, in the glorious and rapt quietude of the blue, blue, blue New Mexico morning, a golden eagle against the blue, a kind of heliograph, and a flashing jewel in the perfect and New Mexico sea of sky. The gold eagle, recapitulent, lost then found as it twirled steady and upward in the shattered light, followed by the tin bird.

Sun knew that he must gain height. All the power of maneuver lay in getting above the tin bird. He knew, too, and from experience that the tin bird could only go a certain height. He knew, too, and from experience that air current he rode up could collapse at once and without warning. He knew, too, and from the experience of several battles now with the bird of tin that the enemy was quick and could spit things out that could pain then kill. All this he knew from experience. But the tin bird was learning, too.

The tin bird jerked upward after the golden eagle. The golden eagle, Sun, wandered upward as though searching and lost. A last and final tryst in the list of Indian Country because now always until now, until now no one killed everything that moved. You always had a chance. Now there was no chance. Soon there would be no Sun.

"Remember, Drago, I've got to stay away from him or above him —he can take us with him. The last time when we got his mate he almost took us with him; I just barely got away when he attacked the rotors—when the rotor goes we go, Drago—we fall like a rock, smash like a glass. They will pick you up with a dustpan."

"Who?"

"Those Indians down there."

"Mr. Osmun, I don't want to play this game."

"You want to save the sheep, don't you?"

"No."

"Why not?"

"I don't have any sheep to save."

"You don't have any sheep, you don't have any children. But you have pride."

"I don't know."

"Then fire when I tell you to and you'll get some."

"I don't know."

"Do you want eagles to take over the country?"

"I don't know."

"Eagles and Indians at one time controlled this whole country, Drago, you couldn't put out a baby or a lamb in my grandfather's time without an Indian or an eagle would grab it. Now we got progress. Civilization. That means a man is free to go about his business."

"It does?"

"Yes, now that we got them on those ropes we can't let them go, Drago."

"We can't?"

"No, that would be letting civilized people down. It would be letting my grandfather down. What would I say to him?"

"Are you going to see your grandfather?"

"No, he's dead. We'll be dead, too, Drago, if you don't shoot. That eagle will put us down there so those Indians will pick us up with a dustpan. You don't want that, do you?"

"I don't know."

"You better find out right smart or I'll throw you out of this whack-bird myself."

"Would you?"

"Someone's got to live, Drago. The eagle doesn't want to live."

"Why do you say that?"

"He knew we were after him. He knew we would get him, he could have left the country. He could have flown north to Canada. He would be protected there."

"Maybe he thinks this is his country."

"No, this is a civilized country. Will you shoot the eagle?"

"No."

"I like the eagle and the Indians as well as the next man, Drago, but we have to take sides. It's either my sheep or them. Whose side are you on, Drago?"

"I guess I'm on theirs."

The helicopter was much lighter now without Drago in it. The copter handled much better and was able to gain on the eagle.

Ira Osmun continued to talk to Wilson Drago as though he were still there. Wilson Drago was one of Ira Osmun's sheepherders and should have taken a more active interest in sheep.

"The way I see it, Drago, if you wouldn't defend me, the eagle would have brought us both down. It was only a small push I gave you, almost a touch as you were leaning out. By lightening the plane you made a small contribution to civilization.

"We all do what we can, Drago, and you have contributed your bit. If there is anything I can't stand, it's an enemy among my sheep."

The copter continued to follow the eagle up but now more lightsome and quick with more alacrity and interest in the chase.

The Indians on the ground were amazed to see the white man come down. Another dropout. "Poor old Wilson Drago. We knew him well. Another man who couldn't take progress—civilization. Many times has Drago shot at us while we were stealing his sheep. We thought anyone might be a dropout but not Wilson Drago. It shows you how tough it's getting on the white reservation. They're killing each other. Soon there will be nothing left but Indians."

"Good morning, Indian."

"Good morning, Indian."

"Isn't it a beautiful day. Do you notice there is nothing left but us Indians?"

"And one eagle."

The Indians were making all these strange observations over what remained of the body of the world's leading sheepherder, Wilson Drago.

"He created quite a splash."

"And I never thought he would make it."

"The last time I saw him drunk in Gallup I thought he was coming apart, but this is a surprise."

"I knew he had it in him, but I never expected it to come out all at once."

"I can't find his scalp. What do you suppose he did with it? Did he hide it?"

"The other white man got it."

"I bet he did."

"They don't care about Indians anymore."

"No, when they drop in on you they don't bring their scalp."

"Please, please," Mary-Forge said, "the man is dead."

"Man? Man? I don't see any man, just a lot of blood and shit."

"Well, there is a man, or was a man."

"Well, there's nothing now," Bull Who Looks Up said, "not even a goddamn scalp."

"Well, Drago's in the white man's heaven," More Turquoise said. "On streets of gold tending his flock."

"And shooting eagles."

"Drago's going higher and higher to white man's heaven, much higher than his what do you call it—"

"Helicopter."

"—can go," Jesus Saves said.

"I don't like all this sacrilege," Mary-Forge said. "Remember I am a Christian."

"What?"

"I was brought up in the Christian tradition."

"Now you're hedging," When Someone Dies He Is Remembered said.

Ah, these Indians, Mary-Forge thought, how did I get involved? And she said aloud, "Once upon a time I was young and innocent."

"Print that!" Bull Who Looks Up said.

"We better get higher up the mountain," Mary-Forge shouted at the Indians, "so when Osmun closes on the eagle we can get a better shot."

"O.K., Teacher."

"There's only one white guy left," she said.

"I find that encouraging if true," More Turquoise said.

"Load your rifles and pull your horses after you," Mary-Forge said.


"My Country 'Tis of Thee," Ira Osmun hummed as he swirled the copter in pursuit of the eagle. You didn't die in vain, Drago. That is, you were not vain you were a very modest chap. We can climb much higher without you, Drago. I am going to get the last eagle this time, Drago. I think he's reached the top of his climb.

Sun watched the tin whack-bird come up. The tin bird came up whack-whack-whack, its wings never flapping just turning in a big circle. What did it eat? How did it mate? Where did it come from? From across the huge water on a strong wind. The evil wind. Sun circled seeing that he must get higher, the tin bird was coming up quicker today. Sun could see the people he always saw below. The people who lived in his country, filing up the mountain. They seemed to be wanting to get closer to him now.

Ira Osmun felt then saw all the Indians in the world firing at him from below. How are you going to knock down an eagle when all the Indians in the world are firing at you from Mount Taylor? It was Mary-Forge who put them up to it, for sure. An Indian would not have the nerve to shoot at a white man. You don't have to drop down and kill all the Indians. They—the people in the East—who have no sheep would call that a massacre. Indians are very popular at the moment. If you simply knock off Mary-Forge, that would do the trick. Women are not very popular at the moment. Why? Because they have a conspiracy against men. You didn't know that? It's true, Drago. The woman used to be happy to be on the bottom. Now she wants to be on the top.

No?

Did you say something, Drago?

I thought I heard someone say something. I must have been hit. My mind must be wandering. What was I saying? It's part of the conspiracy. What's that mean? Something. I must have been hit. What was I doing? Oh yes, I was going to get Mary-Forge—the girl who is queer for Indians and eagles. The eagle can wait.

And Ira Osmun put the copter in full throttle, then cradled the M-16 automatic rifle in his left arm with the muzzle pointing out the door. With his right hand he placed the copter in a swift power glide down.

Sun saw the obscene tin bird go into its dive down. Now would be a chance to get it while the tin bird was busy hunting its prey on the ground. Sun took one more final look over the aerie nest to check the birds. The eaglets were doing fine. Drawing the enemy away from the nest had been successful. The eaglets craned their necks at the familiar shape before Sun folded his great span of wings and shot down on top of the tin bird.

Mary-Forge mounted on Poco Mas saw the tin bird coming, the M-16 quicking out nicks of flame. She could not get the Indians to take cover. The Indians had placed their horses behind the protection of the boulders and were all standing out in the open and were blasting away at the zooming-in copter. Mary-Forge was still shouting at the Indians, but they would not take cover. They have seen too many goddamn movies, Mary-Forge thought, they have read too many books. They are stupid, stupid, stupid, dumb, dumb, dumb Indians. How stupid and how dumb can you get? They want to save the eagle. Standing exposed naked to the machine gun. The stupid Indians. Mary-Forge raised her rifle at the zooming-in copter in a follow-me gesture, then took off in a straight line, the horse pounding, and the flame-nicking copter followed, so did Sun. So now there were three.

The tin bird was alive in flame all at once, something had hit the fuel tank and all of everything exploded in fire, the rotors of the tin bird were still turning and fanning the flame so that it was not only a streaking meteor across Indian Country but at once a boil of fire that shot downward from the terrific draft laying a torch of flame across the desert so that the mesquite and sagebrush became a steady line of flame ending where the tin whack-bird hit into the rocks and went silent in a grand tower of fire.

"It was Sun that did it," More Turquoise said.

The death of Sun.

All of the Indians and Mary-Forge were standing around the dying fire of the big whack-bird in the smoke that shrouded the death of Sun.

"When an eagle," the Medicine Man said, "—when a true bird has no hope—"

"Yes?"

"When the eagle is no more," the Medicine Man said.

"Yes?"

"Then we are no more."

"Yes," every person shrouded in smoke said.

Look up there. It was within three months When Someone Dies He Is Remembered remembered that an eagle named Star by the Medicine Man sailed in one beginning night to reclaim the country of Sun. Now Star's wide shadow passed over the dead tin whack-bird; then he, the great eagle Star, settled on his throne-aerie in awful and mimic splendor, and again admonitory, serene—regal and doomed?

# MAGAZINES CONSULTED

*American Review*—Bantam Books, 666 Fifth Avenue, New York, N.Y. 10019

*Ann Arbor Review*—115 Allen Drive, Ann Arbor, Mich. 48103

*Antaeus*—G.P.O. 3121, New York, N.Y. 10001

*Antioch Review*—P.O. Box 148, Yellow Springs, Ohio 45387

*Aphra*—Box 3551, Springtown, Pa. 18081

*Ararat*—Armenian General Benevolent Union of America, 109 East 40th Street, New York, N.Y. 10016

*Arizona Quarterly*—University of Arizona, Tucson, Ariz. 85721

*The Atlantic Monthly*—8 Arlington Street, Boston, Mass. 02116

*Audience*—241½ 32nd St., New York, N.Y. 10016 (ceased publication 1973)

*Carleton Miscellany*—Carleton College, Northfield, Minn. 55057

*Carolina Quarterly*—Box 1117, Chapel Hill, N.C. 27515

*Chelsea*—Box 242, Old Chelsea Station, New York, N.Y. 10011

*Chicago Review*—University of Chicago, Chicago, Ill. 60637

*Colorado Quarterly*—Hellums 118, University of Colorado, Boulder, Colo. 80304

*The Colorado State Review*—360 Liberal Arts, Colorado State University, Fort Collins, Colo. 80521

*Commentary*—165 East 56th Street, New York, N.Y. 10022

*Cosmopolitan*—224 West 57th Street, New York, N.Y. 10019

*December*—P.O. Box 274, Western Springs, Ill. 60558

*The Denver Quarterly*—Denver, Colo. 80210

*Descant*—Dept. of English, TCU Station, Fort Worth, Tex. 76129

*Epoch*—159 Goldwin Smith Hall, Cornell University, Ithaca, N.Y. 14850

*Esprit*—University of Scranton, Scranton, Pa. 18510

*Esquire*—488 Madison Avenue, New York, N.Y. 10022

*Evergreen Review*—64 University Place, New York, N.Y. 10003

*The Falcon*—Mansfield State College, Mansfield, Pa. 16933

*Fantasy and Science Fiction*—347 East 53rd Street, New York, N.Y. 10022

*The Fault*—41186 Alice Avenue, Fremont, Calif. 94538

*Fiction*—513 East 13th Street, New York, N.Y. 10009

*The Fiddlehead*—Dept. of English, Univ. of New Brunswick, Fredericton, N.B., Canada

*Forum*—Ball State University, Muncie, Ind. 47306

*Four Quarters*—La Salle College, Philadelphia, Pa. 19141

*Generation, the Inter-arts Magazine*—University of Michigan, 420 Maynard, Ann Arbor, Mich. 48103

*Georgia Review*—University of Georgia, Athens, Ga. 30601

*Good Housekeeping*—959 Eighth Avenue, New York, N.Y. 10019

*Green River Review*—Box 594, Owensboro, Ky. 43201

*The Greensboro Review*—University of North Carolina, Greensboro, N.C. 27412

*Handsel*—P.O. Box 558, Lexington, Ky. 40501

*Harper's*—2 Park Ave, New York, N.Y. 10016

*Hawaii Literary Review*—Hemenway Hall, University of Hawaii, Honolulu, Hawaii 96822

*Hudson Review*—65 East 55th Street, New York, N.Y. 10022

*Intro*—Bantam Books, Inc., 666 Fifth Avenue, New York, N.Y. 10019

*The Iowa Review*—EPB 453, University of Iowa, Iowa City, Iowa 52240

*Kansas Quarterly*—Dept. of English, Kansas State University, Manhattan, Kans. 66502

*Ladies' Home Journal*—641 Lexington Avenue, New York, N.Y. 10022

*The Laurel Review*—West Virginia Wesleyan College, Buckhannon, W. Va. 26201

*The Literary Review*—Fairleigh Dickinson University, Teaneck, N.J. 07666

*The Little Magazine*—P.O. Box 207, Cathedral Station, New York, N.Y. 10025

*Lotus*—Department of English, Ohio University, Athens, Ohio 45701

*Mademoiselle*—420 Lexington Avenue, New York, N.Y. 10022

*Malahat Review*—University of Victoria, British Columbia, Canada

*The Massachusetts Review*—University of Massachusetts, Amherst, Mass. 01003

*McCall's*—230 Park Avenue, New York, N.Y. 10017

*The Mediterranean Review*—Orient, N.Y. 11957

*Midstream*—515 Park Avenue, New York, N.Y. 10022

*The Minnesota Review*—New Rivers Press, P.O. Box 578, Cathedral Station, New York, N.Y. 10025

*Mundus Artium*—Dept. of English, Ellis Hall, Box 89, Ohio University, Athens, Ohio 45701

*New Letters*—University of Missouri-Kansas City, Kansas City, Mo. 64110

*The New Mexico Quarterly*—University of New Mexico Press, Marron Hall, Albuquerque, N. Mex. 87106

*The New Renaissance*—9 Heath Road, Arlington, Mass. 02174

*The New Yorker*—25 West 43rd Street, New York, N.Y. 10036

*North American Review*—University of Northern Iowa, Ceder Falls, Iowa 50613

*Northwest Review*—129 French Hall, University of Oregon, Eugene, Ore. 97403

*Ohio Review*—Ellis Hall, Ohio University, Athens, Ohio 45701

*Panache*—P.O. Box 89, Princeton, N.J. 08540

*The Paris Review*—45-39, 171 Place, Flushing, N.Y. 11358

*Partisan Review*—Rutgers University, New Brunswick, N.J. 08903

*Perspective*—Washington University, St. Louis, Mo. 63105

*Phylon*—223 Chestnut Street, S.W., Atlanta, Ga. 30314

*Playboy*—232 East Ohio Street, Chicago, Ill. 60611

*Prairie Schooner*—Andrews Hall, University of Nebraska, Lincoln, Nebr. 68508

*Prism International*—Dept. of Creative Writing, University of British Columbia, Vancouver 8, B.C.

*Quarterly Review of Literature*—26 Haslet Avenue, Princeton, N.J. 08540

*Quartet*—1119 Neal Pickett Drive, College Station, Texas 77840

*Ramparts*—1182 Chestnut Street, Menlo Park, Calif. 94027

*Redbook*—230 Park Avenue, New York, N.Y. 10017

*The Remington Review*—505 Westfield Avenue, Elizabeth, N.J. 07208

*Roanoke Review*—English Department, Roanoke College, Salem, Va. 24153

*Seneca Review*—Box 115, Hobart & William Smith Colleges, Geneva, N.Y. 14456

*Shenandoah*—Box 722, Lexington, Va. 24450

*The Sewanee Review*—University of the South, Sewanee, Tenn. 37375

*The South Carolina Review*—Dept. of English, Box 28661, Furman University, Greenville, S.C. 29613

*The South Dakota Review*—Box 111, University Exchange, Vermillion, S.D. 57069

*Southern Review*—Drawer D, University Station, Baton Rouge, La. 70803

*Southwest Review*—Southern Methodist University Press, Dallas, Tex. 75222

*The Tamarack Review*—Box 159, Postal Station K, Toronto, Ontario, Canada

*Transatlantic Review*—Box 3348, Grand Central P.O., New York, N.Y. 10017

*Tri-Quarterly*—University Hall 101, Northwestern University, Evanston, Ill. 60201

*U.S. Catholic*—221 West Madison Street, Chicago, Ill. 60606

*Vagabond*—P.O. Box 2114, Redwood City, Calif. 94064

*The Virginia Quarterly Review*—University of Virginia, 1 West Range, Charlottesville, Va. 22903

*Vogue*—350 Madison Avenue, New York, N.Y. 10017

*Voyages*—Box 4862, Washington, D.C. 20008

*Washington Square Review*—New York University, 737 East Bldg., New York, N.Y. 10003

*West Coast Review*—Simon Fraser University, Vancouver, B.C.

*Western Humanities Review*—Bldg. 41, University of Utah, Salt Lake City, Utah 84112

*Wind*—RFD Route 1, Box 810, Pikeville, Ky. 41501

*Woman's Day*—67 West 44th Street, New York, N.Y. 10036

*Works*—A.M.S., 56 East 13th Street, New York, N.Y. 10016

*Yale Review*—26 Hillhouse Avenue, New Haven, Conn. 06520